DEATH WISH

Poor Mr. Delancey. His wife Josephine belittles him, controlling his purse strings and managing his life. It's understandable that he might grow a bit resentful. His best friend, Robert Whitestone, is a frustrated artist. Whitestone hates his wife, and is in love with a young girl named Elsie who has come to stay with their neighbors, the Luffs. But Whitestone has a plan to free himself, and naturally Delancey is pulled into the middle of it, willingly or not. And when Mrs. Whitestone is found drowned, what can poor Delancey do? He has to help his friend, no matter what the consequences. If only his wife weren't so hateful about the whole thing, so unreasonable. It's only when young Hugh Acheson comes to visit and begins an investigation of his own that things become really complicated. Poor Mr. Delancey—what's a man to do? It's enough to drive a person to murder.

NET OF COBWEBS

Malcolm Drake had been a merchant seaman, but has returned from the war a changed man, his nerves completely frayed. Now he lives at his brother Arthur's house, with his sister-in-law Helene and her sister Virginia—and their domineering Aunt Evie. Aunt Evie only wants what is best for Malcolm, of course, but when she drops dead one evening at a party, the rumors quickly spread that he had something to do with it. Dr. Lurie is sure that Malcolm had loaded her glass with alcohol, inducing a heart att butler, Ben, even claims to have seen him do it. One Aunt Evie's young protégé, Ivan Jenette, has nev but has conveniently disappeared. T' Kingscrown, believes in his innocenc decidedly strange going on at her house into screaming fits for apparently no reason. A olice have some questions of their own. Malcolm is ed in a net of cobwebs, and the strands are growing tighter by the moment.

ELISABETH SANXAY HOLDING BIBLIOGRAPY

Invincible Minnie (1920)
Rosaleen Among the Artists
  (1921)
Angelica (1921)
The Unlit Lamp (1922)
The Shoals of Honour (1926)
The Silk Purse (1928)
Miasma (1929)
Dark Power (1930)
The Death Wish (1934)
The Unfinished Crime (1935)
The Strange Crime in Bermuda
  (1937)
The Obstinate Murderer [aka
  No Harm Intended] (1938)
Who's Afraid [aka Trial by
  Murder] (1940)

The Girl Who Had to Die
  (1940)
Speak of the Devil [aka Hostess
  to Murder] (1941)
Killjoy [aka Murder is a Kill-
  Joy] (1941)
Lady Killer (1942)
The Old Battle-Ax (1943)
Net of Cobwebs (1945)
The Innocent Mrs. Duff
  (1946)
The Blank Wall (1947)
Miss Kelly (1947)
Too Many Bottles [aka The
  Party Was the Pay-Off]
  (1950)
The Virgin Huntress (1951)
Widow's Mite (1952)

THE DEATH
WISH

NET OF
COBWEBS

Elisabeth Sanxay Holding

Stark Houʃe Preʃʃ • Eureka California

DEATH WISH / NET OF COBWEBS

Published by Stark House Press
1945 P Street
Eureka, CA 95501, USA
griffins@northcoast.com

ISBN: 0-9667848-9-8

Text set in Adobe Garamond. Heads set in Champion and Dogma.
Cover design and layout by Mark Shepard
Cover art by Campbell Shepard

*The publishers would like to thank Roger Schwed
for his help and assistance in making this book happen.*

First Stark House Press Edition: February 2004

0 9 8 7 6 5 4 3 2 1

Table of Contents

INTRODUCTION

We have the Depression to thank for Elisabeth Sanxay Holding's career as a mystery author. Until 1929, she had been writing serious, mainstream novels like *Rosaleen Among the Artists, Angelica, The Unlit Lamp* and *The Shoals of Honour*. She published six novels before the Depression, starting with *Invincible Minnie* in 1920, and ending with *The Silk Purse* in 1928. Early critics noted her expert characterization, and in the *New York Times* review of *The Silk Purse*, the reviewer said: "They are as real a collection of peoples as ever said yes when they wished to heaven they could say no."

So when the Depression hit in 1929 and she was no longer able to sell her leisurely character novels, Holding turned to writing mysteries. Or, more properly, suspense novels. Because, simply put, Elisabeth Sanxay Holding is the precursor to the entire women's psychological suspense genre, and authors like Patricia Highsmith and Ruth Rendell owe her a very large debt of gratitude.

Holding was one of the first to write mystery novels that didn't so much ask whodunit, but *whydunit*. In fact, we know whodunit because it's quite often the main character. It's the "why" that is always the most important part of her books. The psychological underpinnings of her novels form the basis of the mystery. Her characters always act from a very determined point of view. Whether from guilt, discontent, deception, misconception, or even pure altruism, they act out their dramas with very little consideration for other points of view. And therein lies the conflict. They have all got blinders on, seeing just what they want to see, each with their own misguided agenda. They lie when it will get them in the most trouble and tell the truth when it's in their own worst interest. In other words, her characters feel very real to us—we believe in them.

A rich, alcoholic husband grows tired of his well-meaning but lower-class wife. Everything she does irritates him. He decides he must get rid of her but his drinking is making him delusional and easily annoyed. Who can he trust? As he rushes from one hidden bottle, one seedy bar to another, the answer is clearly "no one." When his chauffeur comes to him with a plan to catch his wife with another man, he jumps at it. After all, sooner or later you've got to trust somebody.

This is the basic plot of *The Innocent Mrs. Duff*. What makes the book so compelling is the degree to which Holding gets under the skin of this self-deluded man. She wrote the story in a crisp, staccato style and makes the reader feel every bit of the scheming husband's mounting alcoholic mania. Though casual drinking was more a part of the daily lifestyle in Holding's day, she wasn't afraid to shed some light on its darker aspects. In fact, she had previously explored the theme of the alcoholic male in the *The Obstinate Murderer*—albeit more sympathetically—and clearly knew this personality well.

The Innocent Mrs. Duff and *The Blank Wall* (filmed twice, as *The Reckless Moment* in 1949 and *The Deep End* in 2001) are arguably two of her best works and the only two novels of Holding's that remain in print, thanks to Academy Chicago. Dell published several of her novels in paperback in the 50's, and Mercury published a few in digest form as well. And back in the 1960's, Ace Books published twelve of her books as Ace Doubles. But since then she has almost entirely gone out of print. A sad state of affairs for an author whom Raymond Chandler called "the top suspense writer of them all" in a letter to his British publisher.

All in all, Holding published eighteen suspense novels in her lifetime, beginning with *Miasma* in 1929, and ending with *Widow's Mite* in 1952. Many of these novels were also serialized in national magazines, and almost all were published in paperback and foreign editions, as well as by mystery book clubs. She also published quite a few short stories in magazines ranging from *McCalls, American Magazine* and *Ladies Home Journal* to *Alfred Hitchcock's Mystery Magazine, The Saint, Ellery Queen's Mystery Magazine* and *The Magazine of Fantasy and Science Fiction*. She even wrote a children's story, *Miss Kelly*, the story of a cat who could understand and speak human, and who comes to the aid of a terrified tiger.

Elisabeth Sanxay was born in Brooklyn in 1889, the descendant of an upper middle class family, and was educated in a series of private schools, specifically Whitcombe's School, The Packer Institute, Miss Botsford's School and the Staten Island Academy. She married a British diplomat named George E. Holding in 1913 and together they traveled widely in South America and the Caribbean, settling in Bermuda for awhile where her husband was a government officer. She also raised two daughters, Skeffington and Antonia, the latter of whom married Peter Schwed (until his recent death the executor of Holding's estate and a retired author and publisher with Simon and Schuster).

Holding was thirty-one when her first book was published. Right from the beginning she introduced the theme of discontent that she was to use so often in her mystery books. *Invincible Minnie* starts off slowly—telling at first when it should be showing—but evolves into a fairly lurid tale, the compelling story of a headstrong woman who uses sex to control men and get her way. There's no pat, happy ending either. Minnie runs roughshod over everyone, including her sister and children, and prevails through sheer determination. Holding's lean 40's style was only seen in glimpses in this first effort, but her characterizations were already taking shape in the relentless actions of Minnie and the various people she controlled.

With her second novel, Holding lets the story tell itself, vastly improving over the style of her first book. *Rosaleen Among the Artists,* a bit less melodramatic than *Invincible Minnie,* tells the story of a self-sacrificing young woman struggling to survive and find love in New York City. Though polished off with a sweeter ending, there is much travail as Rosaleen hits rock bottom before finally being united with her soul mate, Mr. Landry. In fact, the two are so matched in the stubbornness with which they hold onto their ideals—tenaciously sacrificing their own happiness at every turn—that they almost wear each other out by the end of the book. Ironically, it is their own principles that almost kill their only chance at love.

In 1929, when the Depression killed her mainstream career, Holding had to do something to help support her two daughters. She could have started writing nice, cozy romantic mysteries. But she just didn't have it in her. The characters she was creating were too contrary, too impulsive—too flawed—and not particularly romantic. They didn't act in their own best interests, holding onto ideals that invariably precipitated trouble. It's as if they felt compelled to do the very thing that caused the most havoc, even if for all the best reasons.

As a consequence, the mystery novels Holding began to write were dark affairs, having more in common with noir than standard detective fiction. It's easy to understand why she was such a favorite of Chandler's. Murder and mania are always lurking in the wings—and the menace doesn't always exist from the outside, but is quite often found from within. These are characters with something to hide. Sometimes there is a happy ending, sometimes not. Sometimes there is a detective, but he's usually as clueless as everyone else. You might say that Holding's characters are quite often lucky if they can make it to the last page with their health, if not their sanity, intact.

In *The Virgin Huntress* we follow young Monty on V-Day as he meets an older woman, Dona Luisa, and is brought into a world of class and culture he had always dreamed of. He is a charming if somewhat insecure young man, somewhat expedient—perhaps too expedient—in his past dealings with women. In fact, he is constantly nagged by secrets from his past, secrets that begin to fracture him as Dona Luisa's niece Rose begins to pry into his past life. By the end of the short novel, Monty has become completely unraveled, the victim of his own expediency. It's not a pretty portrait.

Another of Holding's favorite themes involves fractious family relationships and domestic disputes. *Dark Power* is a perfect example. In the first chapter we meet a young lady, Diana, who discovers that she is quite penniless and soon to be out on the street. Before this happens, however, she is suddenly rescued by an eccentric uncle she didn't know she had. He happily escorts her back to the family home, where she meets such a thoroughly dysfunctional collection of relatives that by the end of the book she barely makes it out alive.

Holding also loved to examine the way stress works on characters, particularly middle-aged men, and would combine this with her theme of domestic disharmony. *The Innocent Mrs. Duff* is an obvious example, but *The Death Wish* is another in which a man, Mr. Delancey, who had always thought himself happily married, comes to a moment of crisis in which he discovers that he actually hates his wife. She has slowly been emasculating him by controlling his purse strings, but when his best friend reveals a similar domestic situation and announces his plans to kill his own wife, Delancey is plunged into a world of self-doubt. At first he is shocked by his friend's confession, and when the wife is found drowned, he hopes that it is the accident that it seems to be. But a seed has been planted, and nothing in his formerly phlegmatic life will ever be the same.

Holding's deft hand at characterization makes all these situations ring true, giving them a psychological perspective that not only presents all her characters' foibles sympathetically, but creates the tension that propels her story along as well. Their actions are understandable, given the circumstances, and all the more frustrating because they are so identifiable. In *The Death Wish*, we watch Delancey try to convince himself at first that his wife is simply moody and a bit insecure. He wants to think the best of her. But the reader knows that his wife's insecure nagging is stifling him, her words little barbs that sink in and latch Delancey to her side, subtly but firmly controlling him. We feel his weakness and frustration, his mounting domestic horror, and nothing that proceeds from this realization seems anything less than inevitable. Not even murder.

This is Holding's true forte, that she can make the commonplace, the ordinary, so horrific and so suspenseful. But make no mistake, whether writing about dysfunctional families or failed marriages, her books are full of mystery. In *Lady Killer,* a young recently-wedded ex-model named Honey is on a cruise ship in the Caribbean with her older husband, who is turning out to be a fussy, fault-finding old crab. At the same time that she begins to realize that a life with this man will be completely intolerable, she also becomes aware that the man in the next cabin might possibly be trying to kill his wife. She begins to set about a campaign to protect this poor, plain and unfortunate woman, who doesn't really seem to want her help. In fact, no one on board seems to feel that Honey has any business stirring up trouble.

But the more Honey finds out, the more mysterious her fellow passengers begin to seem to her. Even her own husband begins to seem alien to her. And when she finds a body, even that isn't quite what it seems. But still the little mysteries pile up, and we are swept up in Honey's suspicions and doubts until even we begin to believe, like her, that *no one* is to be trusted.

Miasma presents us with another set of mysteries. A young doctor named Dennison has just about reached the end of his financial resources when he is contacted by a wealthy older doctor in town who wants him to take up residency in his house and assume the care of his patients. All well and good, except that the doctor's young nurse immediately warns Dennison to leave, mysterious patients come and go in the middle of the night, and his predecessor has gone missing. And then there is the weird drug that the older doctor prescribes to certain of his patients, one of whom is now dead from an apparent heart attack. Holding keeps the mysteries coming until both we and Dennison are wondering what the hell is going on here; daring us to put the book down no matter how late it is and how early we have to get up the next morning.

There is a reason that Dorothy B. Hughes said that "connoisseurs will continue their rush when each new Holding reaches publication." Her books are first and foremost very readable. Not only are they excellent examples of psychological suspense and first rate character studies, they move along at a nice, brisk pace. Holding was never one for overwriting. Her dialog always sounds just right, all the doubtful pauses and self-serving/self-deceptive lies in place. We may not always like these characters, but Holding makes us feel compelled to keep reading about them.

Elisabeth Sanxay Holding's mystery novels have been out of print far too long. Until her death in 1955, she was one of the best, and it is a pleasure to be able to bring her books back into print again, many of which have been unavailable in any edition for well over sixty years. It's time to rediscover Elisabeth Sanxay Holding. Her books may have gone out of print, but they have never gone out of fashion.

Gregory Shepard
Publisher, Stark House Press
September, 2003

THE DEATH WISH

WISH

Elisabeth Sanxay Holding

CHAPTER I

WHITESTONE MAKES A CONFESSION

Delancey lit a cigarette, and leaning back in his chair, gazed across the breakfast table toward the window through which he could see the garden in the green freshness of early Summer. He had eaten with excellent appetite, he had slept soundly all night, he felt comfortable and cheerful; he enjoyed the sight of the clear blue sky; he liked to watch the neat, rosy little housemaid moving deftly about the table.

And, as long as possible, he meant to avoid looking at his wife across the table from him. He was very well aware that there were tears in her eyes, which she wanted him to see; he knew that if he spoke to her, she would answer in a grieved, reproachful voice. Presently, of course, he would be obliged to notice her....

He sighed inaudibly. He liked to laugh, to be easy and careless and good-humoured, and Josephine most effectively prevented that. She made his home life a continual uneasiness, with her affectations, her moods, her sudden changes from clinging affection to hostility. Yet he felt no bitterness toward her, no resentment.

"Makes herself more miserable than anyone else," he thought.

He was a man of immense tolerance; a big, stalwart handsome fellow of thirty-five or so, with smiling blue eyes, and bold features that might have been almost too regular if it had not been for that rather long Celtic upper lip of his, that made his mouth half humorous, half rueful. Something of a philosopher he was, in his own careless way; he relished whatever he found good in life, and amiably endured what was disagreeable.

He finished his cigarette, and dropped the glowing end into his coffee cup, with a faint sizzle.

"Well..." he said, cheerfully. "I'd better be doing a little work, eh?"

He had to look at her now, at that haggard, olive-skinned face, those brimming dark eyes.

"Well..."he said, again.

"Will you be home to lunch?" she asked, with exactly the tone of reproach and challenge he expected.

"I'll try, dear," he assured her.

"No!" she said. "If you've got to 'try'—if it's an effort, I don't want you to come.... You didn't really *want* me to breakfast with you."

"My dear girl, I wanted you to get your sleep," he protested. "I thought—"

"It was horrible!" she cried, with sudden vehemence. "I opened my eyes, and saw you creeping out of the room.... In that stealthy way... You looked—horrible!"

"Now, my dear girl, that's a bit—"

"You frightened me!" she said. "You looked horrible! Like a—"

"Very well!" he interrupted. "We'll leave it at that. I'll ring you up later, about lunch."

Going round the table, he gave her a perfunctory kiss on her cheek that was wet with tears, and went hastily into the hall. Another moment, and he would have lost patience with her. That was a little too much, to tell him he looked "stealthy" and "horrible," when he had simply been going quietly down to breakfast in his own house. Stealthy and horrible, eh...?

"She ought to be a writer," he said to himself. "Extraordinary choice of words...."

He took up his soft hat, and put it on, with a casual glance in the mirror as he passed. And stopped short, staring.

The image he had seen, that man in a soft hat pulled low on his forehead, his eyes glancing sidelong.... Something in the lighting of the hall had given to his healthy, sunburned face a strange look of pallor; the hat brim shadowed his eyes, he looked—

"No, damn it!" he cried to himself. "This is... This won't do!"

He was in a hurry now to get out into the sunshine; his footsteps rang out briskly on the drive leading to the garage. The chauffeur came running down the stairs from his living quarters above, putting on his coat as he came.

"You're early, sir," he said, faintly reproachful. "I'd have been at the house in time, all right."

"I know that, Linney," he answered, affably. "But—well—see here! As long as I am early, we might as well stop by for Mr. Whitestone, eh?"

He got into the car, and Linney set off; a good driver the fellow was, careful and sure and quick. Delancey lit another cigarette, and threw it away at once.

"Bad habit," he told himself. "I've never been a heavy smoker, and I won't begin. Upsets your nerves, makes you short-winded.... The thing is, to keep fit."

Keep fit—for what? It was as if a voice outside himself had asked him that question, profoundly disturbing. His blue eyes clouded with a sort of bewilderment. He was not in the habit of any self-questioning; he was superbly healthy, equable, easygoing, ready to accept life as it was.

"It's Josephine," he thought. "I mean—I've always heard that if you live with someone who's nervous and fanciful, you're apt to be affected by it."

He frowned, with a sudden little qualm of uneasiness. It dismayed him to think that his sane good-humour might be undermined, his cheerful zest in life shadowed. But that passed, his tolerance returned.

"It's worse for her than for me," he thought.

Things always had been harder for her than for him. Even in the beginning, when he had first begun his gallant attentions toward the wealthy young widow she had then been, he had known very well how much more serious the whole thing was for her than for him. He had liked her; indeed, in his way, he had loved her, but it was not her kind of love. Not that fierce, jealous, sombre passion.

"I'm not capable of that," he thought, with a sigh. "Never have cared that way for anyone... I've done my best. I've been faithful to her. I've tried to be considerate.... But it's not enough for her. Well..."

Well, he couldn't give what he hadn't got. He had been fond of her, and if he were less fond of her now than he had been at first, he did not show it. No man could do more than his best, and if he had not made her happy, that was really her fault as much as his. He would not deny that her money had made life smoother for him, but after all, he had made a pretty fair return in patience, in unfailing amiability, for three far from easy years.

"Well..." he said, again. "After all, I'm only at home—say, fourteen hours a day, and I'm asleep for eight of them. Only leaves six hours a day to keep my temper with the poor girl.... Except Saturdays and Sundays."

Unfortunately, this was a Saturday. He would have to go home to lunch, and in the afternoon, if Josephine wanted him to take her out, he would have to do so.

He stopped thinking. He was able to do that; whenever he chose, he could make his mind a blank, and simply absorb, in a half-animal innocence, the sights and sounds and smells about him. They were passing the Luffs' place now, a place he had always admired; something here, some touch of charming carelessness, entirely lacking in his own formal grounds. He liked the way the Luffs' driveway wound through the trees.

"Who's that?" he thought, and in a moment repeated the question to the chauffeur. "Who's that, do you know, Linney?"

"Some relation of Mrs. Luff's, sir," Linney answered, and for a moment his glance left the road, looked where Delancey was looking, at a tall young girl in a striped dress and a wide-brimmed hat, sauntering across the lawn. Delancey had only the briefest glimpse of her face, a grave, beautiful mouth, dark eyes; then they turned a bend in the road, and she was gone, leaving an impression on him of strange charm. She had glanced at them with the aloof unconsciousness of a child, of a creature whose existence is complete, who needs nothing from any other living creature.

"Too bad Josephine had a row with Mrs. Luff," he thought, and sighed again, a resigned sigh. Josephine was always having rows, always shutting doors in his friendly face. Even poor Whitestone...

"Lord knows why she's so down on him," he thought. "He's always very polite to her."

He could see Whitestone's house now, through the trees, a beastly little house, he thought it, damp, hemmed in by those dark pines, a jerry-built little house, with a cheap tiled fireplace, built-in settles on the porch, all sorts of "arty" touches. Poor Whitestone hated it himself, but he had to live in it, just as he had to work in an advertising agency, instead of painting remarkable pictures.

"He can paint, all right," thought Delancey. "Fellow's a genius, I think."

His admiration for his friend was perfectly uncritical. He had admired Whitestone and liked him ever since they had been at a preparatory school together; he admitted candidly that Whitestone was far more intelligent than he was, that it was unfair that he should have so much and Whitestone so little. He wanted very much to help Whitestone; he would have done a great deal for him, if Josephine had not been so disagreeable about it. As it was, he had been able to spare twenty or thirty dollars now and then, had paid the poor devil's club dues, a garage bill, things like that.

"Oh, forget it!" he would say, when Whitestone tried to thank him. "Some day when you're famous, you can paint my portrait."

The car stopped outside the cottage, and Linney sounded the horn. This usually brought Whitestone out in a hurry, glad of the chance to ride so comfortably to the railway station instead of taking a bus. But this morning he did not come. The horn sounded again and again, with no result.

"I'll go in and see..." said Delancey.

"Only fifteen minutes to catch the train, sir," Linney warned him.

In his heart Delancey knew well enough that it made very little difference whether he caught that train, or any other. He had desk room in a downtown office, where he went every day to open and answer such letters as came addressed to The Washproof Button Fastener Company. An invention of his own, this was, a device for fastening buttons to any sort of material, so that they were almost undetachable. A good idea, but not very successful. Needed a few improvements, when he could get round to it....

He went along the brick walk, mounted the steps to the narrow porch, and rang the bell.

"Can't have gone," he thought. "Or I'd have seen him at the bus stop." There was the sound of a quick, light step inside; he smiled to hear it. Rosalind, of course. It was a pleasure to think of her, the one compensation of poor Whitestone's life.

"And a big compensation, too," thought Delancey, somewhat ruefully.

Even the harassments of poverty, he imagined, would not be intolerable with a girl like Rosalind to share them, a gay, valiant, pretty comrade. Their devotion was the most beautiful thing...

"Hello, Shawe!" she said, cheerfully. "Come in! Robert's not going in to the office this morning. Another headache.... Come and have a cup—" Her voice broke; she swallowed, and then went on, cheerful again. "Have a cup of coffee."

Delancey glanced at her compassionately. The poor girl was upset about something; he could see now that her eyes were reddened. Yet she was still so pretty, always so pretty and smart, even in her cotton housedress, her blond hair waved, her hands beautifully tended; she was so slender and straight.

"Thanks, Rosalind," he said. "So Robert's got another of those headaches, eh? Ought to see an eye specialist, I should think."

"I believe they're nervous headaches," she said, lowering her voice. "He doesn't sleep well, you know. And he lets everything upset him."

"Artistic temperament!" said Delancey, seriously. "Where is he? In bed?"

"No. In the dining-room. Drinking far too much coffee. But come in, Shawe!"

He followed her along the narrow hall to the little dining-room which, in spite of its low ceiling, its cheap furniture, he had always found attractive. More than ever so now, with the Spring sun shining in, the fresh blue and white cloth on the table, the willow-pattern china, the tulips in a bowl.

"By Jove!" lie thought, with a sigh. "Money isn't everything.... If Whitestone could realize..."

But Whitestone was obviously in a bad mood this morning. He sat slouched in his chair, his dark hair untidy; a lean, haggard fellow of thirty or so, with something unreasonably boyish about him, something touching.

"Hello, old man!" said Delancey. "What's this I hear about a head—?"

"Got the car there?" Whitestone interrupted. "Run me down to the station, will you, Shawe?"

"Oh, Robert!" cried his wife. "Don't think of going to work when you feel—"

"I want to get some Bristol board," he said, curtly.

"But—" she began, and stopped, and Delancey saw her looking at her husband with a curious intensity.

"Worried about him," he thought. "Poor girl...."

Whitestone had risen and walked into the hall.

"Come on!" he cried, impatiently.

Delancey turned his head to give Rosalind a comforting smile, but the smile never happened. He saw a look on her face such as he had never seen before; he had not imagined that she *could* look like this. Always before he had thought of her as a girl; not now, though. Her skin had a dry, blanched look beneath the powder, her eyes were strained, the lids a little wrinkled; with surprise he realized that when she was not gay and smiling, she was not really pretty. Smart, of course, and attractive, nice figure, but not really pretty—and not young. Not like the girl he had seen strolling about the Luffs' garden. Authentic youth there, with its irresistible and undefinable charm; just the way she had turned her head on her slender neck, the complete unconsciousness of her pose.... Queer how well he remembered that girl....

"Shawe..." said Rosalind, standing very close to him, and speaking in the lowest possible tone. "Poor Robert.... Do remember, won't you, that he's not himself this morning?"

Delancey nodded in kindly reassurance, but he did not want to look at Rosalind again just then. He felt guilty, ashamed to have discerned that she was not young; he felt very sorry for her.

"For God's sake, come *on!*" shouted Whitestone, in a fury.

"Temperament, eh?" said Delancey, with a smile in Rosalind's direction, and made haste to join his friend. They went along the brick walk at a ridiculous pace; Whitestone was almost running.

"Here, now!" said Delancey, half laughing. "What's the idea?"

"Walk a way with me," said Whitestone. "Linney can pick us up."

"O.K.!" said the good-natured Delancey. "May do your head good. We'll get more shade if we—"

But Whitestone was already striding along the dusty highroad, and after a word to Linney, Delancey set out after him.

"If it's a question of money," he thought, "I've got dam' little just now, and that's a fact. If I can unload those Craddock shares for Josephine, she'll give me a commission, and that'll be something.... Thing is, Whitestone lets things get on top of him. Granted he's short of money—and that's no joke. But he's got Rosalind, an ideal home life, sympathy, comradeship, all that. And talent."

He caught up with his friend, and taking his arm, forced him to a more reasonable pace. They went on for a time in silence, the burly, ruddy, handsome Delancey, and his haggard and temperamental friend.

"See here, old man!" said Delancey, presently, troubled by the other's blank aloofness. "What you want to do is, take things a little easier. You upset yourself, and you upset Rosalind—"

"Rosalind?" said Whitestone, turning on him suddenly. "Upset Rosalind? I was just thinking—I wish to God I could kill her."

CHAPTER II

DELANCEY ACCUSED

Delancey stopped short in the road, shocked.

"Robert..." he said, "you're... You shouldn't say things like that, even if you are a bit overwrought."

"Not say it?" said Whitestone, with a smile.

And the smile frightened Delancey. Here on a public road, in the bright Spring morning, he felt a chill run down his spine.

"Is it possible...?" he thought. "I mean, these artists... High-strung, and all that... I mean, is it possible his mind's affected?"

He glanced cautiously at his friend, but Whitestone was looking at him, still with that strange, mirthless smile.

"Look here, Robert," he said, firmly, "you've got to get away—for a rest. A little trip."

"I'm not going away," said Whitestone. "Not when the only thing that makes life worth living is here."

"What do you mean, Robert?"

"I'll tell you," said Whitestone. "I've got to tell you. All of it. I'll go mad, if I don't. I'm in love."

"Lord!" murmured Delancey, immeasurably distressed. "That's... Poor Rosalind..."

"Oh, shut up!" shouted Whitestone, so loudly that Delancey glanced back, alarmed lest someone had heard him. "I know—" Whitestone went on, "that you manage pretty well not to see what you don't want to see, but even you must have noticed.... You must have realized what a hell my life has been with that—"

He used a word that made Delancey wince.

"Robert," he said, "you're going to regret this. The fact that you're temporarily infatuated with some other woman—"

"It's not a woman," said Whitestone. "She's only a girl—a kid. She's the loveliest... God! And at this moment, she's not half a mile from me!"

"Robert, see here! She's not by any chance the girl who's visiting the Luffs?"

"So you did know, did you?" said Whitestone, with a short laugh. "I suppose it's all over the place. And what the hell do I care? The first time I set eyes on her, two weeks ago, everybody could see how it was with me. And I tell you I don't *care!*"

"You've got to care. Whether you like it or not, you've got to consider your wife."

"Come here!" said Whitestone, and taking his arm, drew him into a little glade of birches beside the road. "You're in for it now, Shawe. You're going to hear—everything. I've got to talk—and you're the best friend I've got."

Delancey would much have preferred not to hear any more, ever.

"This'll blow over," he thought. "I mean to say—if I can get him to go off somewhere for a while. Nerves, that's all...."

Things did blow over. He had learned that much from his own experience. So many things. Josephine's tears and tempers, his own rare moods of puzzled misery—all blew over, and left the sky clear.

"I might be able to borrow enough money to send him away," he thought. "On one of these cruises."

Whitestone had lit a cigarette, and was smoking with deep inhalations. If he hadn't been an artist, thought Delancey, he would have looked like a tramp, in his shirtsleeves, with that low collar.... Hadn't shaved, either, this morning....

"I was trapped," Whitestone began. "I never wanted to marry her. She knew it, too. But she 'just felt she could help me so much'... That's the way she put it.... She led me on.... I didn't realize where I was heading until it was too late. She managed so that everyone took it for granted we were going to be married.... I imagined myself that I must have said something—must somehow have given her to understand that I cared for her.

I was ashamed to back out of it.... She was such a damned good woman.... I felt like a brute.... So I went through with it. And as soon as the trap was sprung, I began to see."

"But, Robert... See here! You're prejudiced now. You're forgetting all she's done for you."

"No," said Whitestone. "I haven't forgotten *anything* she's done for me—or to me. I remember it all. I lie awake at night, going over it. The first thing she did was to destroy my faith in myself. 'You're such a funny old boy, Robert.... Of course you forgot to stop at the Electric Light Company's office'... Of course I forgot everything important—like darning cotton and stopping at the dry-cleaner's. I was just a big boy, a poor, helpless boy, hopelessly unpractical.... Wonder I managed to keep alive, before I married her. To keep alive, and sell some of my drawings.... Then she destroyed my work. 'But you funny old boy, we've got to eat,' she said. So I got this damned job. I was to do my poor, pathetic painting on Sundays and holidays—after I'd mowed the lawn and carried out the ashes, and put up the screens.... Oh, I didn't *have* to do a thing. Rosalind would work so hard, and faint, because it was so hot and she was so tired."

"But, Robert—"

"That fainting didn't fool me for long. But even when I knew it was a sham, what could I do?... All those burns and cuts.... You've seen her often enough with her hand bandaged.... I knew, long ago, that there wasn't a dam' thing under those bandages. But, oh God, that brave, bright smile...!"

A profound uneasiness possessed Delancey. He had seen Rosalind often with a bandaged hand. He had seen the brave, bright smile. What if there really were some truth in Whitestone's passionate grievance? He could scarcely endure to think so; for over a year he had taken a benevolent pleasure in the spectacle of their happiness....

"She made me take this job," Whitestone went on. "And then she wasted the money I made. The blood money. The price of my soul. You must have realized that what I made was enough for us, for the mean way we live."

"Well, I—"

"You didn't want to see," said Whitestone. "When I told you I was in trouble, you'd put your hand in your pocket. But you wouldn't *think*. I made enough. We could even have saved a little. My tastes are simple. But she has to go to the Beauty Salon every week. She has to buy special shoes—her foot is so narrow.... She has to spend more for painting her face than I can afford for my canvases. If I don't give it to her, she runs up bills. Which I'm legally obliged to pay."

His mouth twitched; he stopped a moment.

"She's taken away my money, and my work, and my faith," he said. "She's drained me, she's ruined me. Inch by inch. And now—she's so amused about Elsie.... Poor old Robert, without a penny to his name, with his hair getting grey—the pathetic failure—dreaming that a girl like Elsie could ever take him seriously.... This morning at breakfast, she told me, in her cheerful, amused way, that she'd heard gossip about it. 'I'm not going to let people laugh at you, Robert.... I've asked your Elsie here to dinner to-night, so that everyone will see there's nothing in it.' "

"But, Robert, perhaps she—"

"I want you to come to dinner to-night—with Elsie," said Whitestone. "The Luffs are coming too. Then you'll see for yourself. I'll tell you in advance what you're going to see. Rosalind's going to be brave, and humorous. There'll be a beautiful little dinner—and she'll have a bandage on one hand.... Later she'll ask me to bring out some of my paintings—and when I refuse, she'll say what a pity Robert never finishes anything.... Oh, yes; she'll be able to show Elsie what she's made of me—her poor, silly failure of a Robert, who couldn't exist without her."

"By heaven!" thought Delancey, aghast. "I'm afraid that's what she does do...."

"She went a little too far this morning," said Whitestone. "I called her a name she didn't like."

"There's no excuse for that," said Delancey, curtly. "She's a—good woman, and she's your wife. I'm surprised, Robert."

"So was she," said Whitestone, "and she's afraid now. She saw."

"Saw—what?"

Whitestone lit another cigarette.

"She knows now what I want to do."

"You mean you're going to leave her?"

"Oh, no!" Whitestone answered, smiling faintly. "No sense in that. She won't give me grounds for a divorce; she'd never let me go. And I want to be free. No.... *She's* going to leave *me.*"

"But how—?" Delancey began, and was sorry he had begun. That smile of Whitestone's...

He wanted to get away in a hurry, he did not want to hear any more, did not want to guess any more.... He wanted to get out of the glade, away from his friend, back into the cheerful, everyday world.

"See here, Robert!" he said. "You're overwrought. You get along home now, and dress, and come into town. Meet me at my office, and we'll have lunch together."

"D'you know—" said Whitestone, slowly. "I envy you, Shawe. It's a divine blessing, the faculty you've got for shutting your eyes. You're able to live in that comfortable blindness. You've refused to see how it was with Rosalind and me. And you won't see how you hate Josephine."

"Now, look here!" said Delancey. "You're going too far, Robert. That's a *lie.*"

"You—humbug!" said Whitestone, laughing. "It's almost a pity, to try to wake you up. You hate Josephine, and she knows it."

"That's a damned lie!"

"You've told me twice—with that solemn, anxious face of yours—that you dreamed your Josephine was dead. D'you know what that means? *She* does. The second time you told me, she was there. I watched her—and she knew. You were honest—in your dream. It was the death wish, Shawe."

A peculiar sensation assailed Delancey; it was as if cold water trickled down his spine, under his skin. He resented it.

"I won't listen any more to your raving!" he said, angrily.

"You were wishing her dead, Shawe. Wishing that jealous, domineering woman was dead, and out of your way. And that you had your freedom—and her money."

Delancey turned on his heel and walked off.

"Wait!" cried Whitestone, laughing again. "Don't forget that I want you to dine with me tonight. Seven o'clock."

"I'm not coming," said Delancey. "I don't want to see you again, until you're in a different frame of mind. You've said things..."

"Shawe, come back! You can't leave me like this.... Shawe—I tell you I'm at the end of the tether."

His voice sounded desperate, almost hysterical. But for once Delancey ignored an appeal. He was shaken by a great anger.

"He's gone too far, this time," he said to himself, striding along the road toward his car. "I won't forget this in a hurry. He's said inexcusable things. Inexcusable. I mean, making all possible allowances for his temperament and so on...."

The wind stirred the dust in the road, the trees rustled; he slackened his pace, feeling suddenly tired, and very hot.

"It's ridiculous," he told himself. "I shouldn't take it so seriously. No one ought to mind an accusation when it has no foundation at all. To tell me I 'hate' Josephine... Simply ridiculous. Of course, I'm no Romeo. I'm not the kind of man for one of those 'grand passions.' I'm too practical. But I'm as fond of Josephine as I've ever been of any woman in my life. She has her faults—but who hasn't? What's more, she's fond of me. Very. It's—it's an insane thing to say that I... That she knows I..."

Something came into his mind, which made his blue eyes dilate.

"You looked stealthy and horrible!" she had said, that morning. "You looked like—"

Like what? What had she been going to say?

"My God!" he said to himself, in a whisper.

CHAPTER III

THE LUFFS

Delancey had missed his usual train, and the one after it; the people waiting on the platform were strangers to him, not those well-known faces he was accustomed to seeing six days a week. But they were ordinary, decent, comprehensible people; he felt a great good-will toward them; he felt the relief of one waking from a nightmare to familiar surroundings. And he felt, too, the vague terror that a nightmare leaves.

"Whew!" he said to himself. "That was a—very unpleasant experience.... But fantastic, of course."

The word pleased him.

"Fantastic," he repeated to himself, as he boarded the train.

It seemed to dispose in a thoroughly satisfactory fashion of poor Whitestone and all he had said, it gave to the scene in the birch glade an air of unreality. The real world was this, the train, the crowds, the Grand Central Station, the subway, his desk at the office, the amiable stenographer who worked for him when he needed her.

He did not need her this morning; his business was not brisk.

"I'm going to look around for something else," he thought. "A regular job with a salary."

He had mentioned this once or twice to Josephine, and she had protested.

"Oh, don't, Shawe! It's so nice for you to have your own business. I'd hate to think of your working for someone else—being at someone's beck and call."

Very generous, she was. He had his own bank account, in which she deposited a cheque the first of every month. She never asked what he did with it, and if he said he needed a bit more, for his business, she almost always gave it. Almost always. Sometimes, when he least expected it, she would make extraordinary accusations against him, would say she knew he wanted the money to spend on some other woman.... Of course, she had her faults, like everyone else. He had faults himself. But, with the exception of a little scene now and then.... Simply nerves.... She was a high-strung girl, poor Josephine.... Well, not exactly a girl, perhaps. She admitted to being five years older than he, and sometimes he had a suspicion that it was a bit more than that. When she waked in the morning, there was a look about her eyes...

He wished he had not thought of that. He always tried to avoid look-ing at her until she had removed her "night cream" and applied those "ton-ing lotions" and so on.

Suddenly he felt rather sick.

"That damned cheese soufflé last night," he thought. "I need a drink."

He was very temperate by habit; he never drank in the morning; he could not remember ever wanting a drink as he did now. He opened a per-fectly unimportant letter, frowned at it, and rose, with a purposeful air.

"I'll have to see this man at once," he observed, aloud, for the benefit of the stenographer, and taking his hat, went out of the office.

It did him good. He ordered another. Nearly eleven. If he was to get home for lunch, he ought to catch the 12:24. He didn't want to get home for lunch. Well, nothing remarkable in that. Plenty of men he knew, men who appreciated their homes as much as he did, nevertheless liked to stop in town now and then. He might ring up Foster, or Duval. He might go to the club.

"No," he decided. "Josephine was a bit upset this morning. I'd better go home, this time."

Linney was waiting for him at the station, smart looking fellow in that uniform; the car, too, was one of the finest; these men with their shabby little coupés must envy him. There was a rush for the waiting taxis; never enough of them. One young man got left; he stood on the platform, with his bag beside him, and glanced at his watch.

"Hold on a moment, Linney!" said Delancey, and leaning out of his car, addressed the stranger. "See here, going north? Perhaps I can give you a lift."

He often did that, and liked to do it.

"Sorry, but I don't know whether it's north or not," answered the stranger. "I'm going to Mrs. Luff's—if you happen to know where that is."

"That's right on my way! Hop in!"

"Thanks!" said the stranger, gave his bag to Linney, and got in beside Delancey. He was a neat, fair-haired young fellow, slight, rather short, qui-etly dressed, quiet in voice, yet there was something about him which made Delancey anxious to impress him.

"Fine place the Luffs have," he observed.

"Is it?" said the other, politely.

"Yes.... They're neighbours of ours, you know. Delancey, my name is. Shawe Delancey."

"My name's Acheson."

"Acheson...." Delancey repeated. "Yes.... Fine place the Luffs have. Quite an estate. Our place isn't half the size, but my wife's a great gardener. I wish you could see—"

He stopped, with an odd look on his ruddy face. The thought had entered his mind, and would not be banished, that he would not like this quiet young man to meet Josephine.

"Most men of my age have younger wives," he thought. "Girls...."

Then he recalled that this was Josephine's car, and that she was generous to him.

"She's a fine-looking woman, too," he thought. "And she knows how to dress. I mean to say, Mrs. Luff's like a rag-bag, compared to Josephine."

He liked Mrs. Luff very much, though; he greatly regretted that Josephine did not get on with her. When they had first come here, the Luffs had been remarkably nice, had invited them to dinner, had been friendly in a fashion he had never before encountered. With honest humility he admitted to himself that the Luffs were "a cut above him," and above Josephine, too. Their way of living, their simplicity, their ease, the atmosphere of careless comfort in their house, seemed to him about the best thing there could be. He would have liked to live like them; he would have liked to *be* like them.

"Drive right up to the Luffs' house, Linney," he said.

For, after all, he had not quarreled with the Luffs; he didn't even know exactly what had gone amiss between Josephine and Mrs. Luff. Whenever he met Luff, at the railway station, or on the train, they always chatted together. There was no reason why he should not take this young man to the door; and if he happened to see Mrs. Luff, well, he wouldn't be sorry for a chance to say a few friendly words to her. That would be no offense against Josephine.

"Fact is," he thought, "I believe Josephine's sorry now. I believe she'd be glad of an excuse to patch things up with Mrs. Luff. She lets her nerves get the better of her."

His heart quickened a little, to see Mrs. Luff on the terrace. He had always admired that terrace, with the striped awning over it, the comfortable chairs and little tables.

"Suppose she—snubs me?" he thought, and he imagined her speaking with the haughty arrogance he had heard Josephine employ toward the presumptuous.

Mrs. Luff rose as the car stopped, and came to the head of the steps.

"Hugh!" she said. "I'm so glad... And Mr. Delancey.... How nice!"
Her husband had come to her side.

"Delancey..." he said. "Come up and have a drink?"

Delancey was delighted with this welcome; he mounted the steps, smiling joyously.

"Elsie, dear," said Mrs. Luff. "Mr. Delancey, Miss Sackett.... And I forgot—you don't know Hugh Acheson, either."

It was the girl he had seen in the garden that morning, the girl Whitestone said he loved.... She was wearing a sleeveless white dress that made her olive skin seem darker; her face was exquisite, great black eyes, soft and sombre, a wide and sullen and beautiful mouth. She was very young, and her manner was not amiable, yet, for all her immaturity and her lack of graciousness, Delancey knew that she was something rare. Without being at all able to define it, he nevertheless knew that here was the sorcery that men have died for since the beginning of things.

"Poor Robert..." he thought, with a pang. "Poor devil!"

For what could this lovely girl find to please her in the bitter and moody Whitestone, a man certainly ten years older than she, and a married man, too? Yet, if Whitestone's heart had once turned to her, how could he ever forget...? Poor devil!

A parlour-maid brought out whiskey and a syphon of soda on a tray; Luff held out his cigarette case; there was the friendliest air. But for once Delancey's cheerful talk deserted him; he felt unhappy, desolate, and did not understand why. Only that somehow this was the right life; somehow Luff, lean and amiably taciturn, Mrs. Luff in her debonair dowdiness, the quiet young Acheson, the unforgettable Elsie, were the right people, whom he had been longing for, without knowing it. And he couldn't stay here, couldn't ever get back here once he had left.

He sipped his drink slowly; when anyone spoke to him he answered, and that was the best he could do. He wanted to make this moment last.

"You'll stay to lunch, won't you?" asked Mrs. Luff, and he came to, with a slight start.

"Why, thank you," he answered. "I'd certainly like to, but my wife's expecting me home...."

He had to go now, and go forever. Mrs. Luff would simply not be interested in "patching things up" with Josephine.

"It was all Josephine's fault, whatever it was," he thought. "Must have been. Mrs. Luff wouldn't quarrel with people. She must think Josephine is—"

The word came to his mind; it was as if he had heard Mrs. Luff say, in her lazy, pleasant voice—"impossible." That must be what all their neighbours called Josephine. The impossible Mrs. Delancey....

He got into the superb dark-blue car, and he was ashamed of it. He was ashamed of his own bigness, his hearty voice; he sat back in a corner, thoroughly miserable.

"It's no use," he said to himself, over and over. "It's no use."

And did not know what he meant by that, or why he was so unhappy. As his own house came in sight he pulled himself together, tried to shake off his depression. It was really a fine house, Colonial style, big white pillars, well-kept grounds.... The housemaid smiled at him when she opened the door.

"Shawe!" called his wife's voice, imperiously.

She was lying on a couch in the library, tall, looking very slight in a black lace tea gown, with long jade earrings, her olive face powdered, her lips scarlet, her black hair drawn straight back from her forehead. He had seen her before in this same costume, and in this same pose, and he had admired her. "Cleopatra," he had called her.

He did not admire her now. In his mind, he envisaged her on the Luffs' terrace, in the sunlight. He contrasted her low, thrilling voice with Mrs. Luff's clear one; her heavy perfume made him think with nostalgia of the clean scent of cut grass. He thought of that girl Elsie, who was dark and slender, like Josephine, but who was really young. And he felt an overwhelming pity for Josephine.

"Well, Cleopatra!" he said, and crossed the room to kiss her.

"Shawe!" she said, curtly. "Where have you been?"

It would never do to mention the Luffs to her, especially when she was in this mood.

"The train was a little late—" he said.

"That's a lie!"

"Now, see here, Josephine! That's not—"

"It's a lie!" she repeated. "Alice Hampton got the same train as you. She told me she saw you. And she stopped in here twenty minutes ago. You've been *somewhere* for that twenty minutes."

"My dear girl, look here! I ran into a fellow I know, down at the station, and we talked for a while. Naturally, I didn't keep track of the minutes—"

"No!" she said. "It's that girl."

"Good Lord! *What* girl?"

"I heard about it last week, but I tried not to believe it. Someone told me that that girl who's staying at the Luffs' was running after a married man in this neighborhood, and by the way she said it, I felt it was you she meant...."

"Good Lord!" he said, again. "When you say things like that—what can I answer?"

"The truth—if you're capable of it."

"All right, then. Here's the truth. I've never spoken ten words to Miss Sackett—"

"So you know her name!" cried Josephine, sitting up. "You admit then that you know her!"

"Luff happened to introduce us—at the station," he said, for now, less than ever, could he mention his visit to the Luffs' house.

"It must have been a regular little reception at the station," she said, with a sneer.

"Now, see here, my dear girl...! You're working yourself up over nothing. Absolutely nothing. Other women don't interest me—none of 'em—"

"Do you think I'm blind, or a fool? Do you think I haven't noticed the way you look at Annie, my own servant?"

He felt no anger against her, only an immense boredom. These scenes had happened before; she made herself ill by them, by her wildly unreasonable jealousy. He had never been unfaithful to her, or even contemplated such a thing, but he could not convince her of that. The only way to end these miserable episodes was by making love to her, flattering her, letting her "forgive" him—for what he had not done.

"Don't you ever look in the mirror?" he said. "Well, then, do you imagine that a man with a wife like *you*—"

"You needn't try that," she interrupted. "I've listened to you once too often. You've seen the girl once to-day, and you planned to see her again. Your precious Robert Whitestone's wife rang up. 'You'll both come to dinner to-night, won't you? A little party—some friends of Robert's...' I could see through *that* without much trouble. Rosalind Whitestone knows perfectly well that I wouldn't set foot in her house. She asked me because Robert bullied her into it. I wasn't expected to come. It was just an excuse for you to get there. Robert's trying to help you, in your nasty, underhand love affair. You were going to tell me you were dining with them, and you were really going to meet that girl somewhere."

"Josephine, you're—" he began, and stopped. It occurred to him that, in defending himself, he might incriminate Robert. He would have to be careful—and with the alarming insight women had, Josephine might very well discern that he was being careful. That would make it worse.

"You're making a mountain out of a molehill," he said, in a soothing, reasonable tone. "I saw Robert this morning, and he spoke of our both coming to dinner."

"Well, I'm not going, and you're not going either," she said.

He was still not angry, and he was aware of the necessity for caution, on Robert's account, yet he felt that this domineering spirit in her must not be encouraged.

"I want to go," he said, amiable but firm. "And I want you to come too. Wear that new dress—the brown lace, y'know. Rosalind likes you, and if you knew her better—"

"Likes me, does she? Just about as much as I like her. I'm not going, and neither are you."

Their eyes met, and now he felt anger rising in his heart.

"Hold on!" he said to himself. "Keep cool."

He waited a moment; then he said, mildly.

"All right; if you don't want to go… I'll call up Robert and tell him I'll run over later in the evening for half an hour or so. Fact is, I'm worried about Robert. I don't think he's well."

"You're not going there this evening."

The smouldering anger in him was growing, and he feared it. He was so seldom angry.

"I will not have a scene with her," he thought. "We've never had a really serious row yet, and I don't intend—"

"I told Robert you weren't coming," she went on. "What's more, you've got to give up Robert entirely. He does you nothing but harm. Every time, after you've seen him—"

"You're going entirely too far!" said Delancey hotly. "I'm not going to give up an old friend, for some whim of yours. I intend—"

"Then you'd better hear what I intend to do," she said. "I'm going to tell Linney you're not to use the car. I'm going to stop making any deposits to your account—"

"What the devil's the matter with you?" he shouted. "You ought to be ashamed—"

"You're not going to use my money, and my car, to carry on with girls! I've had enough! The affair is getting to be common gossip—you and that girl. And Robert helps you! He's always hated me—"

Delancey turned on his heel, and walked out of the room, out of the house. And he walked as if the devil were after him. Anger goaded him, seemed to gnaw at the foundation of his amiable, easy-going nature.

"She was talking at the top of her lungs," he thought. "The servants must have heard her. Accusing me of making eyes at the housemaid.... And running after that girl over at the Luffs'.... It's enough to *make* me unfaithful, all this disgusting suspicion.... And if she hadn't flown at me the way she did, I shouldn't have needed to lie about stopping in at the Luffs'. We could have had them for friends.... But she won't be friendly with anyone. She doesn't know what loyalty and friendship mean.... Give up Robert entirely.... The hell I will!"

All the time he was aware of something else, some other cause for anger against Josephine, so bitter and savage that he could not face it.

"She said a lot of things she didn't mean," he told himself.

He felt that his anger was a menace, a danger, and he made a determined effort to banish it. After a mile or so, he grew calmer, and he grew hungry. He stopped at a roadhouse and had lunch, a good lunch, and a highball. After he had finished, and smoked a cigar, he was no longer angry.

"Don't know when I've enjoyed a meal more," he thought.

It was after three now, and he contemplated the rest of the afternoon with uneasiness. He had forgiven Josephine, but he did not want to go back to her.

"No," he thought. "Better give her a chance to realize..."

In the three years of their married life, he had never yet stayed away without telling her where he was. Sometimes what he had told her had been a lie, when he had wanted to sit in a game of poker, or to spend an evening with Robert, but harmless lies like that did not weigh upon his conscience. This time he would tell her nothing.

"She really did go too far," he thought. "I mean to say, a man can't let himself be—well—trampled on. I'll go—"

He would go to Robert's, and he would not tell her that he had gone there. That, after all, would be the best course, to tell her in a quiet, good-humoured way that would make her realize he meant to keep his independence.

He took a taxi to Whitestone's cottage, and kept the cab waiting. He was very reluctant to enter; he dreaded the prospect of facing Rosalind, after Whitestone's deplorable outburst.

"Not that it really meant anything," he said to himself. "Pretty nearly all married couples have a row, now and then. The thing has probably all blown over now, and they're happy again."

Nevertheless, he didn't want to see Rosalind just now if he could help it. "I'll take Robert up to the Country Club," he thought. "It'll do him good. We'll have a couple of drinks...."

He was relieved to find Whitestone smoking a pipe on one of the wooden settles built into the narrow porch.

"Hello, Robert!" he said, genially. "Just taking life easy, eh?"

"Oh.... Planning..." answered Whitestone.

"Planning a picture? Well, come on, old man! I'll run you up—"

"No," said Whitestone. "You remember what I told you this morning? There are still a few little details to work out. Because I'm going to do it tomorrow, if the weather's good."

Rosalind's voice came from inside the house, gay and light.

"What are you two doing out there?"

"Talking about you, my dear," said Whitestone.

CHAPTER IV

ROSALIND'S DINNER PARTY

Hugh Acheson sat in his room, looking out of the window, and considering the situation.

It was a situation very familiar to him. How many times had he arrived at a house, and found there a girl—invited only on his account...!

This seemed to him a wrong and unfortunate thing; he always felt apologetic toward these girls, charming girls, pretty, well-bred, intelligent, altogether suitable; he liked them all—but never quite enough. Not one of them had that quality, which he could not have defined, or named, yet which was to him indispensable. Sometimes he had a glimpse of it in a play, an opera; Isolde had it, and Mary of Scotland; he could believe that there had once been women in the world who had that tragic and passionate magnificence. But he had lived for twentyseven years without encountering it in actual life, and the girls he met seemed to him, all of them, a little insipid.

Mrs. Luff's new protégé rather surprised him, although in his eyes Anabel Luff could do no wrong.

She had been a friend of his mother's, and ever since his schooldays he had felt for her an affection and respect he accorded to no one else. If she were so fond of this silent and almost sullen girl, then there must be something admirable in her which he had not yet discerned.

"Her father was Foxe Sackett, you know!" Mrs. Luff had told him, and seeing by his face that the name meant nothing to him: "The musician," she had added. "A composer.... He was really famous, in musical circles. And Elsie plays marvellously, and she's beautiful, don't you think, Hugh?"

"Oh, very!" he had answered, politely.

He sighed now, thinking of Elsie. His chivalrous attitude toward woman was a burden to him; he could not help being deferential to them. He could not let Anabel Luff suspect how little interest he felt in her Elsie; he could not let her know how reluctant he was to go to dinner to-night with this artist fellow. Mrs. Luff enjoyed the society of artists, but Hugh didn't. He admired them, of course; no doubt it was necessary for pictures to be painted, music and books to be written, and so on, but the people who did these things were trying. He did not know how to talk to them. What he understood and liked best were riding, hunting, polo, flying, sailing; he liked to be active physically. To-night, he would probably have to look at this fellow's pictures, and say something....

With another sigh, he rose and began to dress. Dressing was one of the many things he knew how to do well. He was extremely fastidious; his dinner-jacket was a marvel, his trousers were a work of art. Slender, fair-haired, boyish in appearance, he had none the less a sort of dignity about him; he was easy, friendly, polite, but no one took liberties with him.

Anabel was waiting in the hall for him. Her black evening dress did not fit very well; her sandy hair was untidy, as usual, but she was privileged to look like that; she was beyond criticism. Luff was with her, wooden and immaculate.

"We'll have cocktails before we go," he said. "Whitestone's liquor is... Well, Anabel's responsible for this."

"Robert Whitestone's quite charming," said Mrs. Luff, firmly. "And very talented."

"But he doesn't do anything!" her husband objected. "I mean—after all—how d'you know he's talented? Never has any pictures to show."

"If you'd ever seen him at work," said Mrs. Luff, "in an awful little sort of summer-house, full of spiders, and wearing a smock, and his hair ruffled..."

Her husband and young Acheson both smiled with immeasurable indulgence. Anabel Luff was past fifty, there was grey in her hair, but she would always be able to evoke in men that tender amusement.

"You'll see yourself—" she began, and stopped, looking toward the staircase. Elsie was coming down, in a long white evening frock, a rose-coloured ribbon about her dark hair; her appearance was unusual, and as a rule Hugh Acheson disliked any sort of eccentricity. But this girl, he thought, was like some portrait in a gallery, fragile, immature, touchingly lovely.

"You won't want a cocktail, dear...?" said Mrs. Luff.

"I do, please."

"It's not good for your complexion—"

"I need one!" Elsie vehemently.

This seemed to Hugh in poor taste. A kid of her age had no business to "need" a drink.

"Neurotic," he said to himself.

He did not know definitely what that word meant, but he did know what it connoted for him. It signified too much smoking, and too little fresh air, too much emotion, and too little exercise. He was sorry to see her swallow a cocktail almost at a gulp, and hold out her glass for another. For she was authentically young, not more than eighteen or nineteen, he decided, and her youth was exquisite.

She had been badly brought up, though, or else she was bad-tempered. As he sat beside her in the car, he made two or three attempts to talk to her as he talked to other girls, without getting anything better than the curtest possible retorts. So he let her alone.

The Whitestones' house was worse than he had expected, shabbier and smaller; something queer in the atmosphere, too. Whitestone was silent and distrait; Mrs. Whitestone was too gay. Moreover, it made Hugh uncomfortable to be waited upon by his hostess; he found it embarrassing to sit at the table while she hurried back and forth. He wanted to help her, but she would not allow that, wouldn't even let her husband help her.

"But you've hurt your hand, Mrs. Whitestone!" Hugh protested, observing a bandage about her fingers.

"It's nothing," she assured him, smiling. "Just a tiny burn."

She could not suppress the other man, though, that Delancey whom Hugh had met earlier in the day. Delancey seemed very much at home here, jumping up from the table, going in and out of the kitchen, making good-humoured and somewhat pointless jokes. He carried it off very well, but Hugh saw....

It was perhaps because he so seldom read anything, because his thoughts were so largely occupied by sports and more or less impersonal matters, that Hugh Acheson had so great a power of observation. He observed, and he understood, only by the light of his own experiences. There were no other people's ideas in his head. He was that rare creature, a truly independent human being. Moreover, his active and temperate life had sharpened his senses; he had almost the accuracy, the quickness of a savage, and he never thought of doubting his own conclusions. He simply didn't make mistakes.

"Something wrong here..." he thought.

There was something wrong with Delancey, and with Elsie, and with Mrs. Whitestone, and something very wrong indeed with Robert Whitestone.

"That fellow's in hell," thought Hugh, soberly.

Mrs. Whitestone was talking with animation to the polite and unresponsive Luff; Mrs. Luff and Delancey were very cheerful together, and Elsie and Whitestone obviously had no desire and no intention of talking at all, so Hugh thought himself justified in keeping silent, and trying to understand this situation. His quiet grey eyes never seemed to watch; his boyish face never revealed that he was listening, but he saw, and he heard, and every nerve in his alert, hardy body was conveying impressions to him.

Somehow, it was Delancey who interested him most. Beneath that genial air was a strained uneasiness; he kept glancing from Whitestone to Mrs. Whitestone.

"Is he in love with Mrs. Whitestone?" thought Hugh.

He decided not. He had seen plenty of fellows in love, and they had not been like this.

"No," he thought. "He's afraid of something."

Fear, he reflected, was the one emotion that could not be concealed. Hate, love, even pain could be disguised, but not fear, that first great primeval passion and driver of men. At the hangar, at sea in a storm, Hugh had seen men afraid; he knew what that sidelong look, that overhearty laugh meant.

"Why?" he thought. "What's he afraid of? Whitestone? Mrs. Whitestone? Is it blackmail?"

He was well enough acquainted with the less creditable aspects of life; on one occasion an attempt had been made—unsuccessfully—to blackmail him. He knew that such things happened, and he was neither unduly shocked nor distressed about them. He turned this idea over in his head. But whatever was afoot, he decided, the Whitestones were not acting in concert; there was no harmony between them. Mrs. Whitestone wasn't afraid of anything; he felt sure of that. The flush in her cheeks, the forced gaiety of her manner were caused by anger. That was how women behaved when they were angry. And she had cause for irritation, with her husband sitting there silent and haggard, eating none of the excellent dinner she had prepared. She couldn't feel much goodwill toward Elsie, either; the girl did not make the slightest effort to do her duty as a guest; never even glanced at her hostess.

"The kid's miserable," he thought. "And so is Whitestone."

That gave him another idea, and a most unwelcome one, but one that persisted. As always, he fell back upon his own experience, recalling what he himself had seen or heard, and he could not call his idea impossible, or even improbable. Elsie would not be the first poor little fool to entangle herself in a disastrous love affair of this sort, or the last. It happened all the time. And it fitted. It explained her sullen mood, and Whitestone's morose and distrait silence, and Mrs. Whitestone's anger.

But it left out Delancey's fear.

"I don't see..." thought Hugh.

He wanted to see, on Elsie's account, because Anabel Luff was fond of the girl, and because she was so young. He did not want to witness any disaster to her, and he was troubled by the possibility. For, by some sixth sense, which he trusted implicitly, he felt that there was something atrocious overshadowing this cottage.

Mrs. Whitestone, with no servant, and very little money, and, he suspected, very little social training, had however an undeniable social talent; she was the sort of woman, he thought, who could have married a man in a far more exalted position and managed well for him. He didn't like her; he saw her as insincere, vain, and superficial, but he admired her for the valour of that dinner, well-cooked, well-served, if a little over-elaborate. And he pitied her, too, because it was so unsuccessful. She served wine, and that was one thing she did not understand; no one but Delancey drank it. The conversation grew more and more desultory; Mrs. Luff tried in vain to aid her....

Whitestone laughed abruptly, at nothing.

"I've got some whiskey that's really fit to drink," he said, and pushing back his chair, went out of the room.

Delancey rose too, and with an inaudible excuse, followed his friend, through a swing-door that led to the pantry. The door fitted badly; from his end of the table, Hugh heard that hearty voice, subdued to an anxious murmur.

"Now, Robert, see here...! Pull yourself together, old man! I mean to say—with guests in your house—"

"I'll be fine in a little while," Whitestone answered. "I'm going to get drunk."

Mrs. Whitestone had taken Mrs. Luff and Elsie into the sitting-room; Luff sat staring at his glass of wine with gloomy intentness.... Hugh's ethical code was artless as a schoolboy's, but rigid. He considered eavesdropping a discreditable thing, so, much as he wanted to hear more of that conversation in the pantry, he addressed a remark to Luff. Luff, though, was slow in answering, and in the interval, Hugh heard Delancey speak again.

"Oh, shut up about your plan!" he cried, and there was a note in his voice that disturbed the listener. "I know you're only talking through your hat. I know it's simply dam' nonsense—but I don't like it."

"Ah...!" said Luff, at last. "Well, I shouldn't be inclined to back Weyman too heavily.... Seems to me..."

He went on talking, and presently Whitestone re-entered, followed by his friend. Luff and Hugh accepted his whiskey; they praised it politely, but a curious uneasiness possessed them all. Even Luff was restless. They went, presently, into the sitting-room, and it was better there.

"Mrs. Luff does that," thought Hugh.

He had seen her do it before. Once away from the disturbing influence of Whitestone's moody silence and Delancey's forced geniality, her own influence had made itself felt, her cool, light gaiety, her effortless good-humour. Mrs. Whitestone was more tranquil now, Elsie less sombre, and when the four men entered, they too were changed. Delancey was a little subdued, and Whitestone suddenly became animated. It might have been the whiskey, but whatever the cause, he showed a quick, biting wit that was close to brilliancy. For the first time Hugh could see that Whitestone had a certain charm; he was handsome in his fashion, he was clever, and he was appealing. He had the air of a man who laughs in despair.

"That's what gets women," thought Hugh, and glanced at Elsie.

Her beauty dazzled him. Her dark eyes were soft and shining, her lips were parted in a half smile as she listened to Whitestone. She was enthralled, rapt. And Mrs. Whitestone was watching her.

"Lord!" thought Hugh. "This won't do...."

"Robert, dear," said Mrs. Whitestone. "Won't you bring in some of your work? I'm sure—"

"Please!" said Mrs. Luff. "Have you finished that one of the bridge in the twilight, Mr. Whitestone?"

"He hasn't!" said Rosalind, laughing. "He *won't* finish things. I wish you could make him, Mrs. Luff. He's such a provoking boy. All these—"

"He'll do something big, one of these days," Delancey interrupted, so hastily, so loudly as to startle the others. "Thing is, with an artist... You've got to let 'em alone. I mean, they've got to work things out their own way. One of these days Robert'll do a picture that'll surprise all of us. The fellow he used to study with—can't think of his name just now—I remember he said Robert was the most promising pupil he had. And you've got to remember Robert won a scholarship in that art school. I mean, all that shows he's got it in him."

It was difficult, even for Anabel Luff, to find anything to say after this vehement outburst; but, after a brief and embarrassed silence, she did speak.

"But we all feel sure of that, Mr. Delancey! You've no idea.... I use Mr. Whitestone as a decoy. I ask people down to meet our artist."

"Please do!" entreated Rosalind. "What Robert needs is more encouragement. Of course, what I say doesn't count. He can't help feeling that I'm prejudiced—"

"My dear girl," interrupted Whitestone. He rose and lit a cigarette, with a very unsteady hand. "My dear girl—on the contrary! I never forget the things you've said. I can assure everyone that I'd never be where I am, if it hadn't been for you."

It seemed to Hugh astounding that Mrs. Whitestone didn't see.... Mrs. Luff began to talk again, Delancey responded to her. No one seemed to have understood that note in Whitestone's voice, the look on his face.

Hugh himself was so disturbed that Mrs. Luff's move to go home was a great relief to him. He wanted to think over all this, in quiet. They went out to the car, the Whitestones standing silhouetted in their lighted doorway. Luff was helping his wife in, when Elsie touched Hugh's sleeve. He turned quickly.

"I'd like to speak to you," she said, in a whisper.

"Now?" he asked. "Shall we walk?"

"No. I'd rather—I'll come to your room after they've gone to bed," she said, and got into the car.

CHAPTER V

IN THE GRAND MANNER

Not yet in his life had Hugh Acheson misunderstood a woman. It was impossible for him not to know that he was an extremely eligible young man whom girls wanted to marry; he had also met with married women who wanted him to be publicly, obviously devoted to them. But he accepted all this impersonally and without vanity. When he was liked for his own sake, he knew it. And when he was not liked, he knew it too. He had known from the beginning that Elsie Sackett did not like him, and that if she wished to see him now it was not for his beaux yeux.

That didn't disturb him. He was sorry for her, and if she wanted anything from him she would probably get it. He found waiting for her a wearisome affair though; he had got up early that morning, he had ridden in the Park, there had been a difficult and delicate meeting of the Board of which he was secretary, and now he was sleepy. He yawned and yawned, leaning back in his chair, yet he felt it would be incorrect to change his dinner-jacket for a dressing-gown. He put his feet up on another chair, and smoked a cigarette and yawned and looked at his watch. Nearly midnight.

"Regular kid's trick..." he thought. "We could so easily have walked back from the Whitestones' and got this over with."

He remembered another night, a year or so ago, at his aunt's house. One of the girls there, a house-guest, had told him during the last dance that she was "starving." He had offered to get something for her to eat, but that wouldn't do.

"I'll knock at your door later, when they're all in bed," she had said. "And we'll go down and raid the ice box."

He remembered that girl's gay, eager little face; not her name, though. It was the memory of her adventurous young happiness that remained. He had kissed her while they sat side by side on the kitchen table, and she had accepted the kiss with an air of indulgent nonchalance. But it had added to her happiness. She had felt herself to be desirable and lovely.

That was how Elsie ought to be, and he did not know if it were her misfortune or her fault that she was not. She had none of the charming self-confidence of a pretty young girl, no coquetry. Yet she was not incapable of emotion. That look she had given Whitestone was a look of adoration. She might, of course, be simply imagining this thing, making a drama out of it, but on the other hand, she might be seriously in love with him, and it was a bad job either way. Whitestone was unstable, unsound, not a man to trust with any woman's life.

"And he hates his wife," thought Hugh. "He's not just irritated, or bored with her. He hates her. That's a damned ugly thing. I can see that she might be pretty hard to bear, but he could get out, get away from her—not stay and hate her. There's going to be trouble in that quarter, and if someone doesn't stop it, Elsie's likely to be mixed up in it."

A knock at the door brought him to his feet, and he opened the door for her. She passed him without a smile, or a word of greeting, and as he closed the door she sat down in a high-backed armchair. She looked somehow different, taller, almost august, with the gleaming white dress in folds about her feet, her fragile arms extended on the arms of the chair, her dark-browed face pale.

"You'll think I'm horrible," she said, curtly.

"I don't think so now," he answered, with a smile.

"I shan't even try to explain," she went on. "I can't help what you think. I'd never have come to you if I hadn't been—desperate."

"I'm glad you came to me, if I can help you."

"You can," she said. "But there's no reason why you should."

He made no answer to that. He had received her courteously, he had behaved as well as he knew and she had been, from the first moment, challenging, even hostile. He stood before her now, and waited for her to continue. It was obviously difficult for her.

"I want to ask you if you'll lend me a thousand dollars," she said.

He did not show the surprise he felt.

"Will you smoke?" he said, offering her his cigarette case. "While we talk things over?"

"No," she said. "There's nothing to talk over. Either you're willing to lend me this money or you're not."

Now for the first time he admired her. There was something magnificent in her arrogance, something splendid in her self-control. For she was close to the breaking point. He could see that in her pallor, in the set of her mouth, by the faint unsteadiness of her voice.

"As I told you," he said, "I'll be very glad to help you in any way I can."

"You mean you'll lend me the money?"

He lit a cigarette, and in the moment it took to do that, he made up his mind in his own quick, clear fashion. She had said she was "desperate," and he believed that. He believed that if she did not get what she asked from him, she would surely make other and possibly disastrous attempts elsewhere. She would be humiliated and angered by a refusal, but not daunted. Not she!

"Yes," he said. "With pleasure."

That was almost too much for her. Her lip trembled, she turned away her head for an instant. But then she turned back to him and though tears shone in her eyes, they met his steadily.

"Thank you," she said. "I.... Will it be all right if I don't pay it back for six months?"

"Perfectly all right."

She rose.

"May I have it now?" she asked.

Magnificent was undoubtedly the word for her! She considered the transaction finished, but he did not. He meant to find out what she wanted the money for, and he meant to protect her from the folly he suspected.

"Sit down, won't you," he said, "while I write a cheque? And do you want to deposit it or shall I certify it?"

Evidently she didn't understand that; her dark brows drew together in a faint frown.

"Can't I just get the money for it?" she asked.

"If you're known at the bank."

She sat down again, and reflected.

"I didn't know about that," she said. "I've never had a cheque."

His admiration for her increased still further; not before in his life had he encountered such directness. Never had had a cheque...?

A soft breeze blew in at the open window, stirring her dark hair with the rose-coloured ribbon about it.

"Mrs. Luff told me your father was a musician," Hugh said, tentatively. He wanted to make her talk.

"He was," she said. "He was a genius. And he was never appreciated. His life was miserable and dreadful."

"Bad lead," thought Hugh. "I suppose Whitestone's another unappreciated genius. Are you going to study music or take up a musical career?" he asked aloud, not quite sure of the right phrase to use in this subject so entirely outside his experience.

"No," she said. "I don't know exactly what I'll do."

"I hope I'll hear you play tomorrow."

"No," she said again. "I don't practice any more. I live with my aunt, and she hates it."

"Hates music?"

"Yes. She's very poor and her one ambition is for me to live a life like *this.* I'd rather be dead."

"Like this?" he asked, puzzled.

"Week-ends and tennis and dancing," she said. "I hate tennis and I'm a horrible dancer. And I don't care about clothes, and things like that. When father was alive, he wouldn't bother with people who weren't interesting. I hardly ever met people who weren't artists of some sort."

"Lord!" thought Hugh.

"Money doesn't matter to me," she went on. "It never has. I don't even want money—" She stopped, a little disconcerted. "I mean..." she said, "...for the usual things. It's—this happens to be an emergency."

"I understand," he assured her.

"I'd better go now," she said. "Mrs. Luff would be shocked, if she knew I'd come here."

Hugh was quite certain that Mrs. Luff would be no more shocked than he was himself. But if she liked to feel that she was affronting bourgeois prejudices.... He took out his cheque-book and his fountain pen.

He was canny about money; he had been trained to be so. He was more careful than were friends of his who had not a tenth what he had. He was generous, invariably, but his generosity was never slipshod or rash. And he was not reckless or unthinking in this instance. He was taking a risk, with his eyes open.

She could not cash the cheque until Monday morning, and he hoped that during the Sunday they would spend under the same roof, he would find out what she meant to do with it. If she planned something to her own great disadvantage—and he believed she did—he intended to talk to her, or to Mrs. Luff, or to Whitestone. He was very well aware that he might not be able to dissuade her, and that his money might serve only to hasten a catastrophe. That was the chance he took.

When she had gone, he still sat there, thinking over the episode, to see if he could have managed it better. He didn't see how he could have done better or differently. She had come to him defiant, painfully keyed up to make her outrageous request. If he had shown no sympathy, or too much, if he had tried to ask her questions, or to dissuade her, she would have left him at once, and gone away "desperate" as she had said.

"No," he thought. "She's well worth taking a little trouble about..." He reflected. "I believe..." he thought, "that *she's*—one of those women...."

He could not have expressed it in words, but he knew what he meant.

He meant that he discovered in her this strange quality of a heroine. If she were a fool, she would be a superb fool. He respected that.

He slept soundly, according to his wont; when he awoke the sun was up and he felt cheerful, lively and hungry.

"I'll find out why she wants the money," he told himself. "I think I know—but I hope I'm wrong. If she wants it for an elopement with that genius—all right! Then I'll interview *him!*"

It occurred to him that he was taking a good deal upon himself.

"Being an officious ass, very likely," he thought. "But someone's got to be officious where kids are concerned. You can't just let them alone when they don't realize where they're heading."

Mrs. Luff never came down to breakfast, but in due time Luff appeared.

"Up early," he remarked. "Well...!"

They had scarcely sat down at the table when Elsie appeared, dressed in white and entirely too pale.

"I think," said Luff, "that I'll teach you to play golf, Elsie."

"I couldn't possibly!" she said. "I'm hopeless at games, and I hate all of them."

"You'd like golf," said Luff with quiet conviction. "Couldn't help it. Fascination about it. You come up to the Country Club with me this morning and just give it a try."

"I really couldn't!" she cried, and both men were a little disconcerted by the vehemence of her protest.

"Some other time, then," said Luff.

"What about a drive?" Hugh suggested. "My car'll be here presently, if it's not here now. Something went wrong with it yesterday, but the chauffeur said he'd be able to run it out this morning."

"Thanks," she said.

He did not know whether she meant yes or no, and he did not like to ask her. She was so pale, obviously so disturbed.

"Why?" he thought. "She was all right when she left me last night. What can have happened in the meantime? Did she see the genius last night?"

She drank a cup of coffee, and left the table.

"Can't understand the girl," said Luff, when she had gone. "Pretty girl. I'm fond of her. But I never could make her out. Anabel's had her here before, and she's always the same. Never wants to do anything. Doesn't ride, or swim, or play tennis; doesn't like dancing. Sort of morbid, don't you think? Girl of her age...."

"Well, her father being a musician..." said Hugh.

"Ha...!" said Luff, gravely. They understood each other perfectly.

Hugh went out presently, to the garage, and there he found his chauffeur waiting, and his car in condition. He drove it to the house and, entering the hall, he found Elsie there, in a black suit and black beret, with a red scarf about her throat, like a handsome young Apache, he thought.

"It's a good day for a drive," he began.

"I'd forgotten it was Sunday!" she cried, with a tone of passionate accusation.

"But—don't you like to drive on Sunday?" he asked.

She went past him out of the door, and he followed, before he could help her, she had got into the roadster.

"I'd forgotten to-day was Sunday!" she said again. "And you didn't remind me!"

"Does it make much difference?"

"Yes! It does!"

He was just starting the car when Luff came along the terrace.

"See here!" he said, "Hugh—Anabel says will you leave this at Delancey's? He left it here yesterday. Must have dropped it. Might want it."

Hugh put the silver cigarette case into his pocket, and set off down the drive.

"If it's something very urgent," he said. "I have a little cash with me."

"How much?" she demanded.

"Not more than fifty dollars, I'm afraid."

"That's no good," she said, and fell silent.

He felt no resentment at this cavalier treatment; glancing covertly at her, he felt only pity for her misery. The time had come when he ought to talk to her, win her confidence, persuade and convince her. Only now in the cool, bright morning, it was more difficult than it had seemed last night. The very fact of her being so young made it worse. If she had been a mature person, with some knowledge of the world, he could have devised an approach; but she was so self-willed, so blunt and naive, she would probably take offense at the first hint of advice. He glanced at her again, and still could not begin.

"How early tomorrow can I get that cheque cashed?" she asked.

He could not afford to miss that cue.

"I've been thinking," he said, "If there's this—emergency—perhaps I could help you in some better way. I'm rather good at practical things."

It was as he had expected. She grew suspicious at once.

"No, thanks," she said, with a quick, sidelong glance. "I can manage for myself."

"Look here!" he said. "I don't mean to be meddlesome. It's simply that I'm older than you and I've had more experience. I think that if you'll talk this thing over with me, you'd be glad."

She did not answer at all, but a flaming colour rose in her cheeks. She looked so lovely, so furious, so very young, that he sighed inaudibly.

"You saw for yourself," he went on, "that I was glad to do what you wanted, without any questions."

"You knew to-day would be Sunday. You thought you'd have plenty of time to talk me out of it. You knew I couldn't do anything with the cheque until Monday.... I suppose you've told Mrs. Luff."

She opened the purse she carried and brought out the cheque.

"I'll give it back to you," she said. "You never really meant me to have it."

He turned his head, and for a moment their eyes met. And in his steady gaze she saw something that abashed her.

But she could not tolerate that weakness in herself; she would *not* be disconcerted.

"Last night," she said, "I thought you had understanding. I thought you were—rather wonderful about this. But I don't now. Now you want to make me tell you why I want the money. I won't tell you. I'd rather give it back to you."

"There weren't any conditions attached to it," he said, briefly.

"There were. There are. I might have known, from the way Mrs. Luff talked about you. She said you were 'so level-headed.' That means that you couldn't ever have a generous, reckless impulse. Take it back, please!"

"If you don't want it, tear it up," he said. "I'll have to stop here for a moment to return Delancey's cigarette case."

He turned into Delancey's driveway, and there was Delancey himself, sitting in a wicker chair on the veranda, smoking, and reading the Sunday newspaper. He was delighted to see them. He was, Hugh thought, almost pathetically hospitable.

"Sit down for a few moments!" he entreated. "I'll call my wife."

Hugh was pleased that Elsie accepted with a certain graciousness. He realized that he had never felt so uncertain about a fellow-creature as he did about her. If she had turned her back and walked off without a word, it would not have surprised him. But she took the chair Delancey pulled forward, and sat there quietly, hands clasped in her lap, and never glanced at Hugh, until Delancey returned with his wife.

As a naturalist, when finding a new specimen, compares and contrasts it with species already known to him, so did Hugh, when meeting a person for the first time, attempt to relate that person with someone already known to him. He did this unconsciously, because it was his fixed habit to draw only upon his own experience. He looked at Mrs. Delancey, thin, supple, handsome in her somewhat haggard fashion, and he thought—"Jessica!" There was no actual physical resemblance, but in Mrs. Delancey's voice, her smiles, her gestures, he detected his cousin Jessica.

He had been a boy of eighteen at the time of the great Jessica scandal, but he had forgotten nothing of it. He had been alone with her, in her villa at Nice, when she had killed herself. She had been the first person he had ever seen dead; he had not known at first, when he had found her lying on a couch, tall, thin, her black hair elegantly dressed, her handsome face composed, faintly scornful. Only she had not answered, when Hugh reminded her that D'Albert had waited so very long alone in the salon....

Even at eighteen he had understood that *affaire* with an impersonal clarity. It had seemed to him fantastic and distasteful that there should be love between Jessica, a woman of forty and D'Albert at twenty-five. But it had been a genuine passion, and D'Albert had been an ardent and chivalrous lover; he had given her no cause for suspicion or complaint. Yet she would never trust him, never believe him, would never permit herself to be happy.

And now, in Mrs. Delancey's face, he saw the Jessica look, a look of torment caused not by grief from outside, which the spirit attempts to resist, but a pain bred in the soul, not resisted but fostered, encouraged.

She was a little over-affable to Hugh.

"My father used to know a Mr. Acheson," she said. "The famous millionaire financier, Mr. Bruce Acheson. Is he any relation to you?"

"Er—yes," Hugh answered, with immense reluctance. "My father...."

A blank silence followed, and he felt as if he had been guilty of some horrible breach of good taste.

"The telephone, sir," said the housemaid, and Delancey, went into the house.

"My gardener tells me—" Mrs. Delancey began, when her husband's voice reached them from inside.

"What?" he shouted. "What...? Oh, God!... No...! Oh, my God...!"

Mrs. Delancey rose and Hugh with her. They were all facing the door

when Delancey came out. His ruddy face was ghastly, his eyes staring.
"Mrs. Browne telephoned.... My God!.. She says Rosalind's *dead!*"
Hugh caught Elsie as she fell forward out of her chair.

CHAPTER VI

ROSALIND COMES HOME

"What's the matter?" cried Delancey, standing by the sofa to which Hugh had carried the unconscious girl. "Merciful Heavens...! I'll send for the doctor."

"I don't think there's any need for that," Hugh answered. "She's fainted, that's all. The news was a bit sudden."

"I'm a clumsy fool!" said Delancey. "I didn't realize."

"If Mrs. Delancey will ring for water, and whatever you have— brandy...."

"Lord...!" said Delancey, with a sort of groan, and turning to see what new trouble there was, Hugh found Mrs. Delancey lying back in a chair, with her eyes closed.

"You might give Mrs. Delancey some brandy too," he said, briefly.

He was seriously disturbed about Elsie. Not about her fainting; he had once fainted himself, when having a dislocated arm set; he had seen plenty of people faint and recover. It was her emotion that worried him, and her lack of discretion. She might very well say something outrageous when she recovered her senses, and Mrs. Delancey would hear. Mrs. Delancey was not a woman he would have chosen to overhear an indiscretion.

"She could say anything," he thought, looking down at Elsie's white face. "And not necessarily by mistake, either.... If she's hurt, she'll hit back and hit hard."

He wet a towel in cold water, and bathed her face, he saw to it that she lay with her head low, and he was confident that she would soon revive. Her dark lashes stirred, a little colour came back to her lips. She looked up directly into his face, with a blank, clear gaze. Then her eyes seemed to darken. She was remembering now. He could not glance away; he was obliged to watch, dawning in her eyes, a black, bitter fury.

She sat up, without a word, and let him support her with his arm about her shoulders while she drank a glass of water.

"I'm going now," she said.

"Hadn't you better—?" he began.

"I'm going now," she said, and rose to her feet. Mrs. Delancey still had her eyes closed, but it did not seem to Hugh necessary to display much concern about her.

"I'll take Miss Sackett home now," he said.

Delancey left his wife's side, and hastened to help. He insisted upon holding Elsie's arm as she went down the veranda steps; he almost lifted her into the car.

"I can't tell you how sorry I am I upset you this way," he said. "I might have known what a shock..."

Elsie held out her hand to him.

"No," she said. "You're Robert's friend. It's horrible for you.... You're going to see him soon, aren't you?"

"I'm going at once. He hasn't been notified yet. I... They want me to break the news...."

"Wait! I didn't know that. Let me go with you, please."

"No!" protested Delancey, shocked. "Wouldn't do at all."

"Then I'll go alone. I'm going to be there when he hears...."

"Better not, Miss Sackett," said Hugh.

She did not take the slightest notice of him.

"Mr. Delancey, please take me with you!" she said.

Delancey was obviously incapable of resisting her, and Hugh saw that any attempt at interference from himself would be worse than useless.

"I'll take you in my car," he said, addressing Delancey.

"To his house?"

For with Elsie in this mood, he was not going to let her meet Whitestone with no better support than Delancey, who was more unnerved than she. The fellow was shaking like a leaf as he got into the car.

"How did it happen, Shawe?" asked Elsie.

He looked startled at her use of his name, and perhaps by the gentleness of her tone.

"It's—I can't understand it," he answered. "Naomi Browne said she and Rosalind went down to the beach. They often did that.... And Rosalind swam out too far. Naomi missed her after a few moments.... But she'd gone...."

"Where did they find the body?" asked Elsie, her eyes narrowed in a curious intensity.

"They haven't. Not yet."

"Mrs. Browne didn't really *see* her go down?"

"No. She just—"

"Then perhaps she's not drowned. Perhaps she swam round the point and came ashore somewhere else."

"Not possible. In the first place, Rosalind wouldn't do a thing like that.

She'd know how it would worry Naomi. And even if she had, she'd be *somewhere*. As soon as Naomi missed her, she ran along the beach. Then she went back to the road, and stopped a car that was passing, and the people in it helped her to look. If Rosalind had been there, they couldn't have helped seeing her."

"She might have gone home."

"Walked two miles in her bathing-suit? And just left Naomi there without a word? No. It's—it's got to be faced. She's gone. They've got people looking for her—along the shore."

"She might have gone home, just the same," Elsie insisted, with an obstinacy that interested Hugh.

"She wants Mrs. Whitestone to be alive," he thought. "As Delancey wants to believe she's drowned. I don't quite see—"

With infinite patience and kindliness, Delancey was arguing with the mutinous girl.

"No use clinging to false hopes," he said. "I mean, the thing's got to be faced—"

They were very near the cottage now, and Hugh was aware of a sensation he had known before, a queer and very unpleasant sensation in the solar plexus. So had he felt when his cousin Jessica had not answered him, had not opened her eyes. So had he felt when he had gone to tell the mother of one of his sailboat's crew that her son was not coming home to her. Ever. They were going now to tell Whitestone that his wife was not coming home, ever. And the fact that he had hated her would not soften the blow.

"I'll go first," said Delancey, but when he got out of the car, the girl followed him, and doggedly Hugh followed her. Delancey rang the bell, but no one came; he knocked and no one answered. And this had the most singular effect upon him. His face blanched. He stared at the closed door in undisguised terror.

"But he must be home!" he shouted. "I tell you I know he's home!"

"Maybe he's in the studio," Elsie suggested, and Delancey gave a great sigh of relief.

"Of course!" he said. "I'm a fool to have forgotten that."

Hugh said nothing, but his own face had grown a little pale. For in his terror, Delancey had most completely betrayed himself. What he feared was obvious, and not good to contemplate. If Rosalind were dead, he wanted to be sure that her husband was at home—and had been at home. He too, for all that he was not very quick-witted, or very observant, must have seen what Hugh had seen, that Whitestone hated his wife.

However, Whitestone was in his studio. It was a wretched little sort of summer-house, dusty and untidy, and he sat there in a faded brown smock, before an easel, so absorbed in his work that he did not notice their approach until Delancey spoke.

"Robert, old man—"

He turned, and rose, in polite haste.

"Miss Sackett..." he said. "It's nice to see you here."

They all stood facing him, in a blank, wretched silence, and he stared at them with a frown.

"But—what's the matter?" he demanded.

"Robert, old man," said Delancey, in a voice which desperation made over-loud. "Old man, you'll have to—to prepare yourself for a shock."

"Get on with it!" cried Whitestone. "What's happened?"

"Robert... Your wife... Rosalind's met—with an accident."

Whitestone stared at him.

"She—you know she went swimming this morning with Naomi Browne.... Robert, old man—you've got to brace yourself...."

Whitestone turned fiercely on Hugh.

"Acheson!" he said. "Are *you* capable of giving me a coherent account? What's happened to Rosalind?"

"She's missing." Hugh answered in his quiet way.

"Missing? What d'you mean? From where?"

"Mrs. Browne missed her while she was swimming. The shore's been searched but there's no trace of her."

"I'm not going to take Naomi's word for that!" said Whitestone furiously. "She's a fool. I don't believe all this. I'm going there myself.... Rosalind's a good swimmer.... She wouldn't... It's impossible...."

He strode out of the summer-house, brushing past the other three as if he were unaware of them.

"I'll drive you," said Hugh.

Whitestone looked back over his shoulder.

"All right!" he said. "But hurry up!"

"I'll come back for you, Miss Sackett," said Hugh.

She did not trouble to answer that; both she and Delancey crowded into the roadster. She sat on Delancey's knees, he had his arm round her waist. And she had her back turned to Whitestone.

"Drive like hell!" said Whitestone.

Hugh drove as fast as he considered advisable, and he kept his mind on his driving. This wasn't the time to think....

But there was no need for him to go as far as the shore. Little more than half way there, they met Rosalind Whitestone coming home. She came in a hospital ambulance, and Doctor Madison and a young interne were with her. She did not need them, though. Nobody could ever do anything more for her.

Hugh drew up his car at the side of the road, and Doctor Madison got out of the ambulance.

"Try artificial respiration, you damned fool!" said Whitestone. "Often—even hours after..."

"It's no use, Whitestone," the doctor answered. "I'm sorry.... Try to take it quietly. There couldn't have been any pain. She struck her head against a rock. Better get him home, Delancey."

Delancey had taken his friend's arm when that thing which Hugh had dreaded, happened. Elsie put her arm about Whitestone's neck, laid her check against his.

"Try to stand it, Bob," she said. "Bob, my dear darling. I'm with you— all the time."

He did not speak or stir. He stood as if her frail young arm were his sole support.

"Bob, darling, go home now. I'll come later... to be with you. I'll help you all I can."

"Come on, Robert!" said Delancey roughly. "Can you give us a lift in the ambulance, doctor? Then Acheson can take the young lady back to Mrs. Luff's."

She made no demur, but got back into Hugh's car. And already Delancey was trying to explain to Doctor Madison.

"She's very high-strung.... Had dinner with poor Mrs. Whitestone only last night.... She was at my house when we got the news, and naturally... A shock like that... She doesn't know what she's saying or doing...."

The doctor and the interne had nothing to say to that. Hugh wondered if Elsie had heard....

"Do you want to go back at once?" he asked her. "Or would you rather drive a bit?..."

"I want to go back," she said. "And I want never to see you or speak to you again."

"Rather difficult to manage," said Hugh equably. "But I'd like very much to know what I've done."

"It's what you'd *like* to do," she said.

CHAPTER VII

JOSEPHINE GOES TOO FAR

Delancey sat by the window of the little sitting-room of the cottage, rigid, tense with misery. He had no idea what to do, what to say to Whitestone who sat on the sofa, his head buried in his hands. He had so slight a personal experience of grief, he felt so inadequate. His instinct would have been to adopt a tone of hearty sympathy, to cheer up the poor fellow, but this case was too complicated. There must be, he thought, something worse than shock or sorrow in Whitestone's heart.

"He won't be able to help remembering what he said about Rosalind yesterday. Of course, I knew he didn't mean it, but just the same... Now that she's gone..."

In a way, she hadn't gone. She was here in the cottage, lying upstairs in the room she had used to share with Whitestone. Whitestone had insisted upon that, and had insisted, violently, upon seeing her, although the doctor had tried to make him wait until the undertaker's people had done their merciful work. Delancey had not looked at her.

"I'd rather keep the memory of the last time I saw her alive," he had said, and wanted to believe it.

Whitestone had been unmanageable. He had forced Delancey to drive him over to see Mrs. Browne. Poor Naomi had been half-hysterical. Her husband had very warmly resented the intrusion, but Whitestone would have her account of the accident then and there.

"Simply made things worse for himself," thought Delancey. Worse for Delancey, too. The memory of Naomi's tear-stained face, the echo of her broken voice, made the tragedy more harrowing. She was a timid swimmer who had remained inside the cove while Rosalind swam around the rocky point, out of sight.

"She always did that. She'd done it hundreds of times.... I just waited for her to come swimming back.... I'll be looking for her green cap all the rest of my life.... I waited, and when it seemed a long time, I called her.... Somehow it frightened me, to hear myself calling.... I climbed up on the rocks and she *wasn't there*.... There wasn't anything but the sea...."

"You mean to tell me..." Whitestone had demanded of Doctor Madison, "that she could have struck her head and sunk, without calling out even once? She was a strong swimmer. She knew every inch of that shore.

How was it possible for her to do what you say—strike her head with that violence?"

Madison had been very patient with him.

"You'll find it's generally the good swimmers who meet with these disasters," he had said. "They grow overconfident. They take chances.... And there are these jagged rocks just below the surface of the water and quite a surf running...."

"Think she'd swim head on into a rock when she knew the coast so well?" Whitestone had asked, scornfully.

"She might have been floating. She might have had a sudden cramp."

"No!" Whitestone had said. "It's impossible, I tell you! The thing's got to be investigated."

Only it was not impossible. It was true. It had actually happened, so horribly soon after Whitestone had said—what he had said.

"Seems almost like a judgment," thought Delancey.

He wished he had not thought that. It seemed cruel and treacherous, with poor Whitestone there before him in his anguish. It seemed cruel, also, and indecent to feel hungry.... But he had had no lunch, and it was now late in the afternoon.

"I wish I'd had a chance to ring up Josephine," he thought. "She was badly upset. But of course she'll understand how it is."

He was a little surprised by his own position in this affair. The doctor, the undertaker, the Brownes, that young Acheson, everyone seemed to take it for granted that he was the one to take charge of Whitestone. He was more than willing to do all he could, only he wasn't, perhaps, as competent as other people imagined. And there was Elsie, too. She treated him like an old friend, she seemed to have a touching sort of confidence in him.

It made him very uncomfortable to think about Elsie, so he stopped. She was a young girl, a nice girl, and therefore belonged in a particular category. Nice young girls could not be anything worse than silly, and "silly" was what he resolutely called her conduct. He would not admit that he had seen on her face a look that had alarmed him, a look fierce, reckless, dangerous....

"Fact is," he said to himself, "I don't exactly know what I'd better do next."

The sun was beginning to set and here he was, alone in the cottage with Whitestone. Not quite alone, though. The undertaker's people had gone, but Rosalind was there, upstairs.... That was another thing it was better not to think about.... Naturally, he could not dream of leaving Whitestone unless someone else came. Someone else ought to come, neighbours, relations, someone to see about dinner. There ought to be a servant.

"I wonder—" he thought, "in the circumstances, I wonder if Josephine might—"

He confessed to himself, with melancholy resignation, that he really had no idea what Josephine might do, or how she felt. She had often enough expressed her dislike for Robert and Rosalind, and, for all he knew, this tragedy might not have softened her. But, on the other hand, she might be overcome with remorse. He took a packet of cigarettes out of his pocket, and, to his dismay, found it empty. He felt in his vest pocket for the very expensive silver case Josephine had given him. He was very proud of that case, but it never occurred to him to bring it out unless other people were present. Days, even weeks went by without his remembering it. He thought of it now because he needed a smoke, but it was not there.

"Must have left it in my grey suit," he thought. "Now, about Josephine... She's changeable.... Sometimes she's—well—unreasonable. But I've known her to be damn generous to people in trouble."

He began to recall all the instances he could of her generosity, and it heartened him.

"She was certainly upset enough when she heard the news," he thought. "Yes.... Yes, I'll try it...."

He glanced cautiously at Robert, who did not stir, then he rose and went into the hall, closing the sitting-room door after him. There was only a wall-telephone here, and the sight of it caused him a pang. He thought of the five French telephones in his own house.

"We've got pretty well everything," he thought. "And Robert..."

Robert had lost his wife; Robert had no money, no servants to make him comfortable, and apparently, no friend but Delancey. He rang up his house, and asked to speak to Mrs. Delancey.

"She's gone out, sir," the housemaid answered.

"Did she say where she was going?"

"Yes, sir. She went to the beach for a picnic with Mr. and Mrs. Parrish."

"To where—!" he began and stopped. "All right, Annie," he said. "I'll call up again later."

It did not seem possible that after the emotion she had shown at the news of Rosalind's death, Josephine could have gone to a picnic, and of all places, to the beach. Nevertheless, he was not sure. She so often confounded him with reasons, motives he could not have imagined.

"She might have felt she had to get her mind off this thing," he reflected. "Well... I suppose I couldn't ring up Mrs. Luff and ask her to get hold of a—a trained nurse, someone to look after Robert and cook a dinner.... I dare say I could get some sort of meal for us, if necessary."

The thought of going into poor Rosalind's kitchen was far from agreeable; he felt that he would almost have preferred to go hungry. But there was Robert to be considered, and Robert he now regarded as a sort of invalid. He had nothing to smoke, either.... On tip-toe, with the buoyancy common to men of his build, he went back down the hall, and cautiously opened the sitting-room door. Robert might have fallen asleep.

Robert was just putting a bottle of whiskey under the sofa.

In haste, Delancey retreated back along the hall and returned to the sitting-room with considerable noise. Whitestone was sitting now as he had left him, his head in his hands.

"I don't like this," he thought. "I mean, if he wanted a drink, why not take one and offer me one? I could do with it! I mean—there's something—well—I can't help calling it stealthy."

He remembered suddenly that Josephine had applied that very word to him, only yesterday.

Stealthy she had called him, and horrible....

"Robert!" he said, abruptly. "See here, old man! You won't do yourself any good by—by brooding like this. The thing is, you ought to eat, to keep up your strength."

A car was stopping before the house, and Delancey lost no time in going to open the door, to see Elsie descend from a taxi and start up the path. And whether it was some reflection from the faint, pale sky, or some fancy produced by his own fatigue and distress, she seemed to Delancey a creature not quite human. She was dressed in white, her face looked white, her black eyes tragic; she did not smile or speak, only looked steadily into his face as she approached. He drew aside, as if she were capable, like a ghost, of walking through him.

She went straight into the house, and he followed her, closing the door behind him. They stood facing each other in the dark little hall.

"I'm going to stay with Bob now," she said. "Do you want the taxi?"

"But—" he said. "I don't think.... I mean—I'll stay too, and help you."

She took his hand in both of hers.

"No," she said. "I'll do much better alone. You've been wonderful. You really understand. Please go away now."

She was perfectly composed and quiet, for a moment longer she held his hand in her firm grasp.

"You're our friend," she said. "Come back soon."

He got into the taxi, and as soon as the cottage was out of sight, he began to reproach himself.

"I shouldn't have left her. It's not right for a young girl. I can't understand how I left her...."

Only, her appearance, her behaviour had been so resolute, so striking, and he had been a little dazed with weariness.

"Something about her..." he thought. "Sweeps you off your feet. But I'll see that some other arrangement is made at once. I'd like to bring Robert home with me for a few days—until he can make some plans."

Their house looked exceedingly pleasant to him now, with the last rays of the afternoon sun in gold bars across the lawn. Josephine was on the veranda and someone else, too, a woman in a light dress. He was relieved to see her; it was always easier when there was a third person present.

"Oh! You're back, at last?" said Josephine. "Shawe, you've met Miss Phillips."

Her manner of speaking these words at once put him at a disadvantage. She implied that he had no doubt forgotten Miss Phillips, that he always forgot his wife's friends. As a matter of fact, he had an almost royal ability to remember names and faces and even little remarks he had heard. Because he genuinely liked people, and was interested in them; he had in his heart an immense good will for his fellows.

"Certainly I've met Miss Phillips!" he said, heartily. "At the Parrishes'. How's that terrier of yours you were telling me about, Miss Phillips?"

Miss Phillips liked his remembering her terrier, and when she smiled she was attractive, a grey-eyed, brown-haired young woman, self-possessed and good-humoured. He could have sustained a pleasing conversation with her, if he had not recalled the tragic quality of this day. He stopped smiling, and sat on the rail of the veranda, staring heavily at nothing.... Surely Josephine or Miss Phillips would begin to speak about Rosalind....

"It's been nice and cool, hasn't it?" said Miss Phillips.

"But the sunset looks like a hot day tomorrow," said Josephine.

"I don't mind hot weather," said Miss Phillips.

He could not understand them. They both knew what had happened, they must realize that he had been with his friend; how was it possible that they should ignore it, not make even a perfunctory enquiry about poor Whitestone?

"Shawe!" said his wife, "I want to speak to you. Excuse me just a moment, Helen."

She went into the house, erect and imperious, and, filled with secret rebellion, Delancey followed her along the hall to the small room at the end which was called his "study." When they were first married, Josephine had furnished it as a surprise for him. "A place of your very own," she had said. "I know what that means to a man." But it never had been his "very own" any more than anything else in the house. She came into it when she pleased, without even knocking at the door.

"I've asked Helen Phillips to stay with me—indefinitely," she said.

Her tone was openly challenging, but he decided to take no notice of it.

"That's nice," he observed.

Then he saw that she was trembling, and his heart sank. Neither of them had mentioned the disgraceful scene of yesterday morning; she had pretended to be asleep when he had got home that night, and at breakfast she had been very amiable, had not even asked him where he had dined. He had made up his mind to forgive and forget the outrageous things she had said about stopping his little income and not letting him use the car. He had hoped that she felt ashamed of herself. He could hope that no longer; she was obviously in one of her tempers.

"Helen's going to stay indefinitely," she repeated. "I have no intention of being left alone in this house with you."

He had had perhaps the hardest day of his life. He was very tired and hungry, and his usual patience failed him.

"You needn't worry about me," he said, briefly. "I won't bother you."

"After this morning," she said. "I'd be *afraid* to be here alone with you."

"What are you talking about?" he demanded.

"You're not very good at hiding your feelings," she replied, with a short laugh. "You were really a little too obvious this morning. You couldn't even pretend to care how shocked and upset I was when that girl pretended to faint. And as soon as she lifted a finger, you went off with her without even telling me you were going. You've been gone all day."

"Josephine," he said, making a despairing effort to speak quietly. "I'm pretty well worn out. I've been with Robert ever since this morning. The whole thing's been... Well, I should think you'd be able to imagine. I've had nothing to eat since breakfast. I'm not inclined to have any sort of argument with you now. I'll simply say that you're entirely and absolutely wrong about the whole thing. And you're *heartless!*" he added with a violence that surprised him. "You haven't even mentioned Robert."

"*I'm* not a hypocrite," she said. "I've never liked him or Rosalind. I'm not going to pretend to feel what I don't feel. I leave that to you. My whole life lies in ruins. I've given you everything—all my love and trust, and you've betrayed me. For that insolent ill-mannered little fool."

"What the devil can anyone say to a woman like you?" he cried. "I've hardly spoken a word to her—"

"My dear Shawe," she protested, again with that short laugh. "Really—! Of course I was one of the last people to hear of it. It's always that way. But for the last two weeks everyone in the place has been talking about your girl and her married man who's so devoted."

He began to speak, but checked himself.

"Can't give Robert away," he thought.

"I'm not quite blind," she went on. "This morning it was plain enough. I'm simply an obstacle, a nuisance to you. You want me out of your way, so that you can enjoy yourself."

"And that's God's truth," he thought.

The thought was like a physical shock. He sat down hastily in the nearest chair, so white that she stared at him in alarm.

"Shawe!" she said, and began to cry. "Shawe, what's the matter?"

"You... I... can't forgive a thing like that," he said. "You've gone too far...."

"Shawe, I didn't mean..."

"Well, you said it!" he cried. "You said... No! I can't forgive that...."

He rose heavily.

"I'm going," he said.

"Shawe, oh, no! I didn't mean what I said.... I swear I didn't.... You can't go.... Where are you going, Shawe?"

"I don't know. Into town. Let me alone, Josephine! I tell you you've gone too far."

She clung to his arm.

"Forgive me, Shawe. Just this once! I'll never, never... Shawe, I'll go now, this instant and tell Helen not to stay.... You know I *do* trust you, Shawe...."

He pulled loose her clinging fingers and went to the door. But she was there before him, blocking his way.

"Shawe, darling! Just do one thing to please me! Just have your dinner first. I beg you! You're tired and overwrought. If you'll just have your dinner, I know you'll see things differently.... Sit down, Shawe, darling!... Let me mix you a nice little cocktail and bring it to you here where it's cool and quiet...."

He was suddenly at the end of his strength, unable to resist her. He sat down again, and closed his eyes, with a long sigh that was like a sob. She brought him a shaker of cocktails and a plate of hors d'oeuvres. She stood beside him, tearful, solicitous, tender. After two drinks he felt better; he reached in his pockets for a cigarette and again brought out that empty packet.

"Shawe, darling, you don't use the silver case I gave you. Don't you like it, dear? Do you want some other kind of case?"

"No," he said. "No, thanks. I do like it.... I left it in the pocket of my grey suit."

"Shawe, I'll tell Helen to go."

"No," he said. "Don't do that."

"But will you not go away, Shawe?"

"All right," he said. "I won't."

"Shawe, darling. I'm not really heartless about Robert. I feel frightfully sorry. Only it was because I thought— Shawe, you can't imagine what it is for a woman to see her youth slipping away—and then to hear that gossip." A restless movement from him stopped her. "But I'm not heartless, Shawe. If there's anything I can do for poor Robert..."

"Well," he said, "the natural thing would be to ask him here for a few days."

"I'll ring him up now."

"No," he said quickly. "Better leave it to me. Robert's in a bad state.... I'd better run over there after dinner...."

She sat down on the arm of his chair.

"Shawe—Shawe, darling.... Just tell me that you forgive me. That nothing's changed between us...."

He wanted to put his arm around her as he had done a hundred times, he wanted to speak to her affectionately, to reassure her. But he *could not.* Something was changed between them, most horribly and irrevocably changed.

"You're—just overwrought," she said with a sob. "I won't bother you now, poor boy."

CHAPTER VIII

A STORM COMES UP

Josephine suggested his having dinner alone in the study; but the last thing on earth he wanted was to be alone. He went up to their bedroom, shaved, had a cold shower, and dressed in his dinner jacket. When he descended, he found the table decked as for a gala occasion. Josephine, her eyes a little reddened, was wearing a low-cut black frock he had once admired. Miss Phillips, nonchalant and amiable, had dressed too. She looked, Delancey thought, very distinguished and handsome. He wished she would stay forever, so that never again would he and Josephine sit down at the table alone together.

There were pink roses on the table, pink candles, ruby glass, the best china with the gilt edges; the food beautifully cooked. He was half-ashamed of his lusty appetite, remembering poor Robert, half-ashamed of his comfort.

And he put out of his head that thing he had thought, banished it utterly. Josephine had seen that he was overwrought. That was it. He and Josephine had had a little row, and it had cleared the air, wonderfully. He had never seen her gentler, more anxious to please. She even made a point of discussing the morning's tragedy, in a tone of profound sympathy and with an anxious eye on her husband.

"A dreadful thing," Miss Phillips agreed.

But in her tone there was not the slightest sympathy. She had not known either of the Whitestones, she was not in the least affected, and her remark was nothing but politeness. Somehow this pleased Delancey. He began to feel a profound respect and admiration for Miss Phillips, with her rather drawling well-bred voice, her nice, straight little nose, her imperturbable good-humour.

"She'll make some lucky fellow a fine wife," he thought.

He fancied he knew the sort of house she would have, dim, cool, tranquil, nice people, like the Luffs, coming in and out. No scenes, ever....

"Well, Josephine and I get on very well for the most part," he said to himself, as he drove the car down the drive in the sultry evening. "A little flare-up now and then, but what's that amount to?"

As he drew nearer to the cottage, his comfortable, after-dinner mood began to leave him; back came the old oppression. Rosalind lying dead in the cottage. And that girl...

"*She* won't be there," he assured himself. "Mrs. Luff wouldn't allow that. Robert himself wouldn't allow it."

Unless, of course, the poor fellow had been a bit too free with the whiskey. If he had, no one who knew the circumstances would blame him. For he was suffering not only the natural grief any man would feel, but he must be remembering those things he had said only the day before her death.

"I won't deny it," thought Delancey. "He practically said he was going to do away with her. Of course, he didn't mean it, but it'll be bad to remember how bitter he felt against her.... Even though it was only a passing mood...."

Just for a moment he remembered how he himself had felt, at Rosalind's last dinner. He had not thought then that Whitestone's words expressed a passing mood. He had believed them, and he had known a horrible fear. He had even made up his mind to have a private talk with Rosalind, to advise her to go away at once for a visit because of Robert's "nerves"!

"I was a fool!" he told himself. "It was nothing but talk, and talk he'll regret to his dying day."

He was relieved to see lights shining from the cottage windows, lights downstairs, none above where Rosalind lay.

"Poor girl," he thought.

The front door was unlocked; he pushed open the screen door and entered. Rosalind had always been glad to see him. Poor girl...

He was a little surprised at the sight that met his eye. The little sitting-room was brightly lit, and in it were three people, all still and silent. Whitestone and Elsie were side by side on the sofa, and across the room was that young Acheson nursing his ankle and gazing at nothing. None of them looked at one another.

"Hello!" said Delancey in a low, subdued voice.

"Oh... Shawe?" said his friend. "Come in!"

He came in and sat down, with a civil greeting to Miss Sackett and Mr. Acheson, then he too fell silent. A pale sheet of lightning flashed across the sky.

"We may get a storm," said Delancey in the same subdued tone. "Break up the heat."

No one answered this, and he could find nothing more to say. A little gust of wind sent the window curtain fluttering into the room. He remembered Rosalind making those curtains. Very far away there was a mutter of thunder.

"This won't do!" he thought. "I mean to say—Robert shouldn't sit here, brooding...." Yet he did not know how to break the silence; he did not even venture to light a cigarette. Again the lightning played, the curtain billowed out, the distant thunder rolled. His eye fell upon the Sunday newspaper and he had an inspiration.

"Robert," he said. "Did you see what they said about Mallier's exhibition?"

"No," answered Whitestone.

"Ought to interest you," said Delancey, rising and taking up the newspaper. He had read about the exhibition, solely because of Robert. On his own account he would certainly not have read "Art Notes."

"Here it is," he said, folding a page neatly. "The notice is pretty hard on the poor fellow."

"Let's see," said Whitestone, with a sudden awakening of interest. He felt in his pockets and frowned. "I can't find my glasses. Read it to me, will you?"

Delancey did so, a little embarrassed by certain names and words he could not pronounce.

"Fellow's nothing but a charlatan, anyhow," said Whitestone, when he had finished. "He's fooled the public for five years, but the critics have never been fooled...."

Again that strained and painful silence descended. And suddenly Delancey thought.

"I can't take Robert home with me.... I mean—we can't leave Rosalind here alone.... No.... I'll have to stay here with him."

The idea was far from pleasing. The storm was coming nearer, the wind that blew in the window was almost chilly now; there was something tense, ominous in the air.

"But of course I'll have to," he thought. unhappily.

"Miss Sackett!" said Acheson.

His voice was a very quiet one, yet it seemed to ring through the room. They all looked at him.

"Well?" she said.

"There's a storm coming up," he said, amiably. "I think we'd better be starting home."

"I don't mind storms," she said.

"I think we'd better be going. Mrs. Luff will be anxious."

"I told Mrs. Luff not to wait up for me."

"But she will, you know," said Acheson, still amiable, but with a far from amiable glint in his grey eyes. "We'd better..."

"There's the rain now!" said Whitestone. "Take a look at the windows, will you? If you'll go upstairs, with Acheson, I'll see to the downstairs ones."

That was obvious enough. He wanted a word alone with the girl. And somehow, with Rosalind lying upstairs, it seemed horrible.... Horrible to go upstairs, too, in the dark....

"Delancey and I can look after the whole thing," said Hugh, amiably, and in spite of his reluctance to move about in the dark little house, and his feeling that Whitestone and the girl should not be left alone, Delancey followed him. "The wind's south," said Hugh. "We'd better look at the back windows first. D'you know where the switch is?"

As Delancey turned on the light in the dining-room, a clap of thunder sounded very close, and the rain came in a deluge. They hurried through the swing-door into the pantry.

"Broken window-pane here," Delancey observed. "We'll have to close the shutters."

The rain was driving in through a little window high in the wall. Delancey, being the taller, pushed up the sash, drew the shutters in and fastened them. As he stepped back, something wet and cold brushed his face.

"My God!" he cried. "What's that?"

"A bathing-suit," said Acheson. "Hanging on a line."

Delancey felt suddenly sick, physically sick. Rosalind's bathing-suit.... What did they do in such cases...? Dress the poor girl, perhaps, in one of those fresh, gay little dresses she had liked so much...?

"I—can't..."he said.

Hugh had found the switch, in the clear light he was looking narrowly at Delancey.

"What's the matter?" he asked.

"I—this thing's a little—too much for me...."

"Better go and sit down," said Hugh, briefly. "I'll carry on."

When Delancey, sick and shaken, went back to the sitting-room, Whitestone and Elsie were talking together in whispers. They stopped as he entered, and he regarded them with something that was almost hostility.

He could feel no sympathy for his friend now, or for the girl. It was monstrous that they could so affront and ignore Rosalind in her own house. Even if Robert had not loved her very much, even if he had not loved her at all, it was brutal to ignore her, lying dead upstairs.

"Josephine suggested my bringing you home with me," he said, coldly.

"Out of the question," said Robert. And, of course, that was the truth. Rosalind could not be left here alone.

"Then I'll ring up Josephine and tell her I'm staying here with you tonight."

"You needn't," said Elsie. "I'm going to stay."

Delancey was really shocked, and he made no effort to conceal it.

"Well..." he began when Hugh spoke from the doorway.

"We'd better be starting, Miss Sackett."

"I'm going to stay here," said Elsie.

"We'd better start at once," said Hugh.

He was considerably younger than the other two men, he was slight, boyish, unassertive. Yet there was something about him, in his voice and manner, that gave him indefinable authority.

"He's right," thought Delancey. "She's got to be made to realize."

She turned to Hugh.

"There's no need for you to interfere," she said. "I'm not going with you."

"Whitestone," said Hugh. "Will you try to persuade Miss Sackett?"

To Delancey's consternation, Whitestone was silent.

"Even if she doesn't, Robert ought to realize that the girl can't stay here," he thought. "I don't care how upset he is. He ought to realize..."

"Will you remind Miss Sackett that your wife is still in the house?" said Hugh, and Delancey thought he had never heard a voice so merciless.

"You'd better go, Elsie," said Whitestone.

"Do you really want me to go, Bob?"

They looked at each other, as if there no one else present, looked and looked into each other's eyes.

"I think so..." said Whitestone.

She turned then and went out of the house, and Hugh went after her. The screen door slammed behind them.

"She's a fool!" said Whitestone.

Delancey stared at him.

"I don't know what is the matter with you," he said, sternly. "Upon my word—you don't deserve... When she's been so—so kind to you.... And when I think of what you told me that morning, about the way you felt toward the girl—"

"That?" said Whitestone, fiercely. "Couldn't you see for yourself that I didn't know what I was saying yesterday? I was drunk."

"You were not," said Delancey. "Though maybe you are now."

"I was drunk, I tell you!" shouted Whitestone. "Everything I said then was all dam' nonsense. Anyone except you would know that the only woman I ever loved, or could love was Rosalind. Elsie's nothing but a hysterical little fool."

The front window of the sitting-room was open, and Whitestone's voice was clearly audible to Hugh and Elsie as they went along the path in the rain.

Her foot slipped in the mud and Hugh took her arm, but she pulled away from him. He opened the door of the car, she got in and he followed her.

"I suppose," she said, "that even you could see that that was camouflage.... He doesn't want me involved."

"Yes," said Acheson.

But his quiet forbearance did not placate her.

"I'd like you to know," she said harshly, "that Bob and I are going to be married."

A jagged streak of lightning seemed to cut the road for a moment like a fiery sword. The rain was drumming loud on the roof of the car.

"I hope not," said Acheson.

"I know you do!" she cried. "You were horrible to him! Even now— when he's in such trouble—all alone, you went into his house and scarcely spoke to him. You had no right to come!"

"If I hadn't," he said, with that invincible patience. "Mrs. Luff would have come...."

"I told her..."

"I know," he said. "You told her you felt you ought to go. But she looked at it in a different way. And so do I. And I hope Whitestone does. It's impossible for you to be there alone with Whitestone...."

"Do you think that in a tragedy like this, I care a snap of my fingers for stupid, outworn conventionalities?"

"I think," said Hugh, "that you're looking at this whole thing from a point of view that's outworn and conventional and sentimental."

"Sentimental?" she repeated.

"That's the word I'd use."

"Why?"

"You've got this idea... Your father was very unhappy, and you saw what made him unhappy. He was a talented man and he got no sympathy or understanding. You think it's been the same way with Whitestone. You think he's a genius, and that you're the one to make him happy."

"Who told you?" she cried.

"No one. I've listened to what you said and I've watched you, that's all."

"And you call that 'sentimental'?"

"I do. Sentimental and impossible."

"There's nothing," she said, "nothing that can stop me. I know Bob's a genius and anyone ought to be proud to help him."

"You can't help him."

"Why can't I?"

"I don't know anything about geniuses," said Hugh. "But whether Whitestone's a genius or not, he's a man. I know how to judge a man. And he's—"

"Don't dare to say anything against him!"

"I've got to," said Hugh. "I want to make you see now, before it's too late."

A terrific clap of thunder made her jump; the lightning illuminated the road.

"We've gone past the Luffs'," she cried.

"I know. I've got to talk to you—I've got to make you see *now* that Whitestone's no good. He's yellow. Think, won't you? Forget it's you and Whitestone. Think of a man who'd go to a girl, a young girl, with complaints about his wife."

"What makes you think he did that?"

"It's got to be that way," said Acheson, slowly, frowning to himself in the dark. "The Luffs think Whitestone was happy with his wife. You'd have thought so too, if he hadn't told you otherwise."

"I might possibly be more observant," she said, with an uncertain attempt at irony.

"When you spoke to me last night," he went on, "it was on his account."

"Are you trying to be like a detective out of a book?"

"No. I'm not brainy. Not by a long shot. I only see things, and listen, and try to put two and two together."

"Well, *why* are you doing this now? Why don't you let me alone? I'm nearly twenty. I know what I'm doing. Why do you try to ferret out what I don't want you to know? Let me *alone!*"

"I can't," he said. "I can't even wait until tomorrow. You've got to see *now* what Whitestone is."

"Why now?"

"Because," he said, "to-morrow it's going to be harder for you."

"Listen," she said. "I don't know how you guessed it, but what you said about father was true. I saw all his wonderful talent ruined, all his faith in himself destroyed. And I think that's the most horrible thing in the world. You say yourself that you don't know anything about geniuses. Well, I do! The fact that I've got a second-rate talent of my own makes me understand it all the better. I found out last year that *I'd* never amount to anything much. My playing is just good. And I made up my mind then that if I could, I'd do for someone else what nobody ever did for father. I know Bob has faults and weaknesses. I know it better than you can. But do you think that matters? It doesn't! He's got to have infinite sympathy and understanding.... I don't care if you know the whole thing now. You'd find it out anyhow in that detestable way you have. I did want the money on his account. He was desperate. He was frightened!"

"Frightened of what?"

"I don't know. He didn't know himself. He only said that if he couldn't get away, he didn't know what would happen. And I told him I'd help him to get away." She was silent for a moment. "He still wants to get away," she said. "I suppose you're not willing now

"No," said Hugh.

She put her hands over her ears.

"Take me home!" she said. "I won't listen to another word!"

With a long sigh, he turned the car.

CHAPTER IX

ACHESON'S VIEW OF IT

"Come in here, Hugh," called Mrs. Luff.

He had returned to the house, after letting Elsie out, and taking the car to the garage. He was tired and dispirited, and in no mood for talking. But what Mrs. Luff wanted must be done. She was in the drawing-room sitting in the dark by the window, looking out at the lightning that still flickered across the sky. He made his way across the room and dropped into a chair beside her.

"Hugh!"

"Mrs. Luff..."

"That child worries me. She *would* run off to Whitestone.... She was so passionate about it. Her father was like that. A fascinating man and brilliant and such a fool. It bothers me...."

"What was her mother like?"

"Her mother never did a foolish thing in her life, except marrying Foxe Sackett. She was very good-looking and very cool and prudent and rather amused at the world. I think she was the most irritating woman who ever lived. And she's made Elsie feel that there's something splendid in being a fool."

"Perhaps there is," said Hugh.

"Hugh!" she said, with energy. "Don't."

"No..." he said. "I won't. But she's—I shouldn't care to be like your Mrs. Sackett, cool and prudent and rather amused.... I've been thinking to-day that I'm rather cold-blooded."

"What do you think of Elsie, Hugh?"

He did not answer for a long time.

"I'm sorry," he said. "But we don't hit it off."

"Don't you think she's lovely, Hugh?"

"That doesn't seem quite the word."

"Please tell me! I'm so fond of her, Hugh. Is it because she's so reckless and silly about that Whitestone man? Because that's really nothing."

"Mind if I turn on the light?" he said. "I don't like talking to you in the dark. I don't trust you."

She was looking up into his face, dazzled at first by the sudden light, then her glance grew more intense.

"Hugh..." she said. "Something's hurt you."

"I've just found out something I didn't know before. I'm a prig!"

"Oh, I've known it for years, my dear boy! It's one of the nicest things about you. It's so unexpected at your age, and with all your money."

"And I'm hard," he said. "Hard as nails."

"Yes," she said. "You can be sometimes. Hugh... Are you going to do something that will hurt my poor Elsie?"

"Yes...."

"You'd better have a whiskey and soda before you go to bed, Hugh."

"Aren't you going to argue with me about what I'm going to do?"

She shook her head, with a faint smile.

"I'll trust you," she said. "Good-night."

He bent and kissed her on the temple; then he went upstairs to his room, and in fifteen minutes he was in bed and asleep.

But he was up very early the next morning and off in his car, and when Luff and Elsie came down to breakfast, he had not returned.

"Queer, too..." said Luff. "Most punctilious sort of fellow.... Never late. Never fails."

"I can't *stand* people like that," said Elsie.

Luff glanced at her sidelong.

"Well," he said. "In a way, y'know, it makes life easier, to show up when you're expected—to be on time and so on."

"Who wants life to be easy?" she asked.

"I do!" said Luff promptly. "Oh, I do!"

She smiled half reluctantly, and while she drank her coffee, Luff studied her.

"Either she's on one of these fool diets, or she's in love," he thought. "Both of 'em very bad for girls.... Poor arrangement altogether that the time for falling in love should be the time when you haven't any sense. Now, if people only fell in love when they were—say fifty—when they'd had their families and their children were grown up... Much better. Mistakes wouldn't matter so much. This kid... But Anabel will look after her."

He sighed with relief and helped himself to another slice of toast. The clock in the hall struck nine.

"Got to get the 9:30," he observed. "Board meeting.

He went upstairs to take leave of his wife and as soon as he was well away, Elsie went to the telephone in the library and rang up Whitestone's house.

"Hello?" answered a voice that made her gasp.

"I want to speak to Mr. Whitestone," she said.

"I'm sorry, Miss Sackett, but—"

"I *will* speak to him," she said. "You can't do this. Call him at once!"

"No," said Acheson.

She hung up the receiver and stood for a moment, resting her hand on the table, her knees trembling. Then, lifting the receiver again, she ordered a taxi.

"At once, please!" she said. "And tell the driver to wait in the road outside the gates."

As she turned toward the door, she saw Mrs. Luff there, an unusual thing at this hour.

"Elsie, dear..."

"Yes, Mrs. Luff. In a moment. I want to get something."

"Elsie, wait, my dear! Don't go until I've spoken to you."

The girl looked about her, a desperate, trapped glance. One of the French windows was open.

"Elsie! Hugh has just telephoned!"

"I'll come back, Mrs. Luff..."

She was through the window like a flash, and running bareheaded across the lawn, down the drive. The car stood waiting before the house to take Luff to the station. He might try to stop her.... Everyone was trying to stop her. There was some horrible plot—something she didn't know.... The taxi had not come.... Perhaps they wouldn't let it come.... She thought of the Luffs, of Acheson, as people of immeasurable power and prestige, and alone, with them all arrayed against him, that most unhappy, most unfortunate man. She knew he was weak, pitiably so, and he had turned to her for help. He was the first human creature who had ever needed her, had ever depended upon her.

"And now they'll send him away," she thought. "They'll tell him it's best for *me*. They'll make him go now when he's sick and utterly wretched from this horrible shock. I don't know what would happen to him if I deserted him now.... Last evening he looked—haunted.... It's easy to imagine how he must feel. Now he must be remembering all he said about her. It's worse, a thousand times worse than if he'd loved her...."

For had not she herself felt haunted, oppressed with guilt all night, as if, even in listening to his outburst, she had somehow wronged the wife who now lay dead?

"But I couldn't have stopped him," she thought. "He was at the end of the tether...."

It had shocked her, frightened her. She had known the first time she met Whitestone, two weeks ago, that he was attracted to her, and she had been proud. He had shown her his paintings; no one else had seen them, he told her. He had made a crayon study of her head; he had told her she looked like Guido Reni's "Cenci." And she had felt that here was someone she could help, someone who was threatened with the same wretched fate which had overtaken her father, because he had had no one.

She had, all the time, been singularly free from illusions about Whitestone. She had seen that he was unstable, passionately self-willed, that he had a queer strain of something inhuman in him. But her father had had that quality too. He would let his family go hungry while he took what money there was, to go into the country with a friend. She understood that. She could not judge whether Whitestone's work was very good, or not, but she knew that he was an artist. And she knew that she possessed all that he lacked. She had the vitality, the directness that could stimulate him, she had the pride that could win his respect, and she had a loyalty upon which his insecure life could be firmly established.

The night of the little dinner party, he had slipped a note into her hand.

"Burn this as soon as you've read it. I am a fool and a knave to write it. But I can't help it. I love you so. My little beautiful girl, if I could get free of all this, would you marry me? Only if you love me, though. If I had your love, I could do work you'd be proud of. I could do anything. Oh, forgive me. Forgive me, my poor beautiful girl. But I am at the end of everything. If I can't get out of this now, at once, God knows what I shall do. If you care, if you're ever going to love me, just tell me to-night."

She had told him in the room full of other people. She had found a moment to speak to him aside.

"I'll help you to get away," she had said.

"You mean—you care?" he had asked.

And she had answered. "Yes, I care."

She had not spoken on impulse, or recklessly. She had realized fully what her words implied, to what she had pledged herself. She knew very well that this was no romance, but reality, and she had faced it with sombre deliberation.

"*He* won't be able to manage it," she had thought. "I'll have to make all the plans."

And she had made them. She had felt certain that, if the situation were not changed at once, there would be a terrific row between Whitestone and his wife. In his state of intolerable tension, he really needed a violent quarrel; he would not mind that any more than Elsie herself did. Scenes like that cleared the air, in her opinion, and she didn't care if Rosalind got hurt in the process. Rosalind seemed to her small and mean and grasping. But she did mind hurting the Luffs, because she liked them. And she knew also, from harsh experience in her early years, that a scandal is harmful to an artist. She had decided that Bob must go away at once on a trip, making some pretext that it was for his health, or his work. While he was away, he must write to Rosalind and tell her he was never coming back to her. But he must do that decently, and he must, above all, leave some money with his wife when he went. That was another thing Elsie had learned early in her life; that an artist is judged more by the provision he makes for his family than by his work.

She had known better than to approach the Luffs. They would certainly be kind and generous to her, but they would certainly ask questions. So she had gone to Hugh, and she had got what she asked from him, and she hated him.

Her heart was hot with anger against Acheson. From the beginning, beneath his mild and courteous air he had been trying to thwart her and to hurt Bob. He had slandered him. He had interfered persistently.

"And now," she thought. "He'll be arguing with him. Bob's in no condition to argue. He'll agree to anything.... Especially if that—that Acheson drags me into it."

When she reached the cottage, she discovered that she had no money to pay the taxi. That did not disconcert her; she still lived in that child's world in which there was always someone else who would pay. Her clothes had always been bought for her, food and shelter provided, money had little meaning and little value for her.

"Wait, please!" she told the driver, and sprang out. Acheson's car stood before the gate, and she looked at it with scorn. He was one of the Philistines, an outsider who would never understand Bob or herself.

She rang the bell, but no one answered. She tried the door and found it locked.

"But I know Acheson's here," she thought and hurried along the path to the summer-house. They were there. She heard the sound of voices.

"I'll kill you for that, you hound!"

She stopped short, her hand to her heart. That was Bob speaking, in that unsteady, tortured voice.

"No," Hugh answered as if the threat were merely tiresome. "I'm giving you your one chance. Get out now, at once."

"He shan't go!" said Elsie, from the doorway.

She was flushed with haste and excitement, her dark hair was damp on the temples, her eyes were brilliant. The two men faced her in silence, for a moment.

"Bob," she said. "Don't listen to him. Don't think of going away."

"Miss Sackett," said Hugh. "You're giving Whitestone very bad advice. You're—if you knew the harm you were doing—I ask you, for Whitestone's sake as well as for your own, to go home at once."

Whitestone pushed forward the only chair.

"Sit down, Elsie," he said. "I want you to hear this. I want you to know what this hound's trying to do."

There was a strange exaltation about Whitestone this morning. He looked ill, exhausted, yet filled with a passionate energy. His dark hair was disordered, his collar was grimy; beside him the neat, slight, fair-haired Acheson had in her eyes a look of detestable smugness.

"I knew he'd try to make you go away," she said.

"But you don't know *how* he's trying to do it," said Whitestone.

"Whitestone," said Acheson, with a sort of entreaty in his voice. "Tell Miss Sackett to go. This isn't—"

"I'd like you to know, Elsie," said Whitestone. "Acheson's come here to tell me I murdered Rosalind...."

"Oh..." she cried, stretching out her hand toward the back of the chair.

"I want you to hear this," Whitestone repeated. "Because he threatens to go to the police with his theory, if I don't clear out at once. And you might hear of it from someone else."

"You didn't dare...?" she said, turning to Acheson.

He was silent for a moment.

"Won't you go?" he said, presently. "This is between Whitestone and myself."

"It's not," she said. "I want to know everything—every one of the lies you've invented against Bob."

"Tell her, Acheson," said Whitestone. "And see how your story sounds to her."

Again Hugh had difficulty in speaking.

"Whitestone," he said, "this thing you're doing is unforgivable. I said I'd give you a chance. If Miss Sackett doesn't go immediately, you won't get that chance."

"Elsie, what do you say? I'll do as you tell me, Elsie. Shall I run away—?"

"You're not going to make *her* responsible," said Hugh, slowly. He did not look smug now, with his grey eyes narrowed and his jaw set, he looked dangerous and merciless.

"She'll decide," said Whitestone. "I'll go or stay, as she says."

"No," said Hugh. "She shan't have that to remember—that she told you to stay. Because she doesn't—she can't—know what the consequences of your staying will be. No.... You've lost your chance now."

Whitestone sat down on the edge of the table.

"So you're going to the police?" he said. "All right! Go—and be damned to you!"

"I shan't leave Miss Sackett here with you."

"You can't make me go," said Elsie. "Send for the police, if you want. I'm going to stay with Bob."

"Miss Sackett, if I go to the police, they'll arrest Whitestone."

"D'you know what his 'evidence' is, Elsie?" said Whitestone. "He found poor Rosalind's wet bathing-suit hanging up in the pantry."

"It was your suit, Whitestone."

"Only your word against mine, Acheson. Unfortunately I didn't foresee that you were going to play the boy detective, and I took all the things off that line this morning."

"Delancey saw that wet suit, too."

"I'm afraid it would take a little more than that to make Delancey believe I'm a murderer. Just the sight of Rosalind's wet bathing-suit wouldn't be quite enough."

"It's your choice that Miss Sackett has to hear all this," said Hugh. "I didn't want it like this.... Mrs. Whitestone's bathing-suit was removed in the hospital, when they took her there from the beach. It's still there."

"Sorry," said Whitestone, "but she had two suits. It was the one she'd worn the day before that you found. I'm afraid that evidence won't convict me."

"It'll help," said Hugh. "That—and your glasses."

"My glasses?" Whitestone repeated with a sort of fierce hilarity.

"I'm putting all my cards on the table," said Hugh. "I'm taking a chance in letting you know all the case against you. I'm doing it on Miss Sackett's account. Because I hope that when she hears, she'll go away."

"Come on!" said Whitestone. "Let's hear about my glasses."

"When we came here yesterday," said Hugh, "you were painting—without your eye-glasses."

"God!" cried Whitestone, laughing. "You make me think of some of
the advertisements I've made drawings for. 'You will never have another
pair of eyes. It is criminal folly to neglect or abuse them.' So I was actually painting without my eye-glasses! Only I'm afraid that's a crime I've committed before."

"No," said Hugh. "For a certain reason, I made enquiries this morning
about that. I asked Mrs. Browne if you ever wore glasses, and she told me
you were so far-sighted, you couldn't paint a stroke without them. I went
to the optician in the village.... I didn't come here to you, Whitestone,
until *I knew.*"

"Knew I wore glasses, eh?"

"Miss Sackett," said Hugh. "Have I got to go on with this, or will you
go now?"

"Go on!" she said. "I want to hear all you've got to say."

He did not begin at once. He was still very quiet and deliberate in his
manner, but he ran his fingers inside his collar, as if it had grown tight.

"I'll tell you what happened," he said. "Yesterday morning, Whitestone
followed his wife to the beach, without being noticed by her, or by Mrs.
Browne. He knew she was in the habit of swimming round a point of rock
where she couldn't be seen by Mrs. Browne. He swam out and waited for
her there. Naturally she didn't call out. She wasn't surprised or frightened
to see him. He forced her head under the water."

"Stop!" cried Elsie. "It's—"

"Yes. It's horrible," said Hugh. "When she began to struggle, he
knocked her head against a rock. When it was all over, he swam ashore,
took off his bathing-suit and put on his clothes. The whole thing only
took a few moments. It's very lonely there. No one saw him. He went
home through the woods and he met no one. He went here, to his studio,
and when he heard us coming, he took up a brush—"

"Elsie," said Whitestone, "it's hard for you to listen to this. But if the
fellow's going to broadcast his little fantasy—"

"You'll have to stop him, Bob."

"My dear girl, I can't. He's a millionaire's son, and I'm a poor devil of
an artist without a penny."

For the first time, Hugh lost his temper.

"Damn you!" he said, in a sudden fury. "That's something I won't—"

"It's true," said Elsie. "You've invented this—horrible thing, because it
pleases your vanity. It's a lie—from beginning to end. But people will listen to you because you have money. They'll say there must be something

in it, because *you* tell it. Everyone imagines that rich people are disinterested. No one will realize that you've done this—just to make yourself important. I saw last night how proud you were of your 'observation.' You told me you saw things and heard things. So you do. And you draw any conclusion you please from them. I don't suppose anyone ever contradicts you. You live like a king, surrounded by flatterers. But I won't flatter you! I tell you that this is all a *lie!*"

She ended with a sob, but her blazing eyes were still fixed on Hugh's face.

"I'm going to stay with Bob," she said. "And we'll fight you—and your money."

She took Whitestone's hand and laid it against her cheek. Hugh turned away and left them.

CHAPTER X

THE BLOW FALLS

Delancey sat on the veranda, a tall mint julep beside him, and between his teeth a new pipe Josephine had given him.

"I love to see you smoke a pipe, Shawe!" she had said.

She regarded his smoking altogether as if it were the endearing and somewhat absurd amusement of a child; she had given him for toys that silver cigarette case, a leather cigar-case, a humidor, and she liked to show them to people.

"Shawe! Cigars just loose in your pocket? Where's that humidor?"

She did not smoke herself.

"I haven't any objection to it," she always told people. "But I'm well— I suppose I'm overfastidious. I simply couldn't stand the smell of tobacco in my hair, or on my hands."

She had not offered cigarettes to Miss Phillips this afternoon and he hesitated to do so, for fear Josephine would make that remark again. He didn't wish Miss Phillips to hear it.... He felt like a fool, anyhow, sitting here with Josephine watching him fondly, and Miss Phillips rather carefully not looking at him.

"I ought to have gone into the office to-day," he observed.

"But Shawe dear! After all you've gone through—and sitting up half the night with poor Robert!"

He felt sure that somehow Miss Phillips knew he had not sat up half the night.

"I'm not tired," he said.

"And the inquest's to-morrow," Josephine went on. "Will you have to go, you poor boy?"

"I don't think so. I haven't had any summons."

"I'm going," said Miss Phillips.

"Helen!" protested Josephine. "Isn't that—morbid?"

"I've always thought it was morbid *not* to be curious," said Miss Phillips.

"But Helen! In a dreadful tragedy like this, you must feel something more than curiosity!"

"I'm afraid I don't. You see, I'd never met the Whitestones."

A taxi was coming up the drive. Miss Phillips and Delancey watched with the alert interest of the bored. It stopped before the house and to Delancey's surprise, Elsie Sackett descended. She wore a white dress with a frill around the neck, and a wide straw hat with a black velvet band.

"Beautiful girl..." he thought. "Picturesque..."

But what about Josephine? He glanced uneasily at his wife and saw her advance toward the unexpected guest with a gracious smile.

"You're Mrs. Delancey, aren't you?" asked the girl. "I'm Elsie Sackett. I've been visiting Mrs. Luff. Do you mind...? May I speak to Mr. Delancey a moment?"

Delancey was almost angry at her. This was enough to start another row between himself and Josephine. But he forgot that, when the girl turned her dark eyes to him.

"Certainly!" he said, with heartiness. "Certainly! Come in!"

And let Josephine think what she chose.

He let the girl into his study, drew forward a chair for her, offered a cigarette.

"Mr. Delancey," she said. "I've left the Luffs."

"Er—left the Luffs?" he repeated.

"I couldn't stay... A horrible thing has happened. But I don't want to leave this neighborhood. Do you think Mrs. Delancey would let me stay here a few days?"

For the first time he felt the whole crushing weight of his dependence. For the first time all the amiable little pretences that had sustained him crumbled, left him poor indeed. Josephine's house, Josephine's money, nothing of his own. He had not even a moral ascendancy; such influence as he had over her was unstable and tenuous. He didn't know how she would take the girl's request. She might be very pleased to have a former guest of the Luffs', she might be jealous, and openly, outrageously show her jealousy. He didn't know.... He could only stand before the girl, shamed and miserable and silent.

"Mr. Delancey, if that wouldn't be convenient, will you lend me some money so that I can go to the hotel in the village?"

She asked him as a child might ask, with perfect simplicity, and he answered, "Yes. Yes. I'll be pleased to, Miss Sackett." Because somehow he could get money, if not from Josephine, then he could sell something, his cuff-links, cigarette case. "But I'll ask my wife... I don't know what her plans are... May be having people to stay, y'know...."

She seemed to accept this as quite ordinary.

"It's on Bob's account that I want to stay here," she went on. "It was bad enough for him before, but now...! Oh! If you knew what that Acheson man has done!"

"Why? What's he done?"

Elsie leaned forward, clasping her hands.

"It was the most horrible scene.... This morning with Bob half sick from shock—this man came and accused him of murdering his wife."

Delancey turned white and threw down his cigarette.

"Accused... But... He... But... how could he?"

"I want to tell you all of it. So that you can help Bob. Hugh Acheson has money and influence. If he spread a story like that... And he even said he was going to the police...."

"But he—what—what grounds...?"

"He says that last night you and he found a wet bathing-suit in the pantry of the cottage. And he calls that 'evidence' that Bob had been in the sea."

Delancey sat down heavily in a chair. Was this how people felt when they fainted—this nausea—this black whirling in the head...?

"And his other evidence is that when we went to the studio yesterday, Bob was painting without his glasses on," she said, scornfully. "Of course, the police won't pay any attention to him, but other people will. Even the Luffs will. I don't know what he said to them, but when I got back they were different. Mrs. Luff said she wanted to have a talk with me, but I— I couldn't. I left a note for her. I told her I was awfully sorry to go away like this, because she's been sweet to me.... But they're on Acheson's side. They're the same kind of people. People who couldn't ever understand an artist like Bob."

He was thankful that she went on speaking long enough to give him a chance at recovery. But even now he was not sure how his voice would sound, how his face looked.

"Did Robert—was Robert—upset?" he asked.

"Of course. And furious. Can anything be done to stop Acheson from spreading that rumour?"

"I'll think," said Delancey. "Yes, I'll think it over. I'll think it over. I'll..." He checked himself. The one thing he must not do was, to think it over. Not until he was alone. Mustn't think that Robert never painted without his glasses, couldn't do so, in fact.... Mustn't remember that wet bathing-suit that had struck against his face.... Above all, must not—must not remember Robert saying, "I'm going to do it to-morrow if the weather's good...."

"If you'll excuse me," he said, politely. "I'll go and speak to my wife...."

But when he had closed the door of the study behind him, he could go no further. He stood there leaning against the wall, making a desperate effort to summon back his old philosophy, his cheerful insistence that everything was pretty well all right.

"Aren't you feeling well, Mr. Delancey?" asked Helen Phillips' cool voice.

He looked at her with a dazed, sickly smile and he believed he saw in her face something like compassion.

"Thing is," he said. "I wonder if *you'd* ask Josephine... If you'd tell Josephine that Miss Sackett wants us to put her up for a few days...?"

"I'd be perfectly willing..." said Miss Phillips. "But don't you think that if Miss Sackett herself spoke to Mrs. Delancey, they could arrange things better...?"

He saw then that Miss Phillips understood, that she had seen how things were here. On impulse, in his dreadful dismay, he held out his hand to her and she took it in a firm, cool clasp. She was not beautiful, not extraordinary, a slim, self-possessed young woman of thirty, yet he thought he had never seen anyone so benign, and solacing.

"You're right," he said.

"Come into the dining-room and have a whiskey first," said she. She was right again, that was what he needed. And she asked no questions, did not even look at him.

"Mrs. Delancey's on the veranda," she said. "I was speaking to her about Elsie Sackett. Her father was Foxe Sackett, you know."

He recognized that as a lead for him, and he could have blessed Helen Phillips for it. He gulped down another whiskey, straightened his tie, and went out to Josephine.

"Well!" he said. "Here's a nice thing! This little Sackett girl's come running to you.... But you'd better see her. She wants you to put her up.... I don't know... I mean to say, might upset us....

He was watching Josephine's face as he had never watched it before. She was angry before he began, then she was startled, then puzzled.

"But why?" she asked.

He was afraid, afraid of every word he must speak. But the thing must be made plausible.

"To tell you the truth," he said, "she's interested—in poor old Robert. I mean, he's an artist, and her father was a musician. Same sort of people, you know. She..."

"I'll see her," said Josephine, and went into the house.

He knew she was suspicious, half-hostile, but curious. If she refused to take the girl in, then what? He couldn't go away with her, couldn't take her to the hotel, couldn't give her any money now....

"I wish she hadn't come!" he thought. "She's a nuisance... I've got to see Robert...."

He did not want to see Robert. He was afraid to see Robert.... The sound of voices in the hall made him jump; Josephine and Elsie were coming together.

"Miss Sackett's going to stay with us for a few days," said Josephine. "Shawe, will you pay the taxi and get her bag?"

He could not pay the taxi. He knew that, all the while he felt in his pockets.

"Got any change, Josephine?"

"Oh... Find my purse, will you, Shawe?"

Times without number he had asked that question and she had made that response. Even on their honeymoon.... In hotels, in other people's houses, in their own house, he had gone, times without number, to find her purse. The purses themselves varied incessantly, but they were always fragrant with perfume, and always stuffed with money, bills and change. She liked to have plenty of cash on hand, and she could do it. She had so much, and he had nothing. Only this paltry allowance she doled out to him each month.

He found her bag on the hall table and brought it out to her; he stood by while she opened it and gave him a bill. An unendurable bitterness filled him that he must do this in the presence of the Sackett girl and Helen Phillips; glancing covertly at Josephine he saw in her thin face something mean, something miserly which he had never noticed before.

But he had to take the money and he had to bring her back the change. And he had to sit there, on the veranda, with all that bitterness and that sickening fear and dread in his heart.

"Can't even be alone!" he cried to himself. "I need to be alone... To think about—Robert...."

But if he didn't think about Robert, would this blow over...? Or did things like this really happen...? Things such as he read of in the newspapers with interest?

"It's not true," he said to himself. "It's—it's treacherous to think such things about Robert... Best friend I've got. And he *couldn't* have been such a fool...."

That last word disconcerted him. That wasn't the way to look at it. A man who did a thing like that couldn't be called a fool. He would be a criminal of the worst sort. And Robert was no criminal....

"I know that," he told himself over and over. "Good Lord! I've known Robert for years. He's no more capable of a dastardly crime like that than I am."

But if he could only forget what Robert had said that day in the birch glade.... The misery, the fury, the torment he had seen in his friend's face.... That would look bad, very bad....

"But no one else heard!" he thought, with a relief so great that he sighed loudly. "No one else knows how he felt.... He's very well liked here. Who'd pay any attention to Acheson's flimsy evidence? Everyone thinks they were happy together."

"*Lunch,* Shawe!" his wife was saying. "What's the matter with you?"

She was being gay and sophisticated for Elsie Sackett's benefit; it was a manner that had always faintly embarrassed him, but to-day it was almost unbearable. He saw Elsie's clear eyes regarding her with a sort of wonder, and still worse, he saw that Miss Phillips did not look at her at all.

"Why can't Josephine be natural?" he thought. "If she were only different... If I could talk to her... If I could ever tell her I wanted to be alone...."

That wish to be alone was growing and growing into a passion. Yet he dared not express it. If he went up to the bedroom, Josephine would follow him and ask what was the matter; if he went to the study, she would come there, if he went out alone, on foot, or in the car, she would accuse him of Heaven knew what. He couldn't get away from her. He was never going to be able to get away from her....

"Where's my purse, Shaw...?" and she would give him what she felt like giving. He remembered that row on Saturday when she had threatened to stop his allowance, to prevent his using the car.

"No, I can't forget that," he thought. "I told her at the time that she'd gone too far. Some things a man can't forget...."

His sullen anger surprised him.

"This worry about Robert's got on my nerves," he thought. "I've got to think what to do about Robert."

He could not. When he told himself that he must see Robert, something within him balked. He did not even want to talk any more about Robert with the Sackett girl.

"Fine girl," he thought to himself, mechanically. "Loyal to Robert."

But a disturbing girl; impossible to imagine what she might do or say.

"Now, a girl like Miss Phillips..." he thought. "You'd never have to worry about her. She has tact, and all that."

For a moment he allowed himself to imagine the relief of confiding in Miss Phillips. She would listen, he thought, with some extraordinary sort of understanding; she would somehow comprehend Whitestone as he did. But, of course, it was impossible. He could make no genuine confidences to her, or to anyone, without telling more than he intended.

"Well, I'll see Acheson!" he cried to himself in despair. "I'll have a talk with him. Try to make him realize... And there's one thing I'll tell him straight. If he's going to talk about his 'evidence,' the bathing-suit and the glasses, he needn't expect me to back him up. In fact, if things look troublesome for Robert, I'll lie. Robert would do it for me. No.... Then there won't be anything but this fellow Acheson's word. Just this theory..."

They went into the drawing-room after lunch; and through all his obsessive anxiety, he was vaguely aware of the constraint and awkwardness of the moment.

"If Mrs. Luff was the hostess," he thought. "Or Miss Phillips..."

He was standing by the mantelpiece, smoking a cigarette, when Elsie came up to him.

"Mr. Delancey!" she whispered.

He glanced apprehensively toward Josephine. She wouldn't like this girl whispering to him... She was looking, too... He attempted an amused, benevolent smile.

"You're going to see Bob, aren't you?" she went on and anyone could tell that she was speaking of something significant.

"I'll telephone to him at once," he said.

He was glad to get out of the room, and glad he had thought of telephoning. He shut the door of the study and sat down, staring before him with a fixed frown, then he lifted the instrument and asked for Whitestone's familiar number.

But no familiar voice answered. A man, slow and mild, said "Hello!"

"This Mr. Whitestone's house?"

"Yes, sir."

"I'd like to speak to him, please. Tell him it's Mr. Delancey."

"He's not here, sir."

"Who are you?"

"I'm from the McHenry Funeral Parlours, sir. Joe Perley."

With his fondness for friendly conversations, Delancey had acquired a large acquaintance in the little suburban town. He knew Joe Perley; he had often talked to him.

"Know where Mr. Whitestone's gone, Joe?"

"Well... Yes, Mr. Delancey," Joe answered, with a hesitation that Delancey noticed with a start of alarm.

"Where, Joe?"

"They took him to the police station, Mr. Delancey, about fifteen, twenty minutes ago."

"They—they..." said Delancey and had to wait a moment, to conquer that queer stammer. "I suppose—they want to question him..."

"Well..." said Joe. "It seems they had a warrant, sir."

"A warrant to...? You mean...?"

"Well, you see, Mr. Delancey, I got a friend is a policeman.... It seems they found Mr. Whitestone's glasses down on the beach."

"No!" cried Delancey. "I mean—they couldn't arrest a man for anything so ridiculous...."

"Well, you see, Mr. Delancey," said Joe, unable to conceal his immense pleasure in this unprecedented excitement. "The glasses was right near the place where Mrs. Whitestone was drowned. Somebody tipped off the police they was Mr. Whitestone's glasses and the police took 'em down to Charley Eden, and Charley, he could swear they was the ones he'd made for Mr. Whitestone, and, you see, Mr. Whitestone, he'd bin swearing up and down he'd never bin near the beach that morning."

"All right..." said Delancey. "All right, Joe.... "

CHAPTER XI

A RING IS GIVEN

Delancey locked the study door and fell into a chair so heavily that the room shook.

"What'll I do?" he asked himself. "What'll I do? If they ask me questions, all right, I'll lie. I'll deny I ever saw that bathing-suit. I'll swear on my oath that Robert was wearing his glasses when we got to the studio yesterday morning. Oh, God, if I could only see him, just for a moment.... Tell him to stick to it that he was wearing his glasses when we came. Then he could say he dropped them when he went there later on.... If he'll only have the sense to say that, there'll be nothing but Acheson's story and what good'll *that* be, if I won't back him up? But *she* saw him too. I've got to have a talk with her quick...."

Unlocking the door, he rang the bell and sent the housemaid to tell Miss Sackett he wanted to speak to her.

"She'll have to swear he was wearing his glasses," he thought. "She'll do it, for Robert's sake."

He felt so sick and shaken, he longed for another drink. But if he went to the dining-room, Josephine might catch him.

"Shawe," said Josephine's voice from the doorway. "I'd like to know what this means?"

He tried to control the fury of impatience that filled him. The police might come before he had chance to speak to Elsie....

"I sent for Miss Sackett," he answered. "I've got to speak to her."

"And why, may I ask?" she demanded haughtily.

"I'll tell you later. Send her along now...."

"I shall do nothing of the sort! I don't like this at all. I shall—"

He rang the bell again and when the housemaid appeared: "I told you to get Miss Sackett here!" he cried. "Are you deaf, or what?"

"You needn't shout at poor Annie. She delivered your message, but I told Miss Sackett I'd come—"

"Tell Miss Sackett to come here *at once!*" he said, and as the girl hurried away, "Now clear out!" he said to his wife. "I've got to speak to her alone."

"I'll do nothing of the sort!" she began, when he advanced toward her, his face darkly flushed and a look in his eyes that made her retreat in haste. Elsie was coming down the hall.

"Come in!" he called to her and shut and locked the door after her. "Now, see here!" he said. "Please try to take this quietly.... Because you can help a lot. If you don't get excited.... Sit down... I... I'm sorry to have to tell you..."

She remained standing, very straight.

"Do you mean that Acheson's begun?" she asked.

"Yes," he answered, and looking at her valiant young face, he felt for a moment that he could not tell her that other thing... But he had to, for Robert's sake.

"Robert's—been arrested," he said.

She gave a little gasp, but she stood as straight and steady as ever.

"Maybe the police have to do that, if someone makes an accusation," she said. "They'll just ask him questions, and then let him go. They *can't* keep him just because of what Hugh Acheson says."

He was distressed to see in her face no fear, no doubt, only a stern anger.

"You see..." he said, "the police found his glasses down on the beach. Near where it happened."

"Well, he went there in the afternoon."

"No. Don't you remember that we met—the ambulance before we got to the beach? And—and then, there's Acheson's statement that Robert wasn't wearing his glasses when we went to the studio that morning.... And—I'm afraid a good many people know he can't paint without them."

"You mean...!" she cried, the colour rising in her cheeks.

"Oh, never mind what I mean!" he answered, impatient in his torment. "Whatever way you look at it, it's bad for Robert. I've been thinking... The police are certainly going to ask you questions. They'll ask me, too. And I'm going to swear on oath that Robert was wearing his glasses when I saw him Sunday morning."

"It's—that serious?" she asked, and when he was silent, she read the answer in his look. "Then I'll do the same," she said. "If you're sure we've got to lie to get Robert out of this?"

"I'm sure," said Delancey.

And when he said that, he knew, very definitely, what was in his own mind. He had denied it before; he wished to deny it now, but he could not. He believed Robert to be guilty. He *knew* it.

"If you and I stick to that story," he said, "then there's only Acheson's word that he wasn't wearing them."

"Yes..." she said. "I see..."

There was a knock at the door.

"Well?" called Delancey.

"Shawe," said his wife. "Shawe! There's a policeman here to see you."

He flung open the door and came out. He had expected this. It had to come and he was glad it had come. He felt a craving for action. He wanted to do something definite in his friend's defense, even if it could be no more than the telling of a lie. He forgot Elsie, he would have forgotten Josephine if she had not caught his arm.

"What is it?" she whispered.

"It's about Robert," he answered, very low. "He's been arrested. Hush! Keep quiet! Don't say anything *now*. Where is he?"

He was in the drawing-room, an ordinary enough policeman, stoutish, his face red this hot day.

"Officer Monahan, from the Greenvale station," he said, rising. "The chief'd like you to come along with me, sir, down to the station. Just to answer a few questions."

Delancey had not expected this. He had thought the interview would take place here, under his own roof. He had meant to be cool, perhaps a little jocular. But to be taken away...

He stood staring at Officer Monahan, with a great fear rising and rising in him. This stout, red-faced man was not like the traffic policemen he made jokes with. Even his appearance of good-humour seemed to Delancey a sinister thing, veiling a gross brutality. This was The Law. He knew then that his lies would not be the mere matter of effrontery he had thought. He saw that to carry this through required a courage, a quick wit which he had not got. There came to him one of those horrible little flashes of insight which from time to time shot across his mind, and, for a moment, convulsed it. He saw that he was clumsy, slow, easily bullied.

He was afraid. Elsie and Miss Phillips and his wife watched him leave with the policeman and he knew he was going to an atrocious ordeal.

Before Officer Monahan's car turned out of the drive, he saw young Acheson, driving toward them. He saw in young Acheson everything he himself wanted to be, and he gave a groan which he disguised as a cough.

Acheson had seen him and knew where he must be going and why. He did something very unusual for him; he accelerated with a jerk. But he had never in his life felt in such desperate haste. He pulled up before the Delanceys' house and ran up the steps to the veranda, and to his immense relief, he saw Helen Phillips there. She could be counted on to understand things without being told.

"Helen," he said. "Get Elsie Sackett for me, will you, please? I'm in a devil of a hurry. It's important."

"Right!" said she and went into the house.

She found Elsie still in that pathetic "study," standing by the window.

"Miss Sackett," she said. "Hugh Acheson's here to see you in a frightful hurry."

"I don't want to see him!" said Elsie, turning toward her.

"But I should if I were you," said Miss Phillips, amiably. "Hugh really doesn't go dashing around like this for nothing. He's not—temperamental."

Her quiet good-humour had its effect upon the girl.

Hugh was sitting on the veranda railing, smoking a cigarette. He rose as she came out, and they looked at each other.

"I don't know if you've heard," he began.

"That Bob's in jail?" she said. "Yes, I've heard."

"You realize, don't you, that you'll be questioned by the police?"

"I'm ready to be," she said. "And I'm going to."

"Wait, please! They may send for you at any moment. I've *got* to talk to you first. And I don't know how to do it. I don't know how to appeal to you... Is there anyone you care very much for—anyone you don't want to hurt?"

"Just Bob," she said.

"The aunt you spoke of? Mrs. Luff? Anyone you'd want to keep out of a mess—a headline scandal?"

"Nobody," she answered, coldly. "I see very well what you're getting at. You want me to go back on Bob, now that he's in trouble. And trouble that you caused."

"That's one way of looking at it," said Hugh. "Another way would be to think that he was—reaping what he's sown."

"I wish you the same," she said. "I hope with all my heart that some day you'll be repaid for your cruel, officious meddling. I know Bob's been foolish. He hasn't flattered people—like you and the Luffs. He hasn't made friends. He's not being humble enough now, when he's falsely accused of this preposterous thing."

"Elsie," said Hugh. "You've got to see... I told you what happened—what Whitestone has done."

"You told me what you thought he'd done."

"It's not me alone. The police wouldn't arrest him just because I suspected him."

"They might," said Elsie. "You've got up this plausible story... The wet bathing-suit that you say was Bob's, and he can't prove now that it wasn't. Those eye-glasses... I suppose you found them."

"Yes. I never was satisfied about the thing being an accident, and after I'd seen the wet bathing-suit, I knew. The police hadn't bothered to search the beach."

"But *you* did?"

"I did," he said.

"Perhaps," said Elsie, "you put those glasses there yourself. To make a nice, interesting case, with you for the hero."

"You have..." Hugh began, and checked himself, with something of an effort. "I want to help you," he said. "But I can't do anything, unless you'll realize how serious the thing is."

"Serious?" she cried. "Do you imagine I think it's funny for Bob to be in prison? With everyone against him? I know how hard it's going to be for him to clear himself, and how just having been accused is going to affect his whole future."

"I don't like saying this to you. But you'll have to face it sooner or later. The case against Whitestone is very much stronger than you think. It's..." Again he paused for a moment. "There's one thing you can do that would help him."

She looked at him, in an intent effort to understand, to discern if this were a trap, a new menace to Whitestone.

"Let's hear," she said.

"When the police question you, don't try to defend Whitestone. Let them think there was nothing but an insignificant sort of flirtation between you. And say that you're engaged to me."

"Engaged to you?"

"That ought to stop the gossip about you. The gossip you've done everything to increase."

"Do you think I care?" she demanded scornfully. "Let them gossip."

"It hasn't occurred to you yet, has it?" said Acheson, deliberately, "that this gossip is the thing that's going to damn Whitestone utterly."

Her eyes widened; she caught his sleeve.

"No!" she cried. "Don't say that! Oh, it couldn't be..."

He glanced down at her clutching hand; he opened his lips as if about to speak, and stopped, stood stiff and silent for a moment.

"If it can be proved that there was any sort of understanding between you and Whitestone," he said, "that would be motive enough on his part to satisfy any jury."

"I—didn't see that. I didn't think of that."

"You haven't thought at all," said Hugh. "You've simply gone ahead, with no regard for yourself or for anyone else."

There was a cold anger in his voice that startled her.

"You think I've—" she began.

"I think you've been a dam' silly little fool," said Hugh.

She flushed and then grew pale again, the light of anger that had come into her eyes died out of them. She looked down at the floor.

"I guess you're right," she said, not with humility but thoughtfully. "But I can deny all that now—"

"No. You've done your best to broadcast the fact that you and Whitestone are infatuated with each other. A jury won't care how much you and Whitestone deny it."

She was frightened now; she kept her glance upon the ground, and her face composed; but he saw that her breathing had quickened.

"Nobody knows, except Mr. Delancey," she said.

"You gave yourself away pretty thoroughly in front of Doctor Madison and the interne. Mr. and Mrs. Luff know. And I know."

"But you wouldn't...?"

"You'd ask them and me—to lie under oath?"

She could detect no kindness, no compassion in his voice.

"Why did you say that?" she asked. "Why did you tell me to say I was engaged to you?"

"I suppose," said Hugh, "that I'm a fool myself. But I don't think I'd like to see you dragged through a thing like this. I don't think I'd like seeing your pictures in the tabloids: 'Murderer's Girl Sweetheart Loyal to the End' and so on."

"The dramatic part of it is," she said, "that I'm really going—to be loyal—" The unsteadiness in her voice made him wince.

"Very well," he said. "This is the way to do it. You've already mentioned the fact that I have influence and—money.... You can take advantage of them now. As my fiancee, you won't be bothered much by anyone. And, of course, the case against Whitestone will be very much weakened, too."

"I don't understand.... You've taken all this trouble to build up a case against him, and now... It means that, after all the harm you've done, you're *not* really sure he's guilty."

"I know he's guilty," said Hugh.

"And you're willing to help him?"

"It's you I want to help. And unfortunately I can't help you without benefiting him."

She looked straight at him.

"Why?" she asked. "Why do you care what happens to me?"

"I'm afraid I can't explain," said Hugh returning her level glance. "Because I don't quite know why myself."

There was a moment of silence between them.

"I've brought you a ring," he said. "It belonged to my mother. It's small. I think it ought to fit you. I didn't buy a new one, because that could be traced, and we'd better say we fell in love at first sight, and got engaged the first evening I came here."

She took the ring he handed her and held it in the palm of her hand.

"I'm not going to cheat you," she said. "If I do this, it won't be to help myself out of trouble. It won't be because I care what people might say, or think about me. It'll be *only* for Bob's sake."

"I understand that."

"Maybe—" she said, "if you realized how I felt about Bob—how nothing he could ever do would make any difference—you wouldn't be so keen on my wearing your mother's ring."

He slipped the ring on her finger, and her hand closed over his.

"You're a gentleman," she said.

CHAPTER XII

A FLAW

There was one thing Hugh had not said or suggested. But Elsie said it to herself. His words had been a staggering blow to her, but she had no thought of denying them, or of justifying herself. What he had said was true. She had wanted only to be loyal to Whitestone and to make her devotion obvious not only to him but to the world. She could see now that she had been a fool, as Hugh said, and that she had done harm to Whitestone.

And, with her native honesty and courage, she faced another possibility. It was so terrible that her heart grew cold with fear, yet she contemplated it steadfastly.

When she had given Whitestone that answer to his note, had she caused Rosalind Whitestone's death?

Hugh had said that a jury would consider Whitestone's infatuation for her a wholly satisfactory motive. What if it had been the actual motive of crime?

At the sound of a footstep in the hall, she ran down the veranda steps and along a path, seeking in vain, in that ostentatiously cultivated garden, a place where she could be alone and unobserved. The dwarf firs, the neat lawn, the few trees, offered no refuge; she went to the iron fence that bordered the road, and leaning against it, looked back upon the course of her romance with Whitestone.

She did not spare herself.

"I thought I was going to be a sort of guardian angel to him," she reflected. "Well, suppose I was a devil? A devil who tempted him?"

She thought of Whitestone, with such intensity that she could see his face before her, and she asked herself that other question. Did she believe that Whitestone was capable of yielding to such a temptation? Did she believe him capable of murder? And in all sincerity she had to answer to herself:

"I don't know...."

She had thought she understood him. She had seen that he was sensitive, unstable, pitiably vulnerable, and pitiably lonely. He was hurt and maddened by things another man would have ignored. He had been miserably unhappy with Rosalind, and curiously helpless against her. He could fly into a rage, but he couldn't really defend himself. He had that weakness, and that was his claim upon Elsie. For she was not weak. She had believed that her young vitality, her faith in him, would inspire him to work, to a new faith in himself. She realized now that it was possible she had inspired him to something else, something monstrous, awful.

"He could have done a thing like that," she thought.

It was possible. She admitted it.

"If he did," she thought, "it was my fault."

She stood, a charming figure in her white dress, a young girl in a garden on a Summer day, and she was enduring, as best she could, the worst hour of her life.

"Hugh Acheson is right," she thought.

Hugh represented all the qualities, the traditions against which she was in perpetual rebellion. He belonged with the rich, the powerful, the unassailable ones of the world, and she was heart and soul with the others, the oppressed, the mutinous. Yet she respected Hugh. She could not, in her pain, feel gratitude toward him at this moment, but she admitted the debt of gratitude.

"He's tried to help me all along," she thought. "He's been right all along. What he wants me to do is the only possible thing...."

It must be done at once, too. She slipped his ring on her finger. It was a little loose, but not too noticeably so. The diamond glittered in the sun; she thought to herself that probably it was valuable. She marvelled for a moment that any woman could care very much for such things. Then, still with that icy coldness in her heart, she went back to the house.

It was curiously easy to play her part. She had never suspected before how easy it was. She found Josephine arranging flowers in a vase on the hall table, and she went up to her, smiling.

"You're the first I've told, Mrs. Delancey," she said, holding out her hand with the ring.

"My dear!" cried Josephine, with a delight that made her thin face radiant. She put her arms about the girl and kissed her with a warmth touching and surprising to Elsie.

There was, indeed, some honest kindliness in that embrace, but there was so much more than that. This was to the unhappy Mrs. Delancey a supreme triumph, to be the first to hear this intimate news from one of what she called "that Luff set!" She was forever angry, sore, bitter against those people, yet forever drawn to them. Elsie's arrival had been salt to her wounds, for Elsie had come asking not for her but for Shawe, and Acheson, when he came, had not troubled about her at all.

What was more, the girl's lovely youth had terrified her, she had thought amazing things, she had said some of them to Helen Phillips.

"She's been running after Shawe for the last two weeks," she had said. "I know the type! One of those so-called 'society girls'! With no respect for anything or anybody.... And Shawe's a fool about women. Any woman who flatters him little..."

"Oh, I don't think you could call Elsie Sackett a 'society girl,' " Helen had protested. "And I'm quit sure she—" She had paused a moment. "I'm quit sure she wouldn't come here if she had designs on Mr. Delancey."

Her words, her tones, had added to Josephine's unhappiness. She felt that she had astonished the superior Helen Phillips. She felt that she was inept, stupid, an outsider. She had pretended to laugh.

"I'm foolish about Shawe," she had said. "He's so good-looking, isn't he?"

"Oh, very!" Miss Phillips had agreed. And what that tone meant, Josephine could not decide.

It seemed to her, too, that Miss Phillips received the news of Elsie's engagement in a very queer way. *She* did not kiss Elsie, did not show any warmth.

"Hugh's a lucky boy," she said politely.

But that was not going to spoil Josephine's triumph for her. It was under her roof that Elsie Sackett and the dazzlingly rich Hugh Acheson had become engaged, and she wanted that fact proclaimed. "We must have a little dinner to celebrate!" she cried.

"Oh...!" said Helen Phillips.

Again Josephine had that feeling of having committed an unpardonable breach of taste or manners. But Elsie smiled, and Josephine determined to defy Miss Phillips. She became greatly daring.

"It would be nice to ask Mr. and Mrs. Luff.." she said, her voice a little unsteady with excitement. "I mean of course we must have Mr. Acheson, and he's staying with them...."

"Shall I ring them up?" asked Elsie.

Nothing could have suited Josephine better, for she was at heart afraid of the mild Mrs. Luff. She remembered what she had described to Shawe as her "quarrel" with Mrs. Luff, at a lunch party some months ago. "Quarrel" had been a curious word to use for that little scene. Josephine had taken offense at some words of Mrs. Luff's, and had been haughty and implacable. She had intended Mrs. Luff to see that she was offended, but whether or not she had succeeded, she did not know. Nor could she imagine how Mrs. Luff would receive an invitation from her.

When Elsie telephoned, Mrs. Luff was in her drawing-room, one of a little party of four. Herself, her husband, Hugh Acheson and the Assistant Chief of Police from Greenvale. And never in her life had she enjoyed a party less.

The Assistant Chief of Police was a polite enough young man, but it was his job to ask questions not easy or pleasant to answer. Had Mrs. Luff noticed anything unusual about Mr. Whitestone when she had dined there on Saturday?

It was, thought Mrs. Luff, a curious and distressing thing that, the moment one was asked a direct question like that, and knew that the answer was important, it became almost impossible to answer. She really didn't know whether she had thought Whitestone's behaviour odd when she had actually been there, or whether she imagined now that he had been queer, because of what she had learnt it the meantime. She hesitated so long—and then she felt that the nice young policeman would, and must, think her answer calculated and disingenuous.

"I... Well... No... I can't remember that I noticed anything out of the ordinary..." she said.

Had she noticed anything unusual about Mrs. Whitestone?

"No! Nothing!" Mrs. Luff answered, glad to be definite for once. Had she ever, at any time, observed anything unpleasant or strained in the relations between Mr. and Mrs. Whitestone?

"No! Never!" she answered, and then felt that her tone was much too vigorous.

And then the question had come for which she had been waiting in a tense dread.

"Now... This Miss Sackett that's staying with you... I'd like to have a word with her, if you please."

"She's not at home, just now," Mrs. Luff answered.

She forced herself to let her hands lie easily in her lap. She must not clench them. She must not be thinking of Elsie's name in the tabloids, Elsie's picture, Elsie on the witness stand. She must not be afraid of his next question.

"Will you tell me where I'll find Miss Sackett, please?"

How was she to answer that? Was she to tell the truth, to say that Elsie had taken her bag and run off Heaven knew where...?

"Will you tell me—?" he was beginning again, patiently, when Hugh intervened.

"Mrs. Luff probably doesn't know," he said. "But Miss Sackett's still at Mrs. Delancey's. She'll be there over-night."

"Thank you, sir," said the Assistant Chief.

"If there's anything more I can tell you...?" said Hugh, with the greatest willingness, "I could answer any questions you want without your having to see Miss Sackett. Miss Sackett and I are engaged, you know. And she and I have talked this thing over..."

There was a brief silence.

"Thank you, sir," said the Assistant Chief again. "Now, Mr. Luff. Did you at any time—?"

The telephone rang and Mrs. Luff, sitting near the desk, lifted the receiver.

"Mrs. Luff, please.... Oh! It's Elsie, Mrs. Luff.... I wanted to tell you that Hugh and I are engaged...."

Mindful of the Assistant Chief, Mrs. Luff said no more than "How nice!" Because there was so much here she only half understood, so much that might be dangerous.

To Elsie, that brief, amiable little comment was chilling; she went on with a certain reluctance.

"Mrs. Delancey thought it would be nice if you and Mr. Luff and Hugh came to dinner this evening...?"

"Is that what Hugh would want?" thought Mrs. Luff. "Does he want this thing to be—very public...?"

She glanced at him, but he was looking at the floor, his neat, fair head a little bent. She was afraid to ask him, perhaps he wished all this to seem prearranged.

"Thank her so much, won't you?" she said, careful to avoid any names. "We'll be delighted...."

She was alert, pleasant, unruffled, while the Assistant Chief continued with his questions. But when he had finished and gone, she leaned back in her chair and was suddenly pale with fatigue, and strain. Her husband went to her side and laid his hand on her shoulder. She smiled up at him and raised her brows with an expression evidently known to him.

"Hmmm..." he said. "Well...! I'll step out and get a breath of air."

Hugh was still sitting with his hands clasped between his knees, looking at the ground.

"Hugh," she said. "My dear boy... You're *very* generous to Elsie—very chivalrous."

He glanced at her with a smile.

"Isn't this just what you wanted?" he asked. "Isn't this what you expected, when you asked us both here at the same time?"

"It's not what I want—now," she answered, deliberately.

"I'm sorry," he said.

"I'm fond of Elsie," she went on. "I did think that perhaps you'd find her—different from other girls. But now—I wish with all my heart I'd never asked her here. I'm quite sure she didn't realize what she was doing, but after all, that can't make much difference. She's responsible for *all* of this."

"What?" he asked, sharply. "You mean—?"

"Hugh, there's no use pretending. It's—a horrible thing to say, but I'm going to say it. If Elsie hadn't come here, Mrs. Whitestone would still be alive."

"That's going to be the popular idea, of course. And it's unjust. Very unjust."

"You don't need to defend Elsie to me, Hugh. I'm not going to desert her. Both Joe and I want to do everything we can for her—within reason. But what you're doing—isn't reasonable. It's excessive... for you to announce that you're engaged to her just as this wretched scandal is about to break."

"Being engaged won't do me any harm," said Hugh. "And it'll do her a great deal of good. You can see for yourself that it's the only thing for her now."

"Hugh," said Mrs. Luff, not looking at him. "You're not—?"

"In love with her?" he said. "No."

Something in his tone troubled her; she looked at him and he caught her at it.

"D'you know," he said. "I wish I could be."

"Why, Hugh?"

"She's—magnificent," he said.

Mrs. Luff meditated upon that for a time.

"I see what you mean," she said. "But she's done dreadful harm—"

"That's unjust," he repeated. "Granted that she was rash and foolish— that she gave Whitestone encouragement. Still that doesn't make her responsible for his crime. The thing to remember is, that, long before he ever met Elsie, he was capable of what he did. He had it in him. He's violent and reckless by nature. There's no rock-bottom to his character. She didn't make him like that. If he'd never met her, still he'd have done something of this sort, at some time of his life."

"You can't know that, Hugh."

"Well, you see," he said. "I notice things. And I link up what I notice with past experiences...."

"I'll admit you're very observant, Hugh. But you're very young, too. You can make mistakes."

"I know," he said, and his tone was apologetic. "But somehow I *don't* make mistakes about people."

"My *dear* Hugh!"

"I know how that sounds. But it's the truth. I could see that flaw in Whitestone the first time I ever set eyes on him. And it's in his friend, too."

"What friend?"

"Delancey."

"Really, Hugh!" she said, half-vexed. "That's a little too far-fetched. Delancey's the most harmless, good-natured man."

"He has no guts," said Hugh briefly.

"No. Very likely he hasn't. But what of it?"

"You remember when I started to sail down to Florida with Preston a couple of years ago?"

"And you were lost for three days. I'm not likely to forget."

"We had a fellow like Delancey along with us. Big, cheery sort of fellow, that same sort of travelling-salesman manner, nervous underneath it. When we were blown out of our course, things got pretty uncomfortable. The others took it as a matter of course. It was the sort of thing you knew might happen. The only one who made any trouble was that fellow like Delancey. He wanted a bit more than his share of everything. And before we were picked up, he collapsed."

"Very well," she said. "Perhaps poor Delancey wouldn't be very good in an emergency. I can't see that that justifies your very low opinion of the poor man."

"Well, y'see," said Hugh. "Thing is, you never know when there's going to be an emergency." He rose. "Dear Anabel Luff!" he said. "Make Elsie come back here with you, will you?"

She wished to look annoyed with him, but she could not.

"I'll try," she said.

CHAPTER XIII

AN ALLIANCE

Anabel Luff had not only been thoroughly disciplined in social conduct, but she was by nature courteous and amiable. She was not able to like Mrs. Delancey, but if she were going to dine in Mrs. Delancey's house, she would do her utmost to please her hostess. She felt that a somewhat elaborate toilette would be expected of her and, fatigued and resigned, she put on a dark-purple frock with no back, and her diamonds round her neck, and called in the housemaid to help her with her soft, unmanageable sandy hair.

The result did not satisfy her. The strain of this day had left its mark upon her face. Sitting before her dressing-table, she applied a little rouge.

"I look like a harridan—whatever that is," she remarked.

"You probably are one," said her husband, gloomily. "I'd certainly call it a harridan's trick to drag me out to dinner with those people. You've got a string showing."

"I don't wear strings," said Mrs. Luff. "It's a shoulder strap and I don't know anything to do about it."

"Hmm... Anabel! About this engagement...?"

"What about it, Joe?"

"Nothing," said he. "Ready?"

Hugh was waiting for them in the hall. They all got into the car. And they were all a little too talkative, as if in haste to prevent even the briefest silence.

Mrs. Delancey welcomed them with a shade too much nonchalance. She was wearing a severe black frock that swept the floor, with long sleeves. It was an extremely expensive French model, and Anabel regarded it with sincere admiration. But Mrs. Delancey fancied her guest supercilious, she felt that everything was a little wrong, and that Mrs. Luff, actually the most casual of housekeepers, would notice certain little imperfections in her appointments. She detected, moreover, what she believed to be an insolent indifference in Anabel, an absentminded way of answering her.

Indeed, this was one occasion when Mrs. Luff's tact and kindliness had almost deserted her. She was so concerned about Elsie that it was difficult, almost impossible, for her to attend to anything else.

"Elsie doesn't look well..." she said to Mrs. Delancey.

The unhappy Josephine could see a slight even in that.

"She wants to make it plain that she hasn't come here to see me," she thought. "No, it's all her precious Elsie. And that Acheson talking all the time to Helen Phillips. As if this were a hotel." Aloud she said, with a smile: "Well, naturally... It's been an exciting day for her, hasn't it? First getting engaged, and then that policeman coming and asking her questions."

"Oh!" said Mrs. Luff. "Was there a policeman here? "

"For ever so long. I don't know why he needed to bother *her*.... And my poor husband! But of course he was that man's friend unfortunately.... They took him down to the police station and he hasn't come home yet."

Cocktails were served, too many and too strong, Mrs. Luff thought. They all sat drinking and smoking in the drawing-room. Mrs. Luff talked, and Helen Phillips ably assisted her, but Hugh, always before so entirely to be depended upon, was useless now, and Mrs. Delancey was so odd and artificial. And Elsie sat there like a little ghost of her old vivid self.

"Shawe's so late..." said Mrs. Delancey. "Shall we give him another ten minutes?"

She could have cried from chagrin and disappointment. Her dinner was spoiled. It was all wrong. Shawe was late and these other people were hateful, insulting. Mr. Luff hadn't said half a dozen words....

A dreadful pause came. Then Mrs. Luff and Helen Phillips both spoke at the same time.

"Have you—?"

"Did you—?"

They looked at each other and laughed, and it seemed to Josephine a laugh that deliberately excluded her. She rang for the parlour-maid and ordered dinner served, in a haughty voice that startled Mrs. Luff. They had all risen when Delancey entered.

At first Mrs. Luff thought he had been drinking. He stood in the doorway, leaning against the frame. His hair lay damp on his forehead, his face was pallid and grimy, his blue eyes had a fixed, blank stare.

"Shawe!" cried his wife. "What's the matter?"

With a great effort, he turned his blank gaze to her.

"Police..." he said. "I mean to say..." He shuddered, and pulled himself together. "Gave me quite a grilling," he said, with something like his old manner. "I... it tires you.... Didn't know I'd have the p-pleasure of company...."

"Cocktail, sir?" asked Hugh in his quiet voice, and without waiting for an answer, he brought a glass to Delancey.

Mrs. Delancey was recovering now from her alarm. She saw his condition as a fresh disaster to her dinner party.

"You'd better hurry and dress, Shawe," she said sharply. "We've all waited so long."

"Can't I put in a plea for Mr. Delancey this hot evening?" said Helen Phillips. "Can't he come as he is?"

Josephine wanted to cry. "No!" The idea of that pallid, haggard, grimy creature at her charming table was unendurable. But she felt forced to yield.

"All right! Then just wash your hands," she said, in the tone of a mother forced to condone in public an offense she would not forget in private.

"Doesn't she see...?" thought Mrs. Luff. "The man's really *ill....*"

She felt genuinely alarmed for Delancey. After he had two or three drinks, the pallor of his face gave place to a dark flush. He became boisterous. His hands trembled.

"He's ill," she thought.

But Delancey was not ill in body. It was his soul that was mortally wounded. No man can endure life without self-esteem, and his self-esteem was stricken and dying.

He had a wonderful capacity for deluding himself, but he could not do that now. He had seen his own unhappy, naked soul. He had fought and had been entirely defeated. He had done his best, and his best was contemptible. He could not remember half that he had said, but he knew that he had betrayed his friend. The police had questioned him about the wet bathing-suit, and he had said he "knew" it was Rosalind's.

Had he actually seen it? Could he swear to it? What colour was it? He didn't remember... Then how did he know it was Rosalind's...?

He had been defeated about that, and defeated about the eye-glasses. He had asserted that he had seen Robert was wearing his eye-glasses when they had entered the summer-house on Sunday morning. He had said that he would swear to that.

Two men had sat in the sweltering room with him, both staring at him all the time, staring and staring, with cold, watchful eyes.... He had sat there, in a sweat of terror, had tried to assume an air of candid good-fellowship.

"We have a statement here from another witness that Whitestone did not always wear glasses when painting. To the best of your knowledge, is that true, Mr. Delancey?"

Suppose Elsie were the witness who had made the statement? Suppose she had grown confused under their questioning and admitted that

Whitestone was not wearing glasses...? If her statement and his didn't agree... Perjury...

"I... well... yes.... Sometimes he didn't."

"But you're certain he was wearing them that Sunday morning?"

If Elsie had said no...

"Well.... Yes. Yes, he was."

"We found Whitestone's glasses on the beach that morning, Mr. Delancey."

"Well, good God, he could have more than one pair, couldn't he?"

They had abruptly dropped the subject and that was the worst thing they could have done. Had he said something fatally wrong...?

"You're not concealing any facts that might help us, Mr. Delancey?"

He had said no—no. He was a good citizen. He wanted to help them.

"Will you tell us all you know of the relations between Whitestone and his wife?"

"Very—pleasant.." he had answered, feeling the palms of his hands grow damp.

If they had let him take a rest, even ten minutes... if they had let him smoke.... But they wouldn't even give him a glass of water. And he had known, all the time, what they were doing. They were breaking him down. He had heard of that happening to other men. Other men had been shut up like this and questioned without rest, without mercy, until they cracked. But they were gunmen, criminals, or men without strength of character, and of no standing in the world.

"You don't have to answer these questions, but you'd better...."

He didn't have to and he *would* not.... His throat was dry. He wanted a glass of water, a cigarette.... One cigarette.... Those men never took their eyes off him. They would never stop, never, never stop until he told them.... No! He mustn't even think of that. They might read his mind. They might see those words written on his brain. "Whitestone said he was going to kill his wife.... Whitestone said he hated his wife...."

He had flown into a violent rage.

"Now, see here! You fellows have no right to treat a decent citizen like this. I'm going. D'you hear me? And I'd like to see you stop me!"

He had risen, but they sat where they were, still looking at him. And the fact that his fury made no impression on them, frightened him. It was because they *knew* he was ineffectual. *They knew they were going to break him.* He stared down at them, and he had seen in their eyes their cool knowledge of their own strength, and his weakness.

"You were an intimate friend of Whitestone's, Mr. Delancey?"

"Yes, I was! I am!"

"Would you say that you were his most intimate friend?"

"I... Well. Yes. I'd say that."

"Then he'd have been more likely to make confidences to you than to anyone else?"

"Yes."

"Mr. Delancey. Did Whitestone ever tell you he was unhappy in his married life?"

"No. Never."

"You're sure of that? Try to remember."

"I'm sure."

"Then, if you were his most intimate friend, how d'you account for the fact that he told several other people his married life was unhappy?"

"He—probably he was—just talking. He was—he is—a nervous—"

"Didn't he ever talk that way to you, Mr. Delancey?"

"No!"

"You never knew Whitestone and his wife to quarrel, on any occasion?"

"No."

"Mr. Delancey, do you admit that you were present at a picnic given by Mrs. Naomi Browne?"

They had heard about *that* quarrel, then; no doubt Naomi had told them. He shouldn't have made these flat denials.

"Oh, well...!" he had said, trying to laugh. "All married couples have—have tiffs now and then."

"You stated you had never known Whitestone and his wife to quarrel. Do you wish to retract that statement?"

"I meant—not serious quarrels."

They had confused him, tormented him; he hadn't known what would be the best thing to say. And now, now he could not *remember* what he had said. O God! Had he told them—without intending to, without realizing...? Had he in some way let them know about that thing Whitestone had said to him?

He wanted to die. He wanted the wearisomeness of dying to be over and to be already dead, buried, where no one could ever see him, and where he could never hear what they said of him. Everything that makes life good or even tolerable, had been taken from him. He felt eviscerated, nothing but a shell, with no manhood in him.

He made an effort to keep that shell intact, to smile at his guests. But it was not possible.

"I've got to go and kill myself," he thought. "I'm a murderer! I've killed Robert."

He pushed back his chair.

"Excuse me," he said politely. "I've got to go and..." He stopped, just in time. Of course it wouldn't do to tell them.... They'd try to stop him.

"Shawe, if you'd eat something..." said his wife, with that fretful little frown of hers.

"Yes..." he said, absently, and hurried out of the room, stumbling and unsteady on his feet. He imagined he heard Josephine's voice following him all the way down the hall.

"Shawe! Shawe!..." That petulant, dissatisfied voice. Dissatisfied with him.... Like everyone else.... He pulled down the blinds in his study and sat down before the desk. His idea had been to shoot himself at once, before there was any more trouble. He had his Army revolver.... Never had got across to France.... He took out the gun and laid it on the desk.

He knew he was not going to shoot himself.

"It's—the noise..." he thought. "Must be deafening..."

He could not endure that awful, shattering roar that would rush into his head, go spreading and spreading through his brain. It might go on indefinitely—even after they thought he was dead....

Someone knocked at the door and he covered his face with his hands and cried.

"Can't they let me alone...? Can't I have even an hour...?"

He made up his mind not to answer. He didn't care who it was. There was no one on God's earth he wanted to see, could endure seeing.... Tears ran through his fingers.... He was so tired, so unutterably tired and wretched.

Elsie's voice addressed him. Somehow she had got in. He must have forgotten to lock the door.

"I wish you'd go away..." he said. "I don't feel well."

"I will, Mr. Delancey," she answered, in a subdued voice. "Only, I just wanted so very much to know if they'd let you see Bob?"

He took down his hands and looked at her. His face was grimy, his wet lashes gave to his blue eyes a singularly innocent and pitiable look.

"No," he answered, politely. "They didn't."

It was at this moment that Josephine came to the door of the study, and stood outside listening. If the two persons inside the door were wretched, she was equally so. If they were driven by pain and dread, so was she.

"I know you don't want to talk now," the girl went on, "but— Oh! You're the *only* one!"

"I'm not," said Delancey. "Not really."

He was scarcely aware of what he said; as an aftermath of his collapse in the hands of the police that afternoon he was assailed now by a violent desire to break down again, to confess again to this young creature with the soft voice. He was struggling against that desire with whatever strength he had. He tried to light a cigarette, but his hand shook so that he could not. Elsie came to his side, and struck a match and held it for him. He could not thank her, for fear of more tears.

"You *are* the only one," she said, and seeing him so greatly troubled and shaken gave her the strength of despair. "Did you think my getting engaged to Hugh Acheson meant...? It's *nothing!* Oh don't you see that you and I have got to stand together against everyone?"

"We can't," said Delancey. "There's nothing we can do now."

"Please, please, don't look at it that way! Please don't be hopeless! I've been thinking and thinking... What we need now is money. You have money."

"I haven't," he said. "I have no money of my own. Not a cent."

"Well, you can get it, somehow," she said.

That was all Josephine could stand. She had heard Elsie tell Shawe that he was 'the only one,' that her engagement to Acheson meant nothing to her. She had heard Elsie urging Shawe to get money from her, his wife. And he would try. He would come to her, in the old way, with plausible, lying reasons.... She ran up the stairs to her own room and flung herself face down on the bed. Her guests would be surprised by the absence of herself and her husband. Let them be!

"Damn them!" she cried. "I hate them all...."

Her husband in that study of his "very own," which had proved so poor a sanctuary for him, was undergoing a new ordeal. He was able to endure it because exhaustion had numbed him.

"Your wife will let you have some money," said Elsie.

"No," he answered, and made the admission without shame.

"But don't you see...? We've got to get the best possible lawyer for Bob. There's no one but you to do that. You and I are the only ones who have faith in him."

Their eyes met, and the look on her face made Delancey straighten up in his chair.

"Of course we have faith in old Robert," he said in his old hearty voice. "We know, even if no one else does."

"Yes!" she assented.

They were silent for a moment, and their unspoken thought was plain to them both. Neither of them had any faith in Whitestone's innocence. Neither of them had even a hope that he might be innocent.

"It's my fault," thought Elsie. "I made Bob do it."

And Delancey thought:

"If he goes to the chair, I've sent him there. I gave him away to the police."

He rose and laid his hand on her shoulder.

"Don't you worry, little girl," he said. "I'll get the money and we'll find the smartest lawyer there is. We'll get Robert out of this."

It was the one thing he could do, the one atonement he could make. He would go to Josephine, he would ask her, beg her to let him have what money he needed. He would abase himself, do anything, to give Whitestone that chance. He would endure anything she chose to say, suffer anything.

"Don't you worry, Elsie!" he said. "I'll see to it." He paused. "But I think you'd better not stay here—for the present," he said.

"Why?"

"I'll explain later," he said, and was pleased to see that his grave tone impressed her. He did not wish her to know the truth. He knew well enough that Josephine would make trouble about Elsie very soon. She would accuse him of more and more outrageous things. She had been in a bad humour this evening, and Elsie, being young and pretty, would be her pretext for a fresh attack. He really couldn't stand any more.

"We can't have guests," he thought. "We can't have any sort of normal, pleasant life. No."

"Is it really important for me not to stay here?" asked Elsie.

"It is," he said.

"But where shall I go?"

He pretended to think that over for a moment.

"You'd better go back with Mrs. Luff," he said. "You can see that that looks so much better. And just now, appearances are of the greatest importance...."

He was not sure whether his words had any sense or coherence. Only he wanted Elsie to go. He wanted to be alone, to think, to plan some way of getting money from Josephine.

And all the time, he knew he wouldn't get a penny.

CHAPTER XIV

DELANCEY'S CAREFUL PLAN

Miss Phillips was not disconcerted to find herself obliged to play hostess. She made no attempt to explain the absence of the Delanceys, and no excuses for them. She was not responsible for them, and the Luffs and Hugh Acheson knew that.

"I'm pretty well fed up with the Delanceys," she thought. "I'm going home to-morrow."

The Sackett girl had likewise disappeared, and that seemed to make Hugh uneasy. But there was nothing to be done about it. Miss Phillips had no intention of running about the house looking for her.

"Very likely they're all three having a tremendous row somewhere," she thought. "Josephine's desperately jealous of Elsie. And they're like that."

Presently Elsie reappeared. She looked miserable enough but, thought Miss Phillips, it's very hard to tell with kids like that. Almost impossible to know whether they're sulking, or really suffering. Mrs. Luff rose to take leave almost at once.

"Miss Phillips," she said. "Will you tell Mrs. Delancey...?"

Their eyes met.

"Tell her anything you can think of," murmured Mrs. Luff. "I don't know..."

As soon as they were gone, Helen Phillips had one sole idea, and that was to get up to her room before either of the Delanceys would capture her and force her to listen to their domestic troubles.

"I'm sorry for that man," she thought. "But I'm afraid he's never going to know it."

She mounted the stairs apprehensively, dreading that one of them would call to her from below or that a door would open above. The house was quiet, remarkably quiet. Either their "row" was a singularly, repressed one or it was over now. No one intercepted her. She reached her room and with a sigh of relief, locked the door.

"*What* an evening!" she thought. "Poor Shawe looked horrible.... The whole evening was horrible." The sound of a window being closed made her start. "It's a little horrible even now," she thought. "Why did I ever accept that ferocious woman's invitation...? Rhetorical question, dear Helen.... You did it to save money.... But I'm going home to-morrow to be poor and proud...."

She put on her pajamas and lay down on the bed to read. But she was not destined for a peaceful evening. It was not ten minutes later that she heard a "row," such as she had never heard before. A door slammed and Josephine's voice cried in a shrill scream:

"This is the end! Do you hear me? I've *finished* with you. You liar! You thief!" She ended with a gasp and was silent for a moment. But no one answered her. She might have been alone on earth. "Not another penny, do you get out of me! Not while I'm alive and not when I'm dead, either. I'll change my will to-morrow. You can starve if you're too lazy to work.... I won't stay another night under the same roof with you. I'm going—now!"

Still there was no answer, no response of any sort. Miss Phillips, sitting up in bed, shivered a little with dismay and dislike for that horrible voice and the horrible words it uttered.

"Of course, if he had the spirit of a mouse," she thought, "he'd stop her if he had to choke her. But I'm sorry for him, all the same."

"I'm going now!" Josephine went on. "And I'm going to tell your precious Mrs. Luff why, too."

The door slammed again and Miss Phillips leaned back on the pillow. There was a knock at the door.

"I don't think I'll answer," she said to herself.

The knock was repeated, and Delancey spoke her name, in a low voice. She still hesitated for a moment, but some emotion, pity, or perhaps mere politeness, made her get up reluctantly and open the door. Delancey stood there, a deplorable spectacle, with a pale, dirty face and disordered hair; yet he had a new composure about him which was curiously impressive.

"I'm sorry to bother you, Miss Phillips," he said, "but Josephine is in a bad state. I think maybe she'd listen to you. She won't, to me. If you'll just make her understand that I'm leaving the house at once; there's no need for her to go. Fact is, she can't go rushing off Lord knows where."

"I don't think she'll listen to me," said Miss Phillips. "I think any interfering will really make things worse, Mr. Delancey. There's—"

As she stood in the open doorway, she heard Josephine's voice again, shut in her own room now, but quite audible. She was telephoning.

"Hello! Hello! Well, keep on ringing! Hello! I want to speak to Mrs. Luff. No, thank you, Mr. Luff. I've got to speak to your wife. I tell you I've *got* to! It's urgent.... Mrs. Luff? This is Josephine Delancey. I want to tell you that I'm leaving my husband and it's that Sackett girl who's the cause of it. I heard her myself: 'You're the only one! Oh, you can get money for me!'"

Her voice in a falsetto mimicry of Elsie's was not agreeable to hear. Helen

Phillips glanced sidelong at Delancey, and she was surprised by his look, a grave, quiet, untroubled look that gave to his usually rather simple face a virile handsomeness.

"He's a *man,* after all," she thought, wondering.

"Hello! Hello! Give me that number again!" Josephine was crying. *"I know* they're there.... Hello!" But she got no satisfaction, and in a moment she ceased trying and flung open her door.

"So you're there!" she said to her husband.

"I'm just going," he answered evenly. "I was asking Miss Phillips if she'd talk to you.... Goodnight!" He turned away and walked off down the hall, and he never had had that erect, lithe bearing before.

"He never said one word to that harpy," thought Miss Phillips. "He's controlled his temper marvelously.... Yes, he's really a *man. "*

In the lower hall Shawe Delancey picked up his hat.

"I'm going to kill her," he thought.

He sighed with relief as he closed the front door after him and stepped out into the night air that felt like cool, sweet water against his face.

"I've got to kill her," he thought. "There's no other way...."

He set off down the gravel drive with his hands in his pockets, his head thrown back so that he could look at the stars.

"Makes you realize," he meditated, "how petty human affairs are."

Then he remembered that Robert, his friend, could not see the stars, not to-night and perhaps not ever again.

"Unless I can help him!" he thought. "And I can't do that unless—"

Well, unless Josephine died, and died before she had a chance to alter her will.

"I mean—" he thought, "looking at it logically... What good is she to anyone? She's not even happy. She makes even herself miserable. If she goes on living, look what happens. I won't be able to do a thing for Robert. Poor Elsie'll be dragged into Lord knows what, a divorce case, perhaps. And the beast Josephine would tell everyone that Elsie was the cause of her leaving me. I've got to do it."

Again he thought of Robert in a cell, and thought of those two police-men....

"No!" he thought. "My God! I couldn't stand anything like that again. I'd rather kill myself." But he felt so well, so strong, so sane and clear-headed. It was wrong. A monstrous injustice for *him* to die. He had wronged no one; on the contrary, he had been wronged. He had been humiliated, insulted, injured in every way.

"Robert was careless," he thought. "Very careless."

He felt an overwhelming pity for his friend, a sorrowful indulgence.

"If you're going to do a thing like that," he thought, "you can't be careless. I believe it could be done so that no one would ever find out.... It could be done.... It ought to look like an accident. Of course, that's what poor Robert tried to do.... But he was careless. If he hadn't dropped his glasses..."

He wanted to sit down quietly and think. His brain was working marvelously well, but his body was weary.

"I'll go to a hotel," he decided and then remembered that he had no luggage and no money and that he was dirty and dishevelled. There was nowhere he could go. He was here with no roof over his head, no food, not even a clean collar.

"It's her fault, blast her!" he thought, in a sudden rage. "I can starve, can I? If I'm too lazy to go to work! We'll see about that!"

He sat down on the damp grass under a tree and felt in his pocket for a cigarette. One left. And *she* wouldn't let him have any more, wouldn't let him have food, or shelter, or anything.

"I want to get it worked out before I finish this smoke," he thought. "Now, let's see.... She's going to get run over."

That idea came without the slightest effort; he felt a sense of relief and comfort to find his brain working in this clear, easy fashion.

"First thing is to establish an alibi for myself.... There mustn't be any way to connect *me* with the accident."

He saw exactly how he could do it. He had a key to the garage, he would get the car out, push it out quietly so that Linney should not hear him. He knew an excellent place to hide it, half a mile from the house. Then he would go back to the house and he would find a pretext to let Miss Phillips know he was there.

"I'll cut my hand," he thought, "and ask her to tie it up."

The car would be missed in the morning, but no one would connect him with that. He would stay in his own house all night. He would have a bath and a shave, dress himself decently, and take care that the housemaid saw him before he left in the morning. He would get his commutation ticket and go into town, reaching the office before anyone else was there. Then he would telephone to Josephine; he would tell her he was at the Station Hotel in Greenvale and ask her to meet him on the old bridlepath. He couldn't fix the hour now, not until he had a time-table. He would have to use the right tone with her. Well, he could certainly do that.

He might say he would kill himself if she refused this one last interview. But how was he to make sure she would tell no one she was going to meet him?

For a moment that difficulty worried him, and then he had a genuine inspiration. He repeated to himself the very words he would use, in the very tone, low and hurried.

"When I left you last night, I was *desperate*. Felt I didn't care what happened to me. I don't care now, either, if you've thrown me over. But I didn't realize I was dragging you into disgrace. It's all right for me. I've got my gun. I'm going to blow my brains out. But I don't want you in it. I don't want you in the newspapers as the widow of a thief."

He regretted the word "widow": It sounded cynical. But it couldn't be avoided.

"It's only a small matter," he would continue. "If I can see you before the police get me, you can set it straight, without any publicity. Meet me on the old bridle-path, and for God's sake, don't let anyone suspect where you're going."

His mind, working so lucidly to-night, saw a great many flaws in this tale, but they were not, he thought, of any real importance. Josephine was never logical at any time, and this tale told to her in a hurry would confuse her beyond the possibility of analyzing it. She would catch the salient points. In the newspapers as the widow of a thief! Blow my brains out! He knew Josephine so well. He was certain that she would come, and come without suspicion, to meet him so near her own house, in broad daylight.

She would come and he would be ready for her. The bridle path was almost never used. The chances were a hundred to one against anyone else being there.

"And I've got to take some chances," he thought, philosophically.

He proceeded. After he had telephoned to Josephine from the office, he would borrow ten or fifteen dollars from one of his friends in the city and this would not only supply him with the cash he needed but would establish, if not an alibi, at least a supposition that he was not in the vicinity of Greenvale. Then he would return there, not from the Grand Central where he would be recognized, but by a little branch line that left from One Hundred and Twenty-fifth Street. At the end of this line, he would take a bus and then a taxi and then he would walk, taking by-roads until he reached the spot where the car was hidden. Close to the bridle-path that was. He would start the engine and when he saw Josephine coming...

That part of it was not agreeable. He had too vivid an image of her on that narrow path lined with trees. He would have to come toward her, he would have to see her face and she his.

"But it'll all be over in a moment," he thought. "I won't even have to touch her."

Somehow, that seemed to him a most important mitigation. Somehow it seemed to rob the act of any brutality. The cigarette was smoked down so low now that it burned his fingers; he threw it away and rose, sighing. It was a sigh of relief, for now that he had definitely wished the thing, and planned it, it was as good as done.

He walked lightly across the grass to the garage, opened the door with his key. It was easy to push the car out, easy to coast down the hill, and once in the highway, the engine started easily. He had the feeling of doing all this a second time, with the confidence of a rehearsal behind him. He hid the car, and walked back to the house, let himself in with his latch key, and re-entered his study. Now he had to cut his hand, and that was more difficult than he had expected. Very much more difficult....

He tried, even to scratch the back of his hand with his pocket knife, and at the first touch of the steel, he flinched. He sat miserably staring at the knife; he tried to think of doctors who so boldly cut into living flesh.... He took a drink and was steadier, another drink, several more, and at last he made a sort of lunge and cut, deeper than he meant.

It didn't hurt in the least.

"Or maybe," he thought. "I'm not very susceptible to pain. Good nerves.... Very few fellows could do a thing like this...."

His hand was bleeding profusely, and he was proud of it. He went upstairs and knocked at Miss Phillips' door. When she opened it he thought how attractive, how neat and cool and young she looked, in a striped dressing-gown belted about her slim waist.

"Hurt my hand a little," he said. "I wondered if you'd be kind enough to tie it up for me."

She stared at him so.... The blood was dripping from his hand on to the floor, and she stared at him so, her face grown white as paper....

CHAPTER XV

MRS. DELANCEY IS NOT AT HOME

Mrs. Luff saw that she could do nothing with her husband that morning. For a moment she wondered if she could manage to cry, but she had long ago got out of the habit of that, and doubted if she could do it convincingly. Moreover, she was very tired, so tired that she was almost willing to give up to the unmanageable man.

"But I think it's very unkind and very *wrong,*" she said.

Her husband stood beside the bed, looking down at her.

"I wish you could see yourself!" he said, sternly. "You look—like the devil."

"When I've had my coffee—"

"Nonsense!" he said. "It'll take more than coffee to set you right. I won't have it! That damned woman ringing you up in the middle of the night, and the police in the house.... You're not young any more—"

"Joe!"

"Well," he said. "Sorry if I was tactless.... As far as I'm concerned, you're better-looking—you're nicer than you ever were."

She reached for his hand.

"Just leave this to me," he said. "You know I won't be harsh with the confounded kid. I'm sorry for her. But she'll be better off at home, and, after all, *you're* the one to be considered. You come first."

"Joe..." she said. "Of course, a great deal of it is because of my training, but you really are very satisfactory."

"Here's Lotta with your breakfast," he said. "For Heaven's sake, eat something. I'll be back presently, to see..."

On the way downstairs he lit a cigarette, the first time he had smoked before breakfast in years. But he hadn't felt so thoroughly upset in years, either.

Last night there had been that telephone call from the Delancey woman, waking them out of their sleep. Anabel had refused to repeat what Mrs. Delancey had said, but her voice had been so loud that he had heard most of it. She was leaving her husband on Elsie's account.

"Crazy..." he thought, "the girl wouldn't look at Delancey. Whatever else you might say about her, she's certainly no coquette. But she's a trouble-maker...."

When they had got home from Mrs. Delancey's very awkward and uncomfortable dinner-party, there had been four reporters waiting for them. And more would surely follow. Elsie was the magnet who drew them. Elsie was the "heart-interest" in this cruel and ugly crime. The fact that she admitted being engaged to Hugh Acheson made it worse. The newspaper men were singularly well aware of the interest she had, or had had, in Whitestone. Their questions showed that; and after the inquest, thought Luff, nothing could keep them quiet about it. Now what they wanted were photographs and details about "Millionaire Polo Player's Romance," and Elsie, while very brief with them, had not seemed abashed.

Luff wondered about this. Certainly the girl had been infatuated with Whitestone. Did the very suspicion that he had committed murder make her turn instantly against him—and toward Hugh? If that were so, he ought to be pleased, and yet he wasn't. When he saw her sitting at the breakfast table, he felt sorry for her, because she looked so very young and so very unhappy, but he wasn't pleased.

"Altogether..." he thought. "First she leaves Anabel—simply walks off, to stay with the Delanceys. Then she decides to come back.... 'Do you mind, Mrs. Luff?'—That's all. No apologies... Doesn't care..."

She "cared" about something, though, to look as she looked this morning. When he spoke to her, his voice was gentle.

"Elsie... Ha!... My dear girl... I've been thinking... These reporter fellows are just beginning, y'know.... It's going to be... It seems to me, Elsie, that you'd better leave this neighborhood for a bit...."

"But do you mean—?"

"Go home for a bit," he said. "Back to your aunt."

He almost regretted having spoken, but then he thought of Anabel, and did not regret it.

"I'll—have to be here for the—inquest," said Elsie.

He was silent, and so was she, for a considerable time.

"I know how it is," she said, presently. "I know it's horrible for Mrs. Luff.... But I can't leave here—just yet. I can stay at the inn."

"No," he said. "No. You mustn't stay there, alone.... Thing is—Anabel wasn't going to tell you, but I'd think you'd rather know.... Mrs. Delancey... Woman's half out of her mind... She rang up last night.... Very unpleasant.... You mustn't stay here, my dear girl."

"What did she say?"

"That doesn't matter, Elsie. She's not the sort—"

"She's been nice to me."

"Well, she's *not* nice to you!" he said. "Do be a good girl and promise me you won't communicate with the Delanceys in any way."

"I've got to see Mr. Delancey."

"Merciful Heavens!" he cried. "You've— You must not see Delancey."

"I've got to."

"Look here! Mrs. Delancey telephoned last night. Said she was leaving her husband. Said it was on your account...."

"On my account?" Elsie repeated scornfully. "How perfectly insane!"

"It's the kind of insanity that leads to very unpleasant results, my dear girl."

She looked down at her plate for a moment, then she raised her dark eyes to his face.

"I'll try my best not to worry you and Mrs. Luff," she said.

"That's not the point. You've got to think of your own reputation, Elsie."

"I don't—" she began, when Hugh came into the room.

"Sorry I'm late!" he said. "I overslept."

It seemed to Luff that both Hugh and Elsie were almost inhumanly untroubled by what was taking place about them. Their hostess of a few nights ago murdered, their host in prison, a public scandal involving both of them—yet they were so cool....

"Nice morning, sir," said Hugh. "I'm going to give myself one more holiday. Like to take a drive, Elsie?"

"All right, thanks," she answered.

"What about making a start now?" he said. "I've got the car outside."

"She hasn't finished her breakfast," objected Luff. "And you haven't begun yours."

"We can always get something to eat.... This is the best part of the day.... Ready, Elsie?"

"One moment," she said, and finishing her second cup of coffee, rose, and went into the hall.

"Back door," said Hugh.

She followed him through the pantry, and through a side door to the path the tradesmen used.

"Why?" she asked.

"Reporters," he said. "And—I— There's something I'd rather tell you, before you hear it from someone else."

"Something bad?" she asked.

"Yes," he answered. "I'm sorry but—yes."

They went through a gap in the hedge. Two men sprang forward.

"Miss Sackett!" cried one. "What message...?"

Hugh started the car, a camera clicked.

"Got us," said Elsie. "Well?"

"You'll have to know," said Hugh. "Whitestone confessed last night."

He did not look at her but kept his eyes on the road before him. His lean hands were steady on the wheel.

"It may not be genuine," she said, after a pause. "I've read about the police bullying people into confessing things they haven't done."

"This is genuine," said Hugh. "I talked to his lawyer."

He had made no attempt to break the news gently, he was not trying in any way to minimize it. Luff would have thought his way surprisingly crude, even brutal. But it suited her, it was as she wanted it to be. His direct and quiet manner was infinitely more pleasing to her than any expression of sympathy.

"Has he a good lawyer?" she asked.

"Yes. Smart fellow. Vesey is his name."

"Do you think he has much of a chance?"

"No," said Hugh.

"If he had a better lawyer?"

"Vesey's good. He's advising Whitestone to plead guilty... then he'll try to prove emotional instability and extreme provocation."

"What—what will they bring forward as—the extreme provocation?"

"I think it can be proved by the Brownes and one or two others... that Whitestone felt his wife was antagonistic to his work. Made him take that job, and so on...."

"Not good enough," said Elsie.

"It's the best that can be done for him."

"No," she said. "If there was—another sort of provocation, he'd have a better chance."

He turned the car up a lane, and stopped it.

"I'm paying Vesey," he said. "Whitestone has nothing. He'd have had to take a lawyer appointed by the court."

"You lent me a thousand dollars—" she began.

"I stopped payment on that cheque."

Her lip trembled, but there was no softening of her tone, or her glance.

"You're not—really giving him his chance," she said. "I've read newspapers. I know how those things are. If it comes out in court that he—loved me—and I him—there'll be a thousand times more sympathy for him."

"No," said Hugh. "The average man would feel pretty much as I do, about that. And what I feel for Whitestone now isn't—sympathy."

"You're—hard," she said. "Hard—and utterly intolerant."

He glanced at her, and found her eyes shining with tears. But she *would not* shed them.

"There's another thing," he said. "Whitestone himself wants to keep you out of this."

"I don't want to keep out of it. It's all my fault."

"I had an idea you'd be thinking that. But you're wrong. Look at it honestly. He's a good ten years older than you. Whatever he is, he was, long before you ever saw him."

"I encouraged him."

"Not to do—that."

"I don't know," she said. "He may have thought..."

The tears were running down her cheeks now.

"People with money enough—don't go to the electric chair..." she said. "If you'll—save him from that—I'll marry you now—to-day.... I'll do anything you say."

"I don't want to marry you, Elsie," he said.

That startled her.

"You thought that—in the course of time I'd—get fond of you," she said, challengingly.

"I didn't. I know dam' well you'd never get fond of me."

"Then it was—just nobleness?" she demanded, with scorn.

"If you want to call it that. I like you. I've got a sort of admiration for you. I'm glad of a chance to help you, especially as it doesn't mean any particular trouble for me."

She put her arm round his neck, drew down his head, and kissed him on the mouth, a kiss that astounded him, that entirely destroyed for a moment his admirable composure.

"Elsie!" he said.

"That's how I feel about you," she said. "I don't *love* you. I've never loved anyone but Bob. I guess I never will. But I'm fond of you. You're a thousand times finer man than Bob. You're a thousand times stronger, and kinder and more understanding. But he's the man I love. And even if I never see him again, it's the same."

They sat hand in hand, in silence, for a long time.

"You've got to be merciful to people like Bob," she went on. "When you think... Oh, it's almost *unbearable!* What he's enduring—what he's got to endure—is so much worse for him than it would be for anyone like you. Last night, when I thought of him in a cell..."

"I'll tell you a cure for that," said Hugh. "When you find you're feeling too sorry for Whitestone, think of his wife."

She moved away, and then sighed.

"She's out of all her troubles," she said. "But other people aren't. I've made trouble and misery for everyone, right and left.... Mr. Luff told me something new this morning. Mrs. Delancey telephoned last night that she was leaving her husband and that it was on my account."

"*What!*" said Hugh.

"It's ridiculous," said Elsie, sighing again. "He never gave me a thought any more than I did him. But I just seem to be unlucky for everyone else."

"We'd better be getting back now."

"I can't stay at the Luffs any longer, Hugh. Mr. Luff said so."

"Stay to lunch, anyhow," he said. "And we'll talk about it later."

"Why are you in such a hurry?"

"I've got something to do," he answered. "But I shan't be very long."

He drove back as fast as he deemed advisable, and while Elsie was on the veranda, he went in search of Mrs. Luff.

"Please look after Elsie!" he said. "Until I get back, anyhow. Then if she's a nuisance—I'll find a place for her."

"Hugh!" cried Mrs. Luff, bitterly hurt. But he did not hear her, or at least he did not heed her. By the time she reached the window, his car was speeding down the drive.

He had made up his mind that somehow Josephine Delancey was to be stopped from including Elsie in her domestic scandals. He was ready to go to very great lengths to accomplish this. He had even spoken in hostility to his beloved Mrs. Luff.

"That's queer, too..." he thought.

He drove up to the Delanceys' house and rang the bell with more vigour than is customary.

"I want to see Mrs. Delancey, please," he said to the parlour-maid. "Tell her it's Mr. Acheson."

"Mrs. Delancey's not in, sir."

"Expect her soon?"

"I couldn't say, sir," the girl answered and the hesitation in her manner dismayed him. Had the wretched woman left already, gone to spread her poisonous rumours all over the place?

"Mr. Delancey in?"

"I—don't know, sir. I'll see."

She admitted him to the drawing-room and went off, and Hugh stood quietly and tried to think quietly. Almost immediately Delancey came into the room, unsteady on his feet, a witless grin on his face. No use trying to talk to *him* now.

"Will you tell me when you expect Mrs. Delancey home?" he asked.

"S-sorry..." said Delancey. "Couldn't... N-nobody knows where she went."

"You mean she's left? Gone away?"

"Didn't take any bags. Didn't even take a hat.... Just gone. Dis-dis'-peared."

CHAPTER XVI

WHERE JOSEPHINE WENT

Whatever Acheson felt, he kept to himself.

"Afraid I don't quite understand," he said. "Do you mean that Mrs. Delancey isn't coming back here?"

"Dis'peared."

At this moment Acheson saw the very welcome figure of Helen Phillips in the hall, going toward the door, bag in hand. Without troubling to take leave of his host, he hurried after her.

"Helen!" he said. "What's going on here?"

"Oh, my dearest Hugh!" she cried. "What indeed! I don't know. But I'm leaving."

"I'll drive you to the station."

"I've got a taxi."

"I'll get rid of it," he said, and returned presently and helped her into his car.

"Where's that woman gone, Helen?" he asked.

"I don't know and I don't want to know. I hope I'll never see another Delancey in my life."

"I want to find her, Helen. She's disposed to make trouble."

"For Elsie?"

"You know about it?"

"Quite a lot. I heard what Mrs. Delancey telephoned to Mrs. Luff last night and I also heard the prelude to that. She really was in the most unpleasant sort of rage I've ever seen."

"Then you can see that she's got to be stopped."

"I don't see how."

"Perhaps she can be frightened. I could say that if she mentions Elsie's name in connection with her little domestic troubles, there'll be suit brought against her."

"If I were you," said Miss Phillips. "I'd be cajoling, Hugh, instead of threatening. You're really quite a nice boy, when you like to be."

"If you could read my thoughts at this moment," he said, "you'd never call me 'nice.' But how am I going to get hold of the woman?"

"I can't imagine. She simply strolled out of the house, nearly two hours ago. She didn't say good-bye to me, although she knew I was taking the 12:55, and I expected she'd be back."

"Sure she didn't take her car?"

"Oh, that's another thing! Their car was stolen last night. She reported it to the police this morning. And there was another unholy row with the chauffeur. The poor devil swears he left the door locked, but it was unlocked this morning. She discharged him on the spot, with the most libellous remarks.... Altogether, it's been what you'd call such a *different* kind of visit."

"She and her husband had a row last night about Elsie?"

"She really had the row alone. I thought he was remarkably patient. She said she was going to leave the house at once, but he said he'd go. I was beginning to feel dangerously sympathetic toward our Shawe until he came back and woke me up."

"Why did he do that?"

"He'd cut his hand. It was bleeding badly."

"But that needn't turn you against him."

"He was also drunk. And I imagine he's been drunk ever since."

"Did he see his wife before she left?"

"I'm quite sure she didn't even know he'd come back to the house after he left last night. After I'd tied up his hand, he went downstairs, very quietly. And I couldn't get to sleep. I had one of those appealing feminine fears that he'd set the house on fire and I went downstairs. I heard him moving around in his pathetic 'study,' and I hadn't quite the courage to ask him to be careful. So I just lay awake, and smelt smoke for hours. This morning after breakfast Josephine wanted to get in there and when she found the door locked, she was very much annoyed. She said he was always going off with the key in his pocket and that she was going to send to the village for a locksmith. That looks as if she didn't know he was there and didn't expect him back, doesn't it?"

"Yes..." said Hugh. "But all that doesn't help me to find her. She didn't say anything to give you a clue, Helen?"

"Someone telephoned to her just before she went out. I didn't pay much attention but her voice does carry so...! I *think*... I'm pretty sure I heard her say 'My poor boy!'..."

"Is there a boy-friend in the offing?"

"It doesn't seem probable," said Helen doubtfully. "But you never can tell. Here we are now! Au revoir, Hugh! Let me know what happens."

He stood on the platform, staring after the train.

"I've got to find her," he thought. "If she starts talking and the reporters get even a hint of it... No! It's too much! I'm going to find her. Perhaps she said something to one of the servants."

He went back to the Delanceys', once again rang the bell. He greeted the housemaid with a smile which lie felt to be very poorly done.

"Look here!" he said. "It's very important for me to see Mrs. Delancey as soon as possible." He slipped a bill into the girl's hand. "Can you help me at all?" he asked. "Did she happen to mention to you where she was going?"

"No, sir, she didn't. I'm sorry, sir. Oh, excuse me, but there's a policeman now, and Mrs. Delancey told me to take him to the garage and show him the lock and all."

A policeman, burly and solemn, was mounting the veranda steps.

"Like to see Mr. Shawe Delancey," he said.

"If it's about the garage—" the housemaid began.

"Well, it's not," said the policeman. "Just tell Mr. Delancey I'd like a word with him."

"He's asleep."

"Then he's got to get waked up," said the policeman. "I got some news for him."

The housemaid was evidently embarrassed and unhappy.

"Well, you see," she said. "Mr. Delancey's not well."

"That's too bad. But I've got to see him."

She looked at Hugh, entreatingly.

"Better take the officer to Mr. Delancey," he said. "And I'll come along."

Delancey was asleep on the couch in his study, and he was not to be awakened by calling, by shaking him, or any other means.

"Well..." said the policeman, turning to Hugh. "You're a friend of Mr. Delancey's, sir? I was told to tell him personally, but... Maybe you'd be good enough to tell him when he's sober. I mean—when he's better, sir. There was an accident, sir. An automobile accident—and Mrs. Delancey was hurt. They took her to the hospital, and she died on the way there."

As soon as the policeman had gone, the pretty housemaid began to cry.

"Now there's nobody in the house, sir, but me and the cook. However are we going to break the news to poor Mr. Delancey?"

"Let's see..." said Hugh. "It's hard to say when he'll—wake up. You don't know, do you, how long he's been asleep?"

"No, sir."

"Has he been like this all morning?"

"Oh, no, sir! He—" She checked herself suddenly. "I don't think so, sir."

"Why don't you?"

"I don't know, sir. I just—guessed he wasn't."

"It would help a lot if you'd tell me everything," said Hugh, gentle as a dove. But there was a curious excitement in his heart, making it beat fast. The girl was obviously confused, obviously anxious to conceal something. And Hugh was, just now, exceedingly interested in the domestic affairs of the Delanceys. Perhaps the housemaid had overheard another quarrel—about Elsie.

"I—I don't know anything to tell, sir," she said.

"You can see that this accident has changed everything," said Hugh, in a tone so serious, so reasonable, that she accepted the quite meaningless words as valid.

"Well, it couldn't do any harm now," she said, beginning to cry again. "With the madam dead and gone."

"No," Hugh agreed. "Of course not."

"I hope I'm doing right, sir, to tell you, but I saw Mr. Delancey early this morning. He was down here when I got down, sir, and he was—all right then. He said to me, he said: 'Don't let Mrs. Delancey know I've been in the house all night. It's a little joke,' he said."

"I see..." said Hugh and stood staring down at Delancey with an odd look in his grey eyes. An odd look and rather a terrible one, the housemaid thought.

"I hope I've done right, sir," she began, anxiously.

"You have," said Hugh.

And that was the way he saw it. He thought it was very right that he should have heard this.

He got into his car again and drove to the Greenvale Police Station. By good luck he found the young Assistant Chief in, and willing to see him.

"I wonder if you'd mind giving me full particulars about Mrs. Delancey's death," he asked. "My name's—"

"I remember you. Up at Mrs. Luff's. I'll get the report." He rang and the report was brought to him.

"Bad smash," he said. "And it's a wonder it wasn't worse. Fellow named Paulson—radio man—was driving along the boulevard at 11:15 this morning when Mrs. Delancey drove out of that old bridle-path back of Fanning's place and ran square into him. He swears she never sounded her horn, just came out full speed, and rammed him. He was thrown clear, but his car's in splinters. And she was fatally injured; back broken, skull fractured. A taxi happened along just then and the driver sent for an ambulance. Paulson's got off with a couple of broken ribs, but Mrs. Delancey died on the way. There's one funny thing about it," he added.

"What's that?" asked Hugh.

"How Mrs. Delancey came to be driving her own car. She'd reported that car stolen this morning. We sent a man up to see the chauffeur. Fellow told a straight enough story, said he hadn't heard a sound. Said he'd locked the door but that's what he *would* say, anyhow. The lock hadn't been tampered with. He probably forgot to lock it. That's not so strange. But I'd like to know how she got that car back."

"Yes," said Hugh. "That's queer."

"Of course," the young Assistant Chief went on, "people do the damndest things. Especially women. For instance, someone loses a valuable dog. They report the loss, and we put a man on. But before he gets a chance to start, someone'll ring up the owner. 'I can return your dog for fifty dollars and no questions asked!' 'O.K.' the owner tells him and pays the money, refuses to give a description of the fellow who brought back the pup. You can see where *that* leads. But people are always working against the police, the very same ones that are always howling about our 'inefficiency' and 'corruption.'... Mrs. Delancey may have made a private deal like that about her car. Looks like it, to me, her driving out of a place like that bridle-path. It would be a swell spot to hide a car."

"I suppose you've investigated it?" said Hugh.

"Why, no," the other answered. "We haven't any case now. She got her car and we're never likely to find out how."

"There'll be an inquest?"

"Oh, got to be."

"You don't have an autopsy in a case like that, do you?"

"Lord, no!" said the other a little surprised. "Only when there's any question about the manner of the death. There's none here."

"Well, look here!" said Hugh. "I've often wondered... Suppose someone—just an ordinary private person, y'know—isn't satisfied with the result of an inquest. Can he get an order for an autopsy?"

"He could," said the Assistant Chief looking curiously at Hugh, "if he could satisfy the police that there was any good reason for it. But a case like this..."

"Oh, certainly. In a case like this," Hugh agreed, and thanking the other, returned to his car. He was very hungry now. He had had no breakfast and it was long past lunch time. He stopped at a roadhouse and ate heartily.

"I told Elsie I'd be back to lunch," he thought. "I hope to Heaven she hasn't done any more fool things."

If she had, it would be his job to extricate her from her difficulties, and he was ready to do so. He was not by nature tolerant of other people or of himself. He had led a hardy life where the consequences of any transgression were swift and sure and dire. Yet for that girl he had an immense indulgence.

She was sitting on the veranda with Mrs. Luff when he drove up, and at the sight of the latter, he felt a pang of remorse. He went straight to her, before he even spoke to Elsie. He was going to tell her he was sorry for his words, but when he looked down into her face, he knew himself already forgiven.

"Hugh, you tiresome boy," she said. "When you're not coming home to lunch, you must let me know. Minnie will sulk all afternoon now because you weren't here for the braised sweetbreads."

"I've got news that will keep all the Minnies in the neighborhood happy for a week," he said. And sitting down on the rail, glanced at Elsie. Her dark eyes met his, and she gave him a serious little smile that elated him unreasonably. "It's bad news," he said. "Mrs. Delancey's been unlucky."

"Oh! What's happened to her, Hugh?"

"She was killed in an automobile accident this morning."

"Hugh!" cried Mrs. Luff, rising to her feet, and resting her arm on the back of the chair. "Hugh! That frightens me!"

He went to her side, alarmed to see her so pale.

"Frightens you?" he said, gently. "But—"

"Don't you *see...?* We went to dinner with the Whitestones and the next morning that horrible thing happened. Last night we dined with the Delanceys and now—"

"But you don't—you can't believe in that sort—"

"I do—sometimes," she said. "And even if I don't believe in it, it frightens me. I'm going to lie down. No, thanks, Elsie dear. I'd rather be alone."

Hugh looked after her as she went into the house.

"She's the queen of women," he said.

"I know she is," said Elsie. "And I understand how she feels about this.... It is queer."

"Think so?" he said, lighting a cigarette and sitting on the rail where he could watch her face.

"Don't you? How did it happen?"

"I'll tell you," he said. "I'd like to hear what you've got to say about it. To begin with, Mrs. Delancey's car was stolen during the night. She reported the theft to the police about half past eight this morning. At a quarter past eleven, she drove her car out of a by-road, full speed into another car."

He stopped and waited, almost excessively anxious to hear what she had to say.

"Was she alone?"

"Must have been. No one else could have escaped from that smash alive."

"No one saw the accident?"

"No. A taxi driver heard the crash. He got there a few moments later."

"Hugh," she said, her eyes steadily on his face. "You think there's something wrong, don't you?"

"Yes," he answered.

"What, Hugh? Suicide?"

"If she'd been going to commit suicide, she'd have run the car over a cliff or into a tree, don't you think? Instead of deliberately risking someone else's life."

"Then what?"

He did not answer and she too was quiet for a time.

"Have you seen Mr. Delancey?" she asked, presently.

The question gave him a curious thrill of pleasure. Her mind was working along the same lines that his had worked, and without the knowledge he had.

"I saw him twice this morning. He was drunk the first time. And when I left him, he'd passed out entirely."

She gave a little sigh of relief.

"Then I suppose he'd been in the house all morning," she said.

"No. He went out early in the morning. I don't know—yet—what time he returned."

"But, Hugh! In any case—she was alone in the car, driving it herself."

"I'm not sure that she was driving."

"But then—I don't see—if she wasn't driving..."

"I'm not sure whether she was alive then."

"I see," she said. "That's been done before, hasn't it?"

"I believe so. Anyhow, it wouldn't be too difficult."

"Then you think she was murdered?"

"That's what I think."

"By her husband."

"He's the one to profit by it."

Elsie leaned forward in her chair.

"Do the police think that, too?" she asked.

"No. There doesn't seem to be any suspicion at all."

She leaned back again.

"I'm glad of that," she said.

"Why?" he asked, surprised.

"I hope they never will suspect anything."

"You mean to say that even if you believed he—?"

"He's nice," she said. "He's really kind and nice. And she was horrible. You couldn't want to see him hunted down...."

"Couldn't I?" said Hugh, grimly.

"What business is it of yours, anyhow?"

"It's any decent man's business," he said, in amazement and fast-growing indignation.

"Now you're being righteous!" she said. "If the poor wretched man did do this, it's not for you to punish him."

"You'd condone a thing like that? A murder?"

"I don't know whether you'd call it 'condoning' or not," she said, slowly. "I think it's just as horrible as you do. But I think it's still more horrible to hunt down and kill a man like Mr. Delancey. I don't care what he did. He's *not* bad, or dangerous, or cruel. I know that!"

"You can't know it. I can't imagine your taking this point of view. Don't you feel any sympathy whatever for the victim? The poor woman who...?"

"No," said Elsie.

"You don't care whether justice is done...?"

"No."

She rose.

"If Mr. Delancey did do that," she said, *"don't you see why?"*

There was something in her voice, in her face, that shocked him.

"You mean—his wife made him unhappy?" he asked.

"No," she said, again. "Not that. If you think, you'll understand."

She walked past him, into the house, leaving him bewildered, and extremely unhappy.

CHAPTER XVII

ACHESON LOOKS INTO THINGS

He wanted to understand this, and, after she had gone, and he had thought it over a little, it seemed to him that he almost could. Almost. He could understand that, in her mind, Delancey must inevitably be associated with Whitestone, and that, in condemning Delancey, she condemned the crime her lover had committed.

"But there's something more than that," he thought. "To begin with, she's never tried to make excuses for Whitestone. She doesn't even pretend to think he's innocent. She's simply standing by him to the end—as she said. From the way she spoke, she seems to think there's some special excuse or extenuation for Delancey. I don't see... No! I don't see...."

He sighed.

"By the time I've finished," he said to himself, "she'll hate me." Yet he never for a moment considered not finishing.

"Anabel Luff said I was a 'prig,' " he thought. "And 'hard.' Well, she's probably right."

And he was going to keep on being so.

"But I'll try once more," he thought, "I'll try to explain to Elsie."

He looked all over the house for her and at last knocked on the door of her bedroom. She opened the door instantly, and as he looked at her, he saw the marks of tears on her face. He remembered all she had endured and must endure in the Whitestone affair; he remembered that all this had come to her only because she had wanted to be generous.

"Elsie," he said. "Look here, Elsie... I don't want you to imagine I'm without any sort of feeling. But—"

"Are you going to go on hunting him?" she demanded.

"Don't you see? That sort of thing can't be left unpunished."

"You're going to do your duty—like the public hangman," she said. "Go ahead! I can't stop you!"

"Elsie..." he said, a little unsteadily. "Don't you think you're a bit unjust to me?"

"I don't pretend to be 'just'," she said, with a sort of sternness. "I need people to be kind to me instead of just. And I want to be like that to others."

"But a crime like that—"

"I don't care what Mr. Delancey did!" she cried. "You don't understand.... *He's* not a criminal.... Suppose he was driven—goaded to do *one* horrible thing...." Her lip trembled, she stopped for a moment. "If I felt as you do, I couldn't *live*. I couldn't live if I was hoping—wanting Bob to be punished. What he did was hideous. Nothing could be worse. But I hope and pray to God that he gets mercy instead of justice. Good-bye."

She closed the door, and he went off, sick at heart. She had not spoken this like a wilful child. That was her creed. And it was not his. He was going on with this.

He went back to the Delanceys and again sought the pretty little housemaid. Mr. Delancey, she said, had got better and she and the cook had broken the news to him.

"He went right off to the hospital, sir," she said. "He carried on something terrible."

"That's what you'd expect, isn't it?" said Hugh, with a nice air of sympathy. "Perhaps it's a good thing he'd had something to drink."

"That's what I said to cook, sir. It's a blessing, I said, that his feelings is kind of blunted like."

"It must have taken him a long time to reach that stage," said Hugh, thoughtfully. "He must have been at it pretty well all morning."

"Oh, no, sir! He didn't come in till after half past eleven. And he was so hot and all, I felt worried. I mean, they say that those that's sort of heavy-built had ought to be careful in the hot weather. His face was just—" She paused for an adjective, "just flaming!" she said, with satisfaction. "You'd have thought he'd been running."

"Maybe he had," said Hugh, with a smile.

"No, sir. He came in Mrs. Dale's car. She drove him right up to the door."

"Is that the Mrs. Dale who lives on Oak Avenue?" asked Hugh.

"No, sir. This Mrs. Dale lives right up the road. A white house with a tower like."

"I see.... Tell Mr. Delancey I stopped in, will you?"

"I hope you'll come back, sir," said the girl, earnestly. "It's just dreadful, to think of his sitting here alone in the evening. He's—" She stopped, with a sob. "Cook and I both say—he's the nicest gentleman we ever worked for."

As he went away, Hugh thought over that. He wondered what that girl and the cook would say if his suspicions were confirmed. Would they feel as he did, or would they be like Elsie?

Then he thought, sombrely, of Josephine Delancey whom he had seen only a few hours ago, in her modish black gown, with her rouge, her powder, her uneasy affectations. If he were to feel pity, let it be for her, who had had to die and was unregretted.

He went to Mrs. Dale's house, and was fortunate enough to find that lady at home. He had a pretext all ready.

"Sorry to trouble you..." he said. "My name's Acheson. I'm visiting the Luffs just now.... I'd like to ask if you saw a black Alsatian dog anywhere in the neighborhood this morning."

This worked better than he had expected, and even a little better than was necessary. Mrs. Dale was, he discovered, inordinately fond of dogs, and the question excited her.

"I can't *remember* seeing one," she said, "And I'm sure I *should* remember. They're such magnificent animals. Have you lost your dog, Mr. Acheson?"

"A friend of mine..." he said. "I'm making enquiries.... Someone thought he'd seen the dog between here and Delanceys' place. I don't like to ask Delancey in the circumstances—"

She wanted to know what circumstances, and she listened to him with shocked dismay.

"Imagine!" she cried. "And I drove him up from the station.... And neither of us had the *least* premonition of such a thing!"

After a suitable exchange of comments upon the tragedy, Hugh prepared to take his leave.

"I can't ask Delancey about the Alsatian..." he said. "But if you hear—"

"Poor Mr. Delancey couldn't have seen it without *my* seeing it too, Mr. Acheson."

"But perhaps before you picked him up."

"Oh, but I met him at the station! He'd just come out, from the city. He said the heat was simply too much for him, and he did look frightfully flushed.... Mr. Acheson, why don't you offer a reward for the dog? It's so horrible to think of a beautiful animal like that in the hands of goodness knows what sort of people."

It was difficult to get away from her, so great was her interest in the black Alsatian.

"I do hope you'll find him," she said, as he was leaving. "So shocking about Mrs. Delancey, isn't it? I can't say she was a particular friend of mine, but I do like Mr. Delancey."

Not yet had Hugh heard one word of regret for Josephine Delancey. And the more she was thus neglected and disdained, the stronger grew his determination to see that justice was done her. If he were her sole champion, very well. She should not lie forever unavenged.

He was more and more certain now. He believed that he could piece together what had happened.

When Delancey had first told him his wife had "disappeared," a faint uneasiness had stirred in Hugh, and when the housemaid had told her story, he had had a strange glimpse of the truth. He had, as always, trusted in his own instinct, his own vision, and he had, as always, set about verifying it. The Assistant Chief had confirmed his own idea, even Elsie had had the same suspicion. But that wasn't enough. He intended to check his theory, point by point.

As he drove away from Mrs. Dale's, he made a reconstruction of the crime, for his own guidance. He knew that Delancey had left his house early in the morning. He knew that Josephine had left later, after a telephone call. Helen Phillips had heard her say, "My poor boy," and Hugh thought she had said that to her husband, the man who was summoning her to her death. The car had been stolen from the garage by someone who had a key. Josephine had somewhere, somehow, met with the man who had stolen the car. She had gone, and at 11:15 she had died. At 11:30 or so Mrs. Dale had picked up Delancey at the railway station. He could have got there in fifteen minutes from the bridle-path if he had run. And Mrs. Dale had described him as "frightfully flushed." The housemaid, too, had spoken of that. He could have reached the station as the train from New York was pulling in, and without much difficulty have mixed with the arriving passengers. Then he had gone home and begun to drink. He might well drink, with that meeting in his mind.

"He killed her," thought Hugh. "He put her in the car, and started it, straight ahead. I don't know yet how he killed her or how he got the car. But I will know before long."

He drove to the Greenvale hospital and asked if he might see Paulson, the radio man who had been luckier than Josephine. The matron made no objection to that, and, though he knew and understood a good many things, Hugh did not suspect the reason for that. He didn't know how greatly his investigation was simplified by the mere fact that he was Hugh Acheson, a personable young man with very nice manners and a very rich father. He didn't realize and never in his life would realize that other people's requests were not granted so readily. He went into the men's ward, and there was Paulson, in considerable pain, drawn and grey with the shock of his encounter with death but willing, nervously eager to talk.

"I told my wife—my wife just left—I told her 'What did I always say about women drivers?' My wife, she's been wanting to learn to drive our car, but I always said No. I always said women are too blame nervous. I'm not saying they haven't got *brains*. There's women as smart as any man. Only they haven't got the nerves."

He couldn't stop. He was aware of his repetition, his pointless stream of words, and he couldn't stop. Hugh saw that.

"Anything I can do for you?" he asked.

"Well, no, thanks." Paulson answered. "I carried some insurance on my car.... I can get another one, after a while.... Only thing is, my business is a kind of one-man business.... I'm the only one who understands what my customers want, and the arrangements I got with them. In a business like mine, you don't have all your arrangements about installments and all written down—"

There were tears in his eyes, tears of pain and desperate worry.

"I don't want to sue Mr. Delancey," he said. "He's a fine man. Always got a pleasant word.... But it was his wife's fault. All her fault.... My God! I'll never forget.... I... I... I..." He had to stop for a moment. "She came driving right square into me.... I saw her coming.... I knew what was going to happen.... You wouldn't believe the things that come into your head, just in a moment.... She drove right square into me.... If she'd of hit nearer the front of my car, my wife'd be a widow now."

He tried to laugh.

"Mr. Delancey's too much upset to look after things now..." said Hugh. "But I think I can manage something... I've seen him this morning." He could not bring himself to say that he was a friend of Delancey's, but he let it be implied. "If I can help you to tide over... I'll see to all your hospital expenses, and perhaps—"

Paulson's gratitude made him ashamed and exceedingly uncomfortable. It was so little to do for a fellow-creature....

"There's one good thing," he said. "It must have been over very quickly for Mrs. Delancey."

Paulson was silent for a moment.

"Y-yes," he said with a stammer, "I guess so. The taxi came along right away. The driver even heard the smash. And we were both of us unconscious then. She never came out of it.... But just before.... I guess she—she knew what was coming.... She was staring."

Hugh changed the subject hastily, and when he left, Paulson was still in pain, but no longer tormented by anxiety about his wife and his business.

"She was staring..." thought Hugh.

Staring, because she was aghast at what was happening, or because she saw nothing...? If she had been dead, would Paulson have known?

If it had been so, if Delancey had sent that car forward into a main road, he was doubly a criminal. Paulson, the poor young devil with his wife, his "one-man business," might so easily have died too. There could be no mercy for that; there must be no halt now in the search for the truth.

His next step was to return to the Greenvale Police Station. The young Assistant Chief was occupied, but the policeman at the desk was civil in answering his questions.

"I heard that Mrs. Delancey's chauffeur got into a little trouble this morning," he said.

"She changed her mind," said the other. "First she told me she knew he'd had a hand in the theft of the car. But when I asked her if she wanted to make a charge against him, she backed down. He was sore, though."

"Decent fellow," said Hugh. "I might be able to get a job for him if I knew where he was."

"Well, he's right down at the Station Hotel. And jobs aren't so plenty, just now. I guess he'd be glad...."

Hugh found Linney in the dismal little lounge of the hotel, talking with vehemence to another man. At the mention of a possible job, he was interested.

"I haven't saved like I ought," he said. "I couldn't hold out more than a couple weeks. Only, I never had no idea of losing that job. I was glad to work for Mr. Delancey. He was a prince. Even now, if he'd take me back, I'd work for him for less money than maybe someone else would give me. But *her*——! Gawd! If I'd of had money, I'd of seen a lawyer this morning. I'd of sued her, the things she said to me."

"She's dead," said Hugh, curtly.

"I know it, sir," said Linney, unabashed. "But that don't make it right, what she said to me. Telling me I must of lent my key to a friend of mine. Kept on, too, even when I brung my key out of my pocket. Then, 'Well, there's only two keys,' she says. 'Yours and Mr. Delanccey's,' she kep' saying, 'and that door was opened with a key. Unless you left it open. On purpose!' And fires me on the spot. All right. She gets killed, driving that very same car. Looks like it was a judgment on her."

"That's no way to talk," said Hugh.

"No, sir. But if you could of heard the things she said to me this morn-

ing. Always nagging everyone, she was, and Mr. Delancey always as polite
and nice to her as if she was the Queen of Sheba. Like she thought she
was."

It seemed to Hugh as if an evil spirit pursued him, forcing him perpetu-
ally to hear the unhappy woman maligned. Murdered, and unmourned,
unregretted.... As if a rain of blows fell upon her unprotected head.

It was growing late now, and he was tired, more tired than the most vigorous physical exercise would have made him. As he drove home in the
dusk, he thought about Elsie. He was sorry, very sorry, that there must be
between them an unending struggle. He pitied her, yet he could not pity
her enough, in all her suffering, to turn from his course. It was bad enough
for her now, and in a little while it would be worse. When Whitestone was
tried for his life, she would have to endure with him every hour of that
appalling torment. To the end, she had said, and she meant it. And Hugh
was fairly certain what the end would be. Even Vesey had almost no hope.

"There aren't really any mitigating circumstances from a jury's point of
view," he had said. "Mrs. Whitestone was a virtuous woman—good
housekeeper—her neighbours liked her. He didn't kill her in a sudden
rage.... It's going to be almost impossible to prove temporary insanity. And
absolutely impossible to produce any other motive than sheer hate. The
fact that he was infatuated with Miss Sackett won't help him."

"It needn't come out at all."

"It's out already," Vesey had answered. "And she's so young and good-
looking. She'll appear as a sort of victim, that's all. Whitestone himself
doesn't make any excuses. He simply says he wants to get the whole thing
over as fast as possible...."

When it was over for Whitestone, it wouldn't be over for Elsie. She was
very young; she would have plenty of time for remembering all this.... It
was horrible for her, yet pity was not Hugh's chief emotion in thinking of
her.

"I don't know..." he said to himself. "Perhaps it's better to suffer as she
does, and will, than not to care much."

Yes.... One could almost envy the people like Elsie, no matter what happened to them. She had said he didn't "understand" and perhaps that was
true....

He was almost late to dinner. He dressed in a hurry and ran down the
stairs to the lounge, where Luff was shaking cocktails. And he was met by
a curious silence. Elsie was not there. Mrs. Luff lay back in a chair, quite
without her casual good humour. Luff went on shaking and shaking.

"Elsie's gone to bed with a bad headache," Mrs. Luff observed, presently. Hugh was not pleased by her tone, in which he detected a note of reproval.

"So I'm a brute," he thought. "Very well!"

Luff was never talkative, but to-night his taciturnity was accentuated by his wife's unusual silence. And Hugh made up his mind that if she chose to maintain this very unjust attitude of reproachfulness, he would make no effort. It was not an agreeable meal. Once in a while, with an effort, Mr. Luff made some polite remark to which Hugh returned an equally polite reply, and in between their words, were those blank, fatigued silences.

It was hard for Hugh.

"It's not exactly a pleasure to me, to see this through," he thought, with something as near to bitterness as his equable nature permitted. "I don't enjoy hunting down the poor devil. I'm sorry for him.... But it's morbid— it's dangerous—to keep all your pity for the people who break the laws, and have none for the victims. There's no one who gets through life with-out any temptations. Most people are able to resist them, and they're the ones to be considered, not the others. Perhaps Delancey had 'extreme provocation.'... Like Whitestone. There's certainly a fundamental weak-ness in Delancey and perhaps he can't help that. But the fact remains that he's not to be trusted. He's broken down once, under provocation. No matter what remorse he feels, that same weakness will always be there. And if there's another provocation..."

For a moment he wished he might have a chance to say all this to Elsie, but with a sigh he renounced the hope. It would do no good. Justice meant nothing to her. And, indeed, most of the people he had met seemed heartlessly indifferent to Josephine's death. He would have to go on alone, and if he were successful, no one would be pleased.

In his own mind he was sure now, but he did not consider his evidence anything like sufficient to present to the police. To-morrow he meant to analyze Delancey's movements, to dissect his actions. He wanted evidence that the telephone call which had summoned Josephine to her death had come from Delancey; he wanted to prove that Delancey had taken the car from the garage. That, he thought, would be enough to induce the police to order an autopsy.

He was not certain, however, whether an autopsy could prove that Josephine had been dead *before* the accident. He knew very little about such matters, only what he had read in an occasional detective story. He saw that his case was weak, would still be weak even if he got his evidence, because he could not adduce what to him was the all-important fact, the fact of Delancey's fatal and dangerous weakness. He knew this, but other people wouldn't believe it. They would see Delancey, big, burly and ruddy; they would take into consideration his goodhumour, his popularity; his air of assurance would be accepted as valid, and everyone would say he was not the sort of man to do this atrocious thing.

"And in a way he isn't," thought Hugh. "He s weak, but it's the sort of weakness that would make him conform to all the laws and regulations, not rebel against them. Elsie was right, when she said he wasn't 'bad.' He'd never have done a thing like this, without some tremendous provocation."

He tried, with intense concentration, to imagine what the provocation could have been. Not love. Delancey wasn't the man to commit a crime of passion. Money...? It was possible if he were driven to desperation by lack of money. But how could it be so? His wife was undoubtedly infatuated with him; she would not have let him want, and he must have known that.

"No..." he thought. "No. I don't see..." Then he remembered again, what Elsie had said.

"If Mr. Delancey did do that, *don't you see why?*"

No. He didn't see, he couldn't see why. But he was beginning to see.... Elsie had given him the clue. She knew. She knew, because she loved Whitestone; because she understood Whitestone....

"That's it!" he cried to himself. "That's what she meant! It was White-stone who made Delancey do it. Whitestone put the idea into his head. Delancey may not even know that. Suggestible people often don't realize where the suggestions come from that they act on. Whitestone was his great friend. Whitestone must have talked to him about *his* wife...."

He remembered many things now. When they had gone to Whitestone, to tell him of Rosalind's death.... Delancey had been frightened when they had found the cottage empty. Frightened, because he suspected the truth—or because he knew the truth.

At that dinner party, the last dinner Rosalind Whitestone was ever to eat, Delancey had been frightened. There had been that discussion in the pantry. "Oh, shut up about your plan!"

"Delancey knew even then," thought Hugh. "Whitestone must have told him...."

It was incredible to imagine Delancey listening to such a plan, and taking no steps to prevent it. Unless he had been entirely under Whitestone's influence. Or unless he hadn't believed in it.

Then a new idea came to Hugh, suddenly. Whitestone had confessed....
What if Delancey could be brought to confess? It wouldn't be difficult....

"No!" he thought, rebelling. "That's not my job."

Not his job to trap that wretched man into a confession.

He rose as Mrs. Luff got up, and they went into the drawing-room, but
Luff did not follow them.

"Hugh!" said Mrs. Luff. "What did you say to Elsie?"

He considered this a most unfair question which he did not intend to
answer.

"Sorry..." he said.

"Hugh," she went on, "if you've said anything to make matters worse for
Elsie, it was—cruel."

"It's not my intention to be 'cruel' to anyone," he answered briefly.

"But you see, Hugh, you're so hardy," she said. "You don't know how
other people feel. Even I—This whole thing..." He was almost tempted by
the break in her voice. "I'm not directly concerned. I didn't really care much
for either Mrs. Whitestone or Mrs. Delancey.... And yet... I can't sleep...."

He seized her hand, dismayed by the sight of tears in her eyes.

"Imagine what it means to Elsie!" she cried.

In a moment she recovered herself.

"I know you're not cruel," she said. "We won't talk any more about it.
But there's one thing that's quite a relief.... One thing that seems—human
and not distressing. Helen Phillips telephoned me. She'd heard about the
accident and she wanted to know who was staying with poor Mr.
Delancey. And when I told her nobody was, she said *she'd* come back."

"She can't do that," said Hugh, curtly.

"She'll bring someone with her, of course. She's got some sort of old
aunt, you know, quite a nice old lady, but perfectly destitute."

"She can't go there!" Hugh repeated.

"I can't see why not. She told me she was so very sorry for the poor man,
and he's absolutely alone. And she *likes* him. It really might not be such a
bad thing..." said Mrs. Luff with a thoughtful look in her eyes. "He may
not be exactly her sort of person, but after all..."

Hugh saw very well what that expression of hers meant. She was con-
templating the possibility of a match between Helen Phillips, the penniless and respectable adventuress, and Shawe Delancey....

It seemed to him for a moment as if everyone on earth were leagued
against him to defend and comfort Shawe Delancey. Everyone was sorry
for Delancey....

"One thing's certain," he thought. "Helen can't go there."

Helen, like himself, was what Mrs. Luff called "hardy," but even she would be badly upset to find herself a guest in that house, if Hugh succeeded in what he intended to do. He had known Helen a long time. He liked her. He had no intention of letting her become involved in the coming disaster.

His first idea was to telephone to her, and warn her not to come. But he decided that that would be useless. She could insist upon his explaining, she would be tiresome about it, she would talk about "poor Shawe Delancey." He felt very little confidence in women this evening.

"And suppose I'm wrong?" he thought.

He had always admitted that possibility, but now it occurred to him that perhaps the very opposition he had met with was making him over-confident, over-anxious, to prove his case. When the housemaid's words had first aroused suspicion in him, he had tried to check every surmise, he had sincerely desired to be open-minded and fair. But perhaps he had not been. Perhaps he had been grossly mistaken in his estimate of Delancey's character, and upon that estimate rested his entire case. Perhaps he had been a callous and cock-sure fool.

He felt like one. He was, apparently, the only living creature capable of suspecting Delancey.

"I'll have to see him again," he thought. "And it had better be to-night, too, before Helen has a chance to come."

It seemed to him a matter of vital necessity that he should confront Delancey again, before he went on with his investigation. He must make sure that Delancey really was as he believed him to be. This doubt was entirely new to him, and it was not quite genuine, his faith in his own observation could not vanish so easily. It was not much more than a faint uneasiness. Yet if everyone were against him, he must not be arrogant.

"Elsie agrees with me, though," he thought. "She thinks he could have done that. She thinks he did do that."

He wished to see Delancey at once, and talk to him without prejudice. He sought in his mind for a pretext, and one was most providentially supplied to him. In his pocket he discovered Delancey's cigarette-case, which he had left here the afternoon before Rosalind's death, and which Hugh had never remembered to restore to him. That would do, if Delancey showed any surprise at his visit; probably, however, he would not. Probably it would seem to Delancey no more than ordinary kindness.

"I think I'll take a walk," he observed.

"Don't be late," said Mrs. Luff, mechanically. It was what she always said to the young people who visited her.

He set out in the cool, breezy night, and he tried his utmost to banish all preconceived ideas from his mind.

"If I knew only these facts," he thought, "and the man in the case was a fellow like Luff, for instance, would I think they were serious?"

Hypothetical cases did not appeal to him. He couldn't consider a man like Luff in this situation. It was Delancey who was involved, and he had, whether he wanted to or not, formed a definite opinion of Delancey. A decent sort of fellow, genuinely kind and amiable, but with a fatal flaw in his soul, a fellow who could be stampeded into an action he would eternally regret. He would do what was suggested to him, and he would justify himself.

"Whitestone..." thought Hugh, and had a mental image of the haggard, violent Whitestone whispering to his friend that horrible suggestion.... He banished this image, as too fantastic to suit him. He meant to meet Delancey as if he had never seen him before. He wanted to look at him dispassionately, soberly, in absolute honesty. He had never before made a mistake in his judgment of men, but he was, like all mortals, very liable to error. And it was likely that his troubled concern for Elsie, his uneasiness over the Whitestone affair, had clouded his naturally clear insight. He would see Delancey, this one more time, and he would trust utterly to that thing inside himself, compounded of observation and experience and instinct, that had not yet betrayed him.

It was a matter of extreme importance to him. He walked slowly, trying not to think of anything, trying above all not to think of Elsie.... The wind blew the dust in eddies along the road. The clouds were travelling fast tonight, in black and ragged wisps.

"It's going to rain," he thought.

Delancey's house was brilliantly lighted, from top to bottom.

"Suppose the fellow's been drinking again?" he thought. Then it would be still simpler to weigh him, the barriers would be down. He rang the bell and waited a long time, rang again and heard two people coming along the hall. The housemaid opened the door, and behind her stood an older woman.

"Oh, it's you, sir!" she cried, in obvious relief. "I'm so glad... Mr. Delancey's here, all by himself... And it's so kind of queer in the house... I didn't like to come to the door alone."

She regarded Hugh as an old friend of the family now. She was respectful to him, but none the less was she aware that he was young and a man, and she was young and a pretty girl.

"I'll tell Mr. Delancey, sir," she said.

She was back again promptly.

"He's in the study, sir," she said. "Will you please step this way?"

Hugh followed her down the hall. Last night Josephine Delancey had walked here, and never would again.... He mustn't think of her, either. He must simply look at Delancey and make up his mind whether he was persecuting an innocent man, or seeking justice....

Delancey was sitting at his enormous writing-table. He did not rise as Hugh entered and he did not smile.

"He looks damned ill," was Hugh's first impression.

But an innocent man could look ill as well as a guilty one.

"Sit down, won't you, Acheson?" he said. "Very kind of you to drop in. I... Very kind... I..."

He was sober now. His eyes were clear, the flush had gone from his face, leaving it pale. But his voice was unsteady and his hand, fidgeting with a box cover on the desk, was trembling.

"I... They've been asking me..." he said. "I mean if I... If I... want her... brought back here.... She's at the funeral parlour now.... I don't—I mean to say—when—when a person's gone... Can't matter to *them*.... I mean—how do you feel about it?"

"It's more or less a matter of sentiment," said Hugh.

He must not stare at this shaken and wretched man. But he must observe, every gesture, every word. He must make up his mind whether this was a weak man's dread of death in any form, or the horrible shrinking of a guilty man from the presence of his victim.

"I can't decide..." Delancey went on. "I—went over to the hospital... I-I *saw* her... "

He was dangerously close to breaking down. If he did break down, he would almost inevitably betray himself, but that was further than Hugh was prepared to go. Guilty or innocent, Delancey was a man, and whether or not he deserved punishment, he did not, in Hugh's eyes, deserve humiliation.

"Better not talk about it just now," he suggested. "Won't you try a cigarette?" He reached for his case. "And by the way," he said, bringing out the other case. "This is yours, isn't it?"

A horrible thing happened. As if his casual words had been some unholy spell, Delancey's face changed before his eyes, grew grey with a ghastly pallor, even to his lips. He stared across the table at Acheson, stared and stared.

Then his trembling hand flung aside the box cover on the table and seized what had been lying beneath it. And Acheson found himself looking into the barrel of a revolver.

CHAPTER XVIII

THE DEATH WISH

The hand that held the revolver was wavering, but that made little difference, at such close range it was almost impossible to miss a target entirely. And if his hand were shaking, Delancey's gaze was steady enough. His dilated blue eyes were fixed upon Hugh with a sort of glare.

In that moment of extreme danger, Hugh felt no fear, nothing but a tension within him as if every nerve, every muscle had made itself ready for what was to come. There would be a shattering report, and then that tension would be violently released like a tightly-coiled spring, and all that made Hugh Acheson would fly into pieces.

"Now you—you get out of here!" said Delancey.

It took a long moment for the taut nerves to convey that message to Hugh's brain. It was as if a soldier waiting for the signal to go over the top heard instead the order to dismiss.

"Get out of here!" Delancey shouted.

Hugh rose to his feet, and, with a little click, his brain began working again. He had no doubt about Delancey's guilt now, no doubt about the look in his eyes. He was utterly desperate, like a cornered wild beast. He wanted only to escape, and the realization of that roused in Hugh the immemoriably ancient lust of the chase. The dangerous quarry should not escape. If he could not, at the moment, overpower Delancey by force, he could outwit him.

He took up his hat, and then, with an extraordinarily quick movement, dashed the electric lamp off the desk and crouched down in the dark. A shot should have followed at once; the silence was atrocious. He waited and waited, in the dark, longing for the shot to ring out.... Only darkness and silence. Was Delancey able to move toward him so noiselessly...?

Then he heard a long, long sigh.

"Acheson?" came Delancey's voice, almost in a whisper. "Have you gone away?"

Hugh did not think it expedient to answer. He stayed where he was, very quiet, crouched down, ready to spring. He heard footsteps now, but moving away from him, and away from the door.

"The window...?" thought Hugh.

A light sprang up; Delancey had turned on an electric candle in a wall bracket. He looked about him, but he did not at once see Hugh. He moved forward, and Hugh sprang at him with a flying tackle, and brought him to the ground with a crash.

He lay still, but his eyes were open. The automatic lay on the floor. Hugh picked it up, and always with a wary eye upon the other, he pulled loose from its hook the silk rope that tied back the heavy curtain.

"Sit up!" he said to Delancey, and Delancey obeyed. He was docile and unresisting while Hugh tied his wrists behind his back, then with Hugh's hand under his elbow to assist him, he struggled to his feet and sat down behind the desk again.

"You've given yourself away, Delancey," said Hugh.

"I know," said Delancey, and began to tremble violently, his teeth chattering: "Oh, my God!" he cried. *"Why* didn't you let me do it? I could have done it... then. If you hadn't come... Why didn't you let me blow my brains out? I tell you, I could have done it.... But when you smashed out the light... When it got dark... I—I can't stand the dark... I'll never have the nerve to do it now.... *Why* didn't you let me?"

He had broken down now, hopelessly. He had no defenses now. Hugh would see now what he had determined to see, the very soul of this man. And he regretted it; he wished to Heaven that he had not come. This man before him was in torment, and must endure more and more torment. He wished that he had left him to escape, by the only road left open to him.

"You were going to shoot yourself?" he asked.

"Like Robert..." said Delancey, with a sob.

"Whitestone! You mean—?"

"I did *that* for him, anyway. For—both of them...."

"What do you mean, Delancey?"

Delancey straightened himself in his chair.

"She asked me to," he said. "Elsie, you know. She said that if I pulled wires, I could get to see him. I'm pretty well known in this town—and I did. I was allowed to see him and I smuggled a gun to him. He thanked me... He... It was the only thing left to do for him.... He shot himself—just before you came.... He's got out of it.... They'll find out that I gave him the gun, but I don't care. I—I *didn't* care—because I thought... O God!"

His voice broke, he slumped in the chair.

"O God!" he cried. "It would have been so much easier than going to the chair.... Only now... All that will take so long... If you'd only let me alone—it would all have been over now... It's going to take so long...."

Justice was triumphant. All Hugh had to do was to telephone to the police; they would take away this bound man, and he would never be free again. But it would be a long time, as he said, before it was all over.

"Do you want a spot of whiskey?" asked Hugh.

Because it was unbearable to see this fellow-creature utterly without hope, without even the will to hope.

"No," Delancey answered. "That's done. I made up my mind—after I'd seen Robert—for the last time—that when I went, I'd go sober. The way *he* did. He wasn't afraid. All he cared about was getting it over quick. He wasn't even sorry about Rosalind. I wished he had been a little. Rosalind was—Rosalind was..." He had to stop for a moment. "All right," he said. "If it's got to be—this way—the long way.... If the p-police are coming, I'll go with them sober."

There was something in Delancey after all, that was not broken. He was still shaking, he was white about the mouth and nostrils, but there was something... Hugh had the strange idea that that big, sturdy body was going to pieces, and that only a shining spark of spirit kept the man together and whole.

"If you thought I—I was threatening you—with that gun..." Delancey went on, "you were wrong. I just wanted you to get out—and give me a chance... I... I... Hurry up, for God's sake! Send for the police! I can't stand... I can't stand..." He made an effort to control himself. "Let's get it over with," he said.

"I'm sorry," said Hugh, and he was. The excitement of the chase had vanished, there was only pain in the sight of the quarry brought down, trussed, to be taken to the ordeal. With all his heart he regretted that he had come too soon. He wished he might have found Delancey dead, and he was glad Whitestone was dead.

"You needn't be sorry," said Delancey. "You couldn't help it. It's fate. It had to be you. Like it was with—Robert. It's *just* the same! It's just what happened to Robert!"

"I don't quite..."

"Don't you see? You found Robert's eyeglasses down on the beach. That was what did for him. And now you've found my cigarette case the same way. I'd forgotten that case. I missed it a while ago, and I felt pretty sure it was in the pocket of my grey suit. But when I put on my grey suit yesterday, I never thought of looking in the pockets for it. I forgot it. And it's fate for everyone to forget just one thing, like that. Of course, it must have dropped out of my pocket, on the bridle-path, and you found it there."

It seemed to Hugh now as if he had won his victory by a contemptible trick. He had not meant it to be so, he had produced the cigarette case without a suspicion of the result that would ensue. Now he wished it had not happened.

"It's fate," Delancey repeated, a look of dim sorrow in his blue eyes. "All right. Whatever I get is coming to me.... It's just like it was with Robert. I'll confess, like he did. I'll tell you exactly how it was."

"You needn't confess to me! "said Hugh, in haste. "I'm not your judge, Delancey."

"You're the one who was sent," said Delancey. "You're the one who found the case. You're the one that stopped me from blowing out my brains. I dreamt about you last night. Fate..."

His voice trailed off, he sat there, hands tied behind him, not trembling any longer, but intolerably resigned. "I think I knew—all the time—that I'd have to pay.... You don't know what it's like—paying for a thing like that.... Robert felt like that. He wasn't sorry, but he said he knew you always had to pay—for doing things like that. He knew what I was going to do, too. He never knew it *had* happened and I didn't tell him, but he knew before. He said I'd do it.... I forget the day... The day before Rosalind—went... He told me then. He said—I felt the—death wish."

"Whitestone told you you were going to—?" said Hugh. And he wondered if that could be used in Delancey's defense, that his friend whom he had so loved and admired, had suggested this horrible thing to him.

"Robert said I had the wish—the death wish. And when you've got that, the rest doesn't count.... The rest came—without any trouble. I thought out the whole plan while I was smoking one cigarette.... I'd like a cigarette now, Acheson. You could untie my hands. You've got the gun."

Hugh dropped the automatic into his pocket. He wished he had never come here, never suspected this crime. But he had suspected, and he had come, and now he had to see it through. Delancey would never again summon the courage to shoot himself, and he could not be allowed to go free, after what he had done. Josephine was dead, and unlamented. It was her right that she should at least be avenged.

"I'll ring up the police now," he said, with a sort of gentleness.

"Wait a minute!" said Delancey. "If I tell you and you write it down, maybe they'll let me alone—until to-morrow morning. Because I'm— *tired*. I want a good night's sleep."

A strange and dreadful thing to want.

"I'm sorry," said Hugh, "but I'm afraid you'll have to make your statement to them."

"Even if I say I plead guilty?"

"Even then."

"I'll have to answer their questions?"

"Afraid so."

"It's all straight in my mind," said Delancey, with a sigh. "Haven't forgotten a single thing. I mean to say, they can't get me all mixed up, like they did before.... I thought it all out while I was smoking a cigarette... Last cigarette I had in my pocket... I did it all just as I'd planned it. First, I got the car out of the garage. Shoved it out and down the hill before I started the engine. Then—"

"Look here, Delancey! You mustn't do this... You mustn't talk—until you've seen a lawyer."

"I'll have to talk to the police," said Delancey. "They know how to make you answer questions. Anyhow, I don't care now, Acheson. It's a sort of relief... I mean to say, I feel as if I'd been—shut away from everyone—ever since it happened... I'd rather tell you first. I think you—sort of understand things."

His lack of any rancour, any resentment, was pitiable thing, a touching thing. And a dreadful thing, for this man who had cornered him.

"I drove the car to the bridle-path," he went on.

"I hid it in the woods there. Hardly anyone ever goes there. Then I came back here, and I cut my hand with a pen-knife. I wanted Helen Phillips to know I was in the house, so I asked her to tie it up for me. I'm sorry I did that now. She was—nice to me... She didn't know—what was in my mind... I'm sorry I'm never going to see her again...."

He stopped for a time, inhaling his cigarette, and again there was sorrow in his eyes, as if he could envisage in a moment all the delights of life that were lost to him.

"I spoke to Annie in the morning, too. I wanted it known that I was in the house. I thought that would keep people from suspecting I had anything to do with the car. I did it all, just the way I'd planned. I went to my office early in the morning, and I telephoned to Josephine. That's the meanest part of the whole thing—the lie I made up to tell her... The devil himself couldn't have thought of a dirtier trick.... I told her I'd got in trouble—told her a friend had given me some money to buy certain bonds with, and I'd invested it in something else and lost it. I asked her to meet me on the bridle-path, and I'd tell her how to help me out of the jam. I was going to appeal to her pride, you know. But—she was—just sorry for me... She called me 'poor boy'... That's going to stay in my mind till I die. Maybe after I'm dead."

His voice grew unsteady again. He picked up the silver cigarette case and opened it, took out a cigarette and tapped it on the desk, went on tapping and tapping.

"That made me realize... That was when I began to—to pay. I felt—I can't tell you how I felt. But I had to go on with it. You can see that. I tried to think of a way out, and I couldn't. If I told her I'd got out of the trouble by myself, she'd have made me answer a lot of questions. About whose money I'd taken and what stock I'd bought and so on.... And—you don't know what it's like to be asked a lot of questions you don't want to answer. That's what the police did with me—about Robert. I couldn't tell her the truth, either. Couldn't tell her—the idea I'd had—no matter if I was sorry... You—you can see that I couldn't live with her again—ever—after that idea—that wish had come into my head. No. I had to go on with it. Had to meet her there. And when I saw her, coming down the path... Oh, my God!... I know a lot of people didn't like Josephine... But she had— she had—so many good qualities."

Hugh turned away his head, so that he need not see Delancey. It was incredible. Even after he had "realized," Delancey had gone on, he had seen that woman, defenseless in her utter lack of suspicion, walking along the path toward him, coming to help him, and still he had gone on with it.

"She was—I never saw her so—kind..." Delancey went on. "O God! When I think of it... She was just sorry for me... Didn't blame me.. She was really fond of me."

Still Hugh said nothing and still he could not endure to look at Delancey. He felt no pity for the man now, nothing but an icy contempt. Delancey was beyond measure baser than Whitestone had been. Whitestone had killed his wife because he hated her and loved Elsie, but Delancey had felt no hatred, no passion of any sort. He had killed, had committed a murder, because he could think of no easier way out of a complication.

"She wrote a cheque for me," Delancey went on. "I've got it in my pocket now. To help me out. She believed the lie I told her. I said I'd have to go away—leave the country for a while... She cried... I pretended I'd write, and she could join me later... She kissed me... Then—"

"I— You needn't tell me any more," said Hugh.

He felt indeed that he could not listen to any more of this. He felt that there could be no forgiveness on earth or in Heaven for this man.

But Delancey still talked.

"She got into the car and drove away. I watched her go. I knew I'd never see her again."

"*What!*" cried Hugh.

"I couldn't live with her again, after I'd had that idea. I watched her go. I saw the whole thing. *All of it.* She must have stepped on the accelerator by mistake. She was always doing that. She was the worst driver—"

"What are you saying?"

"I'm telling you how it was!" Delancey answered. "I saw the whole thing. I saw her drive square into the other car.... I knew she was killed, but I was afraid to go and see. I ran to the station."

"Delancey! Look here, man! You—gave me to understand that—you'd killed her."

"I did," said Delancey.

The idea came to Hugh that the man was mad.

"But if she was killed in the accident...?"

"She was. But I killed her. If I hadn't wished her dead, it wouldn't have happened. Don't you *see?* It was—the *death wish* that brought her to that place—that killed her. I take all the responsibility."

CHAPTER XIX

ELSIE

Hugh sat immobile staring before him. He knew the bridle-path well enough. He had visited it only to-day. In his mind he could see it now, a lane bordered with trees, green and quiet. He thought of Delancey waiting there, sick with horror and dismay, Delancey who was capable of the wish to kill but not of the deed. God only knew how many other men went about the world harboring such wishes and were not ashamed? Yet Delancey thought he must pay for his intention with his life.

"*Please,* Acheson!" he cried, with a sort of despairing impatience. "Call up the police, and let's get this over."

"No..." said Hugh, rousing himself with a start. "I'm afraid you'll get into trouble over the gun you smuggled in to Whitestone—"

"Oh, that?" said Delancey, with a faint frown of weariness. "Elsie's arranged that. Whitestone sent word for me to bring him a package of stuff from his house. Elsie fixed up the package—some paints and so on, as if it had just come from a shop. They knew me over at the prison. They didn't search the package very thoroughly. Elsie did it that way, so that I could have said I didn't know the automatic was in it. I'd have done that for Robert, anyhow... I saw him...."

He fell silent and Hugh respected his silence. He too thought of Whitestone, and of Elsie.

"Let's get it over with," said Delancey again.

"But—don't you see...? Apart from bringing the gun, you haven't done anything, Delancey."

"I have! I planned it. I brought her there, to the bridle-path. If I hadn't, she'd—be alive now."

"There's no way of knowing that, Delancey. Accidents—"

"I planned it," said Delancey. "I had it in my heart. I'm responsible for her death—and I ought to pay."

"It's not a matter for the law," said Hugh. "See here! No one else knows—what you've just told me. No one else need ever know it."

Delancey looked at him, with a sort of wretched bewilderment.

"I'm responsible..." he said.

"No," said Hugh. "Delancey... I want you to come along with me, to Mrs. Luff's...."

"*She* wouldn't want *me*—"

"She would," said Hugh. "She does. Come on, please! I want to see Elsie."

"She's at the cottage."

"Whitestone's cottage? Alone?"

"I don't know," Delancey answered. "There was somebody else there—a cousin of Robert's—but I don't know."

"We'll stop by there then."

It was difficult to get Delancey started. He had been tried beyond his endurance, and he would not quickly recover. He was dazed and stupid, and Hugh was obliged to display a patience he was far from feeling.

"She's capable of that..." he thought, while he tried to hurry Delancey. It was Elsie he meant, and it was death of which he believed her capable. There was death in the air, Rosalind, Josephine, Whitestone.... Not Elsie, Elsie must not die.

He got Delancey's car from the garage, he hurried Delancey into it, and he drove, very fast, to the cottage. He was afraid, greatly afraid. If Elsie wanted to die, die she would, leaving the world with scornful impatience. She would accept life only on her own terms, and if she didn't like it, she would fling it away.

"She's too young..." he thought. "I've *got* to be in time."

He stopped the car before the cottage.

"Wait here, will you?" he said to the subdued and docile man beside him.

As he hastened up the path, it occurred to him that this wasn't a good place for poor Delancey to wait in, but that could not be helped; wait there he must, outside the little house with lighted windows where his friend had lived. Hugh ran up the steps of the porch, and rang the bell. And no one came.

Somehow he had felt it would be like this. He rang again; then he tried the knob, and the door opened. He entered that most desolate little house....

He went through it quickly; it was plain to be seen that Elsie was not here. Then he remembered how he had come here before, with her and Delancy, and no one had answered the bell.

"The summer-house," he thought.

It would be—a bad thing, to find her there. It was bad, even to think of her having gone there, alone. He opened the back door, and he saw a light there, at the foot of the little garden. The tree-toads were whistling, with a sort of eerie gaiety, the leaves stirred in the breeze, it was such a quiet night, he thought.... Such a lonely garden, with Rosalind and Robert Whitestone both gone.... Had Elsie come here, in the dark, to a dreadful rendezvous...?

He did not think of knocking; he pushed open the door and there she was, standing beside a table, leaning over and writing something on a paper. She straightened up as he entered, and looked at him, and there was no surprise in her glance. She looked preoccupied, cold, very tired.

"Elsie..." he said.

"I've seen Bob's cousin," she said. "He's a horrible man. Cruel and stupid. All Bob's work—all these pictures—will belong to *him* now. And do you know what he said? He said: 'I suppose they'll have a certain value now, after all this...!' After—all this..."

She sat down on the edge of the table, and pushed her hair back from her forehead, her hand left a grimy mark on her brow, her eyes, dark with fatigue, looked enormous. She was young, fragile, alone, yet she could endure everything. She could face death and sorrow and loneliness without help.

"Elsie," he said, "will you marry me?"

She shook her head.

"No," she answered, casually.

He sat down beside her.

"I wish you would," he said. "I don't believe there's another girl like you in the world. I don't expect you to love me—"

"No. I've finished with *that,*" she said, in the same matter-of-fact way. "But I like you. When you asked me to marry you, was it just because you were generous and wanted to help me?"

"Well... Not entirely," said Hugh, with a faint and rueful smile.

"Because if you want to help me," she went on. "I'll tell you what I want."

He was silent for a moment. He looked at her exquisite face, but she was not looking at him. And not thinking of him. Then and there he renounced forever a hope he had had.

"What can I do?" he asked. "I'll be glad."

"Lend me the money to buy Bob's pictures from his cousin," she said. "All of them. I've been making a list of them.... I'll rent a place, and exhibit them—decently. I'm going to see that people know the truth about Bob. I'd like to get out a little book about him and his work.... The truth—about his life. Not about his—poor, miserable end...."

There were two slow tears running down her cheeks, and her face was wonderfully transfigured, rapt.

"I'll be glad," Hugh said again.

She did not thank him.

"Bob—was a genius," she said. "A great man. I want to spend my life—making people see that."

Whitestone's pictures stood about the room, and whether they were good or bad, Hugh did not know. But he did know that a legend was being created here, the legend of Robert Whitestone as a great man, a hero. And he thought it would grow, until the lie seemed a truth, because Elsie was herself a creature of heroic mould.

THE END

NET OF COBWEBS

COBWEBS

Elisabeth Sanxay Holding

To Henri

Chapter One

Malcolm Drake waked early that morning; a little after five. It was a fine September morning and he felt fine, simply fine; he went into his bathroom and took a cold shower, and then there was the thermos bottle of hot coffee on the table. Virginia left it there every night; she was always trying to help him.

He sat down at the table, in nothing but jaunty candy-striped shorts, and poured out a cup of coffee, black and steaming, plenty of sugar in it. I feel fine, he said to himself, and he looked fine; he could see himself in the mirror set in the bathroom door. He was brown and hardy, neatly built; only he did not like his face so much, with dark curly hair growing too low on his forehead, and little, deep-set dark eyes, and two vertical creases in his lean cheeks that made him seem to be smiling, in a sad, doggy way.

He lit a cigarette with the second cup of coffee and leaned back comfortably in the chair. His windows faced the west, so he could not see the sun, but the sky was clear and pale blue. A fine day for a little exercise, he said to himself. Plenty of exercise, that's the idea. I'm coming out of this, all right. Getting better every day.

Coming out of what? What was it he had got into, what dim little hell, like a trap of cobwebs? Never mind. Never mind. He felt fine now. The only thing that bothered him was to see the bed unmade. It would be a long time, hours, before the housemaid came around, and who wanted to sit in a room like this?

He made the bed himself, very carefully; he turned the mattress, made the sheets and the blanket smooth and taut, tucked in the corners of the white spread, laid the pillow exactly straight. He took the two overflowing ash trays and emptied them in the bathroom; he got yesterday's shirt out of the hamper and dusted with it. I like things tidy, he thought. My cabin was always—

Never mind about cabins. He was living on shore now, a new life. The thing was to get started, get going. Get dressed, that's the first step. He put on a clean blue shirt and a dark suit and his well-polished shoes; he lit another cigarette and stood by the window, looking out at the wide green lawn that ended in a belt of trees. He liked the neatness of this landscape, and the different shades of green, the pale-green birches and the dark-green pines. I might go out and take a walk, he said to himself. I think I will.

He finished his cigarette, standing there, and he lit another. Might do a little reading, he told himself, and turned back to the table, where a couple of nice books lay, picked out for him by Virginia. Wonderful girl, he thought, and still standing he opened one of the books.

He could not read. He tried. He read the first paragraph over and over, and his hands began to tremble, his mouth twitched. No... I'll go out, get out in the fresh air, he told himself.

But he could not go out.

The whole thing was coming back, like a towering wave rushing at him. He stood facing it, breathing fast, and out of the wave came a bony wrist and a thin hand. That was Alfred. Jump, you damn fool! he had yelled to Alfred.

Now... No! Look here! he said to himself. This is the bad time, early in the morning. Nobody else awake in the house. In the world.

He went like a blindfolded man, lifting his feet too high, to the closet; he opened the door and fumbled among the clothes hanging there, and in the back, in the pocket of his winter overcoat, he found his little bottle.

It was hard to get the top unscrewed, and it was hard to shake out a capsule into his hand. Bright, vivid blue they were; very fine little pills. If you took four at night, you slept; if you took just one, times like this, the whole thing slowed down, that shaking stopped; you could feel yourself coming together again.

Drake, Dr. Lurie had said, I don't want you to take any more of those capsules. Yes, I know the doctor in Trinidad gave them to you, and I consented to give you a prescription when you first came here. But you've been here six weeks now and it's time you made an effort. I'm not going to renew your prescription, Drake, and you can't get the capsules without it. Personally, I don't care for these sedatives, in a case like yours. Dangerous.

Doctor in Trinidad told me you could take a whole bottle of them and never turn a hair, Malcolm had said, and he had been pretty proud of himself for thinking that up on the spot. It had been a pleasure to see Lurie sort of foam up. A bottle of those capsules would kill you, Drake.

Just what he wanted to know. He had ten bottles now. He had called up the druggist in the village. Send over a couple of bottles of those capsules, will you? he had said. I'll give your boy the new prescription when he comes. Then when the boy had come, Malcolm had said he would send the prescription by mail. Not so good; every time he did it, it made him nervous. But the druggist didn't seem to care, and Malcolm bought everything else he could dream up from the man. And the great thing was to get perhaps fifteen bottles and hide them, and be safe.

He put the bottle back into the overcoat pocket and was going to the bathroom to get a glass of water when there was a knock at the door.

"Just a moment!" he called.

But the door opened, and in came Aunt Evie, trim and dainty in a flowered print dress, her blue-white hair all in little curls about her rose-pink face. Her blue eyes flickered at his clenched hand that held the capsule; her cupid's-bow mouth smiled.

"Malcolm boy," she said winningly, "let's go out and take a little walk in the nice fresh air, shan't we?"

"Th-thank you," he said. "L-later."

He was stuttering, and that always worried him.

"Oh, let's go now!" she said, advancing toward him in a faint cloud of perfume. "Right now!"

She thought she was helping him and saving him, and it was all wrong to feel like this about her. Only if she doesn't get away from me, I'll be sick. I'll heave. I'll go crazy. Get out! Get away from me....

"Malcolm boy," she said, and laid her hand over his clenched one. "You're not—taking anything, are you?"

Make her go. Please make her get out. "Malcolm boy, Dr. Lurie doesn't want you to take anything now. Not *anything.*"

He jerked his hand away and popped the capsule into his mouth. He could not swallow and he was going to choke. But he did swallow it.

"Oh, Malcolm!" she cried.

"I'm s-s-sorry," he said. "I'm s-sorry, but would you mind...? D'you mind going away—just a few moments?"

"Oh, Malcolm!" she said in a stricken voice. "You want to get rid of me!"

He did; indeed he did.

She went toward the open door and in the hall she paused and looked back at him with a piteous and forgiving smile. Over her shoulder Malcolm saw the silly gaping face of Ben, the butler-handy man; he closed the door on both of them and looked around his big, comfortable room in desperation.

Don't know what to do. Don't know what to do, he thought. He locked the door and got out the jigsaw puzzle Virginia had given him. He cleared off a table and dumped all the pieces out on it; he drew up a chair and set to work on it with his shaking hands, his broad shoulders hunched. He tried, breathing hard, and when he fitted two pieces together that made half a lamb, he felt better. He got interested in the puzzle, only the sky was difficult; all those clouds.

The doorknob rattled; that was Arthur.

"Come in! Come in!" Malcolm cried and jumped up, knocking the puzzle all over the floor. He unlocked the door and his brother stood there, pale, gloomy, his light hair ruffled on the crown of his head, his tie crooked. Yet somehow he had a look of the greatest elegance, with his long, sharp nose and his tall, lean body.

"Malcolm?" he said. "How's everything?"

"Everything's fine," Malcolm answered, and they went along the hall and down the stairs together. Funny thing, Malcolm thought, but I always feel better with Arthur. He's not cheerful, he's not calm, not any of those things they say are good for you. But I feel better when he's around.

They went into the dining room. "Ah! Aunt Evie's not down!" Arthur said very low. "Maybe she's sick. Maybe she's laid up."

"She isn't," said Malcolm. "She came into my room this morning."

"To bring you joy."

"Oh, yes. Y'know, I wish the old girl didn't think I needed quite so much saving."

"She thinks everyone's a drunkard and a gambler and a lecher," said Arthur. "It makes her very serene and happy. Hi, Lydia!"

"Yes, sir?" said the little housemaid.

"This it, Lydia? This the new brew?"

"Oh, yes, sir!" she answered, with a dimpled smile. "Mrs. Drake told me specially, sir."

"Try it, will you, Malcolm?"

Malcolm took a sip of his coffee.

"It's a new account," Arthur said. "I've thought up this name for it— Don Carlos Coffee. Not too bad! Only I haven't got an angle. I mean, why should anybody buy it! Don Carlos, the Coffee That Is No Different.... Switch today to Don Carlos—just for the hell of it."

"Good morning, boys!" said Aunt Evie.

She was standing behind Malcolm; as he tried to rise she laid her hand on his shoulder.

"Try to eat, Malcolm boy," she said.

Her sweet perfume enveloped him; appalling things to say came into his head, things that would have made her blue-white curls rise up on her head. "I will," he said. "I will." Get out. Go and sit down. Get away from me.

"Such a lovely, lovely day," she said. "You will get out in this wonderful sunshine, won't you, Malcolm?"

"Yes, I will, he said. "I will," and at last she moved away.

Arthur pulled back her chair for her with the formal and elegant courtesy that was natural to him. He seemed so distrait and preoccupied, yet he never neglected little things like this; he never overlooked anybody.

"And this is the new Don Carlos, Arthur?" she asked.

"How did you know about it?"

"But I heard you talking to Helene, dear. It must be very, very hard to have to praise a thing you really despise in your heart."

"Despise Don Carlos?" said Arthur. "Not I."

"Money makes us do such strange, unlovely things," said Aunt Evie gently.

"Aunt Evie," said Arthur, "this is the best brew you ever set tooth to. Try it."

"I don't notice what I eat or drink, dear boy."

"But you notice aroma," said Arthur. "Just get a load of that aroma, Aunt Evie. You can help me infinitely if you'll tell your many friends about Don Carlos."

"I will, dear. But I did think, from the way you were talking to Helene, that it made you just a little heartsick to have to sing the praises of something, just for money, that you really—"

"You're mistaken!" said Arthur gravely. "My only worry is how to get people to try this king of brews. How to arouse curiosity."

"Curiosity killed the cat," said Aunt Evie with a silvery laugh. "Satisfaction brought it back. How would that do for your slogan, Arthur?"

"It's very punchy," said Arthur. "Only I'm afraid it's not quite realistic enough. I mean, with all the scientific knowledge now available, I'm afraid the consumer won't believe that cats are killed by curiosity."

Aunt Evie laughed again.

"Aren't people *funny*, with their poor bits of so-called scientific knowledge?" she asked.

"Oh , they are," said Arthur.

She began upon her breakfast now, and Malcolm sat stirring and stirring his cup of Don Carlos, and thinking about her. About her awfulness.

When Arthur had married Helene, two years ago, he had accepted the necessity of long and frequent visits from Helene's and Virginia's Aunt Evie. After all, she had brought up the two orphan sisters; they were used to her.

The home life of Aunt Evie was something Malcolm could never imagine. She was well-todo and lived in an apartment hotel in New York; she talked of the little parties she gave there, in the roof garden. She belonged to a cult which was called, quite simply, Joy. The motto was *Joy Now,* and when you waked in the morning you stretched up your arms and Accepted Joy. It came, if you did the thing right, flooding all your being, and you were able then to give it out to others. She got it, all right. She was never tired; she was radiant from morning till night, and helpful.

She explained that she could not help people unless she *knew* things. And she found out everything. She had a sleepless, unwearying curiosity, and great skill in putting two and two together. She believed in candor, too; what she found out she told.

"Good morning, people!" said Virginia.

She was a notably handsome girl, tall and broad-shouldered, with fine dark eyes and a fine color in her olive cheeks, a serious, quiet girl with an air of distinction in her gray flannel suit and blue blouse.

"Where's your naughty sisters?" asked Aunt Evie.

"She went to sleep again," said Arthur. "That's not naughty." He pushed back his chair and rose. "I'll have to hurry," he said. "It's my day to taxi the neighbors."

"The good-neighbor policy!" said Aunt Evie, with a merry laugh, and Arthur gave a polite and spasmodic grin and went out of the room.

"Helene is a very, very fortunate young woman," said Aunt Evie. "So many men would resent it, if a young and healthy girl wouldn't come down to breakfast. But in Arthur's eyes, Helene can do no wrong."

There was no response to that.

"Ah, well—" Aunt Evie began, when Lydia came in.

"Mrs. Foxe to speak to you on the telephone, Mrs. Chatsworth," she said, and Aunt Evie rose. She was very fond of telephoning.

"Malcolm," said Virginia, "would you like to come with me this afternoon to see someone about the new bond drive?"

"Oh, certainly!"

"I called up this Mrs. Kingscrown and she seemed very nice. She asked me to come to tea and bring anyone I liked."

"That'll be very fine," said Malcolm.

"Then let's start around four...?"

She was cutting a slice of toast into neat strips; she looked downcast and troubled.

"I hope I don't really hate Aunt Evie," she said.

"You don't hate anybody," said Malcolm.

"But, Malcolm, suppose I hate her subconsciously?" she asked with anxiety.

She worried altogether too much about things like that, about her motives, about her duties, and she had a way of asking Malcolm for advice that made him unhappy. God knew he didn't have any advice to give her or anyone else.

"Well, that kind of hate couldn't do any harm," he said.

"It could do me harm, Malcolm. Hate can warp your whole nature."

"Your nature isn't warped," he said. "You're as good as gold."

"D'you know what she did, Malcolm? I heard her. She called up Dr. Lurie, and she asked him to come in this afternoon and just have a look at you without your suspecting anything. She said she thought you were slipping back. She said you had some sort of queer hostility toward her. She told Dr. Lurie she thought you were *dangerous.*"

He gripped the handle of his cup, to stop the shaking of his hands. The handle broke, and the cup turned over, and a brown stain like mud went running over the clean white cloth. Dangerous, he said to himself in despair. That was what he dreamed in his ghastly nightmares, that was what he dreaded, all the time. Being dangerous.

Chapter Two

"But, Malcolm!" Virginia said. "You don't mind anything she says."

"No, no," he said. "No... no... no. Excuse me, Virginia. Got to—got to—write some letters."

He had to get into his own room, quick, and shut the door. All right, he thought. I'm crazy. And she knows it, Aunt Evie does. 'Shock,' that damn doctor calls it. People like me don't get 'shocked.' I went through a bad time, yes. But so do plenty of other people, and they get over it. But me...? Two days in a lifeboat, forty-eight hours; what's that? Look at what other people take. Women, children.

But some of them go mad. You hear about that. Raving mad, try to jump overboard. Some people go through with it all right—and some don't.

As he reached the top of the stairs Helene opened her door and came out, tall and exquisite, in a black taffeta house-coat fitted in to her tiny waist.

"Oh, Malcolm!" she said. "I thought it was Arthur."

"Well, no..." he said seriously.

He felt a profound respect for Helene, but he was never at ease with her. She was very courteous to him, and she was kind, but there was a dainty formality about her. She was beautiful and perfect and, to Malcolm, not quite human. She smiled at him, and he smiled at her, and she sought for something to say.

"Ivan Jenette's coming out this afternoon," she said.

"Oh, is he? Fine!" said Malcolm.

"You remember him, Malcolm?"

He didn't know whether to say yes or no. Was this Jenette someone he ought to remember, and possibly did, or could remember if he tried? So he tried.

"It's a lovely day, isn't it?" said Helene.

Her gentle, friendly words did something horrible to him. She had seen, of course, that he didn't know whether or not he remembered this Jenette, and she had tried to make things better for him. But what she really did was to point out to him her own quiet, controlled sureness and his deep confusion.

"Lovely day!" he said with great heartiness. "Lovely!"

He went into his room and locked the door and stayed there until lunchtime. He had plenty to think about.

He went down and had lunch with Helene and Virginia and Aunt Evie. He was the only man; other men went to work. Only he didn't, because he couldn't.

"Shall we start about four o'clock, Malcolm?" Virginia asked.

"Start? Oh, yes!" he said. "Yes. Four o'clock. I'll finish my letters now, if you'll excuse me."

At ten minutes to four he opened the door of his closet. There were three hats on the shelf, two felt ones and a Panama; he stood looking at them, trying to make up his mind, and sweat came out on his forehead.

Now, see here! he told himself. It doesn't matter a damn which hat you wear. Just take one of them—any one—and get going.

He could not. So he closed his eyes and reached up and his hand touched one of the felt hats. He picked up his stick and he put a fresh pack of cigarettes into his pocket and went downstairs. Virginia was standing in the hall below and Aunt Evie was with her.

"Going out, children?" she said. "Don't let Malcolm overdo, Virginia."

She fluttered away, and they went out of the house and down the drive.

"She's been after Helene," said Virginia. "Telling her she ought to learn to cook, so she could do with one servant. And she had a booklet for me, about teaching physical fitness to girls. Malcolm, maybe she's right."

"Maybe she is," he said.

He tried to think of some way to change the subject and avoid any talk about what was right and what everybody ought to do, but he could think of nothing.

"I've got to do *something,*" Virginia said. "Only I don't know where I'd be most useful. I wish you'd give me some advice, Malcolm."

"Virginia, I—wouldn't know..."

"Malcolm," she said, anxious, a little hesitant, "maybe if you'd try to help me, it would help you, don't you think?"

Poor kid! So that was why she kept pestering him for 'advice.' To help him. If you can get your mind off your own troubles, Dr. Lurie had said. How do you get your mind off a nightmare?

The air was thin and clear as crystal; the leaves were falling everywhere, and walking through them on the roadside made him think of the days when he and Arthur used to go scuffling through leaves like this on their way to the Military Academy. Fine snobbish little school, fancy uniforms, capes, white gloves.

Alfred had never had anything. He had grown up in a Brooklyn slum; when they signed him on, he was sixteen. I guess I'll study and be an officer, he had said to Malcolm. That was what he had been told. Fine chances for promotion with this line, my lad. Work hard, study hard, take your examinations. Only he hadn't had much time to study. Ten days at sea was all he got.

"You're awfully quiet, Malcolm."

"Yes, I do seem to be," he said apologetically.

"Malcolm, do you think Dr. Lurie is helping you, really?"

"Oh, yes! Sure. You bet!"

"I don't know if I like him much."

Virginia, don't talk any more. Please. You're such a nice kid, such a nice, good, beautiful kid, won't you please shut up and just walk along beside me?

The road was lined with stone walls and wire fences, enclosing big, well-kept estates. People with money, he thought. Like Arthur. I never bothered much about money. When they made me Purser, I was satisfied. And now... Never mind. Someone was burning leaves and that was a fine smell. Halloween, he thought. Mother used to make lanterns out of pumpkins. She was a quiet woman. Happy—but quiet about it.

They were coming to another high wire fence and he was tired of them.

"Quite a long way, isn't it?" he said.

"It's only three miles. Why? Are you tired, Malcolm?"

"Oh, Lord, no! I just thought it was quite a long way."

"I'm afraid you are tired. Oh, Malcolm, I'm *worried* about you!"

"Well, don't be," he said.

But that wouldn't do; that wasn't good enough. He took her hand and smiled at her, a grin from ear to ear; he kept her hand in his and they went on like that. This is better, he thought. He liked to hold her hand, balled up inside his, warm, soft as velvet, with nice little bones. A good kid, she was, quiet now.

"Here we are, Malcolm. This must be the place."

They turned into a gravel drive that led to a three-storied wooden house with a cupola and a lot of fancy scrollwork.

"Who's this we're going to see?" Malcolm asked.

"I've never met her, Malcolm. Only, at the last wardens' meeting, someone said she'd be a good person to get for the drive. Kingscrown... That's a funny name, isn't it?"

As they came to the steps that led up to the veranda, he loosened his hold on her hand. But her fingers closed around his. Well, nothing you could do about that. If she wanted to go calling hand in hand, very good.

He rang the bell, and then she let his hand go. The door was opened by a pale, red-eyed maid.

"Will you please tell Mrs. Kingscrown that Miss Chatsworth is here?" said Virginia.

"She's out," said the maid.

"But she was expecting me!"

"Well," said the maid, without much interest, "you could come in and wait."

She led them into a sitting room furnished in a modern style, very low white leather armchairs, a low couch with a cover of brown and blue tweed, a glass-and-chromium table at each end, a bare floor with a rug striped black and white, all airy and sunny and, to Malcolm, very agreeable. Then, as he sat down and looked around, he saw other things. On each step of a zigzag bookcase there were little things; he saw a glass cart drawn by two silver llamas; he saw a plaster replica of the Taj Mahal, a tiny Persian rug, a carved gourd in a silver stand, and other things of that sort, interesting as a toyshop. On a white leather chaise-longue that stood by the open window he saw a purple velvet doll with blond hair and extremely long legs.

"Look!" said Virginia in a low voice.

She was pointing to the iron doorstop. It was made in the form of a short lamppost, and beside it sat a lump of a black dog, winking one eye. It made Malcolm laugh.

"Do you think it's funny?" Virginia asked, surprised.

"Well..." he said apologetically.

Someone was coming up the veranda steps; the door opened and a woman came in, red-haired, tall and limber in dark slacks and a black sweater that outlined a fine full bosom.

"Sorry to be late," she said in a good clear alto voice. "Did Gussie explain?"

"No," said Virginia. "But it doesn't matter a bit, Mrs. Kingscrown. I'm Virginia Chatsworth, and this is Malcolm Drake, my brother-in-law."

"I'm Lily Kingscrown," said the hostess. "I'm sorry Gussie didn't explain, but sometimes she forgets, and sometimes she gets sort of contrary."

"Maids are so terribly hard to get, these days," said Virginia, "I suppose it's only human nature for them to take advantage of it, a little."

"Well, Gussie was just born to be taken advantage *of*," said Mrs. Kingscrown. "I told her to tell you they might keep me a little late at the asylum. I go there most afternoons, to help out."

"Oh, an orphan asylum?" asked Virginia.

"Lunatics," said Mrs. Kingscrown. "Mental hospital is what they really call it."

She opened a door and spoke to Gussie; then she sat down, crossing her long legs; her red hair curled up like petals from her strong-boned face with a big, beautiful good-humored mouth.

"What do you d-d-do there?" Malcolm asked.

"Well, I help out with the occupational therapy," she said. "Of course, I'm not trained, but still there are a lot of things I can do."

"But isn't it terribly depressing?" Virginia asked.

"Not as much as you'd think," said Mrs. Kingscrown. "For one thing, quite a lot of them get well. And then there are quite a lot of them who don't realize how they are. You can do a lot for them. We make gardens, and weave, and rainy days we do jigsaw puzzles."

"I think jigsaw puzzles are fascinating," said Virginia quickly. Too quickly.

Gussie was coming in now with a very lavish tea, hot buttered muffins, two kinds of sandwiches, a big layer cake.

"My husband was English," said Mrs. Kingscrown. "He was always crazy for his tea, and he got me in the habit. It is cozy, isn't it?"

She looked straight at Malcolm, with her big jolly smile, and he felt instantly and completely reassured. She knows, he thought. She knows all about things like that.

He felt very hungry now, and this was the best food he had ever tasted; he drank three cups of tea and he ate and ate. Virginia and Mrs. Kingscrown were talking about the bond drive; he did not listen to their words, but he liked the sound of their voices; he felt unbelievably happy and relaxed. This Mrs. Kingscrown, he thought. If she works in a place like that, she knows. Lots of people get well, she said.

A portly yellow cat came into the room, with the observant yet aloof air of a policeman on patrol.

"Hello, Skipper!" said Mrs. Kingscrown.

The cat winked at her, and jumped up on the chaise-longue beside the purple velvet doll; he made himself comfortable there, and purred for a while, staring at Malcolm with clear topaz eyes. Then, as if satisfied, he closed his eyes and went to sleep, in a bar of sunshine.

"Malcolm, I'm sorry..."

That was Virginia's voice, very close to his ear. He opened his eyes and looked into her eyes, dark and anxious.

"Malcolm, I'm sorry, but we'll really have to be going."

So he had fallen asleep, at Mrs. Kingscrown's tea party. He rose quickly, dazed and unsteady with sleep, and horribly ashamed of himself. The
big room was shadowy; the cat was gone; the scene was chilly and strange.
"I'll drive you people home," said Mrs. Kingscrown.

"Oh, don't bother!" said Virginia.

"It's no bother. My car's right out there, and I've got plenty of gas."
Malcolm was deeply relieved to think that he did not have to part just
yet from Mrs. Kingscrown. He could not bear to be parted from her; he
hated to leave her house.

"Is—is S-s-skipper gone?" he asked. "That's a nice name."

"He's a seagoing cat," Mrs. Kingscrown explained. "He belonged to my
husband, and he was a skipper, you know."

My God! thought Malcolm, overwhelmed.

"What line?" he asked.

"The Bell Line."

"No!"

"Why?" asked Mrs. Kingscrown. "D'you know anybody in that line?"
I did, he thought. That was my line. But not now. I'm not going to talk
about that now.

"If you're ready...?" Virginia suggested, and they all went out of the
house.

The sun was gone; there was a lemon-colored light in the west and the
trees looked black against it; the autumn landscape seemed vast and sad.
Malcolm felt cold. Arthur's house looked sad, too; he hated to go into it.

"Come in and have a drink?" he said to Mrs. Kingscrown.

"I'd love it!" she said.

Ben, tall and bony and gangling, in a clean white jacket, opened the
door.

"Mrs. Drake is in the library, sir," he said, "and Dr. Lurie—"

"Let's have some Scotch, Ben, and ginger ale. In the d-d-drawing
room."

The drawing room was the coldest room he had ever been in in all his
life. The lamps had white shades, frosty; the carpet was pale; the sun was
not coming in here.

"Malcolm," said Virginia, very low, "don't take a drink. Please, Malcolm."

"One won't hurt me, Virginia. I'm—cold."

"Please. Malcolm! Dr. Lurie told me it was the worst thing in the world
for you."

"He could be wrong, Virginia."

She looked at him and then moved away, across the long room; she stood at the window, looking out. I've hurt her, he thought. I didn't mean to do that. He wanted to go after her, but he did not know what to say. He did not know what to say to Mrs. Kingscrown, either. She was sitting on a sofa, and he sat down beside her; he hoped she would talk, and she did.

"Did you read in the papers about the two French sailors in the Brooklyn subway?" she asked.

"No," Malcolm said. "I—don't seem to read the papers."

"Well, it doesn't matter," she said. "There's no law about it, is there?"

Ben came in then with a tray, and Malcolm got up at once to mix the drinks.

"Virginia?" he said. "L-little drink?"

"No, thank you," she said, without turning. It was growing dark in the room; Mrs. Kingscrown's face looked pale in the dimness.

"After all," she said gravely, "there's nothing like Scotch, is there?"

"Nothing!" Malcolm said. "Nothing!"

The drink was beginning to help; the blood was running warmer in his veins, the numbness in his heart was thawing.

"Malcolm boy!" cried Aunt Evie.

She was coming toward him, in a lavender chiffon dress with floating sleeves and a purple jet butterfly in her blue-white curls.

"Oh...!" she said, peering at Mrs. Kingscrown; then she turned on the lamp and her smile.

"This is Mrs. K—K—Kay—" said Malcolm.

"How do you do, Mrs. Kay," said Aunt Evie. "Are you a neighbor of ours?"

"Yes, I live a couple of miles down the road."

"Have you lived here long, Mrs. Kay?"

"Only since April."

Aunt Evie's curiosity was not subtle; many people resented it. But not Mrs. Kingscrown. She seemed perfectly willing to answer questions.

"Are you a New Yorker, Mrs. Kay?"

"I'm from Brooklyn," said Mrs. Kingscrown.

"Oh, are you? I have friends in Brooklyn, very dear friends. They live on the Heights. Malcolm dear, what are you drinking?"

"Scotch."

"Dear boy, put down that glass, won't you? Alcohol is poison for you."

She turned to Kingscrown. "Malcolm's been ill, you know," she said. "So very, very ill. Dr. Lurie—"

Shut up! cried Malcolm to himself, and finished his drink quickly, so that she couldn't get it away from him.

"Why don't you try a drink, Aunt Evie?" he said. "You'd be surprised." That made her angry; her blue eyes glittered.

"Dear boy, I've never touched alcohol. I never feel any *need* for artificial stimulants. Or *drugs.*"

She was looking straight at him, and he knew what she meant. She always called those capsules 'drugs.' If she says anything to Mrs. Kingscrown about my taking drugs, he thought, I'll have to choke her, that's all.

"You ought to try some of this alcohol," he said. "Just to see what it could do to you."

"Very well!" she cried. "I *will!* Fix *me* a drink, Malcolm."

He poured a glass almost full of ginger ale and added a dash of whisky; he was handing it to her when Helene came into the room, followed by two men.

"Here I am, tippling!" cried Aunt Evie.

That fell flat, because Helene had caught sight of Mrs. Kingscrown and came toward her with the look of delight she had for guests. Malcolm said nothing, and Aunt Evie took charge.

"Helene, dear," she said, "this is a Mrs. Kay. From Brooklyn."

"I'm so glad," said Helene. "This is Dr. Lurie."

"Mrs. Kingscrown and I are old friends," Dr. Lurie, stepping forward, a slender, straight man, with a trick of carrying his head thrown back and his square chin out; he wore his grey hair in a sort of pompadour over his broad brow and he had a look of proud suffering.

"And this is Ivan Jenette," Helene said.

This Jenette was a stocky, broad-shouldered young fellow, black-haired and sallow, with sad, bilious dark eyes. He gave Mrs. Kingscrown a foreign-style bow, heels together; then he looked sidelong at Malcolm, with considerable distaste.

"Ivan, you and Malcolm know about each other," said Helene.

"Oh, yes," said Malcolm politely, but with no truth, and Jenette said nothing at all.

"Everybody's drinking whisky in here," said Helene, "while we were so nicely having tea. Will you have a drink, Dr. Lurie and Ivan?"

"*I'm* taking a drink, Dr. Lurie!" cried Aunt Evie. "My very firstest one— and who knows what will happen? I do hope I shan't talk too much and say the *wrong things.*"

Malcolm glanced quickly at her, and their eyes met. God! he thought. That's just what she means to do.

The amount of whisky he had given her couldn't, he thought, have any genuine effect upon her or anyone else. But if she chose to put on an act, to start babbling, saying the 'wrong things'... About me, he thought. About my pills and all that. I wish she'd choke.

She began to choke.

"Good gracious!" she said, coughing and gasping. "It's like liquid fire!"

Ivan Jenette took her glass from her and set it down on a table while she went on coughing.

"But I will finish it!" she said. "Every drop! Ivan, where is my dreadful drink?"

He handed her the glass and she sipped and choked again.

"Aunt Evie," said Virginia, coming across the room from the window, "don't take any more."

"I agree with Miss Virginia," said Dr. Lurie.

"I'm going to be naughty!" said Aunt Evie. "Malcolm poured it out for me and he wouldn't let me have too much. I'm going to finish every drop of it!"

"I'm afraid I'll have to be going now, Mrs.Chatsworth," said Mrs. Kingscrown.

"Oh, don't hurry away!" said Aunt Evie. "I wanted a little chat with you about Brooklyn."

"Come and see me some time, why don't you?" said Mrs. Kingscrown, with perfect good humor. "Good-by, Miss Chatsworth."

"Good-by," said Virginia briefly.

"I'll go out to your car with you," said Malcolm.

For he couldn't bear to see her going away. They went out on the terrace together and it was full dusk now.

"It's nice," she said.

They stood side by side, looking out over Arthur's peaceful domain. Her car stood there, and she was surely going to get into it and go away. There was so little *time*.

"Thing is..." he said. "I made—an error of judgment."

I called out—jump, you damn fool! And Alfred jumped. Like that joke about the volunteer fireman. He called out to the fellow in the burning house—jump into the net, and the fellow jumped. And cheese it, I had to laugh. There wasn't no net.

"I gave bad advice," he said.

His mouth twitched, the bridge of his nose twitched. God, if I could *tell* it! If I could *say* it!

"I gave bad advice," he said. "He was only a kid. Only sixteen. He was frightened sick, right from the start. I told him—nothing to worry about. I told him everything would be all right."

I killed him. The others on the deck—the ones who didn't jump—they were all taken off, safe and sound. Only Alfred... I told him to jump and he did. He landed flat against the thwart of the lifeboat and it caught him on the chin and broke his neck.

"The fellows on deck," he said, "they looked like gnomes. They were on deck in their life belts and they looked—very small. They looked as if they didn't have any necks. He was only sixteen."

Oh God, let me tell it, let me say it, this once....

"It was cold," he said. "It was a cold day."

She had not spoken at all; he could scarcely see her now in the gathering dusk. But he knew she was listening.

"I g-gave him bad advice," he said.

"And he died?" she asked.

Her voice sounded gentle and far away. But she was standing beside him, near him. We couldn't keep the kid in the lifeboat. He was dead. We had to put him overboard. If I tell *you*—

"Mr. Drake!" said Lydia's voice, high and urgent. "Mr. Drake, are you there, sir? Mr. Drake!"

"Yes, I'm here," he said.

"Oh, Mr. Drake, sir!... Mrs. Chatsworth is dead!"

"What?" he asked, puzzled.

"She fell right down dead on the floor, Mr. Drake."

Chapter Three

"Excuse me, just for a moment, please," he said politely to Mrs. Kingscrown, and followed Lydia into the house.

The drawing room was empty; he looked into the library and saw nobody there.

"Where are they all?" he asked.

"The doctor and Mr. Jenette, they carried poor Mrs. Chatsworth upstairs, and Mrs. Drake and Miss Virginia—they went up, too, sir," Lydia answered eagerly.

"I'd better go up, don't you think?"

"I don't know, sir," said Lydia.

"No. No, of course you don't," he said apologetically.

"What shall we do, sir?"

"Well, who?"

"Ben and me and Mrs. Jordan, sir. What did we ought to do, sir? Go right on about—" She lowered her voice. "About dinner, and all, sir?"

He looked at her blankly.

"L-l-later," Malcolm said. "I'll l-let you know l-later."

So he was in charge. He was to tell people what to do. He stood in the hall, and his knees felt weak. I've got to take charge. Give orders. What'll I do? You tell me. Where shall I go? Where do we go from here? Upstairs. Only, when he looked at the stairs, they were so extremely steep and long he could not start climbing them. Lydia was looking at him, waiting.

"You'd better—better—better tell me—exactly what happened," he said.

"I was just going into the room, sir, with some fresh canapés Ben made, and Mrs. Chatsworth, she sort of sunk down right on the floor, and then Dr. Lurie he knelt down beside her, and you could see by looking at him that it was terrible serious."

She was crying a little, but she could not help relishing the drama of this.

"Right while I was standing there," she said, "she must of died."

"Well, why?"

"Why, sir? Well, the doctor didn't say. But don't you guess it was a kind of stroke, like?"

"Must have been. I'll get along upstairs now."

He could not start climbing those stairs. Arthur must be on his way home now, he thought. Arthur'll know what to do when he comes. Only, right now... If Aunt Evie falls down dead, you have to do something. Be helpful. Go on! Begin!

Dr. Lurie was coming down the stairs, and Lydia went away.

"This is a shocking affair!" said the doctor sternly.

"Yes, it is," said Malcolm. "It is."

"And *reprehensible,*" said the doctor.

Reprehensible. Repersensible, Malcolm said to himself. Sounds like an Amos 'n' Andy word.

"Mrs. Chatsworth had had a heart condition for some time," the doctor went on, with the same sternness. "It was not unduly serious, but at her age—she was well over seventy—"

"Over seventy, was she? Didn't know that."

"No doubt someone thought it highly humorous to give that elderly woman with heart trouble an extremely strong drink," said the doctor.

"Oh, no," said Malcolm. "Nobody. What she got wouldn't have hurt a baby."

"Mr. Drake, there's no use telling that to *me.* I'm a physician. This attack of Mrs. Chatsworth's—this fatal attack—was induced by an excessive dose of alcohol."

"M-mistaken," said Malcolm.

"What d'you mean by that? Are you implying that my diagnosis is incorrect?"

"Only mean that the drink I gave her wasn't excessive. Tiny, it was."

"And what's your idea of a 'tiny' drink, Mr. Drake?"

"It wasn't more than a couple of teaspoonfuls."

"I can assure you Mrs. Chatsworth had a good deal more than that."

"Well," Malcolm said, "I suppose she could have poured herself out another drink, not knowing."

"I doubt it," said Lurie. "I was observing her fairly closely, and I should almost certainly have noticed it if she'd poured any more liquor into her glass. I should have protested, very strongly, against any such thing. As it was, I had accepted your assurance that the drink you gave her was extremely small."

"Yes, it was," said Malcolm.

"I'm signing a certificate," said the doctor. "Mrs. Chatsworth was my patient, and I was present when she died, so I can properly do so. But if it wasn't for the high regard I have for your brother and his wife, I should put down alcohol as the contributing cause."

"Look here," said Malcolm. "I didn't give her a big drink because I thought it would be funny. I know what I gave her."

"Mr. Drake," said the doctor, "I understand that you've been taking some medicine—some drug—on your own responsibility. You've chosen to disregard the advice I—"

"Oh, go lay an egg!" said Malcolm.

"*What!*" said Dr. Lurie.

Malcolm felt very happy about saying that and about the outraged look on the doctor's noble face. It was a long time since he had felt even an impulse to hit back at anyone and it did him good.

"I said—" he began, very willing to repeat. But a key was turning in the lock; the front door opened, and Arthur came in.

"Hello," he paid amiably. "How's everything?"

"Drake," said Dr. Lurie, and laid his hand on Arthur's shoulder. "I'm sorry, Drake, very sorry. Mrs. Chatsworth—"

Malcolm did not want to hear any more of that; he wandered off into the library and there he found Jenette, slouched in a big chair, smoking a pipe. He looked up at Malcolm with his cloudy, dark eyes.

"This is a hell of a thing to happen, isn't it?" he said.

"Yes, it is," said Malcolm.

"It gets on my nerves," said Jenette. "A death in the house—"

She's *dead,* Malcolm thought in a sort of astonishment. She's lying upstairs, dead. Poor old girl was hopping around, so lively, and now it's finished for her. It's damn pathetic. I mean, it's all right for some people to die. They can take it. But Aunt Evie...

His thoughts were growing confused and miserable. Thing is, he thought, she was so *little.* Hopping around...

Mrs. Kingscrown! he thought suddenly. She's gone home, I suppose. She wouldn't still be out there, would she?

"Excuse me," he said to Jenette, and went along the hall and out on the terrace. It was dark now, and only Dr. Lurie's car was standing there; she was gone, and he missed her. I'd like to say *au revoir,* he thought. Don't like to leave it this way. I just walked off and left her out here. I'd like her to know...

He went back into the library, where there was a telephone, and he was glad to find Jenette gone. He looked in the telephone book. Kingscrown, Mrs. Lily. There it was. He dialed the number, but nothing happened. Virginia came into the room.

"I don't get any answer," he said, frowning.

"Who are you trying to get, Malcolm?"

"Mrs. Kingscrown," he said. "I want to speak to her but I don't get any answer."

"Probably she's not at home."

"But the house ought to answer. Ought to be a servant—somebody around."

"You can try later," said Virginia. "We're going to have dinner now, Malcolm."

"Dinner?" he repeated.

"Things have to go on, Malcolm."

"I'll try the number again," he said, but still there was no answer. "This worries me," he said. "The house ought to answer."

"Well, you can try again after dinner."

"I think I'll go over there and see if everything's all right."

"But dinner's ready, Malcolm!"

"I don't seem to feel like eating, Virginia. Worries me, y'know, not to get any answer.

"Malcolm!" she said. "That's really rather silly. That Mrs. Kingscrown certainly knows how to look after herself."

"I can't help it," he said. "You know how you get these ideas."

"No, I don't," said Virginia. "Malcolm, please come and eat your dinner. Please don't be so obstinate."

He was sorry about being obstinate.

"I mean, there ought to be somebody in her house. I mean—the maid—somebody."

"I *wish* I'd never taken you there!" Virginia cried. "But I didn't know she'd be like *this.*"

"Well, like what?" he asked anxiously.

"So common—"

"She's not common, Virginia."

"She is! A big, red-headed wench. What's more, she's at least thirty-five."

"Well, why not?" he asked. "I mean, what's that got to do with anything, Virginia?"

"Malcolm," she said, "I'm pretty upset and unhappy about Aunt Evie. After all, she brought us up. Malcolm, I ask you as a favor to me to come in to dinner now."

"V-V-Virginia," he said, desperately anxious to explain to her. In his mind was a picture of Mrs. Kingscrown's house, dark and solitary, and it worried him; it more than worried him. It frightened him. He was in a hurry to get there. "I-I'll come right back, Virginia, if everything's O.K. I'll just t-take a look."

"All right," she said, turning away. "You've let me down, just when I need you."

Her voice was unsteady; he thought she was crying. Going away from her, hurt, disappointed, let down. I let everybody down, he thought. That's what's wrong with me.

But he *had* to go and see about Mrs. Kingscrown. He did not bother with a coat; he simply walked out of the house and down the drive. It had been a long time since he had gone walking in the dark alone, and it was strange. It was strange to hear the insects chirping in the grass and the rustle of the trees; it was strangest of all to look up at the sky, it was so unexpectedly wild, pallid, with thick black clouds streaming across it. He didn't like it; it reminded him of something.

The long-haul trucks were moving along the highway with dim lights. All this going on, he thought, war or no war. Things have to go on, Virginia said. All right, but I don't. I stopped... Never mind. I'll get in the Army when I've got over—this—this.... The Army. Not the Navy. You don't have to go to sea again. Don't have to go near the ocean again. Don't have to think about it.

He walked fast; he was in a hurry. Damn queer that the house didn't answer, he said to himself. I last saw her out on the terrace, and how do I know if she ever got home? Plenty of accidents.... A truck went by, and his heart began to beat too fast. If her house is dark... he thought.

When he turned into the driveway, he saw a lighted window at the side of the house. He was afraid the light would go out before he got there, and he turned off the drive and ran across the grass.

The shades were up and he could see her. She was sitting alone at a table spread with a lace cloth, with four candles in silver holders; she wore a green dress and her red hair glittered. She looked lonely, but she looked all right.

He felt tired, but he felt pleased; he felt as if he had done something for her in return for some immeasurably greater thing that she had done for him. Anyhow, she's all right, he thought. All by herself in that house. That nice house.

Now that he was going back, he slowed down, he took it easy. And the nearer he got to that other house, the less did he want to go into it. I'll be late to dinner, he thought, and that's not quite the thing, in the circumstances. Better get a bite on the way.

The thought made him sweat with anxiety, even fear. I don't know any place to go, he said to himself. Don't like to walk into a place you don't know anything about. It might look queer.

My God! he thought. I used to do it. Went in anywhere, any port, even where I couldn't speak the language. I mean, if I could do that now. Just once?

He walked on to the village, and near the railroad station he saw a restaurant, white-tiled, glaringly bright; he saw two waitresses in bright green uniforms moving around. He stood outside, and he did not see how he could do this. I might stumble, trip, fall down, he thought. It's been a long time....

A man went by him, in through the revolving door, and Malcolm started after him, fast. He got in, all right; it was done; he was in a restaurant alone. He sat down at a table and picked up the menu. It was a very faint purple and very blurred, and he could not read it. Something wrong with my eyes, he thought. It couldn't be that bad. A waitress was standing beside him.

"Wh-what's good tonight?" he asked.

"That depends," said she.

"On—on—on what?"

"Quit your kidding," said she, with mechanical coquetry.

"Veal!" he said suddenly.

"Tea or coffee?"

"Coffee and p-p-pie."

"Prune, custard—"

"Apple!"

He felt proud of himself; he felt strong and masterful, capable of quick and vigorous decisions. He enjoyed his dinner; he left a quarter for the waitress, and there was absolutely no trouble getting through the revolving door. Maybe it's over, he thought.

Maybe from now on he could go freely about in the world, talking to people. That was the supreme happiness. And maybe that was coming back now.

There were lights upstairs and down in Arthur's house and that bothered him. He felt so fine that he did not want to think about things, he did not want to talk to anybody. He went to the side door, and it was not locked; he went in quietly.

But Helene came out of the drawing room.

"Malcolm," she said in a low voice, "could I speak to you just a moment?"

"Certainly!" he said.

"Let's go up to your room."

He knew something bad was coming, and he rebelled against it. Only not against nice little Helene. He went up the stairs ahead of her and turned on the lamp in his room; he stood waiting, and as she entered the room she smiled and he bowed a little. She sat down in a chair by the window and he stood facing her.

"I thought I'd better tell you," she said. "It's not really serious, but I thought I'd better tell you."

"Oh, certainly!"

He saw her hands moving restlessly. She's nervous, he thought. This is something bad.

"I'm going to send Ben away," she said. "I don't *like* him. I don't think he's reliable."

I'm not understanding this, Malcolm thought. I don't know what she's talking about.

"He came to me and told me. I told him not to *mention* it to anyone else, and he promised he wouldn't."

"Tell? Tell?"

Her pretty little smile looked contorted.

"He told me he'd seen you pour a drink out for Aunt Evie—a very big drink. Almost a whole glassful."

"I did not! I did not!"

"Malcolm," she said, anxiously and earnestly, "please don't mind. Whatever happened was nothing but a mistake. There was a bottle of ginger ale open there; it looks so much like whisky. And you'd had a drink yourself—"

"One! One jigger. One!"

"I know, Malcolm. But you hadn't had anything for a long time, and—"

"I did not!" he said. "I did not!"

"Anyhow, Malcolm, you didn't know Aunt Evie wasn't supposed to drink anything at all."

"I didn't do it," he said. "I did not."

"Well, Ben could easily have been mistaken," she said. But he could tell from her face and from her voice that she did not believe that.

"Anyhow, Malcolm, it doesn't *matter*. Don't let it worry you, Malcolm; please don't. I only told you so that in case there was any silly gossip..."

"Arthur...?" he said. "What does Arthur say?"

"I haven't told him," she said slowly. "I'd rather he didn't know, Malcolm. He's rather worried about his business just now, and I'd rather he didn't have anything more." She looked up at him, a steady and almost stern look. "You know what he's like. So high-strung, and so terribly loyal. I'll get rid of Ben. It'll be easy enough for him to get another job, and probably the whole thing will blow over. But Arthur shouldn't be worried about it, Malcolm."

Now she was not vague and sweet, but very definite. She had welcomed him here with the kindness of a sister; she made him feel completely at home. But now she let him see beneath that pleasant surface.

"There's nothing Arthur wouldn't do for you," she said.

Look now at what he has done for you. Taken you in here, to stay week after week, with no plans, no talk of any future. Look at your fine big room. Everything done for you, everything given to you. By Arthur. Because he's so terribly loyal. And now you've gone and killed Aunt Evie. That's what she means, he thought.

"Don't let it worry you, Malcolm. No matter what happened, it was simply a mistake."

Another mistake. Another error of judgment. Dangerous, Aunt Evie had called him. You're damned well tooting I'm dangerous.

Helene went on talking.

"I'll get rid of Ben at once, and we'll just forget the whole thing."

He could not talk, because he had to keep his teeth clenched so that his jaw should not tremble. He nodded his head, in a sage and thoughtful way.

"Only, I did think I ought to tell you, Malcolm."

"Um-mm," he said, nodding his head again.

She rose. "Good night, Malcolm," she said, smiling and holding out her hand.

He took her hand in a quick grasp. "Night!" he said.

As soon as she had gone he locked the door and got out the bottle of capsules in a hurry. Two at bedtime. Repeat in half an hour if necessary. Sez who? The hell with you!

Chapter Four

It was half-past five when he waked, but maybe it had been early when he went to bed. He felt completely rested and ready to think. He lay stretched out flat on his back, trying to remember how many of those capsules he had taken last night. More than four?

I think I remember taking four at once, he said to himself. I was standing in the bathroom by the washbasin. I think I remember that. Then I got into bed, and I left the bottle on the table here, and a glass of water. Well, the water's gone. Did I take any more of them?

He was deeply interested in this, and a little anxious. Thing is, if you took too many, would it do anything to you? Make you—queer, any way?

He shook all the capsules out of the bottle and counted them. The bottle held fifty and there were twenty-eight left. But I don't know how many there were to start with last night. I've got to get this straight. This is important.

No. He knew what he had to think about and he started on it. It was clear now, clear as crystal.

Yesterday morning, he thought, Aunt Evie came in here. Into this room. She stood there, where I'm looking. She said, you want to get rid of me. And I said, yes. Not out loud, but I said it.

She told Lurie I was hostile to her. I didn't mean to be. But Virginia talked about hating people subconsciously. Could be that way, couldn't it? Aunt Evie told Lurie I was 'dangerous.'

All right. I don't *know.* But I'm not taking any more chances. I'm going.

He took a cold shower and dressed with his usual extreme neatness. Then he got his checkbook and figured his balance. Very little left, after those payments to the hospital and the doctors and all that. Only some four hundred dollars. He had gone to sea at seventeen, straight from boarding school, and he was now twenty-eight. Four hundred dollars to show for eleven years of work. Why didn't I try to save?

Because I'm a fool. Right and good. Now I'll get a job. Lot of things I can do. Keep books—accounts: I can type. I can speak Spanish, and a little Portuguese. Strong, too. Good muscular tone, one of those doctors said. Strong and willing. Only...

He went and stood before the mirror, and his face, he thought, with the deep-set little eyes and the long vertical creases in the lean cheeks, had a look of monkeylike anguish. Dumb animal pain. Not human.

"Shut up!" he cried aloud, and then he was afraid. He was afraid someone might have heard him and would come to see what was wrong.

He waited, very still, but nobody came. It was early, not six yet. But
there was no time to lose. He started to pack a suitcase, and he did it beautifully, everything folded just so. Don't want to forget anything. And now,
how about a note? A note to Arthur?

No, he said. I can't write a note. I'll call him up in his office later.
Now...! He put on his light overcoat and a felt hat and unlocked the door.
The sweat broke out on his forehead. His hands were damp and cold. This
was the last time. Suppose somebody met him now? Sneaking out, with a
bag? Lydia, maybe, or the cook, or Ben?

Ben had been standing in the hall, and he saw me fix—that drink. Ben's
an oaf, a clumsy lubber. But he wouldn't make that up, would he? He's got
nothing against me. No reason... If I met Ben now? Or Helene?

Helene would be glad to see me going. On account of Arthur. Doesn't
want Arthur all upset by his brother getting in trouble. How much trouble could it be?

It was dark in the hall, and he went carefully, cautiously down the stairs;
he heard his own breathing, loud and fast. Like an animal panting. He
took the chain off the front door, and his fingers fumbled and it rattled.
But he got the door open, he got out into the incredibly sweet fresh morning air. He went along the drive, walking as quickly as he could, and now
he had got away.

Now he was out in the world, alone. It was a very bad feeling. No roof
over his head, no walls around him, no corner to back into. The long-haul
trucks were rolling along, into the city; they moved slowly and shakily, he
thought, as if they were weary. They made him nervous; he thought they
would tip over. The suitcase was heavy and he had to go so fast.

"Want a lift, mister?" someone called.

It was the driver of a car labeled Merry's Paint and Varnishes. Merry is
a nice name, he thought.

"Hop in!" said the driver, and Malcolm climbed up beside him. "Going
to New York?"

"No, no," Malcolm answered. "Just down the road a little."

"You're around early," said the driver.

He was a big burly fellow with a blue stubble on his jowls; he was a
tough guy. But he seemed happy.

"Selling something?" he said.

"Me? No," Malcolm said.

"I thought when I seen that bag maybe you were selling something."

I must seem pretty damn queer, Malcolm thought. Walking along the road this hour of the morning, with a suitcase. All right, I *am* pretty damn queer.

But he was extremely anxious to talk to this tough guy, to explain himself, to be friendly.

"Thing is," he said, "I've been at s-s-sea."

"You can have it," said the driver. "You can have it. Only thing I got against this war is you got to take a boat ride to get to it. I'll be going next week."

"Oh, you will?"

"Yep," said the driver. "And that's O.K. by me. What I mean is I haven't got no wife or kids or anything. As for the girls, well, I guess there's girls everywhere you go, hey? How's about it, sailor?"

I *can't* talk any more, Malcolm thought. Not like a man. Sailor, he called me. I'm not a sailor any more. He made himself laugh.

"Sure!" he said with loud heartiness. "You bet!"

The man laughed too, and it was better.

"Well, there it is," he said presently. "Well, better be on the outside, lookin' *in*, hey?"

"What? What is it?"

"There," said the driver. "Up on the hill. The loony bin."

"The l-l-loony bin," Malcolm said.

"That's right," said the driver. "Say, y'know, they say they got a lot of guys—women, too—they get put in there that aren't any more crazy than you or me. What I mean is, to get their money, d'you see. They get them shut up there and then they can't make no will."

The subject interested him; he went on, and Malcolm looked back at the big red brick building on the hill.

"Oh!" he said suddenly. "Let me off here, will you? Thanks for the lift."

"Nothing to it," said the driver benevolently.

Mrs. Kingscrown's house looked lovely this morning. Malcolm remembered the little village his grandfather had used to set up around the Christmas tree when they were kids—a fence, a lot of arsenic green grass, sheep with a shepherd, cows, barns, white square house, like this one. She shouldn't live so near the loony bin, he thought.

He crossed the grass to look in at the windows, and the big room was empty. That stopped him. Now he didn't know what to do. It's too early to ring the doorbell, he thought. I thought she'd be there. I can't ring the doorbell.

Then he heard some little kitchen sounds, little clinkings of metal and china, and he went around to the back of the house. Mrs. Kingscrown was in the kitchen, with the back door wide open; she was wearing blue pajamas, her red hair curling up like petals from her clear, strong-boned face. She turned her head at the sound of his steps on the back porch.

"Hello!" she said, unsmiling. "Come in; I'm just getting breakfast. Eat with me?"

He felt prodigiously strange, in his hat and overcoat, bag in hand; he set down the bag and took off his hat. She paid little attention to him; she was frying bacon, making toast and coffee, but he was satisfied that she was glad to see him. She just does one thing at a time, that's all, he thought.

She began carrying things into the other room, and he wanted to offer to help her, only he felt strange and clumsy in his overcoat.

"I like a big breakfast," she said. "It's my favorite meal."

He stood in the middle of the kitchen watching her.

"All ready?" she said. "Don't you want to take off your overcoat?"

"Thank you," he said, and laid it over the back of a chair.

She had spread a blue linen cloth on a round coffee table drawn up before the couch, and set it with gray pottery; everything cool and quiet. They sat down side by side, and she poured out two cups of coffee.

"Are you going away?" she asked.

"Yes," he said. "I'm going to get a job."

"Where?"

It bothered him for her to ask that. Because his idea was to take his bag and go on, until he got somewhere that seemed right, or something definite came into his head. It would. It would. Only not yet.

"I'll get a job," he said, polite but evasive. "Work.... That's the answer, I guess."

"Sometimes," she said. "But sometimes it's not such a good idea to go off all by yourself."

"Yes," he said.

He would have given anything he had to tell her what had happened. What he had done, or maybe not done. But Helene didn't want him to tell anyone.

"I suppose these things—wear off," he said. "Shock, they call it. I don't know—I can't see why it happened to me."

She was looking at him with her bold blue eyes. She wanted to hear what he said.

"Let's eat now," she said.

Two fried eggs, crisp bacon, toast, coffee, orange juice; all so very good. "The thing is..." he said. "The worst thing was those fellows in the U-boat. I mean, they were standing on deck, and one of them chucked a pack of cigarettes into our boat. I mean—d'you see...? There was that boy Alfred, with his neck broken, and the ship going down—standing on her nose—and they did *that*. I mean, it wasn't a battle—a fight. It was—"

He was making a frightful effort.

"It was—assassination," he said. "No fighting. And then they chucked cigarettes to us. I mean—if they're devils, for God's sake, let them *be* devils and not—like that."

He put his finger inside his collar.

"You know," he said. "I could see them. See their faces. Well... One of them looked like Alfred. Same age, I should say. There they were—looking at me—and us looking at them. I mean... "

They should not have looked with human eyes, with curiosity.

"—don't seem to get over it," he said. "I don't know why. Other people do."

"You will," she said.

"Thing is, you don't know what to do. How to fight it."

"I don't think there's much fighting you can do," she said. "Just take it easy and try to look at things as straight as you can. You just get over things. I had pneumonia once—about the only time I've ever been really sick—and I used to think a lot about that. About how I just got better, day by day, without doing a darn thing, not even trying."

This idea puzzled him and fascinated him.

"But the thing is," he said, "you don't always get over things."

"Just mostly," she said. "I guess that's good enough."

Without trying too much? Without such a weight of guilt because you didn't fight more?

"I telephoned you last night," he said.

"I heard the phone ring," she said. "But Gussie was sick and I was busy with her and I didn't answer it."

"Is Gussie better now?"

"Oh, yes! Have some more coffee?"

"Thanks," he said, and she poured it out for him.

This is peaceful, he thought. This is what I want. A good breakfast in this nice little house. Not necessary to be fighting all the time. Take it easy. Take it easy.

Lily Kingscrown rose and went into the other room and came back with a little box, which she set on the table before him. It had a snow scene painted on the lid in bright, clear colors.

"Cigarettes," she said. "Help yourself."

As he raised the lid, the box began to play *For He's a Jolly Good Fellow* in a gay, confused little tinkle. It made him laugh, and she laughed too, standing before him, tall and limber and easy in her blue pajamas.

"It's cute, isn't it?" she said.

"Darn cute," he said. "Mrs. Kingscrown—"

"Make it Lily," she said.

"Thank you," he said, pleased beyond measure. "My name's Malcolm."

"I know."

He felt so fine and so happy; only, he wanted her to understand how things were.

"I just stopped by..." he said, and then could not get on with the explaining.

"I'm glad you did," she said.

"But I mean—maybe you think it's—it's queer..."

"To come and see me?" said Lily Kingscrown. "Well, no, I don't." Her bold blue eyes rested on his face. "I've had other people that liked to come and see me," she said serenely.

"I can believe that," said Malcolm.

"You wouldn't kid me?"

"*Me?*" said Malcolm.

How he loved this! This was the way he knew how to talk. They sat facing each other, both smoking; he raised the lid of the little box again and again it began to play *For He's a Jolly Good Fellow,* and again they both laughed, looking into each other's eyes.

A car was stopping before the house, and he sprang to his feet in wild alarm.

"It's probably Dr. Lurie," said Lily. "He said he'd stop in to see Gussie this morning."

It seemed to Malcolm an unimaginable disaster for Lurie to come now, at this moment. It seemed to him that he had been on the verge of saying something of vital importance.

Lily went to open the door. And it was not Dr. Lurie; it was Virginia; much worse.

"Oh, I'm sorry," she said, "but I was looking for Malcolm..."

"Come in!" said Lily.

Virginia was wearing a black skirt and a white blouse with long sleeves;

her black hair was pushed back from her forehead and she looked tired and worried and very handsome. I just walked out on her, without a word, Malcolm thought. Nothing I can say to her.

But Lily could say something. Lily could save him. Virginia's a wonderful girl, but *I can't go back with her.* It was for Lily to save him.

"Come in and have a cup of coffee," Lily said.

"Thank you, but—things are rather upset, just now. Aunt Evie's lawyer is coming and—there are so many arrangements to make. We really *need* Malcolm—"

And Lily said nothing. She did not try to save him; she did not explain to Virginia...

"Will you come now, Malcolm?" asked Virginia.

"All right," he said, and came toward her. He stopped in front of Lily. "Thank you," he said.

"You're welcome," she said seriously.

He went out of the house and got into the car beside Virginia. She's done a lot for me, he told himself. She's been very kind and loyal. But she shouldn't have done this.

He sat still, looking steadfastly ahead of him. He was struggling not to feel—the way he did feel about Virginia. I owe her a lot, he thought. But, by God, she doesn't own me. She shouldn't have come after me—like this.

"Malcolm," she said, "could you possibly lend me five hundred dollars?"

Startled, he turned his head to look at her. But she kept her eyes on the road.

"Afraid I haven't got quite that much," he said. "But if four hundred will do...?"

"Well, I..." she began, and stopped. "Thank you, Malcolm," she said. "Can I have it as soon as we get back to the house?"

"Certainly!" he said.

Then, when it was too late, when he had committed himself, he saw what he had done. He was giving away his chance to be free. He saw now how desperately he wanted—and needed—to be free. They turned in at the drive, and there was the house, and it was like a prison. He was going back to all that, going back to Aunt Evie.

Chapter Five

Helene was sitting at the breakfast table, alone, in a black sweater and skirt; she looked elegant and pale and tired. And she looked surprised to see Virginia and Malcolm come in.

"Oh, you've been out *early*, haven't you?" she said, with her charming and meaningless smile. "I'll tell Lydia..."

Malcolm sat down at the table. There was death in the house, and it would not be correct to say that he had already had breakfast. That he had tried to run away.

"Arthur's making arrangements to have the funeral tomorrow," Helene went on. "Virginia, is there anybody else we ought to notify?"

It was a curious thing, which Malcolm had noticed before, that in spite of her dignity and poise, Helene couldn't run things, couldn't manage things. She turned to Arthur, and very often to Virginia.

"Well, Cousin Julia—" Virginia said, and Helene wrote down that name, in the little book she had near her.

Lydia brought in another breakfast for Malcolm, and while he drank his coffee, he watched the two sisters. Helene was twenty-two and Virginia was twenty-four; they were lovely girls, fine girls.

But they bore me, he thought.

He was astounded at such a thought; he was ashamed of himself. The trouble is, he told himself, I've never lived on shore since I was seventeen. Not used to a normal, quiet life like this. All right. Maybe I'd better get used to it. Because what else...?

"Mr. Pond will be here for lunch," Helene said. "You won't mind sharing your bathroom with him, will you, Malcolm?"

"Oh, no! No. Not at all. If you'll excuse me—some letters to write."

I always say that, he thought. And it's crazy. Everybody knows damn well I haven't got all these letters to write. I never write *any* letters. I don't know what to do, that's the truth.

As he went up the stairs, he wondered about Aunt Evie. Still here? he thought, looking at the closed door of her room. You couldn't very well ask anybody about that. He went into his own room and closed the door and looked about him in despair. Arthur doesn't need me, he thought. Nobody does. Nothing I can do. She shouldn't have brought me back.

A knock at the door, and there she was.

"Malcolm, I'm terribly sorry to bother you, but if you could give me a check..."

"Certainly!" he said, and sat down at the table to write it. Signing away everything he had. All right, I owe it to her, he thought.

"There's a bill I—want to settle," she said.

No. he thought. You wouldn't have any bill for five hundred dollars. Couldn't have. You just want to get my money away from me. For my own good. All right. Here it is.

"Here you are!" he said, rising.

"Thanks ever so much, Malcolm. I'll pay you back—in a little while."

"Very glad to be able..." he said.

But you're not going to keep me here. I'll get away somehow, money or no money.

She stood there with the check in her hand, and he stood before her, with his head bent. Because he did not want to look at her.

"I hope this doesn't put you out, Malcolm," she said.

Oh, no! Keeps me in, he thought, and forgot to answer her. And in a moment she went away.

He sat down in a chair by the window and lit a cigarette. Could borrow some money from Arthur, he thought. Just enough to keep going until I find a job. Could go to the company's office, and see about a shore job. No. They might think... No. Somewhere else. Look in the newspapers.

Later in the morning, when he was working on the jigsaw puzzle, he heard someone go into the bathroom, his bathroom. Mr. Pond, that had to be. It made him unhappy; he didn't like to see new faces. He went down to lunch with reluctance, but he was cheered by finding Arthur there.

"My brother, Mr. Pond," Arthur said.

"How d'you do?" said Mr. Pond.

He looked like an Indian, Malcolm thought, lean and impassive, in a gray suit with a white pin stripe; flat cheeks, a coppery skin; black hair parted on the side. He was pleasant, but he was mysterious.

There were six of them at the table, and Ben came in to help Lydia. This was an innovation. Helene seemed surprised to see him, in his white jacket, waiting on people with great style.

Malcolm studied him with absorbed interest. So he thinks he saw me do that, fix that drink, he mused. That's a queer thing...

Very, very thin, Ben was, with knobby wrists, and a big nose, and a worried, woebegone face. He stooped to pass the dishes; he almost cringed. He's always like that, Malcolm thought. Servile. Tries to please—too much. You see that type in a ship now and then. A steward... And you don't trust 'em. Because they'll say anything, do anything, they think will please you.

Did he tell that story about the drink to please somebody? But please whom? It was Helene he told, and it certainly didn't please her. Is there anybody who'd *want* to believe I did that? That I killed Aunt Evie?

And did I kill Aunt Evie? That sickening doubt and panic came back over him in a wave; he had to get away. Quick... Everyone was nearly finished, just drinking coffee, and Jenette still eating his dessert.

"If you'll excuse me, Helene," Malcolm said. "Letter I—I—I've got to finish."

"Mr. Pond's going to read the will, Malcolm," said Arthur.

"Oh, *now?*" said Virginia.

"Unfortunately I can't stay. I shan't be able to attend the—ceremony," Pond said. "I have to go to Washington tonight."

Where's Aunt Evie? Malcolm thought. Upstairs, is she, the poor old girl? Or did they take her away? I don't want to hear her will. But if it's the proper thing...

The two girls went out of the dining room, and Pond and Arthur and Malcolm went after them. And Jenette. Jenette shouldn't come, Malcolm thought. This is a family thing. But Jenette did come—he sat in a chair beside Helene, and crossed his legs, one ankle on his knee. He looked impudently at home.

"I, Evelyn Rounsay Chatsworth..." Mr. Pond was reading, holding the document well away from him. Farsighted, Malcolm thought. Keen Indian eyes.

"To my niece Helene, wife of Arthur Drake, the sum of five thousand dollars..." And the same to Virginia. Poor old girl wasn't so well off, after all.

"To Malcolm Drake, at present residing in Willow Bridge, Connecticut, the sum of twenty thousand dollars—"

"Hold on!" said Malcolm.

Mr. Pond glanced at him, and went on reading.

"In consideration of his handicapped condition, and to mark my confidence in his ultimate rehabilitation—"

She's got no right to talk like that! Malcolm thought. Handicapped and rehabilitation... *No!*

Mr. Pond was still reading. Malcolm heard Arthur's name, and then:

"To my beloved friend and teacher, Marian Jancy Foxe, the sum of ten thousand dollars in recognition of her invaluable work in forming Joy Now..."

Did he say twenty thousand—for me? Malcolm thought. It's—it's a trick. He wants to see if I'm all right, normal, and so on. Aunt Evie thought this up, and it's a nasty trick. All right! All right! Nobody's going to get a rise out of me.

He lit a cigarette and leaned back, and Mr. Pond ceased his reading.

"Is that all?" Jenette asked.

"Oh, yes. Yes, that's all, Mr.—"

"Jenette is the name. Ivan Jenette. Nothing about me?"

"Why no, Mr. Jenette. No."

"The damned old bitch!" said Jenette.

"Look here!" said Arthur.

Jenette rose.

"Good-by, Helene," he said, standing before her and giving her a stylish bow, heels together.

"Oh... Must you go, Ivan? Now?"

"Oh, yes."

"I don't know about trains," she said. "Ben will drive you—"

"I don't care about trains," said Jenette. "And I'll walk, thank you."

Helene was plainly trying to keep this from being a scene.

"We'll see you soon, Ivan?" she said earnestly.

"No," he said, with a smile. "You certainly won't, Helene. Good-by, *la compagnie.*"

He went out of the house, leaving behind him a blank, stiff silence.

"Ivan's a musician, you know," said Helene. "Very—artistic. Very highstrung."

Her attempt to adjust the situation was a failure; her pretty, forced little smile was a failure. Mr. Pond looked at his watch.

"I'm sorry to hurry away, but—"

"Have a drink?" said Arthur.

"Oh, thanks..."

Malcolm got up and walked out of the room and up the stairs, making for his own room. Jenette's door was open and he was in there packing a bag. He turned his head and looked at Malcolm.

"Brother, can you spare a dime?" he asked.

"Well, how d'you mean?"

"I haven't got any money," said Jenette. "If you could lend me a hundred dollars—or a thousand would be better..."

"Well..." Malcolm said, not knowing if this was a joke.

"I haven't any money," said Jenette. "No train fare. I can't get back to New York and my stinking little room."

He was strangely tranquil about this; he moved around the room, putting things into his suitcase, and Malcolm stood in the hall, watching him.

"How much can I have?" Jenette asked.

"Thing is, I'm pretty broke," said Malcolm.

"You're going to get my twenty thousand dollars," said Jenette.

"How is it yours?"

"That damned old bitch—"

"Don't say that again."

"Aunt Evie promised to provide for me," said Jenette. "She's been 'providing,' you know, for the last two years. In a very niggardly way, but better than nothing—"

"You mean, she's been helping you out?"

"Yes. You know how she helped people. She'd pay my room rent, but not *every* week. Sometimes it would run two or three weeks, and my landlady would start bothering me. You see, it isn't as if I could go out and look for a job."

"No?"

Jenette looked at him in gloomy surprise.

"I'm a singer," he said. "A concert singer. And there are damn few concerts, these days. I've tried radio, but for some reason my voice isn't right. My personality doesn't get across. Not obvious enough, probably."

It was a funny thing, thought Malcolm, that Jenette didn't seem to have any personality at all. He now observed that the cuffs of Jenette's shirt were frayed, his trousers were shiny; he thought that Jenette was not so young as he had been, not so slim, not so handsome.

"Aunt Evie got me a few engagements," Jenette went on. "Musical afternoons for clubwomen—things like that. My God! How I had to cringe and fawn and kiss hands! My God! And *she* liked to choose my programs. She called me her 'protégé.' And she hasn't left me one damned cent."

He was gloomy and bitter, but not exactly angry; it was as if he had been disappointed for so long that he now expected very little.

"You've got that twenty thousand," he said. "You might lend me what you can."

"I haven't got it yet. In fact, I'm pretty broke, just now."

"You've got *something,*" said Jenette, annoyed.

Malcolm put his hand into his pocket, but that was pure impulse and habit. He didn't know how he felt about this fellow.

"I've got a ten-spot," he said.

"Well," said Jenette, with a sigh. "I'll take that, then."

Chapter Six

I'd like to know where Aunt Evie is, Malcolm thought, sitting at the table in his room and working away at the jigsaw puzzle. Here, is she, in her room?

He was very much bothered about that. It seemed to him that if he knew where she was, he could think about her; and it was obviously the right and decent thing to think about her. But when you want to think about someone, you have to have some sort of picture in your mind.

And he had none of Aunt Evie. She had drifted off like thistledown; he had stood near her in the library—and then he had never seen her again. Only, you don't like to ask about a thing like that, he thought. Shouldn't like to ask even Arthur. Oh, by the way, where *is* Aunt Evie?... No...

Maybe they take people away, to funeral parlors and so on. It's better at sea. No waiting. But on shore, I don't know what people do. If she's there, in her room, I'd like to go and take a look at her.

Here was a good idea, a good way to find out. He got up at once and opened his door; he went quietly along the corridor to Aunt Evie's room. But there he stopped. Anybody in there with her? he thought. Maybe they keep somebody there all the time. Trained nurse, maybe.

So he knocked at Aunt Evie's door.

"Malcolm!" said Virginia's voice.

He gave a violent start and turned his head, and Virginia was on the stairs. Their eyes met, and he saw, or thought he saw, a sorrowful compassion in hers.

"We're going to have cocktails," she said. "I came to see if you wouldn't like one."

"Why, thanks! Yes, I should," he said, but with shame and wretchedness.

That looked crazy all right, he said. Knocking at a dead person's door. And maybe she's not there at all.

It made things worse to find Dr. Lurie in the library, and a woman he had met before, but whose name he did not remember—a thin, pretty woman with an air of fervent sincerity. She treated Helene like an invalid; if there's *anything* I can do for you, darling... any errands in the village tomorrow? I'll bring you a frightfully interesting book I've just found; it will take your mind off things.

And all this was done for Arthur, you could see that. She would look at

Arthur, with a curious significance., and he would look back at her, a steady, steely glance.

Ben brought the materials on a tray, and Arthur began to mix the drinks. He rose and handed the first one to the woman.

"Sibyl," he said, and bending, he spoke to her very low. She listened with her lashes down.

It's nothing, Malcolm thought, and stopped thinking about them. I don't know... Maybe I'd better explain to Virginia. I mean, how I thought maybe there was a nurse in there. Only, if they've taken Aunt Evie away... It must seem queer for me not to know that...

"Telephone, Mr. Malcolm, sir!" said Ben, and Malcolm sprang to his feet.

It's Lily! he thought, delighted.

"I put the call on the extension in the hall, sir," said Ben. "And, Mr. Malcolm, would you be wanting me to stop at the drugstore for you this evening?"

"No, I wouldn't," said Malcolm curtly, and sitting on the edge of the hall table, he took up the instrument.

"Malcolm Drake?" asked a man's voice. "Oh, Jenette here."

"Where?"

"At a place called the Tavern Something."

"I know. The Willow Tree Tavern. But why are you there?"

"I stopped in for a drink and I liked it. I took a room for a week, but I haven't the money to pay for it. I'd like to see you, Drake."

"Well," said Malcolm. "I'm afraid I couldn't manage that just now."

"Yes, you can. Bring along another twenty or so, and I'll tell you something."

"I'm sorry, Jenette—" Malcolm began.

"Oh, is that Ivan?" said Helene's voice beside him. She and Virginia were standing there hand in hand, in a way they had. The Sibyl friend was in the doorway of the drawing room, talking earnestly to Arthur.

"If that's Ivan," said Helene, "won't you ask him if he'd like to come back here to dinner?"

"I'll tell you something about Aunt Evie," Jenette was saying.

"Thanks, but—"

"I met Dr. Lurie," said Jenette, "and he gave me a lift. And we got talking about Aunt Evie. Bring me along a little more money and I'll tell you exactly how and why she died."

"You mean you—you—you've got information?"

"Yes, I have. I didn't realize until I got talking to Lurie. But I didn't tell him what I know."

"I'll come," said Malcolm. "Right after dinner."

He hung up the instrument.

"You didn't ask Ivan?" said Helene.

"Well, no... I'm sorry. No. I didn't."

The two sisters moved away, and he sat where he was, on the edge of the table, in the dimly lit hall.

What does Jenette mean he saw me fixing that drink? But he didn't, because I didn't fix her a big drink. But if he thinks he did... This could be blackmail.

But what if it's something else? If it is—if I could be—absolutely sure I didn't—make any sort of mistake...

"Well!... said Dr. Lurie. "Are you meditating on your extraordinary good fortune, Drake?"

"No!" said Malcolm.

"Oh, merely not feeling sociable?"

"Tired."

"I shouldn't give way to that sort of mood, if I were you, Drake," he said. "It's a very bad, a dangerous thing, to withdraw into yourself."

"If I knew how to do it," said Malcolm, "I'd be doing it now."

"I'm sorry you've chosen to adopt this attitude of hostility, Drake. It's bad for you. I'm your physician... and naturally concerned with your welfare. I can help you—"

"Don't bother," said Malcolm.

As always, these brushes with Lurie gave him a great sense of well-being and happiness. He was pleased to see the dark flush in Lurie's face.

"And the day will come," said Lurie, "the day will come, Drake, when you're going to need my help very badly."

"I'll—" Malcolm began, but Arthur's voice checked him.

"Sorry you can't wait and have dinner, Doctor."

"Thank you, Drake," said the doctor. "Another time."

He put on his overcoat and took up his hat and went out of the house, and the two brothers remained in the hall.

"Take it a little easy, Malcolm," said Arthur.

"There's something about that fellow—" said Malcolm.

"There's plenty about him," said Arthur. "But compromise is the art of living. There's no sense in getting his back up."

"He won't let me alone."

"Nobody gets let alone," said Arthur somberly. "Just take it a little easy, Malcolm. Come on back now and have a little drink."

That feeling of almost joyous excitement remained with Malcolm. Jenette's going to tell me something, he thought. It has to be something new, something I don't know about the poor old girl. If I can know—for sure—that I didn't make any kind of mistake...

I think I'll be all right again if I know that. I'll be able to walk out and get a job, start living again.... It was nice in the drawing room; it was cozy; the voices of the three women were light and sweet. He glanced at Virginia and found her looking at him; he smiled at her and her answering smile was warm and infinitely kind.

The Sibyl woman took her leave and Helene went out into the hall with her.

"Could I use the car after dinner?" Malcolm asked Arthur. "Just for an hour or so?"

"Well, but it's Ben's night out, and you don't drive."

"I'll drive you, Malcolm," said Virginia.

"Thanks, Virginia, but it's..."

Back came the feeling of being trapped in the house and not able to get out. He was expected to explain, if he wanted to get away, and he could think of no explanation with any sense to it.

"B-business," he said.

"All right," said Arthur. "I'll send for a taxi. What time?"

"Eight-thirty," said Malcolm, with immeasurable relief. And in a very low voice: "Could you lend me some money?"

"I've only got forty bucks," Arthur said. "Here..."

Arthur never bothered him; never asked him questions. Never seemed to think he was queer. Arthur seemed to think he had as much right as anyone to come and go and not explain. That made dinner all right. A nice dinner, two sisters and two brothers, all friendly and cozy.

It was a very fine thing to get into the taxi and set off—alone. I ought to go around alone more, he thought. It was a sweet night, mild, a little misty, and he felt fine. I'm damn well sure I didn't—do that, he thought. Make that mistake about the poor old girl. But once I—I hear it, definitely, from somebody else...

The Willow Tree Tavern looked very nice, a long, low, red brick building flush with the street, the lighted windows rosy. He went into the lobby and it was attractive; chairs with chintz cushions, red-shaded lamps. It would be nice to stay in a place like this, by myself, he thought. Just for a while.

He went up to the desk; there was no clerk there, only a woman with dyed red hair at a switchboard.

"Yes-s-s?" she said, with a cross hissing.

"Mr. Jenette, please," said Malcolm.

"Mr. Jenette has checked out."

"Well, no—look here! Try his room, will you, please?"

"Mr. Jenette has *checked out,*" she said angrily. "It's right here, on my list—"

"But just try him, won't you?"

She plugged in, angrier than ever. "No answer," she said.

"Well—maybe there's a note for me? A message?"

"What name?"

"Drake," he said. "Malcolm Drake."

"There's no message for any Mr. Drake."

"Can you tell me when he checked out?"

"No, I cannot. I just came on at eight o'clock."

"Well... Who was here when he left?"

She answered an incoming call, and he waited.

"If you could tell me who was here when Mr. Jenette checked out—"

"Mr. Price, I suppose."

"Can I speak to him?"

"He's gone home. Willow Tree Tavern. *Good* evening!"

Something wrong about this, Malcolm thought. Jenette wanted me to bring along some money; he said he didn't have his fare into New York. Some mistake. He's got to be here.

There was a bellboy sitting on a bench, an elderly bellboy, growing bald, with an anxious face.

"Look here!" Malcolm said to him. "I had an appointment with Mr. Jenette, and they tell me he's checked out. They—if you could find out whether he's left a note in his room for me... And if his bag's gone."

"His bag's gone, sir, because I saw him take it. Because when he came off the elevator and I asked him if I could take his bag he said no."

"When was that, about?"

The elderly boy mused.

"About six o'clock, sir, he said. "Around then."

"Take a look in his room for a note, will you?"

The elderly boy went up in the elevator and came down again.

"No, sir," he said. "There isn't any note."

Malcolm gave him a dollar, and went out to the taxi. He felt nothing but an unbearable fatigue, a leaden weight on his heart. He was not thinking, he did not want to think; he wanted to go home and go to bed. The fog was thick around him now, and he was helpless, stupefied, lost.

Maybe I misunderstood Jenette. Maybe he didn't say—any of that. I don't know... Maybe I don't get things right. Maybe I don't remember things. Anything... I don't know. I could take a couple of those little pills and go to sleep.

I don't want any of those pills, he thought. I want a drink. Only not here. I don't like this place. The bar here is the darkest little hole I ever saw. Sissy place, with tables and electric candles. Like a tearoom. No, I'll find a nice little bar in the village, and I'll get talking to someone.

It was only a mile to the village and he walked it fast. He was in a hurry to get talking to someone. I wanted to hear what Jenette had to say, he thought. I never wanted anything so much as that. Because if he knew something that would make me sure... Only, God damn it, I *am* sure.

He found a place with a red neon light and there was a jukebox playing inside. It was a fine tune, loud, brisk, and martial; it made him feel good. He went up to the bar and ordered a straight rye and a glass of water.

There was a man sitting on the stool next to him, a middle-aged man in spectacles, with a round face. He looked like the kind of man you get talking to.

"What's the latest news?" Malcolm asked.

"It's pretty bad," said the man. The loud music stopped and it was very quiet. "People don't realize," said the man sternly. "You look around you and you see all these people—they don't know what war *is*. I was over in France, in the other war, and I happen to know. But these people, they don't know a thing."

"N-n-no..." said Malcolm.

"These people," said the man, "don't know what sacrifice *means*. They make me sick."

"Y-y-yes," Malcolm said.

He finished his drink quickly and paid for it and went out. I can't talk to people like that, he thought. A fool, he thought. I wish I had somebody of my own. I mean, somebody who'd be there... I don't know what to do...

He didn't want to go in any more bars. Loneliness made him almost desperate; he called up a retired ship's captain he knew in Brooklyn.

"Come along over," the man said. "The wife and I—we'll be happy to see you, Drake. Come right along over, and we'll have a glass of beer, and talk over the old days, the good old days. Take the Eighth Avenue subway, get out at..."

"Yes, yes," said Malcolm earnestly. He was not able to explain that he was not in New York.

"Then you get a trolley and—"

"Yes, I see!" said Malcolm. "I'm going to try to make it first thing next week."

"Come along now," said the old man.

"Thank you, sir," said Malcolm, "but I can't make it *tonight.*"

He came out of the telephone booth in the drugstore, and a franticness seized him. I don't know what in hell to do. I don't know where to go. Too early to go to bed. Unless I took some of the little pills.

That's not a good idea. And why isn't it a good idea? I might go home and take a double dose of them, and sleep till morning. I might take more than that—and sleep longer than that.

No. I'd rather get drunk. That's better. You're around with other people, and you can get talking to someone, and you feel good, after a few drinks.

So he set off to get drunk and get talking to somebody. Only he didn't seem to get drunk, only cold and sick. He didn't get talking to anybody, either; he sat at the bar in this place, wherever it was, and nobody spoke to him. Every time he looked up, he saw his own face in a mirror, and I look like a monkey, he thought. A sick gorilla. This stuff might as well be water. I *can't* get drunk.

Cold and sick, that was all. He got up, and left this place, wherever it was, and when he stepped out into the street, into the raw damp air, he began to stagger. No, this is all damn nonsense! he told himself. I'm *not* tight.

But just the same, he couldn't walk straight, and as he went weaving along the street, he gave a loud hiccup. He was ashamed of that. There was a taxi standing near the corner; he got into it and gave the address of Arthur's house. He realized now that he had left his hat behind, in that bar, whatever the name of it was; he hiccuped again, and the whole thing was disgusting and beyond measure wretched.

He stumbled going up the steps and fell on his face. He picked himself up, and there was a cut on his forehead; he wiped off the blood with his handkerchief and he remembered he had no key. If the side door is locked. I'll have to ring the bell, he thought.

The side door was opened, and there was Virginia.

"Oh, God!" he said.

She didn't say a word, just took his hand and drew him inside; she closed the door and helped him off with his coat. She took his hand again and led him up the stairs to her room; she sat down on the divan beside him, and put her arm around his neck, and laid her cheek against his.

The room was infinitely tranquil in the light of the shaded lamp, and she did not make him talk. She took her own handkerchief and wiped the little cut on his forehead; she kissed his check, very gently.

He was cold and drunk and horribly lonely, and she said, "Malcolm, I love you." He laid his head on her shoulder, and closed his eyes.

Chapter Seven

Virginia had been saying Malcolm, Malcolm, Malcolm for a long time, hours, but he was miles away and could not answer.

"Malcolm, dear, *honestly* you'd better wake up and get back to your own room."

He opened his eyes, and she was sitting on the bed beside him; she was wearing a wine-red house coat and her dark hair was loose on her shoulders. She gave him a serious and very kind smile.

But, oh, God! he said to himself. He was in bed, in her bed, wearing his shorts, and covered up with a sheet and a blanket.

"Do you feel all right, Malcolm?"

This was awful, so awful that he was stunned. He wanted to look at his watch, but he could not bring himself to take his bare arm out from the covers.

"If you could—lend me a dressing gown . .?" he said.

"Here's your own, Malcolm."

He sat up in bed and put it on with all possible modesty. He could not get out of bed because she was still sitting there.

"Virginia..." he said. "Did you—? I mean—how did this h-happen?"

"Well, you were a little bit tight," she said, smiling again.

"But, Virginia, why didn't you boot me out?"

"Why should I? You said you wanted to stay here."

"But, Virginia...! Virginia!"

"There's nothing to be so upset about," she said gently. "You were just dazed and miserable and you didn't want to go away. So I helped you to get to bed, and I lay down on the couch and went to sleep."

This was awful.

"I-I apologize," he said.

The color rose in her olive cheeks.

"I wish you wouldn't," she said. "I wish you'd think of me as if I were a trained nurse—someone who just wants to help you. I'm only glad you came to me."

But I didn't. You came downstairs and got me. And you're not a trained nurse. He tried to remember everything about last night. He remembered how he had felt when he had come in at the side door and had met Virginia. Pure panic. But he had come up here with her; he had sat with his head on her shoulder.

He remembered that she had said, "I love you, Malcolm." My God! Get me out of this! he thought.

"Malcolm, don't be upset," Virginia went on earnestly. "I'm not shocked at your drinking too much. Only sorry, because it's bad for you. I'm honestly not narrow-minded, Malcolm."

"No! Certainly not!" he assented. "Thing is, I don't know—I don't remember if I—said anything..."

"You said sweet things," she told him with a half smile.

What did I say? he thought.

"Listen!" he said, in an attempt at a matter-of-fact tone. "I'd better clear out now, Virginia."

But she did not get up, so he could not get out of the bed. He sat up straight, with the dressing gown buttoned across his chest and spread out around him.

"Wh-what did I say, Virginia?"

"I don't think I'll tell you," she answered. She looked beautiful; her dark eyes were soft. "It wouldn't be fair. You'd been drinking, and you said things that maybe you'd never have said otherwise."

Oh God, get me out of this! This is the worst...

"Wh-what did I say, Virginia? I—want to know."

She did not answer for a moment. Her dark lashes were lowered; she looked grave and a little tired.

"You said you needed me. You said I helped you. You said sweet things, Malcolm."

He had said sweet things to other girls, and it had meant little enough to him, or to them. But Virginia was different, so utterly different from the careless, laughing girls you met in one port or another. Had he come into his brother's house, Helene's house, and talked in any light, any wrong way to Virginia?

There was a knock at the door.

He seized her wrist and they were both motionless. The knob turned, and Helene came into the room.

"Oh!" she cried in horror.

"It's nothing," said Malcolm in a loud, harsh voice. "Absolutely nothing."

Helene moved backward toward the door.

"Wait! Wait!" said Malcolm. "Please... Thing is, I got drunk last night and Virginia—Virginia looked after me. I—couldn't get to my own room. I fell down. So you see..."

Helene had grown very white; she stood there, in a long loose negligee of pale blue silk; she looked like a stern angel, or a doll, with her shining hair tied back by a blue ribbon. She looked outraged, and she had no business to look like that.

"Why didn't you call Arthur?" she said to Virginia.

"Because I didn't want to," Virginia answered. "You haven't any right to act like this, Helene. I'm not a child."

She was giving a wrong impression.

"I was drunk," said Malcolm. "Virginia—"

"You ought to go away," said Helene, looking straight at him.

"Helene!" cried Virginia.

"You ought to go away *at once,*" Helene repeated.

"If Malcolm goes, I'll go too," said Virginia. "And you're not to talk as if he'd done anything wrong. You know he's not well."

Helene turned away.

"Wait!" said Malcolm, but she did not wait. She went out of the room, closing the door behind her.

Virginia rose and went over to the window, and Malcolm sprang out of the bed and belted the dressing gown snugly about his waist.

"V-Virginia...?" he said.

She did not answer, and when he went to her side, he saw that she was crying, quietly.

"You poor kid," he said. "It's a damn shame... Whole thing's my fault entirely."

She gave him a wretched misty smile, but the tears were still running down her face. Poor kid! He laid his hand on her shoulder, and she nestled her wet cheek against it.

He could not pull away his hand; he could not escape. He forced himself to stand still and to speak in a quiet and reassuring voice.

"I'll fix this up with Helene," he said. "Don't worry, Virginia."

She raised her head to look at him, and he got his hand away.

"How, Malcolm?"

"Leave it to me," he said. "I'll be seeing you."

He got back to his own room. He took a shower and dressed, with great attention to detail. I've got to find a way out of this, he thought. A decent way out. Any way out.

Certainly he could not go down to breakfast with Arthur and Helene—and Virginia. He did not know where he could go, what he could do, how he could carry on any sort of existence. I'll go to that place where I had dinner, he thought, and I'll get some breakfast. The walk will be a good thing. I can do some thinking.

He wanted to wear his light overcoat this cool, rainy morning, but he could not find it. Then he remembered that he had left it at Lily Kingscrown's house, and a wave of relief came over him. Got to stop by there and get it, he thought.

Chapter Eight

You do everything over and over again. Just the same. Going cautiously through the house, getting out into the fresh air. Only this morning it was gloomy outside and a light drizzle was falling. He walked down the drive, just like yesterday; the same thing over and over again, and nothing came of it.

Too early to go to Lily's, he thought. I'll do something different, this time; I'll go along to the village and get some breakfast. It was a good, fine thing to start off along the highway, not as he had gone yesterday, but in the opposite direction. When you do something different, you feel better. Today was *not* like yesterday. It was different.

The trucks were rolling along, but they were different trucks. The headlights were blurred in the rain, and they were going slower. He was going slower, not hurrying, as he did yesterday. No reason why things shouldn't change.

"Hey! Want a lift, brother?"

He stopped, and looked up into the face of the man who spoke. All right. It wasn't *that* man. This was an older man, with a scrawny neck, and a face like an eagle's.

"I was looking for a place where I could get something to eat," said Malcolm.

The eagle stared at him for a moment.

"Well... O.K.," he said. "Hop in."

Malcolm climbed up beside him and they started off, rattling and jolting.

"What's your trouble?" asked the eagle.

"Trouble? My trouble?"

"*All* right. *All* right!" said the eagle. "Take it easy."

That was what Arthur had said.

"Why the hell should I take it easy?" Malcolm demanded. "I want something to eat, that's all. I'm hungry."

"All right," said the eagle. "If you're hungry, I'll stake you to a feed."

"Stake me?"

"Don't you know English?" asked the eagle.

"Yes, but I mean—why?"

"I'm like that," the eagle said with simplicity. "Anybody's hungry, all right. I'll stake them to a feed and no questions asked."

But it was not going to be that easy.

"You'd ought to get you some kind of a coat," said the eagle. "And a hat, or a cap, or something."

"I've got a coat."

"Well, you'd ought to wear it, then. It looks noticeable, like, going around in the rain without no hat and coat."

"What do I care?"

"*All* right! *All* right! Only giving you good advice, *that's* all. I thought maybe you didn't *want* to be picked up—"

"Picked up?"

"My Gawd! Don't you know English?"

"Mean you thought I was—running away?"

"It don't matter what I thought," said the eagle. "I'm not asking you no questions."

Very good. That's how I look to everybody. Queer. Crazy. Strolling along in the rain, this time of the morning.

"We'll stop at Pete's Diner," said the eagle, "and I'll stake you to a good feed..."

"Well—thank you," said Malcolm.

"I would do it for anyone," said the eagle briefly. "It's my policy."

The inside of Pete's Diner was strange, filled with a blue haze of smoke through which the lights twinkled. Three men sat on stools at the counter; they did not speak or look up; behind the counter stood a man with an old-fashioned big black mustache.

"How are you?" he asked quietly.

"O.K., and how's your good wife?" the eagle replied politely. "Listen, Pete, look after this here friend of mine. A good feed."

He put fifty cents down on the counter, and he was gone, without a word of thanks from Malcolm.

This was a dream, and everything in the dream was hazy. Malcolm ate; he had coffee, fried eggs, muffins, more coffee, and nobody spoke to him. More men came in.

"You would be entitled to a piece of pie," Pete said. "Apple, cokernut, or rhubarb."

"Apple, thanks," said Malcolm.

When he had finished eating he was at a loss.

"Mind if I stay here awhile?" he asked.

"I don't mind," said Pete. "You can sit over there. Want a cigarette?"

"I've got some, thanks," said Malcolm.

He sat on a chair, in the corner; men came in and out, and he watched them for a while; he had a couple of cigarettes, and then he went to sleep.

It was after nine when he woke and found the diner was empty; even Pete was no longer behind the counter. He went down the steps, and it was still raining, still a gray twilight. He walked to the railway station and got a taxi and gave Lily's address. He was well aware now of how strange he looked, hatless, his hair damp, his expensive dark suit damp.

All right, so I look funny, he said within himself to the taxi driver. Want to make something of it? But the driver said nothing.

I don't want to go tooling up to the door in a taxi, Malcolm thought. I'd rather be walking. So he got out of the cab at the entrance to the drive-way, and paid the man and started off toward the house. I'll just get my bag and my hat and coat, he thought. I'll just say good-by to Lily.

She would be there in the big room where they had had breakfast yesterday. She would ask him to sit down for a few minutes, and then he would.

Somebody came flying around the corner of the house, a tall, thin, gawky figure in a pink kimono, carrying a paper bag under her arm. He stopped to watch, and he saw her go running to the garage. Then she did a queer thing. She pushed back the sliding door and threw in the paper bag; she closed the door and went racing back, around the corner of the house, never having glanced in his direction.

I'll have to tell Lily about that, he thought, and hastened his steps. He rang the doorbell and waited. He thought it was a long time, but maybe it wasn't. He rang again, and he couldn't hear any sound within the house. He kept his finger on the bell, and after a while he began to knock. But nobody came. Nothing stirred within.

That girl in the pink kimono must have come out of here, he thought. No other houses near. She must have gone back in here. There's something wrong.

He banged on the door, and a window upstairs opened.

"Mrs. Kingscrown ain't home!" screeched a voice.

"All right. When will she be home?"

"Lunchtime."

"Let me in. I'll wait for her."

"I'm not allowed to let in *nobody,*" screeched the voice.

"I'm a friend of Mrs. Kingscrown's. You can let me in."

"No, I can't! I'm sick in bed."

"Well, you've got to," said Malcolm, "or I'll break down the door."

There was a moment's silence.

"Come on," said Malcolm, encouragingly.

"You got to wait till I dress," said she.

"All right. I'll give you fifteen minutes," said Malcolm.

And in the meantime, he thought, I'll just take a look, just see what Gussie threw in at the door.

It worried him. A very queer thing it was, for the girl to come running out in the rain in a kimono and throw a paper bag into the garage. He went across the wet grass that felt spongy and springy underfoot; he reached the garage and pushed open the door. He saw the paper bag lying on the floor; it had burst open, and he saw slices of bread, and a chicken leg, and a big bone.

Does she keep a dog in there? he thought, and after a moment he whistled.

But no dog appeared. No dog had come after the bones.

Nothing here, he told himself, and took out his handkerchief to wipe his face. Nobody here.

But he knew he had to do better than this. He would have to go in there and look around. He pushed the door back as wide open as it would go, so that the gray light of the rainy day came in, and he stepped forward.

Jenette was sitting on the floor in a corner, leaning against the wall.

"For God's sake!" said Malcolm, "what are you doing here?"

But Jenette only stared at him and said nothing.

Malcolm tried to make his breathing more even.

"You're—dead, aren't you?" he asked.

Jenette did not deny that.

Chapter Nine

In this hot, damp place Jenette was very cold.

Malcolm touched his hand and his forehead, and then he felt sick.

But he got the better of that. He looked carefully at Jenette, and he could not see any sort of wound, any blood, anything wrong with him except being dead.

He went out, closed the big door after him, and went to the house, almost running. The door stood open, and he went in.

"Gussie?" he called, but she did not answer.

There was a telephone on a stand in the hall; he looked in the book for the number of the asylum, and dialed it.

"Is Mrs. Kingscrown there?" he asked.

"Oh, yes," said a bright little voice. "I'll call her—"

"Never mind, thanks," he said, and hung up. She was safe, and that was all he wanted to know. Nothing he could tell her on the telephone. No reason to make her hurry home. He had to make up his mind now what to do. He could not make up his mind, but he had to, just the same.

Arthur, he thought. I'll call up Arthur.

No. Arthur had nothing to do with this. It's a matter for the police, Malcolm thought. You notify the police at once if you find a body. But I'm not going to do that, not until I've seen Lily. There may be some special way she'd like this handled.

You could not reasonably expect anyone home for lunch until noon, but it was after ten now. That would not be so long. He rose, and then he saw his bag standing in a corner, his overcoat on a hanger, and his hat over it.

Very nice of her, to put my coat on a hanger, he thought. She's considerate. I want to be considerate toward her, want to do whatever she'd like, about this. About Jenette.

He walked up and down the big room, smoking, taking good care not to drop any ashes on the floor. Very queer, for Jenette to be sitting there dead. But the worst part of it was that girl, throwing bones in at the door. Like some kind of savage rite. Give Jenette a bone to keep him quiet.

I'll never hear now what he was going to tell me, Malcolm thought. And then, unexpectedly, his brain began to work in a nimble way he had almost forgotten. Well, could it be *that?* he thought. Did Jenette know something about Aunt Evie's death that was dangerous to someone, and did he get killed to keep him quiet?

It was not a very startling idea to him. Long before the war he had encountered violence in many forms, he had seen men killed in many ways, in brawls and accidents. He had seen a man killed with a broken bottle in Guadeloupe; in Rio one of the crew had come stumbling on board to die of a knife wound. He had often enough had to deal with the police; he knew that murders happened.

The thing is, he said to himself, what *could* Jenette have known about Aunt Evie? She died of a heart attack, brought on by taking too big a drink. All right. Nobody forced the drink down her throat. Nobody. Not me or anyone else. Whoever had made that long drink couldn't be convicted of murder. Jenette couldn't have been dangerous enough to kill, just for knowing that.

Well, what if she didn't die the way Lurie thought? Or the way Lurie *said?* You don't have to believe Lurie. Maybe he was mistaken, and maybe he lied.

With an immeasurable delight he felt his brain working, concentrating, weighing, examining. No haze in it now. The first thing, he thought, was to make sure that Jenette had been killed. If he had died from natural causes there was no case.

But every circumstance of his death seemed unnatural. He had asked Malcolm to bring him money at the Tavern, and he hadn't waited for it. And what natural, possible reason could he have had to go into that garage to die, alone?

The bag of bread and bones had to mean something, too. Gussie—

A car was coming up the drive; he looked at his watch and saw that it was eleven-thirty. She was coming early. I'll have to tell her carefully, he thought. Not upset her. He went into the hall, opened the door, and there was Dr. Lurie coming up the steps with his little black bag.

"What are *you* doing here, Drake?" he asked sternly.

"I can't see that that's any of your damn business," said Malcolm. "What are *you* doing here?"

"I have a patient here. Stand aside, please, and let me in—"

Malcolm did not move out of the doorway. Suppose Gussie tells Lurie? he thought. Then he'll notify the police, of course. I wanted to wait for Lily, but after all, why? There's no keeping the police out of it. No way to prevent a lot of worry and bother for her. I can't very well stop Lurie from seeing his patient.

He stood aside and Lurie went past him and up the stairs. He stood in the hall, waiting for Lurie to come down again. If Gussie tells him, he thought, then Lurie'll go out there to see for himself, before he calls the police. And then it will begin, all the questions, all the headache. I wish it didn't have to be like that for Lily.

He waited, and Dr. Lurie did not come down. And now another car was coming; he went back to the door again, and this time it was Lily Kingscrown. He watched her getting out of her car, tall, unhurried and nonchalant, in a belted white raincoat and with a blue bandanna tied over her red hair. She knows what she's doing, all the time, he thought.

"Hello!" she said, with her big smile.

"Hello!" he answered.

"Have you come to lunch with me?" she asked.

He had to tell her now.

"Something's happened," he said. "I'm sorry you have—to be worried about it, but I'm afraid it can't be helped. You remember Jenette, that you met at my brother Arthur's house?"

"Yes."

"He's out there, in your garage."

"What's he doing there?"

"I'm sorry, but he's dead."

Her brows drew together in that fierce little way.

"Dead?"

"I'm sorry."

"Did you find him?"

"That's a queer thing about it. I was coming along the drive, and I saw your maid Gussie come running out in a pink kimono. I saw her go up to the garage and throw something in. After she'd gone back to the house, I thought I'd better take a look, and I found Jenette there."

"What did Gussie say about it?"

"I haven't spoken to her."

"What did she throw in?"

"A paper bag," he answered. "It had some slices of bread in it, and a chicken leg, and a bone."

She was silent, her blue eyes fixed on him. "That's Dr. Lurie's car," she said. "Does he know?"

"Gussie may have told him. He's upstairs with her now."

"Listen!" she said. "Keep him in the house for a minute. I want to go and see—"

"Don't do it, Mrs. Kingscrown. Don't go there alone."

"I'll be all right, Malcolm," she said. "I've got to see. Just keep Lurie till I come back, will you?"

He did not want her to go, to see Jenette sitting there. But he did not think that she would faint, or scream, or be too greatly frightened. And anyhow, he could not stop her.

"All right," he said, and she set off across the grass.

Lurie was coming down the stairs. Malcolm turned back to meet him in the hall.

"I heard Mrs. Kingscrown's car," said Lurie. "Where is she?"

"Stepped out. She'll be back—"

"I'll go after her," said Lurie. "I want to speak to her."

"I'd like a word with you, please," said Malcolm.

"Mr. Drake, I have no inclination to talk to you," said Lurie. "You've been consistently antagonistic and offensive to me—"

"Let's talk it over," said Malcolm.

He did not care what he said to Lurie; anything to hold him for a few moments.

"There's nothing to discuss," said Lurie. "You've obviously made up your mind to dispense with my services, although you've never had the courtesy to notify me. You have disregarded all my advice. You've made a deliberate effort to discredit me—"

"No, I haven't."

"I say you *have!* I know for a fact that you've maligned me."

"That's a mistake. I never talked about you to anyone."

"You're not speaking the truth, Mr. Drake."

"Who d'you think I maligned you to?"

"I'm not going to discuss the matter. But when the proper time comes, I shall take action, Mr. Drake—very vigorous action. I consider you completely irresponsible, and a very dangerous man."

Lily was coming up the steps, and Malcolm turned his back on the doctor. She did not look pale or agitated in any way.

"Morning, Dr. Lurie," she said.

"I'd like to speak to you about Gussie, Mrs. Kingscrown," he said.

"Just a moment, Malcolm," she said. "Come into the living room, Doctor."

Malcolm lit a cigarette and waited in the hall. I don't think Lurie knows, he said to himself. Lily wants me to wait until he's gone before we notify the police; and that's rather a mistake. We've got a doctor here, and his report could be useful.

Before the cigarette was smoked, Lurie and Lily came out into the hall.

"Then you'll let me know, Mrs. Kingscrown?" he said.

"Yes, I will," she said. "Good-by, Doctor."

"Good-by," he said. He glanced at Malcolm and conceded him a stiff nod, and out he went. They stood in the hall until his car started.

"Do you want to call the police?" Malcolm asked.

He had never before seen her hesitant, as she was now.

"Well, no," she said.

"I'm afraid it's got to be done," he said.

"No," she said again. "You see, Jenette isn't there. There's nobody there."

Chapter Ten

"D'you mind if I take another look?" he asked.

"Of course I don't. But, honestly, there's no one there."

"I'd just like to take a look," he said, and she went with him.

She had left the door open, and he went straight to the corner where Jenette had sat. He was not there.

"The bag," he said. "I'll show you."

But he could not find the bag.

"Lily..." he said. "I don't know... I don't see..."

"Jenette must have been just ill, some way," she said.

"He was dead. He was cold."

"Perhaps there are things that make people cold, Malcolm. Chills and fits. I don't know."

"He was dead. Not breathing. And—you can tell... There's a look..."

"There's a cataleptic trance that's like death, Malcolm. Perhaps that was it. Then he got over it and went away."

"But—but—but—the b-bag...?"

"Let's go back to the house, Malcolm, and talk there."

The rain fell, steady and fine; a little stream ran down the drive.

"Mrs. Kingscrown... has Gussie got a pink kimono, anything of that sort?"

"I don't know. But I'll find out, if you want."

"Yes, I—I do want. Is—is she too sick to be asked questions?"

"We'll ask her questions, Malcolm."

They mounted the steps again.

"You ought to have a doormat," he said. "My feet are muddy."

"I'll get one."

"There's just one thing—" he said.

"Yes...?" she waited. "Yes, Malcolm?"

But, after all, he could not ask her that. *Do you believe I saw all that?* Even if she were to hesitate, or if she were to answer yes in the wrong tone, it would be beyond his enduring.

"We'll go and see Gussie," she said, and he followed her up the stairs.

She knocked at a door. "It's me," she said, and a shrill voice answered, "Come in, ma'am!"

Gussie was sitting up in bed, wearing a light blue sweater, her dull yellow hair loose on her shoulders. She was pale, her eyelids were red, but she had a certain washed-out prettiness to her.

"Oh, my *goodness!*" she cried at the sight of Malcolm, and pulled the sheet up higher.

"We'll only stay a minute," said Lily. "Why did you go to the garage, Gussie?"

"Me?" Gussie cried. "Why, I never did!"

"Don't upset yourself, Gussie," Lily said quite gently. "I don't care if you did. I'm sure you had a good reason."

"Mrs. Kingscrown, I been lying here in this bed the whole day, excepting when this here gentleman made me open the door for him."

"Gussie, do you mind if I look at your shoes?"

"No, I don't! Go on, ma'am, and look at anything here! I don't know what kind of a story somebody's cooked up against me—and I don't care, neither!"

"Nobody's going to do you any harm, Gussie. I'll just take a look in your closet—"

"Well, look there. Look! I s'pose you think I got your silver spoons in there, or something. It's mean! It's just wicked to come up here and act like I was a thief!"

She was growing hysterical, and that alarmed Malcolm. But Lily went straight ahead; she looked into the closet; she picked up all the shoes and looked at the soles.

"All right!" Gussie screeched. "And what did you find to use against me, ma'am? What did you find?"

"Nothing, Gussie. Thank you for letting me look."

"What have I *done* for you to bring this gentleman right up in my room, and look at all my shoes and clothes and all? I been faithful and true to you—and look at how you treat me!"

"Malcolm," said Lily, "will you please go downstairs and get a glass of sherry for Gussie?"

"I wouldn't touch it!"

"Wait for me downstairs, will you?" Lily said, and he went down.

But as he reached the bottom of the stairs Gussie began to scream, to shriek. He went back, and stood outside the closed door. Gussie screamed and screamed, but he could not hear a sound from Lily. Not a word of soothing, of remonstrance, not a sound from her, only that frantic, crazy screaming. What was Lily doing? Just standing there looking down at that girl?

That troubled him, and he ran down the stairs. Now what? he said to himself. Now what? What can I do? Now how can I make her believe me.

And do you believe yourself? something inside him asked. Jenette sitting there dead, and the bones. The bones. Completely irresponsible, Lurie had said. That means not to be believed, not to be trusted. How do you know you saw all that monkey business? You're irresponsible. You're—

He knew exactly what was happening to him. He was going to pieces. You hear people say that, and here it was. All the little cells that made him were pulling away from one another; all the little flickering images in his brain that made thoughts were flying apart. Gussie was shrieking and screaming, and it wasn't such a bad idea. He rather liked hearing her.

There was one thing that hadn't gone yet. It stood like a rock, with everything else whirligigging around it. If he could put his mind on that... He thought it over and over—his name. Malcolm Drake, he said to himself. I'm Malcolm Drake. I can stop this.

For a minute, you have a choice. You can either go to pieces, which would be easy, and much more fun. Or you can tell all this whirling and swirling to stop. Stop! he said.

He sat down on the divan, and he noticed that Gussie had stopped screaming. Everything was quiet. Very quiet. So he sat quietly, until he heard Lily coming down the stairs, and then he rose, and waited for her, standing.

"Dr. Lurie upsets Gussie," she said.

He upsets me, too, Malcolm thought.

"She's very romantic," Lily went on. "She's always looking for what she calls Truelove. She's been jilted twice, poor girl; she had a trousseau all ready in a trunk. There's no sense in Dr. Lurie's telling her to live for others and forget her troubles."

She's trying to make things easy for me, Malcolm thought. Talking about Gussie, not Jenette and all that. And he made up his mind that he would meet her on her own ground. He would not ask her that question: Do you believe what I told you? He felt that he knew the answer now, and he was not embarrassed or distressed in any way.

"I'll get some lunch for us," she said. "And then we can talk."

"Oh, thank you," he said. "Thank you, Lily, but I'm afraid I can't stay. I'd like to, very much, but I've got to go."

"Can't you have lunch first?"

"Thanks. No, thanks. Thanks very much."

She was very nice, very kind. But she doesn't believe me, he thought, and who would? That about Jenette sitting there dead, and Gussie and the bag of bones.

But as long as I believe it, I'm all right. It's only if I start thinking that maybe I didn't see that.

I did see that. Just the way I told it.

"Well. G-good-by," he said.

"You left a coat here, Malcolm," she said. His coat was there, on a hanger.

"That's—that's very kind!" he said. "That's extremely kind..."

"What is?"

"To put my coat on a hanger."

"Well, I'm glad you think so," she said. "Malcolm, come again soon. You're welcome, any time you feel like coming."

She put my coat on a hanger, he thought. She said, any time you feel like coming.

He walked home in the rain, trying desperately to concentrate on his personal problem. I told Virginia I'd fix things up with Helene, he thought. All right, and just how?

You wouldn't expect Helene to behave like that. She's generally so damn polite and formal. But she ordered me out of the house.

And why the hell don't I go? It's what I want, and it's what I need. Arthur'd understand. And Virginia? Tell Virginia I'm going to look for a job, and that she'll hear from me. In the end it's got to come to that. The right and honorable way is to say things to people. Look here, Virginia! I'm no good to you. I'm sorry, Virginia, but you *don't* help me. You try, but you don't. I'm sorry, Virginia, but *no puedo mas*. You're young and you're beautiful and you've got some money. You can do better than trying to help me.

Good. That's just what I'm never going to say to her. I couldn't. And I won't. I'm going to run away, and write her a letter. I'm sorry, but that's all I can do. I'll tell Helene I've decided to go away.

He rang the bell, and Lydia opened the door, unfamiliar and incredible in a short tight little black dress and a saucy black hat with a veil. She looked very pretty.

"You look very pretty," Malcolm said.

"Oh..." she said, pleased. "Well, you see, I haven't had a chance to change yet, Mr. Malcolm. This is what I wore to the ceremony."

"C-ceremony?"

"Well, the funeral," she explained.

"I'll be damned!" said Malcolm.

Is that still going on? he thought. It seems as if the poor old girl had died weeks, months ago.

"It was just beautiful!" Lydia told him. "Such a lot of flowers, and there was a lady preacher or something, all in white. And Mrs. Chatsworth looked just exquisite."

I am a peculiar character, Malcolm thought. I never showed up at the poor old girl's funeral. I just walked out of the house and didn't come back.

"Where are they all?" he asked, very low.

"They're just sitting down to lunch, Mr. Malcolm."

"Lydia, could you possibly bring me up a sandwich and a cup of coffee?"

"Why, yes, of course, sir. Don't you feel good?"

"Not very," said Malcolm. "Toothache. Will you tell Mrs. Drake I have a toothache? Big double tooth."

"Oh, there's nothing as mean as a toothache!" said Lydia with warm sympathy.

"Nothing," Malcolm agreed, and ran up the stairs.

He found a white silk scarf in a drawer, and standing before the mirror, he tied it round his jaw, with a knot on the top of his head. He could still talk, but nobody would expect it of him.

"Mrs. Drake says she's terribly sorry about you having a toothache, Mr. Malcolm," Lydia said when she brought up his tray.

There was only one sandwich and he wanted a good deal more than that. But there was nothing to be done about it. When Lydia had taken away the tray, he got out the jigsaw puzzle. This is what they like, in the loony bin, he thought. Why not, indeed?

But you ought to leave it out, Malcolm, Virginia had said. I'll get you a bridge table, and you can just leave it there and work on it when you feel like it. She was trying to help him, but he had not wanted it that way. He liked to start all over again each time. There were two corners he could do quickly now; he liked doing them. He sat working at it, having a little bother with cigarettes because of his tied-up jaw, and presently there was a knock at the door. It was Helene.

"I came to ask how you were feeling," she asked politely.

"Well... Tooth not so good," he mumbled.

"I'm sorry. Is there anything I can do for you?"

"No, thanks. No."

"Virginia said you wanted to have a talk with me," she said, and her tone was very chilly.

"Well, yes. But just now..." He touched his bandaged jaw and smiled anxiously.

He could tell nothing from her charming little face. If she doesn't believe in this toothache, he thought, I hate to think how I must look to her.

"Would you rather have your dinner up here?" she asked.

"Tell you the truth, I would," he said. "Big double tooth."

"That's too bad," she said, and went away.

He knew Virginia would come. He pulled down the dark shades and lay down on the sofa, and she did come.

"You poor boy!" she said. "Don't try to talk if it hurts. Do you think you'll be able to eat anything, Malcolm?"

I could eat a horse, he thought.

"I wouldn't know..." he said.

"I'll fix a little tray for you," she said.

She believed in his toothache. She's so kind, he thought. She's such a fine, wonderful girl. What's the *matter* with me?

She brought up his dinner herself; a very little dinner, it was. She came back later, with a hot-water bottle, and she had some raisins in a little covered pot of boiling water.

"This was one of Aunt Evie's remedies," she said. "Try putting one against your gum, Malcolm."

He put a raisin, fiercely hot, and soft, into his mouth; he lay with his cheek against the hotwater bottle. He felt ashamed of himself, and at the same time he felt triumphant and wanting to laugh.

"I've brought up a bottle of brandy, Malcolm," she said. "Arthur told me it was the best thing for a toothache."

"Well... So they say."

"I'll leave the bottle here," she said. "You'll know how much is good for you."

Showing confidence in me, he thought.

"Do you think you'll be able to sleep, Malcolm?"

With a bottle of brandy and ten bottles of capsules?

"Why, yes, thanks, I do, Virginia. Thanks, Virginia, for everything."

"Good night, Malcolm, dear."

"Good night, Virginia, dear."

The door closed softly after her. For a time he lay perfectly still, with his face on the hotwater bottle; he quietly chewed up the raisin. She had left one lamp lighted, the bed turned down, the thermos bottle of hot coffee ready for the morning. He hated the look of the big, airy, tranquil room. Like a sickroom, he thought.

It seemed safe now to get up and lock the door. Then he took off the scarf and sat down by the open window, to cool his burning cheek. This is contemptible, he thought. This is the worst thing I've ever done. The meanest, cheapest, stinkingest thing.

If I don't get out of here, I'll do more things like this. Because I can't fight anyone here. I can't fight Helene. Or Virginia. I can only lie and cheat and hide. Oh, Virginia! I'm honestly damn sorry...

I don't want to think tonight. Not about Virginia. Not about Jenette. I'll take some capsules and get a good night's sleep, and perhaps tomorrow I'll have the courage to run away.

He went to the closet to get the current bottle from the pocket of his heavy overcoat. It was not there. O.K., I suppose I forgot to put it back. There was another bottle in one of his shoes. It was not there. All right. There was one in the little leather box where he kept studs and cuff links. None there.

Nine of the bottles were gone. He took out a key and unlocked a drawer of the desk. There were three bottles in there; he stood looking down at them with a feeling of nausea.

Somebody had taken the others. Somebody knew the shameful and ludicrous secret of the little hidden bottles. Well, who? Virginia? Helene? Lurie? Hardly worth living, if people knew things like this about you.

He shut the drawer and locked it. Scarcely worth sleeping, if it cost this much.

There was a spot of shaving cream on the bathroom mirror. He cleaned that off, and he tried to polish the glass, but it did not get bright. All right; it had to. He tried some brandy on it, and that was better.

Twelve o'clock. Four o'clock is the zero hour. Baloney! He had some very fine shoe polishes he had got in England; fine creams; he had chamois cloths, brushes, everything. He spread a paper on the table and set all his shoes on it and went to work on them. One o'clock and all's well. But four o'clock is the zero hour. That is when your vitality is at the lowest ebb. Ebb tide, when life is going out; when people die. All right, then die at four o'clock, and be done with it.

He set the jigsaw puzzle up again, but it bored him. He tried to read, but the books were terrible. Three o'clock is certainly a quiet hour. What the hell is the matter with all the little crickets and things? Too late in the year? Or is it the rain? Or is it because I—can't hear them?

Four o'clock is the zero hour. Then let it be. You've got to be dead or alive, one or the other. Not like this.

I'll lie down, he thought. But he could not lie down, because then he could not breathe. His heart gave a horrible leap, and he was choking; he put his hand to his throat. The thudding of his heart shook him; sweat ran down into his eyes, so that he was blinded.

Take it easy. This has happened before. All right, but how do I know—this isn't it? Let it be. Go ahead and get it over with. And see if I care...

Chapter Eleven

A knock at the door made him jump. He got out of bed and went to unlock the door, blank with sleep.

"Looky!" said Arthur. "There's a cop here."

"Oh, a cop?" said Malcolm.

Virginia opened her door and came out into the hall, fresh and neat in a blue-and-white-checked gingham dress.

"He wants to ask all of us some questions," said Arthur. "It's about Jenette."

"Ivan?" she said.

"Yes. The poor devil's dead."

"Ivan?" she said. "I don't believe it!"

"Oh, yes," Arthur said. "It happens."

"But how?"

"They found him in a field, in the rain—"

"Arthur, *how* did he die?"

"I don't know," Arthur said. "One of those things, I suppose. One of those things life-insurance agents tell you about. Stroke. Heart attack, something of the sort."

"What field?" asked Malcolm suddenly. Because he was beginning to think and to remember a little.

"Who cares?" said Arthur.

"I'd like to know."

"A field behind the Johnsons' house. Their gardener thought he'd take a short cut home that way last night, and he found the poor devil."

"Stroke?" said Malcolm. "But wasn't he too young—?"

"No, no!" said Arthur. "Anybody can have a stroke at any time. Then your little son becomes a newsboy and your wife spends the rest of her life looking out the window at the rain with sad gray eyes. She has a bit of sewing in her lap, but I bet she never touches it. Just a prop, that is, for the newsboy."

"I don't *believe* Ivan is dead!" said Virginia.

"You sound a little like Aunt Evie," said Arthur. "It may be a hoax, but personally I think the cops know. Looky, Malcolm! This cop is waiting. Better get dressed and come on down, won't you?"

Malcolm was awake now, but even a cold shower did not bring him the feeling of alertness he wanted so badly. The thing is, he thought, there are too many threads. The Virginia thread—which is the worst—and the Jenette thread. And the pills. And the bag of bones. And last night... If you think you're going crazy, you'd better keep your mind on that. It's like a cobweb.

Cobwebs are pretty. I've looked at them. I saw a bee caught in a cobweb once. It was getting dragged along, by the littlest spider in the world. Dragged into the web. The bee could break one thread, and another thread. But in the end there were just too damn many threads. Each one of them is so little, you think, well, I'll bust out of this. But then there's another. And another... The bee looked enormous, furry, like an animal. I thought I'd do something about it. But then something happened; I don't remember what. When I came back, the bee was dead, finished. By the little tiny spider.

No. It doesn't have to be like that. You don't have to be a damned, stupid, furry bee. You can be a fine, bold bee.

But he did not feel fine and bold when he went down the stairs. Arthur was in the dining room with the cop; almost at once the two girls came in.

"This is Captain Rutgers," said Arthur. "Captain Rutgers, this is Mrs. Drake. Miss Chatsworth. My brother, Malcolm Drake."

The way he said that was good. As if his brother was something special.

I'm glad to see you all together," said Captain Rutgers. "I won't take any more of your time than I can help."

He was a slim fellow, not in uniform, but in a neat dark suit with a bow tie; he had a bright and happy face, with arched black eyebrows, and ears that stood out. He stood, with a pleasant smile, until the two girls were seated side by side at the table; then he sat down himself on the arm of a chair.

"We're making an inquiry into the death of Mr. Ivan Jenette," he said. "Now, if anybody can give me any information—"

"Of course, I've known Ivan for years," said Helene.

"Can you give me the names of any relatives or close friends of his?"

"He didn't have any relations in this country," Helene said. "Only some cousins, in France. And he didn't have close friends. He was a rather detached sort of person."

"I see," said Captain Rutgers with sympathy. "Now, I'm sorry to put these questions to you, Mrs. Drake, but you'll understand that under the circumstances... When did you last see Mr. Jenette?"

"The day before yesterday."

"And what was his—well, his mood, Mrs. Drake? Would you say he was in good spirits—or not?"

"But why...?" Helene asked. "Why are you asking me that, Captain Rutgers? Is there something—something queer about Ivan's death?"

"He died from an overdose of some barbital preparation, Mrs. Drake."

"In a f-field?" said Malcolm. "Out in a f-field?"

"We don't know where he took this dose, Mr. Drake, and the doctor says there's a certain amount of variation in the time the drug takes to act. It depends on several factors. For instance, if Mr. Jenette was in the habit of using any such preparation—"

"He was," Virginia said. "He told me so."

"If you could tell me about that, Miss Chatsworth, in a little more detail...?"

"He showed me some little blue capsules, and he said he took them to make him sleep."

"Did he say he took them frequently?"

"Almost every night," she said.

He thought this over for a moment, with a look of bright, alert consideration.

"Miss Chatsworth," he said, "do you know if Mr. Jenette had had any recent trouble—financial trouble—anything that disturbed him seriously?"

"Yes," she said.

"Can you tell me the nature of this trouble?"

"I'd—rather not," she said.

"I understand how you feel, Miss Chatsworth," he said gravely and gently. "But we've got to arrive at some verdict."

She sat there with her dark head bowed; she looked so young, so gravely troubled, it seemed a shocking thing to press her.

"Ivan was sure that my aunt was going to leave him some money," she said. "When he found that she hadn't, he was—" She paused. "He was—in despair. He told me—"

"Yes?" Captain Rutgers said, still more gently.

"He told me—he didn't think he—could go on. He said he was going to—"

"Yes, Miss Chatsworth?"

"He said he was going to kill himself."

"For God's sake...!" said Arthur mildly.

"But he'd said that before, Arthur, often. I didn't take it seriously."

"You're willing to state, then, that Mr. Jenette had threatened more than once to commit suicide, Miss Chatsworth?"

"Yes," she said reluctantly.

"I've heard him, myself," said Helene.

Malcolm looked at them, sitting there side by side. And they're lying, he thought. Lying like hell. They never thought of suicide until just now. I don't believe Jenette killed himself. I don't believe he took sleeping medicine. Blue capsules, she said, same as mine. No. He wasn't that type. Not nervous or jumpy. Resigned, he was. He was mad enough about not getting anything from Aunt Evie, but I'll be damned if he was suicidal about it. No.

"You'd be willing to sign a statement to that effect, Miss Chatsworth? That Mr. Jenette threatened to commit suicide?"

"If it's necessary, Captain Rutgers."

"And you can corroborate, Mrs. Drake, that Mr. Jenette had threatened suicide at other times?"

"Yes," said Helene.

Hold on, now, thought Malcolm. I mean, this is pretty hard on Jenette. I mean to say, to call the poor devil a suicide and just shove him out of the way. When he's been murdered.

"The thing is," he said, "why does it have to be suicide?"

"You mean it might have been inadvertent, Mr. Drake?"

"Well... no," said Malcolm.

There was a silence.

"You suggest he was given this dose, by force, Mr. Drake?" Rutgers asked.

"I mean, it could be that way."

"Well, of course, in a case of this kind, we always consider that possibility, Mr. Drake. But in the case of Mr. Jenette, there's been nothing to suggest foul play."

"Ivan had never been out here before, Malcolm," said Helene. "He didn't know anyone here."

Both she and Rutgers spoke with a sort of kindly protest, as if trying to reason with someone pathetically unreasonable. As if he were a stubborn and troublesome fool.

"It we come across anything," said Rutgers, "anything at all that suggests foul play..."

I could tell you something, Malcolm thought. I could tell you plenty.

Chapter Twelve

Arthur had time only to swallow a cup of coffee; then he hurried off to catch a train, leaving Malcolm to breakfast with the two sisters. He did not relish this; for a few moments he tried to devise wild little ways of escape, but they were no good. The toothache was absolutely out; no one had mentioned it, not even Virginia.

I'll have to tell Rutgers about Jenette, he thought. But not until I've warned Lily. I don't exactly mean 'warn'; I mean, she ought to know what's coming before she gets mixed up in a murder case.

I don't know why Helene and Virginia told that suicide tale. They're mighty quiet now; not saying a word. So much the better. I want to think.

He thought about Jenette with a curious resentment. Fellow can't simply be shoved aside like this, he thought. Can't be murdered, and then be made to take all the blame for it. When Rutgers hears my story, he'll take a different view of it. But I can't tell Rutgers without letting Lily know. It's bound to involve her, to some extent, when I found the poor devil on her premises.

I'm sorry to cause her any trouble, he thought. But she can take it. She'll understand that I've got to tell the police now. It would be a damn shame to let Jenette be buried as a suicide.

And what made the two girls lie like that? Well, I don't know. To smooth things over some way? That's what Helene always wants to do. She doesn't like scenes, doesn't like anything awkward or embarrassing. He glanced at Helene, sitting at the foot of the table, and it occurred to him how very much she would dislike having anything at all to do with a murder.

Oh, what is the use of bringing all that up, Malcolm? she would say. Let's not *discuss* it, please. No, he thought, she'd throw Jenette to the wolves rather than have a scene.

I'm very fond of Helene. And I'm very fond of Virginia. But I'm going to break out of this. I'm not going to stay here, and I'm not going to see Jenette shoved away as a suicide.

"I think I'll walk down to the village and buy some magazines," he said.

"I'll drive you down, Malcolm," said Virginia.

"I'd like some exercise, thanks," said Malcolm.

"It *would* be a nice morning for a walk," said Virginia. "I'll come with you, Malcolm."

"Why, thanks, Virginia," he said. "But the thing is, I'm going to the barber's, to get a haircut."

Lily didn't exactly believe me, when I told her what I saw, he thought. But she will now. And the reason she would believe him now was that his confidence in himself was complete. He was happy, moving along the road in the cool, breezy morning. Some little animal I read about, he thought. Forgotten which one, but it'll bite its feet off to get out of a trap. That's me.

All right. The thing is not to make any more mistakes. I want to tell Rutgers exactly what I saw in that garage. Get everything clear. With Rutgers. With Virginia. The way things are now, it's like being caught in a net.

He thought that maybe Lily would be in the kitchen again; he hoped so; he wanted everything to be exactly as it had been before. He took the gravel path at the side of the house, and as he neared the back, he heard a loud titter. Rising on his toes, he looked in at the kitchen window, and there he saw Ben sitting in a chair, with Gussie sitting on his knees.

"You're crazy," Gussie said archly.

"You *like* the purse all right, don't you?" Ben asked.

"Oh, I've seen better," said Gussie.

"Twenty bucks I paid for that purse."

"Go on!"

"I did!"

"Go on!"

Malcolm moved away. They were, he thought, as unattractive a couple as you could find, the tall, gawky Ben, the pale, red-eyed Gussie. He did not like the sight of them there in Lily's nice house. He went to the front of the house and rang the bell, and presently Gussie opened the door.

"Mrs. Kingscrown in?" he asked.

"Oh, no!"

"Know when she'll be back?"

"No."

"Back to lunch?"

"I guess not."

It came into Malcolm's head now that this might be an opportunity. He had never believed Gussie's frantic denial of her visit to the garage. What if he could trap her into some sort of admission before he went to Rutgers?

He took a folded dollar bill out of his wallet and handed it to her. Artlessly, she unfolded it and looked at it and did not seem enthusiastic. He took out another one.

"Well, thank you," she said. "She'll be back to dinner."

"Will you tell her I'll stop in this evening, then?"

"She might have company," said Gussie.

"Well…"

"She has lots of company," said Gussie. "She likes a gay life."

"Who doesn't?" asked Malcolm.

"Oh, well!" said Gussie. "Even if she ever gets married again, I don't have to worry. After my mother killed my father, Mrs. Kingscrown she said to me I didn't have to worry because she'd always look after me."

"T-tough luck—about your parents," said Malcolm, profoundly impressed.

"Yes," said Gussie. "My father'd been drinking, and he came home and he picked up my little baby brother by the leg and Mommer went for him with a big heavy milk bottle. You couldn't blame her. She got let off. It was only natural."

"Were you there when—it happened?"

"Oh, yes!" said Gussie. "And did I holler! I couldn't stop. I been hysterical ever since."

"That's too bad," said Malcolm, fascinated.

"Yes," said Gussie with pride. "Right to this day, I get spells. I holler and scream. But all the doctors say I'll outgrow it."

"How old are you?" he asked.

"What would you guess?"

Thirty, he guessed.

"Twenty-three?" he said.

"I'll be nineteen in November," said Gussie. "If I live that long."

Such a blurred and faded eighteen.

"Oh, you'll live—" he said.

"You never know," said Gussie. "Anyways, if I had to die right now, I'd have a clear conscience."

"That's certainly something," said Malcolm.

He remembered now that this conversation had been begun with a purpose, and here was an opening.

"Still," he said, "I suppose everyone does something a little wrong, now and then."

"Not me," said Gussie.

"Never even told a little fib?" he asked, with a crafty smile.

"That's not what I mean," said Gussie. "I mean I never did anything *wrong*, and I never will. I don't know if I'll even get married."

"Oh, you're sure to get married," said Malcolm gallantly.

"*I'm* not sure," said Gussie. "I've had plenty of chances, but I don't know if I want to. You never can tell about men. You marry a man and he starts drinking and he might kill you."

"That doesn't happen very often."

"I don't know... A girl we knew, she married a policeman and one day he took out his gun and shot her dead. I don't know as I feel much like taking a chance on that happening to *me*."

"Still, most husbands don't," said Malcolm.

"Well, there's plenty that do," said Gussie. "Believe you me!"

There was a silence, which Malcolm did not know how to break. He looked at Gussie, negligently leaning against the newel post, and he admitted to himself that he had no idea how she could be trapped.

"Well," said Gussie, "I'll tell her you said you'd be in tonight."

This was a dismissal and he accepted it and turned homeward. The police will know how to make her talk, he thought. She's certainly in this thing, up to her neck. She knew Jenette was in the garage, dead. She probably knows who took him away.

Of course, he thought, Helene and Virginia don't know it's murder. It would never come into their heads. No... I suppose they had some idea of—smoothing things over. I don't quite get the idea, and I don't like it. Pretty low, I call it, to try to pin a suicide on the fellow, no matter what reason they have. Damned if I can see what reason they *could* have. Only, women have reasons you'd never figure out. Anyhow, it's something respectable.

Helene was sitting on the terrace, knitting a dark-blue Navy sweater that looked enormous in her small hands; she looked delicate and lovely in a dark wool dress.

"Hello, Malcolm!" she said, glancing up with a smile.

Malcolm forgot to answer. I told Virginia I'd talk to Helene and fix it up. Fix what up? Say what to Helene? You ought to go away at once, she told me, and she was right. But it's got to be done with tact. You have to be very tactful with girls like Helene and Virginia.

"I-I-I—" he began, and was dismayed by the stammer.

"Sit down and smoke a cigarette," she said. "There's plenty of time before lunch."

Her polite tone, her softly rounded little face that was so completely unreadable, almost frightened him. She had turned on him with amazing hostility in Virginia's room, had judged and condemned him and told him to go; she had looked at him with something like horror. She must still feel like that, he thought.

"Been thinking over what you said. And I'm g-g-going—"

"Oh, are you?" she asked with bright interest. "Where, Malcolm?"

"N-New York. Best place to find a j-j-j—"

He clenched his teeth and sat down on the stone balustrade, sweating with humiliation and fury. Stop this! he said to himself. You can talk, you fool.

Helene went on knitting. "Malcolm," she said presently in a low tone, "I'd like to tell you something. But please promise not to tell Arthur."

"Wh-wh—"

"Will you promise, please, not to tell Arthur?"

He was not going to promise that, and she saw it in his face.

"Then I'll trust you not to tell him," she said. "I can't think you'd want to worry and distress him."

She waited, but Malcolm said nothing. Arthur was unalterably his friend, but very definite in him was the feeling that Helene was his enemy; he had to be on his guard against her.

"Virginia's paying blackmail," she said. "To protect *you.*"

He stood up; he looked down at her, and their eyes met squarely. No doubt she was his enemy, striking at him without pity.

"She's been borrowing from me," Helene went on, "but I can't lend her any more. This can't go on."

"Who's getting the blackmail?"

"Ben," she said.

"Very good," said Malcolm. "I'll put a stop to that."

"How?"

"I'll have a talk with him."

"I've had a talk with him. I gave him a month's pay and sent him away. But Virginia meets him somewhere."

"Very good. I'll find him. If I can't make him shut up and clear out, I'll turn him over to the police."

"And let him tell about Aunt Evie?"

"I've no objection."

"I wasn't thinking of you," she said. "I was thinking of Arthur."

"Arthur wouldn't give a damn if Ben told that tale all over the place. It's a lie, you know."

"Have you really thought about it?" she asked. "Do you think you'd be allowed to inherit Aunt Evie's money, if there were a rumor that you'd killed her?"

"Helene!" he said.

"Can't you see what a horrible, disgraceful scandal it would be? In the newspapers—everyone talking. Arthur would stand up for you, through thick and thin. But how do you think he'd feel? You know that he's always trying to protect you—"

"I don't need to be 'protected,'" he said shortly. That hurt.

"If you'd go away," she said, "there'd be no object in Virginia's paying Ben anything more, and she'd stop. Nothing would happen."

"Did Virginia tell you about this blackmail?"

"Yes. But I'd suspected it before, when she borrowed from me. She never borrowed before. There's nothing she wouldn't do for you."

"Does she believe Ben's story?"

"Yes," said Helene.

She was an enemy without pity.

"Everybody would believe it—a little," she said. "Everybody would say—there must be something in it. You know that. And the police would have to investigate it, if they heard a rumor. You see, there's no way for you to *prove* you didn't give Aunt Evie that drink."

"Very good," he said. "I'll go. Now. I'll start to pack."

"You'd better wait until after lunch," she said. "And you'd better not pack. Virginia would notice. You're not going to tell her you're going?"

"No. I'm not going to tell her."

"I'll send your things after you, as soon as you're settled," she said.

"Very good," he said, and wondered why he said that. Like a butler. Very good, madam.

As he went toward the door, Helene took up her knitting again; model of a charming young wife. And that's what she is, he thought. He could feel no anger against her. She was fighting for the peace and the grace she had made here for Arthur; he could not blame her.

She had told him, in effect, that he must run away, making no attempt to defend himself. I'll go, all right, he thought. But I'll see Ben first. With a gun.

Arthur's got a gun; I'll borrow it. I'll run Ben out of town. He won't bother Virginia any more, and he won't go to Lily's house again.

He caught sight of Virginia in the library, writing at a desk; he went past with stealthy haste and up the stairs. When he got to the top he looked

down; nobody in the hall below. He opened the door of Arthur's room—
and Helene's. It was a fine room, large, exquisitely neat; there was a faint
perfume in it. It was an outrage for him to be here.

He opened a bureau drawer, and closed it at once, seeing neatly rolled
silk stockings, veils, a little blue satin envelope. His heart was beating fast
now; it would be a bad business if Helene should come in now. Very bad.
You're a criminal lunatic! she could say. What are you looking for? A gun?
You—with a gun! Help! Help! Malcolm wants to get hold of a gun.

He opened another drawer and saw things of Arthur's in it; he felt
through them, set them neat again. Sweat came out on his forehead; he
saw for himself that certainly he would *look* crazy, if anyone saw him.

He went all through the bureau; nothing there; he started on a chif-
fonier; he opened the middle drawer, and then he could not close it. He
tried lifting it a little, pulling it down; it would not go back. It was impossible to search the drawer beneath until he got this one back. It had to be
done, and it could be done, with patience. Only, his hands were damp, he
was breathing hard; there was no time for patience. If Helene should come
in...

He gave the drawer a tug, and it fell out on the floor with a loud thump.
She would hear that downstairs, and she would come up. In a sort of fury,
he started groping through the drawer below.

"Looking for something?" asked Arthur's voice.

He was standing in his dressing gown, in the doorway of the bathroom,
and maybe he had been there a long time.

"Y-yes," Malcolm said.

The door into the hall opened, and Helene came in. All right. Now
they were both looking at crazy Malcolm rummaging through their private effects.

"Oh...!" Helene said. "It's that drawer. I thought I heard something
fall."

The two men said nothing.

"Are you feeling any better, Arthur?" she said.

"Worse," he said. "Much worse. I'd like a whisky-and-soda and a ham
sandwich."

"Oh, but that couldn't be good for a headache!"

"Who knows, after all?" said Arthur. "Who knows whence cometh a
headache? Probably the price you pay for an almost superhuman intelli-
gence. See you downstairs, Malcolm, in half an hour?"

And now will they talk about me? Malcolm thought. It's kinder not to *say* anything to poor Malcolm when he does these *peculiar* things....

He went into his own room and stood beside the closed door. I'll have to see Ben without a gun, he thought. I'll have to run him out of town — some other way. I can. He doesn't look like what you'd call a formidable character. And you don't expect a blackmailer to be heroic.

Something else was coming into his head. But if Ben's been hanging around Lily's house? Now, take it a little easy. Ben's been blackmailing Virginia. On account of my giving Aunt Evie the big drink. All right. Jenette said he'd tell me something about how she died. But he didn't. All right. Who'd be interested in seeing that he didn't tell me?

The blackmailer.

There was a light rap on the door; it opened a little, and Arthur put in his hand, holding a small automatic.

"This what you wanted?" he asked.

He handed it to Malcolm, and went away, closing the door behind him. He handed me his gun, Malcolm thought. He doesn't think I'm too crazy to have a gun. That makes you feel pretty good. Pretty fine.

Chapter Thirteen

Arthur did not come down to lunch, and that was not so good. Not so good to sit here with the two sisters.

Virginia was quiet; she looked pale and tired and very serious. But Helene was incredible. There was no trace of hostility in her; she was amiable and easy, making conversation. Malcolm responded as best he could, and he tried not to look at Virginia and not to think of her.

Yet he was aware of her all the time, as one is aware of some great pain dormant beneath a drug. Maybe I'll never see her again, he thought. She thinks I killed Aunt Evie, and she doesn't care. Only stands by me, tries to help. Paying blackmail to help me.

And now I'm walking out on her. But God knows there's nothing else I can do. I'm no good to her, that's all. She'll get over it. She'll forget. Only it's sad. So damned sad.

After lunch, he went up to his room. After half an hour, he thought, I'll just walk out of this house, and never come back. If she sees me, if she asks me where I'm going, I'll tell her another lie. And then it's finished. I'm sorry. Here's this jigsaw puzzle she got for me, the books, the thermos. I'm sorry.

"Malcolm!" she said, knocking at the door.

He was frightened; he did not want to see her. But there was no escape; he opened the door and she came in.

"Malcolm, Captain Rutgers is here, to see you."

"M-me?"

"Yes. Malcolm, you *must* be careful what you say."

"Well, no," he said gently and anxiously. "I haven't done anything, Virginia."

He wished that he could make her believe that before he went away.

"Don't say anything about Ben to him, Malcolm. Please promise you won't."

"I don't expect to," he said curtly.

It would be unbearable to discuss the blackmail matter with her. It's damn good of her, he thought, loyal and all that, but...

But she wouldn't be paying blackmail to Ben unless she believed his story. No, he thought. I'll deal with Ben myself.

"Virginia," he said, "I want you to know this. Before I go away. I didn't give Aunt Evie the big drink."

"That's not the point, Malcolm—"

"Virginia, it is the point—for me."

"Malcolm, you see you couldn't *prove* that you hadn't. You'd say you hadn't, and Ben would say he saw you. And Dr. Lurie would say—"

"The hell with Dr. Lurie!"

"Malcolm, please think. If you say anything to make Captain Rutgers suspicious of Ben, he'll begin to investigate, and that might be—horrible."

He was sorry for her in her anxiety and distress, but he was exasperated, too. She brushed aside his assurance of innocence without even a pretense of interest.

"I'd better not keep Rutgers waiting any longer," he said.

"Promise you won't say anything about Ben?"

"Couldn't promise, my dear girl. I'll have to answer his questions the way they come. But I shan't volunteer anything. Don't worry," he added perfunctorily, and went down the stairs.

He was pleased to observe that he was not in the least nervous about this interview. He felt well able to hold his own; he felt nonchalant, even jaunty.

"Afternoon!" he said.

"Good afternoon!" said Rutgers, with a nice smile.

They both lit cigarettes and sat down.

"I won't keep you any longer than I can help," said Rutgers. "Just a few things to clear up. You'd met Jenette before he came here, hadn't you, Mr. Drake?"

"We-ell..." Malcolm answered, "I'm not quite sure about that. There was some talk about our having met, but I don't remember it, and he didn't mention it."

"You don't recall any former conversations with him?"

"No. If I ever did see him, it must have been at some party. You know how it is."

"Certainly!" Rutgers agreed cordially.

He looks like Reddy the Fox, Malcolm thought. Only I don't remember whether Reddy is one of those good animals or a little rascal.

"I understand, Mr. Drake, that you went to the Tavern to see Jenette the night before his body was found."

Powie! thought Malcolm. I'd forgotten about that.

"Yes, I did. But he wasn't there."

"Did you want to see him for any particular reason, Mr. Drake?"

How much do you know?

"Well, he called me up and asked me to come."

"Did he give any reason for this request?"

"Well, yes. Yes. He asked if I could lend him a little money."

"Did you agree to do so?"

"Yes. Yes, I did."

"You had a drink in the bar with Jenette?"

"No, I didn't see him at all. He'd checked out."

"When you left the Tavern, Mr. Drake, where did you go?"

"I w-went to a bar."

"What bar was it, Mr. Drake?"

"Didn't notice the name."

"And when you left this bar, where did you go, Mr. Drake?"

"I—I went to another bar."

"Did you notice the name of this second bar?"

I don't like this, Malcolm thought. I mean, I'm not making a good impression. I don't like it.

"Well) no," he answered. "I mean to say, you—often d-don't look at the n-names of b-bars."

"That's true. Mr. Drake, had you been abstaining from all alcoholic beverages for some time?"

You are very smart, Reddy, and I see where you are heading.

"Yes. More or less."

"Was this on your doctor's advice?"

"Doctor in Trinidad said I might as well lay off for a while."

"Did your doctor here advise you that you might resume?"

"I haven't any doctor here."

"I see! You've been ill for some time, Mr. Drake?"

"Not ill. J-j-just—run-down."

"I've heard about your experience at sea, Mr. Drake. I'd like you to know that I have every sympathy with a man who's been through what you've been through."

Every sympathy? All right, then, shut up and let me alone.

"But we have to follow through with these things. You understand that, Mr. Drake."

"Sure! Sure!"

"I'll ask you to consider the following questions very seriously, Mr. Drake."

Malcolm was not nonchalant and jaunty now. He was sweating now; he was considering a lot of things seriously.

"Returning to the evening when you went to the Tavern. Are all the events of that evening perfectly clear in your mind, Mr. Drake? Or are there certain periods about which you are—let's say, hazy?"

"No!" Malcolm said. "All c-completely clear."

Except after I got home. And that's not your business.

"It's often the case that, after abstaining from alcohol for some time, even one or two drinks will have a pretty marked effect."

"That so?" Malcolm asked brightly.

"You entered only two bars?"

"Yes," Malcolm answered.

Or was it three? This sort of thing—bothers you.

"Did you talk to anyone?"

"I said a few words to one man."

"Could you identify him, Mr. Drake?"

"I'm afraid not. He looked—he looked—like a l-lot of people. I mean, a lot of other people."

"I see! Mr. Drake, at any time during your illness, did you take any barbital preparation?"

I don't want to talk about that. I won't talk about that.

"The doctors gave me a lot of stuff. They never tell you what it is."

"Were you given any sleeping medicine, Mr. Drake?"

"Yes," Malcolm said after a moment.

"Have you any of this medicine now, Mr. Drake?"

How the hell can you answer, when you can't tell how much Reddy knows? He may have found out from Lurie, or the drugstore, or someone in the house. This is the one thing I—don't like.

"I don't know," he said.

"Will you take a look, Mr. Drake? We'd very much appreciate it if you'd give us a sample of whatever sleeping medicine you have in your possession."

We? You and who else?

"You already know, Mr. Drake, that Jenette's death was caused by a barbital preparation. We're considering the possibility that the drug may have been stolen from this house."

My God! thought Malcolm. But that could be it! Ben could have stolen those bottles.

"Will you see if you can find me a sample of this medicine, Mr. Drake?"

"L-later."

"I'd very much like to have it now, Mr. Drake."

"Look here, Reddy— Oh God! Captain... I don't know whether this is quite fair. I mean to say—I don't have to do this, do I?"

"No. Mr. Drake, you don't have to. Simply, you'd be assisting the police in the performance of their duty."

"Anyhow, you said it was s-suicide."

"I don't remember saying that, Mr. Drake."

"You seemed to think so."

"The circumstances—at that time—seemed to point to suicide."

"Any new circumstances?"

"Yes. We have a witness now, Mr. Drake, a waitress at the Tavern, who can testify that she saw Jenette being helped into a car by a man in the lane behind the Tavern at approximately eight-thirty that evening."

"What does that prove?"

"We don't know yet, Mr. Drake." He paused. "It would make a very favorable impression, Mr. Drake, if you'd give me a sample of this drug. Now."

It's not a drug. Just a little capsule. I don't take drugs. I don't imbibe alcoholic beverages. Once in a while I take a drink, and I used to take some little pills. Only not any more. I'm not going to talk about all those little bottles. It—makes me sick.

"Will you get one for me now, Mr. Drake?"

"No," said Malcolm.

There was a moment's silence; then Rutgers rose.

"I'm sorry," he said, pleasant as ever.

But he had something up his sleeve; you could see that. He was going away without the capsule, and without the favorable impression. Another mistake? Another error of judgment?

Chapter Fourteen

"What did you tell him, Malcolm?"

"Why, nothing, Virginia. He asked if I'd seen Jenette the night he must have died, and I hadn't, so there you are."

"What did you tell him about Ben?"

"Name wasn't mentioned."

"Malcolm, are you sure you *remember?*"

"Yes, damn it, I am sure!" he shouted, and then was ashamed. "I'm sorry, Virginia. Very sorry."

"It doesn't matter, dear. I know how wretched all this must be for you."

"No worse for me than for anyone else. Nobody likes to be b-bothered."

"Of course not!"

All wrong to feel like this about Virginia. Only, she's talking as if I had to be humored. As if I—well, never mind.

"Would you like a cup of tea, Malcolm?"

"No, thanks. Thanks very much. I think I'll take a little stroll."

"Would you like me to come with you, Malcolm?"

"Why, thanks, Virginia, but I'm going to the barber's."

I said that before.

"I told the barber I'd start some treatments today. Scalp treatments. I mean to say, my hair is—needs—treatments."

"Back in time for a nice cool drink?"

"You bet!"

He was never coming back. She was such a damn good, dear, faithful girl; a beautiful girl, too, and he was treating her like this. They were standing in the upper hall, where she had been waiting for him; she had been anxious; she was anxious now. She looked like a kid, in her blue-and-white-checked gingham dress, and he was very fond of her. He bent and kissed her on the temple, and that was a mistake. She put her arms around his neck and kissed him on the mouth, a kiss that made him gasp.

"Malcolm! *Malcolm!*" she said in a fierce whisper.

"T-take it easy, dear."

"All I want in the world is for you to be well and happy."

"I am well and happy. Absolutely."

"No! You—"

Lydia was coming up the stairs now and Virginia let him go. He went into his room and got a hat, laid his light overcoat over his arm. His arm was shaking, and his knees. I'm never coming back. I don't care if I haven't got a cent, or a roof over my head. I'll never come back.

When he was out of sight of the house, he stopped to count his money, and he was pleased to find that he had nearly twenty-seven dollars. It was only four o'clock and he did not know where to go. He left the road and went into a little wood; he lay down on a bed of pine needles and lit a cigarette. He smoked for a time and then took a little nap, and then it was five o'clock. He lit another cigarette and lay watching the clouds that were gold where the westering sun touched them. He was not thinking about anything. I'll stop in to see Lily after dinner, he told himself. But certainly he was not thinking about Lily. In a way, you couldn't think about her. She was simply there, that was all. She existed, as independent as a tree.

He got up presently and walked to the village, to that same cafeteria. He had the same waitress, but she did not seem to remember him. Maybe he had the same menu, too, blurred and faint purple, so he ordered veal and apple pie again.

"Tea er cawfee?" the waitress asked.

"Cuper cawfee," he said.

He made the dinner last as long as he could, and it was dark when he went out into the village street. The little lighted shops looked very cozy; the railroad station looked like a nice little house all lit up for a party; he stopped on the bridge for a while, looking down at it. No reason on God's earth why I shouldn't get on a train and go somewhere, he thought. I'll see Lily and tell her what I've got to do. Then I'll telephone to Rutgers. I'll go to New York and telephone him from there. I'll tell him what I saw in the garage. I'll tell him anything, only not about all the little bottles.

No. Hold everything. I've got to see Ben. I can't leave here until I've settled with Ben. I can't leave Virginia with that worry. But if I could make Rutgers see things the way I do, he'd put Ben in jail and that would be very fine. Only I don't feel like talking to Rutgers. I don't like the way he talks. About alcoholic beverages. Drugs. Silly.

No. Oh, no. He's not silly. He's an excellent fox. What do foxes go for? I don't know. I am not smart. I am-pretty mixed up... I am not quite absolutely well and happy.

Very good, sir. One step at a time. See Lily. Telephone Rutgers. What was it our French nursery governess used to teach us? *Petit a petit, l'oiseau fait son nid...* Very good. Very fine. But that *oiseau* knows what she's doing, when she puts in all those little twigs and what not. And I don't know what I'm building.

When he turned into the driveway, there were a lot of lights in Lily's house. And he was startled by a loud burst of music. Excerpts from *The Gondoliers,* played on the piano by a great virtuoso. Could *she* play like that? he thought, and he thought that he would not be too surprised if she could. She had that air of ability. If she played at all, she would play like this.

He rang the bell, and Gussie opened the door.

"She's got company," said Gussie.

"Did you tell her I was coming?"

"Yes, I told her."

"What did she say?"

"Nothing," said Gussie.

"Well, will you tell her I'm here now."

"All right," Gussie said reluctantly and went away, leaving him standing in the hall.

The loud, brilliant music ceased, but in a moment it began again; *Pinafore* this time. Maybe she doesn't want me here just now, he thought, and a cold depression came over him.

He could see that the sitting room and the dining room were empty. Then where's the party? he thought, and it depressed him still more to realize that there were parts of her house he had never seen and knew nothing about.

She came through a door at the end of the hall, with her easy, limber walk; she was wearing a long black taffeta skirt that made her look taller, and a sheer lavender blouse with a ruffle down the front. Her red hair sprang up from her temples; she was so young, good-looking, and alive, so glad to see him, that he gave a long sigh of relief. Everything was all right.

"Hello!" she said.

"Hello!" he answered.

"You'll be surprised when you see who's here," she said. "Come on in!"

"If you don't mind, I won't... I won't go in."

"Why?"

"I'll tell you why I stopped in." He paused for a moment, to get it straight. "The thing is— Why are you smiling?"

"The way you're always saying that. 'The thing is...' Go on!"

"You know Ben?"

"Gussie's boy friend? Yes."

"He told—people I'd given Aunt Evie a very big drink. Enough to kill her, with the weak heart she had. I didn't, but he said he'd seen me do it."

"The son-of-a-gun!" said Lily angrily.

"Well, there was that. The next point is, the evening Jenette died, he called me up from the Tavern and asked me to come and see him. He said he'd tell me how the poor old girl died. He never did, because he got killed."

"But I thought he'd committed suicide. That's what the local paper said."

"No. Not suicide. Rutgers doesn't think that any more. He came to see me today." He paused again, wanting to avoid anything to do with the capsules. "He said he had a witness who'd seen someone helping Jenette into a car behind the Tavern. He asked me if I didn't have a drink in the bar with Jenette. Well, I didn't. He'd gone when I got there; I didn't see him at all. But Rutgers seems to think—I don't know..."

"He thinks it's a murder?"

"That seems to be it. I thought so, anyhow, from the start. But what I'd like to do now is tell him what I saw in your garage. I'm sorry to get you mixed up in this, but I think it ought to be done."

"Yes. Certainly," she said.

"I'm afraid they'll come and ask you questions."

"Well, I can bear it," she said. "Only, it won't be so good for Gussie. She's a hysterical little thing."

"She must know something. She ran out there with that bag."

"If it was Gussie that you saw."

"It was Gussie, all right. And I think it was Ben who brought poor Jenette there and later took him away."

"You think Ben killed Jenette?"

"It makes sense," Malcolm said. "I didn't tell you before, but Ben's been collecting blackmail from—my family, to keep quiet about what he said he saw. I—don't want to tell Rutgers that, if I can help it. You can see, it's pretty complicated.... I think I'll be getting along now."

"Going home?"

"No," he said. "I'm going to New York."

"Does Captain Rutgers know that?"

"Why, no."

"You mustn't do that, Malcolm," she said. "It's the worst thing you could possibly do for yourself."

"You mean guilty-looking? I hadn't thought of that."

"You'd better go back to your brother's—"

"No," Malcolm said.

"Then stay here," she said.

"Lily! Look here! I mean, people—"

"Malcolm," she said, "I'm a widow, and I'm twenty-nine. I've got what's called independent means, and I'm damn independent. If you'd like to stay here, I'd like to have you. I've got a cute guest room all ready."

"Lily..."he said, "Lily..."

"Listen!" she said. "You come in and meet my friends and have a drink, and after they've gone, we'll talk the whole thing over. Right?"

"R-right," he said.

"And who d'you think I've got here?"

"I don't know, Lily."

"MacQuail!"

"N-not T-Tom?"

"None other."

"Not-the B-Bell Line...?"

"Yes! I told him you were coming, and he said he'd be very glad to see you again. Come on!"

"Wait, just a minute. Lily, did you—fix this up—for me? I mean—arrange for me to meet him?"

"I did not," she said. "I've known Tom MacQuail for years, and he knew my husband even before we were married. And I wasn't trying to help you. I never thought you needed such an awful lot of help."

"But you—you can see—I'm not—"

"No, I don't see," she said. "You went into a tailspin, but you're straightening out." She paused a moment. "You know, in the work I've been doing, I've seen the real thing."

"Mean my troubles are—imaginary?" he asked in great anxiety.

"No, I don't," she said. "It's like having a nightmare. You can't help it. You can't wake yourself up out of it. Something happens to you that's too much for you. But after a while you digest it, and you wake up, and it's over."

"If—if you make an effort."

"No use making much of an effort about a nightmare," she said with a sort of rough good humor. "You try to run, and your feet are stuck. You try to call out, and you can't make a sound. But after a while you wake up, and it's over. Come along!"

He followed her down the hall and through the door at the end that opened on a veranda enclosed in glass and furnished with wicker chairs with brilliant chintz cushions. At one end was a player piano, and seated on the bench before it was a short man, bald as an egg, dressed in a snug-fitting dark suit. He was pedaling away, to unwind a roll, so busy that he did not notice their entrance.

The great MacQuail was leaning back in a chair, glass in one hand, his ankles crossed, his face like weatherbeaten stone, his thin gray hair neat on his hollow temples. He rose.

"Oh, Drake, is it? And how are you now?"

"F-fine, thanks," Malcolm answered.

"Then you'd better come back with us," said MacQuail. "We need every man we can get. Did you hear we'd lost poor Maillard? And Johnny Parr."

The man at the player piano had risen and was looking up at them with an appealing shyness.

"D'you know Captain O'Hare? O'Hare, this is Drake, one of our pursers. He was on the *White Tower.*"

"Ah!" said the little Captain, shaking his head.

"Drake, you'll have heard plenty about our James O'Hare here. Our first and only skipper to ram a submarine."

"Hush! now! Hush!" said the Captain.

"Why, James, they're going to have it in all their booklets, after the war," said Lily. "Cruise the Caribbean with the great O'Hare—"

"Hush, now, the two of ye!" he cried. "I'll find some more music. It's that I came for, and not this sort of talk."

He went over to a stack of music rolls in a cabinet and bent over to inspect them, hands on his knees. MacQuail lit a cigarette. General manager of the line, he was now; manager of the Bell-Brazil Line he had been when first Malcolm, at seventeen, had met him. It's a grand line to be with, my lad. A fine future....

"D'you know, Drake," he went on, "we've been combing the whole of Brooklyn, digging out the old fellows who thought they'd swallowed the anchor and 'settled down.'" This made him smile. "Old Captain Peterson," he said. "You could hear him roaring a mile away. What! he says. Go back to sea and risk my life to line your pockets? But he came. He came."

"Another drink, Tom?" asked Lily.

"A wee one, and the last. You know, Drake, we've put the old *Badger* back in commission. That's what I have in mind for you. She's refitting now. You can go to see Captain McLane next week, and he'll tell you as much as it's fit for you to know."

Malcolm lit a cigarette for himself and looked at MacQuail in a secret rage. The old *Badger...* Go and see Captain McLane and arrange to go to hell....

"Is Vesey still with you, sir?" he asked.

"Oh, yes! He lost that young brother of his, you know. In the Pacific." Isn't it all just fine and dandy?

"Things have changed now, Drake. The *Badger*'ll carry two guns now. Yes... We fight 'em now."

Sure. A poor little old tub like the *Badger* will fight the Luftwaffe and the U-boat packs. Bring 'em on. Let them all come. The ship's insured, and the cargo, and you can always get more men. Fine career. Chance of a lifetime.

But I'm going back, he thought, in wonder and anger. I don't know when, and God knows I don't know why. But I'm going back.

"Drink, Malcolm?" Lily asked him.

"Thanks," he answered.

She had sandwiches, too, and they were very good.

"Here's a good one!" said O'Hare. "Southern Medley."

"Sam was crazy about that one," said Lily.

There they were, O'Hare putting wonderful expression into the *Mockingbird* and *Massa's in the Cold, Cold Ground,* Lily and MacQuail, each with a glass of whisky and soda, soft-eyed and half smiling about the *Swanee River.* Three tough guys—and look at them. *Carry Me Back to Old Virginny,* that got them. For God's sake, why? They all brightened up for *Dixie;* Lily began to sing, and MacQuail tapped it out with one foot.

"Well, Skipper?" said MacQuail, when that was finished. "We've each got a wee wifie waiting. What about it?"

"Mine's not so wee," said O'Hare. "But you're right. Time to be off."

"A wee doch-an-doris?" said Lily, and they both laughed indulgently. They liked everything she said; they liked to be here in her house. You felt good here.

But I've got to go, too, Malcolm thought in a panic. It wouldn't look right.... He rose when they did.

"Malcolm," Lily said, "will you stay just a few moments? I want to ask you about something."

She made it as simple as that. Now they were all saying good-by.

"You'll see Captain McLane next week?" said MacQuail, and it was scarcely a question. "Good luck to you."

The telephone rang, and Lily went along the hall and took the telephone out of some sort of box.

"Oh... Miss Chatsworth?" She looked over her shoulder; her bold blue eyes met Malcolm's. He shook his head. "I'm sorry, Miss Chatsworth, I haven't seen him.... Sorry."

When MacQuail and O'Hare were gone, Lily went into the sitting room; she sank down into one of the low white armchairs, clasping her hands behind her head. Malcolm sat facing her, frowning, filled with a deep and vague anxiety.

"Who told you about Ben's story?" she asked.

"H-helene. My brother's wife."

"She doesn't believe it, does she?"

"Well, you see, the thing is..."

"Does that Virginia believe it?"

That Virginia?

"Well, you see, I mean to say—"

"Your brother?"

"He doesn't know about it. But he wouldn't. I mean to say, if I said not."

Very anxious, he was. There were a good many things he would not and could not tell Lily. When he telephoned to Rutgers, there were things he was not going to tell him. Nothing was plain, clear, straight. Before you answered a question, you had to do a lot of thinking. He was not doing a lot of thinking.

There was one definite thing, though.

"I've got to find Ben," he said. "I've got to have a talk with Ben."

"Gussie can tell us where to find him," Lily said. "Listen, Malcolm. Let's not talk any more tonight. In the morning we can go over everything, and I'll work on Gussie."

"She's a queer sort of girl."

"She's got reason to be," said Lily. "I'm very fond of Gussie, and she's fond of me. She's not too bright, but—I don't know—she's got something."

"Yes..." Malcolm agreed.

"I'll show you your room," said Lily. "Just wait, will you, till I see if the back door's locked."

But he rose and followed her when she went, her long skirt rustling. The back door was locked, all right. Then he followed her upstairs, and she showed him the room.

"Good night, Malcolm," she said. "Sleep well."

You did not have to talk to Lily; you did not have to say anything. He closed the door and leaned against it. This was a nice room; the wallpaper had a lot of little Chinese scenes on it: men carrying buckets on a yoke, women crossing bridges; a nice, clean, cheerful room.

I haven't got a thing, he thought. No razor, no toothbrush, no pajamas. Not a damn thing. I don't live anywhere. If you asked me, I couldn't give any address. It makes you feel queer.

No jigsaw puzzle here, no book to read. It makes you feel sad....

He wandered around the room, and on the chest of drawers he found a silver porcupine, very sturdy, with a pad of green velvet in its back, where pins were standing upright. That's a regular Lily thing, he thought, and he liked it. She has a good time, he thought.

Chapter Fifteen

I've been over all this before about not sleeping, Malcolm said to himself. So you can't get to sleep? So what?

There was a lot of air, though, and that was a good thing; a cool stream of air, with the smell of autumn in it. I'd never want to live in the tropics, where there's no autumn, he thought. You can have the spring. It's lovely, and all that, but, for me, autumn's always been the time when things started. School started, and you saw your friends again. Football started.

Harvest festival. Thanksgiving. You see? It's in the autumn that you give thanks, not in the spring. Christmas somehow starts in November.... My God! What couldn't Lily do with Christmas?

I did do some sleeping, he thought. But how could it be only eleven o'clock?

It was only eleven o'clock because his watch had stopped at that hour. He got out of bed, naked as a worm, and went to the window; there was a gray mist outside, but it was day. He could see the garage. And that made him remember all of it. Murder, blackmail, grief. Who wouldn't sell a farm and go to sea?

He went stealthily along the hall to the bathroom, and his own image in the mirror there upset him badly. I've got to get a shave somehow, he thought. I look like a gangster. A gorilla.

He did not want to turn on a bath; it made too much noise. He washed his face furiously with the green pine-scented soap he found, but he could not rub away the bluish stubble. I can't look like this, he thought. But that was the way he did look.

If I only knew the time, he thought. Maybe there's a barber open somewhere. This is the big day, and I want to look decent. This is the day when I telephone to Rutgers, and the day when I have that talk with Ben.

It wouldn't upset me too much to shoot Ben, he thought. I mean, I'm not setting out to do that, but if it happened... If he jumped at me, for instance... They don't come any lower than Ben. Holding up Virginia like that. Telling that lie about me. Finishing off Jenette that way. Anyhow, Ben's going to talk. When I see him, I'll know how to make him.

There has to be a clock downstairs, he thought, and he dressed and went very quietly down the stairs. In the kitchen, he thought, but there was no clock in there. It was a nice, neat little kitchen with a good smell, coffee, he thought, and cinnamon, maybe. Only it was stuffy; he opened the back door and stepped out into the thick mist. The gravel underfoot was wet and gritty, the little bushes were wet; there was no sound of traffic from the road, no sound anywhere. It must be early, he thought.

He stopped short. The kitchen door wasn't locked, he thought. I simply turned the knob and walked out. It was locked last night, but it isn't now.

His heart began to race. I'll take a look at the front door, he thought. He went on along the path and up the steps of the veranda.

The front door was locked, all right; he moved to the window and looked in. There was Ben, taking a nap on the chaise-longue.

Damn him! thought Malcolm in a fury. Drunk, is he? All right. I'll sober him up. He tried the window, but it was locked; he moved along to the next one, nearer to Ben.

Ben was stretched out comfortably in the chaise-longue, on top of the purple velvet doll; its platinum-blond hair hung over the edge of the seat. His mouth was open and his eyes were a little open.

Malcolm went running back along the path and in at the back door, to Ben. He touched his hand and it was cold. He's dead, Malcolm thought.

Now what? he thought, and a black and crushing despair rushed over him. This is the finish, he thought. I cannot cope with this. He could not think of anything to do. This is too much, he thought, and sat down in a chair, facing Ben.

This was the end of everything, the end of the one plan he had had. He had been going to see Ben, and settle things, and now Ben was dead. First Jenette was going to tell him something, something of immense importance, and when he found Jenette, he was dead. And now Ben. It's too much, he thought.

This will make trouble, bad trouble for Lily, he thought. He was sorry about that, but he couldn't help her. He couldn't lift a finger. He sat looking at Ben's vacant silly face, and it was too much.

Someone was coming down the stairs. He was so tired and heavy that it was an effort to rise; he turned his head as Lily came into the hall. She was wearing a white terry robe; she looked marvelously clean, gay, and bright.

"Hello!" she said. "I thought I heard someone running along the path."

"Yes," he said, standing between her and the chaise-longue. "It was me."

"Like some coffee?"

He did not know how to tell her about this.

"Malcolm," she said, "is there anything wrong?"

You don't know how to begin. He could feel her blue eyes fixed on his face, but he could not look at her; he stood with his head bent; he felt beyond measure clumsy and helpless.

"*What's* the matter?" she asked coaxingly, and when he did not answer, she came forward and looked over his shoulder.

"Well, for God's sake!" she said. "What's Ben doing here? Is he drunk?"

"No," Malcolm said.

"Let's have a look."

"No, don't!" he said. "Lily, he's dead."

"Let's see," she said, and went past him. He could not stop her; he could not do anything.

"I'll send for Dr. Lurie," she said.

"No use. Too late. He's dead, Lily."

"I don't think we'd know, Malcolm. People get queer attacks—fits."

'Ben—*and*—Jenette?"

"Well, let's leave it up to Dr. Lurie," she said.

"All right," said Malcolm.

He didn't care. He sat down again, facing Ben; he was not sorry about Ben, not astonished, not really interested. He heard Lily's clear voice telephoning, but he did not hear the words. Nothing else could happen, because everything had happened.

"I'll make some coffee," said Lily. "I guess we could do with some. Malcolm, if Gussie comes down, don't let her see Ben, will you?"

"All right," he said.

He heard a foghorn somewhere; a dull roar that buzzed in the heavy air. Ships were moving out in the Sound. The convoys. We didn't have a convoy, that trip. We went out alone. Things have changed now.... I could do with a cup of coffee. I'm very tired. Drowsy.

Gussie began to scream. There she was, standing in the room behind him, in her pink kimono, her light hair long and dank; she screamed and screamed and it made him wince.

"Gussie," said Lily, "you'll have to run upstairs and scream. Go on! You can't scream here. The doctor's coming, and we can't have this."

"Ben! He's dead!"

"We don't know yet. Go on upstairs," said Lily, perfectly matter-of-fact, "and you can yell your head off if you like."

Gussie was staring at Ben with fascinated intentness.

"I didn't ought to have left him here," she said in a hushed voice.

"Well, why did you?" Lily asked.

"Because he got fresh!" Gussie answered. "I told him I wouldn't stand that from anybody. I told him to get right out, and he said he wouldn't."

"How did he get in?"

"He threw pebbles up at my window and I came down and let him in. He never tried to get fresh before, and I didn't *know* his true nature. He was always a perfect gentleman, other times, and he brought me nice presents, and all."

"Did you ever let him in like this before, Gussie?"

"Just once. Just one time. He came and he said there was a friend of his dead drunk and he wanted to put him in our garage to sleep it off. He asked me for the key and I didn't want to give it to him, but he said if he didn't kind of protect this friend of his, he'd lose the new job he just got, and he was going to give me a watch."

She was speaking louder now and faster.

"Take it easy," said Lily.

"I never said if I'd marry him, I wasn't so crazy about him. And if I'd known his true nature, I'd of told him right at the start where he got off. But I didn't know. He was always a perfect gentleman till last night. And then in he marched, with a bottle of whisky! I've got no use for that. When they start drinking is when they lose their heads and *kill* you."

"You're all right now, Gussie. Tell me, did you help him put his friend in the garage, that other night?"

Gussie began to cry.

"No! I didn't! I didn't want anything to do with any drunk. I didn't even see him. Only the next morning I went to see had he gone and he looked funny in there. Kind of weak, he looked, and I thought I'd give him something to eat. So I gave him some food I didn't think you'd ever miss. I wanted him to get back his strength so he'd go *away.*"

"It's all right now, Gussie. Nothing to cry about."

"Well, anyhow, that drunk did go away, right while Dr. Lurie was here about my nervous digestion. I looked out the window and I saw Ben go in the garage, and I guess he sort of argued with the drunk to make him get up and go away. I just can't stand drunks! I told Ben last night, if you're going to drink any out of that bottle, you can get right out of here."

"Did he say why he came?"

"He said he was looking for Mr. Drake, and I said he was right here. I told Ben to throw that bottle out the window or I wouldn't speak to him, and when he wouldn't, I just walked off into the parlor. I didn't think he'd have the nerve to come in there after me, but he did. I said, 'you've got a nerve, coming right in Mrs. Kingscrown's parlor,' and he said, 'Don't worry about her. She's not going to kick about anything you do,' he said. He said, 'You can shake her down for plenty, on account of how she's got this Mr. Drake here.' I got mad then. I said, 'Mrs. Kingscrown is a perfect lady and she wouldn't ever do anything wrong. And even if she did,' I said, 'I would be the last one to shake her down, after all she's done for me.' "

"Don't hurry, Gussie. Take it easy."

"Well, but it made me mad for him to talk like that about you. Then he sat down in that chair and he began to drink out of the bottle and he talked sort of mumbley-jumble and I got scared of him. I went upstairs and I locked my door and I put the sheet over my head."

"You could have called me, Gussie."

"I didn't want to. I didn't want you to go down and get arguing with Ben. I was afraid he'd kill you."

Nobody thought about calling me, Malcolm said to himself. Just as well. I couldn't have done anything. He stood leaning against the wall with his hands in his pockets, watching Gussie and listening to her with great interest. It had nothing to do with him, but it was a damn interesting story.

"What happened to the pink kimono?" he asked.

"Oh, yes!" said Lily. "What ever did happen to your kimono and your wet slippers after you came back from the garage, Gussie?"

"That was kind of funny," said Gussie. "I didn't wear any slippers, just rubbers, that I left in the hall closet downstairs. And my kimono got muddy, so I put it in the washtub to soak out. When you brought Mr. Drake right in my room, it made me nervous. I get nervous about men if I don't know them."

A car had stopped before the house, and Lily went to open the door.

"Come in, Doctor!" she said.

He came in, with his proud, noble face and his crest of white hair; he looked at Malcolm with stern astonishment.

"What—?" he began.

"Here's the patient, Doctor," said Lily, and he went over to the chaise-longue.

He did not take long about that.

"Madam," he said, "this man is dead."

"Is he?" said Lily.

"My goodness!" said Gussie.

"You run up and get dressed, Gussie," said Lily. "I've started the coffee."

"Mrs. Kingscrown," said Lurie with increased sternness, "I shall have to call the police."

"Certainly!" said Lily. "Go on, Gussie!"

After all, Malcolm thought, it's none of my business. Nothing I can do. I'm tired. Lurie was telephoning in a low, important voice. Being the physician, Malcolm thought. He's enjoying himself—but he bores me.

"Mrs. Kingscrown," said Lurie, "who found the body like this?"

"Let's wait for the police," she said. "Let's all have some nice hot coffee in the kitchen."

"Thank you, no," said Lurie stiffly. "I'll wait here."

"Come on, Malcolm!" she said.

He went into the kitchen with her, but he did not want any coffee. The smell of it made him sick; he had a moment of horrible nausea, and when that was gone, his teeth began to chatter a little. He sat down at the table, because he was too tired to stand up, and Lily set a little glass before him.

"Wh-wh-what's this?" he asked, looking trustfully up at her.

"It's whisky, honey," she said. "I thought maybe you'd like it."

He didn't like it or not like it; he drank it. And then Gussie came into the kitchen, wearing a funny little black dress with a lace yoke.

"All dressed up," said Lily.

"Well, it's respect for the dead," said Gussie with complacency, and sat down opposite Malcolm.

Too bad about Lily, Malcolm thought. Nobody around but Gussie and me. Two zombies.

"Well, we're all in for a bad time now," said Lily.

"Why?" Malcolm asked.

"The police just aren't funny," she said. "I've been through this before."

"How—how come?"

"It was after Sam died, and I had a little apartment in New York. I came in one night and I found a friend of mine there, with her head in the gas oven. Dead. She'd left all her money to me, too, and that made it worse. There was a detective who nearly drove me wild. He said he could see marks where her wrists and ankles had been tied. Well, nobody else could see them, not even the doctor, and the whole thing blew over. But it wasn't so good while it lasted."

I can't help you, Malcolm thought. I wish to God I could, but I can't. I'm too tired.

"The thing is," she said, and looked at him with a half-rueful smile, "just answer their questions, all their questions, just the way they come, and never mind what they seem to mean."

"Oh, yes! Of course!" he said politely.

Because she seemed to be worried. But he wasn't. She took away the little glass and brought it back full.

"But I mean to say..."

"It won't hurt you, honey," she said.

More people had come into the house; there were voices and footsteps.

"I'll have to go, Malcolm," she said. "Just stand by for orders."

He swallowed the drink and then he put his feet up on another chair. Might as well be comfortable, he thought. Nothing I can do.

He lit a cigarette and he was very careful to get every fleck of ash into the little glass. He liked everything nice and neat.

Chapter Sixteen

He heard the resonant and pleasant voice of Reddy the Fox from the sitting room, and then he heard Lily's voice, always very clear.

"All right," she said, "if you want to be responsible. But he's in shock."

"I don't agree with you," said Lurie. "I saw him when I first came in, and I consider him quite capable of answering questions, Captain Rutgers."

Me, that is, Malcolm thought. Rutgers had come to the doorway of the kitchen now, and Malcolm brought down his feet and sat up straight.

"I'd like a little information, Mr. Drake," Rutgers said in his nice way. "I understand that you were the one who found the body?"

"Yes."

"If you'll tell me the circumstances—"

"I looked in the window," Malcolm said, "and I saw him, in that chair."

"At approximately what time?"

"I don't know. My watch had stopped."

"Mr. Drake, did you come here this morning in a taxi or by bus?"

"He stayed here all night," said Lily.

She shouldn't have said that, but it made things a lot simpler.

"In that case, Mr. Drake, if you were staying in this house, how was it that you first saw the body through a window?"

"I was outside," Malcolm explained.

"What were you doing outside?"

"I don't know... Wait! Wait a minute! I came down to see if there was a clock in the kitchen. There wasn't, so I went out."

He paused. He was very anxious to get all his answers straight, so that Reddy would shut up and leave him alone. He had a headache, only it was one that did not hurt. "I went out—to get some fresh air. The back door wasn't locked, and I thought I'd go and s-s-see if the front door was locked. I happened to look in the window, and there he was."

"What did you do then, Mr. Drake?"

"Went along to the back door and into the house."

"And then?"

"Then? Then I sat down, in the room where he was."

"You summoned Mrs. Kingscrown? Or Miss Reedy?"

"Who's Miss Reedy? Oh, Gussie? No. No, I didn't. I sat down—to think things over."

That sounds queer. That sounds crazy. But I can't help it. I don't care.

"Captain Rutgers," said Lurie, "I feel obliged to give you certain information about this man—"

"Let's not bother with him," said Malcolm.

"You can see for yourself, Captain," said Lurie, "he's extremely hostile to me. That's the reason—or one of the reasons—why I gave up the case. I explained that to his brother, Arthur Drake. I advised his brother to get another physician at once. I told him that, in my considered opinion, Malcolm Drake was dangerously irresponsible."

"Look here!" Malcolm said. He knew what was coming. The one thing he did mind.

"Captain," Lurie went on, "it's come to my knowledge—from a source I prefer not to divulge—that Drake had obtained a very large supply of a certain barbital preparation—without a prescription. I had refused to renew a prescription for him."

"What effect does it have?" Rutgers asked.

"Mental haziness, general lack of responsibility—"

"My God!" said Lily. "I know people who've taken that stuff for years, to make them sleep, and *they're* not irresponsible."

"You're not a physician, by any chance, madam?" Lurie asked with cold scorn.

"No," said Lily. "Just one of the public, with a little common sense. Malcolm's not irresponsible and he's not drugged. He's in shock."

Lurie caught sight of the little glass; he picked it up, emptied out the ashes, and sniffed it.

"Drake has been drinking again," he said.

"I gave him a little drink," said Lily. "Why not?"

"Captain Rutgers," said Lurie, "I warned Drake against drinking anything at all. It is my considered opinion that while intoxicated, or semi-intoxicated, he gave Mrs. Chatsworth the drink that was directly responsible for her death."

"You didn't report this, Dr. Lurie."

"I did not. Out of regard for Drake's brother and his wife, and Miss Chatsworth. Moreover, I thought at the time that this excessive drink had been given by mistake."

"You've changed your opinion, Doctor?"

"In view of the circumstances, yes."

"What's your present opinion, Doctor?"

"I believe that Drake deliberately gave Mrs. Chatsworth a drink which he knew—or hoped—would be fatal. I also believe that he killed Jenette. And it is my considered opinion that he killed this man Ben."

Malcolm wanted to laugh. He turned to look at Lily, to see if she was laughing. And he saw her so pale, so deadly serious, that his heart grew cold.

"But that—" he said. "That's—just damn silly."

"Captain Rutgers, Drake had in his possession a large supply of the drug which caused Jenette's death. I believe that an autopsy will disclose that this man Ben died from a dose of this drug."

Reddy the Fox was looking at Malcolm; Lurie was looking at him, and so was Lily. He got up, because it was better on your feet. Because this was danger.

"Drake left his brother's house without a word to anyone," Lurie went on. "Miss Chatsworth was greatly disturbed. He took nothing with him, no bag, nothing at all. I should say it was very likely that he had had a rendezvous here with the man Ben."

"Is that the case, Mr. Drake?"

"No," said Malcolm.

"Both Jenette and the man Ben must have taken the drug from someone they knew and more or less trusted," said Lurie. "Certainly it wasn't forced down their throats."

"What was your object in coming here last night, Mr. Drake?" asked Rutgers.

"I just stopped in. There were some people here—a man I knew. We played the piano, talked, so on."

"Had you intended to return to your brother's house?"

I can't answer that, Malcolm thought. I can't say Helene told me to go.

"Did you notify anyone in the household that you would not return?"

"I—no, I didn't." He paused. "I was drunk," he said.

"Can you corroborate that, Mrs. Kingscrown?"

"No," she said. "He wasn't drunk."

He glanced at her, and he thought her blue eyes looked steely.

"It's better to get things straight," she said. This was danger. The real thing.

"What was your object in coming here last night, Mr. Drake?"

"You asked me that before."

"Tell him," said Lily. "Tell him about seeing Jenette in the garage."

Malcolm told him.

"What was your reason for withholding this information from the police, Mr. Drake?"

It was difficult, it was almost impossible, to answer these questions, to try to remember all his past confusions, his delays, his evasions.

"I was going to tell you today. Had it planned like that."

"Why didn't you tell me when I went to see you yesterday?"

"The thing is—I felt pretty sure Ben had killed Jenette. And I wanted to find out a bit more—have something definite, d'you see, before I talked to you."

"How did you expect to find out anything definite, Mr. Drake?"

"I thought I'd have a talk with Ben."

"Did you have a talk with Ben, Mr. Drake?"

"No. I didn't see Ben—alive."

"Why did you assume that Ben had killed Jenette?"

That was another question he could not answer.

"Oh, some little things," he said.

"Tell him," said Lily. "You've got to."

"No!" he said, looking straight at her. But she was relentless.

"Then I will," she said. "Ben was blackmailing Malcolm's family."

"Why, Mr. Drake?"

"No," Malcolm said. It was all he could say.

"Ben had a tale that he'd seen Malcolm give Mrs. Chatsworth a big drink of whisky. The family was paying him to keep quiet."

"Good God!" said Dr. Lurie.

"Then Jenette called Malcolm up from the Tavern," Lily went on. "He said he had some information about Mrs. Chatsworth's death."

Now it was complete. Now she had handed Rutgers the whole case complete with motives. Motive for killing Jenette, motive for killing Ben. Anyone could find the motive for killing Aunt Evie.

It seemed to Malcolm as if, for a long time, he had been heading straight for this. It was as if everything he had said and done, for a long time, had spun another thread for this web. He was caught now.

"Have you any of these capsules on you now, Mr. Drake?"

"No."

"I'll have to search you now. Raise your arms, please."

"No. I won't."

"Malcolm," said Lily, "you've got to."

She too was helping to weave the net around him. He couldn't fight. He raised his hands, and he felt utterly helpless, humiliated, darkly, obscurely menaced.

"Where did you get this, Mr. Drake?"

It was Arthur's gun that Rutgers had taken out of his pocket.

This was the last straw. This was the finish. There was no way for him to explain why he was carrying this gun. He had never quite known what he meant to do with it. He had not been quite clear about any of these things Rutgers asked him about. It was the very vagueness of his acts that had made the net.

"Why were you carrying this gun, Mr. Drake?"

"He ought to see a lawyer before he talks any more," said Lily.

"I think you're right," said Rutgers. "We'll get along now. Ready, Drake?"

He had been heading straight for this for a long time. He had no address, no bag, he belonged nowhere. But he was going somewhere now, all right. To jail.

Chapter Seventeen

Out of this world, Malcolm thought, sitting on a cot in the cell. Detained, they called this. Detained on suspicion. You feel—surprised, very much surprised that anyone believes you're a murderer. Sort of thing you don't expect.

This surprise, this astonishment, was about all he felt. You can't do this to me, he thought. It's preposterous.

It was a clean little cell, and there was a tree in the yard outside the barred window. From time to time a little breeze stirred the thick mist, and the leaves, red and yellow, fluttered down. It was very quiet here.

An amiable guard came and asked him what he wanted for lunch.

"I didn't know they did that in jail," said Malcolm.

"This is just the police cells," said the guard, "and you haven't been indicted yet. You can get anything you want, long as you got the money to pay for it. Only, no likker."

He was a big, slow-moving fellow with a red neck and thick hair that seemed to grow in three layers, each a different shade of yellow. Malcolm liked to talk to him.

"What kind of people do you get here?" he asked.

"All kinds. All kinds. Some of 'em make trouble, yelling, acting crazy. Some of 'em won't say a word, just sit around like wild animals. Some of 'em are sociable, like you."

Yes, Malcolm thought, I'm sociable. Always have been. I don't like being in jail. It's too quiet. It's lonely. The guard brought him cigarettes and magazines, but he could not read. Arthur'll be along any minute, he thought. And some lawyer.

He had been allowed to call up Arthur in his office.

"Look here, Arthur!" he had said. "I'm sorry about this, but the thing is, I'm in jail. For murdering Ben."

There had been a moment's silence.

"All right!" Arthur had said. "Take it easy." And had hung up.

Time drags in jail. Every time you hear footsteps or voices, you think it's for you. You think something is happening. This isn't a real prison. In a real prison it would be quieter than this, maybe. And you would know, absolutely, that footsteps and voices were not for you.

In a real prison you would damn well have to settle down, knowing that nothing was happening, or going to happen. In a movie I saw a fellow suddenly go haywire, begin to yell, shake the bars. You can see how that could be. How it could come over you, the feeling that you can't get out. It starts in your stomach and comes up into your throat. I want to get *out*....

No... Look here! Suppose I got sick? Got a heart attack—a fit. Nobody would know. Nobody would come. I feel damn queer... Choking... I can't take it. I've *got* to get out....

He stood up, and his knees were shaking, sweat was ice-cold on his forehead, and he was choking. He could not swallow. Nobody was coming. Not Arthur. No lawyer.

Horror closed over his head like a wave and he was drowning in it. He stumbled back on the cot and sat with his hands at his throat, choking. Only, something in him was fighting. He was not yelling. I'll die before I yell.

No little pills to help now. No likker. No nurses and doctors. Nobody at all. Just me—alone. Sink or swim. Alone.

He was not choking now, so he lay down and stretched out, exhausted. Well, I didn't yell, he thought, and a calm, fatigued pride rose in him. I can take it.

This is a funny thing to happen to me. It used to make me laugh, those things you have to fill out. Have you ever been in prison? All right. Here I am. This is real.

He was immeasurably tired, but with none of the stupor he had known before. This was the fatigue of a victor at the end of a violent struggle. I didn't yell, he thought. That's over.

All of that was over. He had broken out of the net of cobwebs, and a prison cell was infinitely better. The thing is, he told himself, to think it out, get everything straight before this lawyer comes.

Tell me in your own words how this happened, Mr. Drake. How the hell did you get yourself locked up for murder? Dr. Lurie did it; he pinned it on me. And why?

But, good God! he thought. Somebody did it. Somebody killed Jenette and Ben. Put that in your pipe and smoke it. If you didn't do it, who did?

I never thought of that. Never tried to figure it out. All right, I'd better start. Because that looks like the only way I'll get out of here. To find out who did do the killing.

Somebody gave Jenette and Ben a lethal draught. And who's the one who has lethal draughts handy all the time? One person. Dr. Lurie.

Who tried to pin it on me? Dr. Lurie. Who's got a damn venomous disposition? Same party.

Motive? I wouldn't know. Maybe he's loony. Psychopathic case, ha-ha. But there could be motives. When Jenette said he had something to tell me about Aunt Evie's death, maybe it was something about the Doc.

If Ben was blackmailing Virginia—poor Virginia—maybe he was blackmailing Lurie, too.

He lay on the cot, thinking about this with great wonder. He lit a cigarette, and when it was finished he got up and wandered around the cell. His watch was still stopped, and there was no sun for a clue, only the gray mist. But there was the feeling of late afternoon. I've been here a long time, he thought. I came in the morning, early. I had lunch—long ago. Queer that Arthur hasn't come, or this lawyer. All day long in the oubliette, where they forget you.

Only that's not so damn funny. Something could go wrong. They might have forgotten to write it down when they locked me up. No record. Maybe Arthur came and they said sorry, no record here of any Malcolm Drake. Sorry, somebody must have been kidding you.

Things like that don't happen. Oh, don't they? This happened. Everything happens.

He lit another cigarette and took up a magazine; he made himself look at the pictures. That made him remember a little girl he had seen on the deck of a ship, a very little girl with long bright hair. She had been sitting in a deck chair with a book, pompously turning the pages as if she were reading, only so very fast.

There were footsteps again now. That may be for me, he thought, and it may not be. In any case, here I am, nonchalantly reading and smoking. In my cell. What I care, *hein?*

It was Captain Rutgers, with a young policeman.

"Drake," he said, "I'm going to take you along to listen to some new evidence."

"What's that mean?" Malcolm asked.

It seemed to him that Reddy looked definitely less pleasant. But maybe you just think things like that when you are in jail and anyone can push you around.

"Miss Chatsworth says she has important information, and she insists upon giving it in your presence. I don't see any objection to that. But we're not releasing you, Drake."

"All right," said Malcolm briefly.

His dread of facing Virginia outweighed anything else he could feel, relief, even curiosity. She knows now, he thought, that I simply walked out on her last night. Without a word. He had injured her cruelly; he had not meant to or wished to, and even now he could not see quite how it had come about that she believed he loved her. But, one way or another, he had done that. And one way or another, at some time or another, she would have to know the truth.

Rutgers went along the corridor ahead of him and the policeman followed; it seemed a long way, with many turnings. He did not remember having come this way before. Rutgers opened a door, and they were at the top of the steps that led to the courthouse. It was raining; a girl went by with a red umbrella, and she looked so nice, so gay and free, it gave him a pang. It was as if he had not seen anything like her for years, or anything like the wet, glistening streets, the cars, the people. Across the road was a cigar store and the lights were on there, this dark afternoon; it looked fine in there, shelves and shelves of bright boxes.

"How about stopping to get some cigarettes?" Malcolm asked, because he wanted to go in there.

"Your brother's waiting in the car," said Rutgers.

There was Arthur sitting in the car, leaning back, his arms folded, his soft hat pulled low, his face pale, sharp, almost wolfish. He watched them come down the steps, and then he opened the door.

"Hello!" he said somberly. "I've got you a fine lawyer. Coming any minute. Pond doesn't handle criminal cases."

The young policeman took the wheel and Rutgers sat beside him; Malcolm and Arthur sat together in the back. The window beside Arthur was wide open and the fine rain blew in.

"We're going to Mrs. Kingscrown's house," Arthur said.

"Well, why?"

"Because she doesn't mind, and I wasn't going to have this in my house, that's why."

"Not going to have what?"

"Whatever this is. Great revelations. Virginia's very pompous about her 'information,' but I don't see what she could know about anything. Anyhow, I didn't want Helene around." He paused. "She's been damn miserable about all this," he said in a lowered voice. "She thinks Virginia's been rushing you a bit."

Malcolm said nothing.

"All this blackmail hocus-pocus," Arthur went on. "If either of the girls had said a word to me... Because, y'see, I knew all the time who'd given Aunt Evie the big drink."

"Who?"

"Jenette. He told me so himself."

"But why, for God's sake?"

"He didn't think there was any harm in it. He told me before he left for the Tavern. He didn't know the drink had had anything to do with her dying. He just thought it would be funny to see the poor old girl tight. 'Ironic, wasn't it?' he said to me. 'Just when she might have started to be amusing, for the first time in her life, she fell down dead.' I didn't say anything about it. What was the point of getting him in trouble?"

"Maybe that was what he was going to tell me," Malcolm said.

"Must have been. Y'see, when Jenette left our house, Lurie gave him a lift, and Lurie talked. He says himself that he probably talked a little too much. About the party with the perverted sense of humor who had given Aunt Evie the fatal draught. And he probably let Jenette see he thought it was you."

"I don't see why Lurie's got his knife into me this way."

"You could almost be sorry for Lurie," Arthur said.

"Not me."

"He's so crazy about Virginia."

"He is?" said Malcolm. "I never thought of that." He was silent for a moment. "Then, look here! If that's the case—" He lowered his voice to a whisper. "He'd want to stop Ben from bothering her, wouldn't he?"

"Could be," said Arthur. "Anyhow, I wish to heaven Virginia wouldn't do things this way. If she's got any information—which I doubt—why the hell couldn't she tell it to Rutgers quietly? What worries me is that she'll make a big, dramatic accusation, and it'll be wrong. Because—I don't know whether you've noticed it—but Virginia is always wrong."

"I hadn't noticed. No."

"She never gets people right. Never anything right. Look at this Ben thing. Here she's been paying blackmail to Ben, to keep him from telling his tale, and it never came into her head that maybe you hadn't done it. I'd have known you hadn't. You couldn't. If you'd been as drunk as a fool, it wouldn't have been your idea of a good joke to get Aunt Evie tight."

"Well, no," Malcolm said.

"But Virginia believed it, without any trouble."

"And Helene."

"I dunno. I don't think Helene cared much about it, one way or the other. All she wanted was to get you out of the house before there was a shotgun wedding."

"Well..."

"Helene's very fond of her sister, but just the same she didn't think Virginia was giving you much of a break. Helene talks to me, you know. Not to anyone else."

The car turned a corner, and Lily's house was in sight.

"I don't know what to do about Virginia," Malcolm said very low.

"What you do is run," said Arthur.

"I can't run when I'm in jail."

"This fine high-priced lawyer is going to get you out of jail."

"I could bear it," Malcolm said. "I don't like jail."

As the car stopped, Lily opened the door. She was wearing a black dress that made her skin look very fair; in the gray light her red hair was misty. She looked different, Malcolm thought, and maybe a little queer. Maybe she didn't like this meeting in her house, police and all that.

She led the four men into her sitting room, and Malcolm turned his head toward the chaise-longue. It was gone. Then he caught sight of Dr. Lurie, leaning back in an armchair, his knees crossed, a look of haughty aloofness on his face. All right, Malcolm thought, anybody who likes can be sorry for him, only not me.

Then he saw Virginia. She had risen and stood waiting for him; she was wearing a dress he had not seen before, gayer than was usual with her, a small-figured pattern of blue and red and black, with a square neck and short puff sleeves. She looked desperately anxious, poor girl; her dark hair was ruffled, as if she had pushed it back from her forehead. I'd forgotten how upset she'd be about all this, he thought.

"That's a very pretty dress," he said.

He had said that to her often enough before; he knew it pleased her, and he was sorry for her now and wanted to please her. Her eyes filled with tears.

"Oh, Malcolm!" she said. "What a *horrible* thing for them to do to you!"

"Perfectly all right," he said hastily.

"When you've been so ill—"

"Miss Chatsworth," said Rutgers, "I understand you have some information for me. If you'll sit down—"

But she remained standing, and it was Malcolm to whom she spoke, not Rutgers.

"It's going to be very hard to tell all this," she said. "Try not to let it upset you, Malcolm."

Lily and Arthur and Rutgers and Lurie were all seated, but he and Virginia were standing, facing each other. It's—embarrassing, he thought.

"When I heard that Tom—Dr. Lurie had accused *you* of all these things, I saw that I'd have to tell everything, all of it. But it's hard... I'd always meant to tell *you*, privately, later on. But now it's too late. Tom said he was sure you'd given Aunt Evie that horrible drink. Well, of course, I know you didn't. I'd have seen, if you had."

"But, Virginia, you did think—"

"Never, Malcolm! Never for a single moment!" she said, her brilliant dark eyes fixed on his face. "I wanted you to think you'd done it because I thought that would help you. I thought the shock of believing that you were responsible for poor Aunt Evie's death would keep you from slipping back."

"You mean—you tried to make me think—I'd done that?" he asked, frowning in his effort to grasp this and all that it implied.

"Yes, I did, Malcolm. I was so worried when you started drinking with Mrs. Kingscrown—"

"I didn't drink *with* anyone."

"And that evening, after poor Aunt Evie had gone... I knew why you were so anxious to get back to Mrs. Kingscrown's that you wouldn't even wait for your dinner. I knew you felt ashamed to drink anything more in our house—in the circumstances, so you wanted to get back to her house—"

"Look, Virginia, please!"

"I'm not blaming you, Malcolm, or Mrs. Kingscrown, either. She couldn't know that you shouldn't drink anything. And after you'd had one drink, you had to go on. I understood—"

"Why did you pay Ben blackmail if you didn't believe his tale?" asked Arthur sharply.

"Because Ben kept threatening to tell Malcolm what had happened. You see, I paid Ben fifty dollars to tell Helene he'd seen Malcolm pour out a huge drink for Aunt Evie. I was quite sure Helene would tell Malcolm, and I thought it would be better that way. More convincing. I thought that if I told him myself he might suspect it was some plan to help him."

Help me? Malcolm said to himself. My God! My God! He looked at Virginia, but her earnest glance did not falter.

"Did you know who did give that drink to Mrs. Chatsworth?" asked Rutgers.

"No. I thought it was probably a mistake."

"Miss Chatsworth, have you any information relative to Jenette's death?"

"Yes," she answered. "Although I don't understand how it happened. If Ben had done as I told him—"

"Let's have this from the beginning, please," said Rutgers.

"You see," she said, "I was in the hall when Ivan telephoned to Malcolm, and I heard Malcolm say, 'Oh, you've got something to tell me about Aunt Evie's death?' or something of the sort. I thought then that Ivan probably did know what had happened, and I didn't want him to tell Malcolm. I honestly thought it was very important for Malcolm to think *he* was responsible. I thought that would keep him from slipping back and drinking with— well, drinking. So I had a talk with Ben. I pointed out to him that if Ivan told what had really happened, Ben might get into serious trouble for going to Helene with a lie. All I wanted was to stop Ivan from talking just then."

"Smith!" said Rutgers, and the young policeman standing in a corner sat down and took put a notebook and a pencil.

"Miss Chatsworth," said Rutgers, "you understand that anything you say will be taken down in writing and may be used in evidence?"

"Yes," Virginia said without hesitation.

"Virginia," said Arthur, "you'd better not talk any more until this lawyer comes."

"Drake is absolutely right," said Dr. Lurie. "Don't say any more now, Virginia."

He was frightened, and Arthur was uneasy. Only Virginia was untroubled.

"I don't need any lawyer, Arthur," she said. "I'll simply tell Captain Rutgers exactly how things were." She turned to Rutgers now and Malcolm saw her face in profile, serious and handsome. "I didn't want Malcolm to find out just then whatever it was that had really happened to poor Aunt Evie. I thought it might make Malcolm lose confidence in me, and then I couldn't do *anything* for him. What I planned was to give Ivan just enough of that drug—"

"Virginia!" cried Lurie.

"Please let me alone!" she said with a little frown. "*You* told me two of those capsules would be perfectly harmless—"

"Virginia! No doctor could say such a thing! There are any number of circumstances—idiosyncrasies—"

"I asked you once. I asked you if two of those capsules would kill anyone, and you said no."

"You gave this drug to Jenette?" asked Rutgers.

"I emptied the powder from two capsules into an envelope and gave it to Ben. I told him to go and see Ivan and give him some money from Helene and me and treat him to a drink. Ivan would let *anyone* treat him. I told Ben to slip the powder into Ivan's drink and as soon as he got drowsy to get him into the car and drive him to New York. There's no telephone in his horrible house, and Ivan never had any perseverance. I felt sure that if Ben left him in his room, with some money, he wouldn't bother about trying to tell Malcolm anything. Anyhow, not for a while. And Malcolm might get back on his feet—"

"What did you think when you learned that Jenette was dead, Miss Chatsworth?"

"I was shocked," said Virginia.

"What did you think was the cause of his death, Miss Chatsworth?"

"I thought probably he'd taken something else."

"Did it occur to you that Ben might have given him more of those capsules?"

"Yes. I asked Ben, and he swore he'd only given Ivan just what I'd put into the envelope. He said he'd easily persuaded Ivan to get into the car, but that almost as soon as they'd started, Ivan toppled over and Ben saw that he was dead. I don't know how he got him into that field; I never asked him. It was just sad and horrible."

Malcolm sat down heavily in a chair and left her standing there alone.

"I can assure you, Miss Chatsworth, that Jenette had had a good many more than two of those capsules."

"He could have taken more himself," she said.

"Miss Chatsworth, did it ever occur to you that you were responsible—"

"Don't answer, Virginia!" said Lurie.

"I wasn't responsible," she said with spirit. "I wouldn't have done Ivan any harm for worlds."

"You were paying blackmail to Ben so that Malcolm Drake should not learn the truth about Mrs. Chatsworth's death. If Jenette were to make the facts public, the man Ben would no longer be able to extort money from you. Didn't it occur to you, Miss Chatsworth, that Ben had a stronger motive than you for keeping Jenette silent?"

"No."

"It never occurred to you that possibly you had instigated a murder?"

"That's enough of this," said Arthur. "Here's where we quit."

"Miss Chatsworth is under no compulsion to answer. I simply put the question. Miss Chatsworth, have you any information as to Ben's death?"

"No," she said.

"Have you any theory, Miss Chatsworth, as to why he died here in this house from an overdose of the same drug that killed Jenette?"

"No," she said again. And there was some sort of change in her now; she was defiant.

"Miss Chatsworth, we found an empty whisky flask beside the body. We've already ascertained that the whisky had been heavily drugged with a barbital preparation. Have you any idea where Ben got this drugged whisky?"

She did not answer at all.

"Nothing further to say, Miss Chatsworth?"

"No. Nothing," she said.

"Smith!" said Rutgers. "Handcuffs. We'll get going, Drake."

"You can't take Malcolm back to jail!" cried Virginia. "I've told you about Jenette."

"It's Ben I'm interested in just now," said Rutgers.

The young policeman approached, and Malcolm rose; the handcuff snapped around his wrist.

"Don't!" said Virginia. "You don't realize what you're doing to him! You don't know how ill—"

"Look here!" Malcolm said. "I don't *care.* Please don't—*bother.*"

He did not care. He longed with all his heart to get back to his cell. Away from Virginia. Away from hearing anything more.

"Virginia," said Arthur, "this is a trick. Don't talk."

"Very well," said Rutgers. "If you haven't anything more to tell me, Miss Chatsworth, we'll be going."

He waited a moment.

"Well, I've got something," said Lily in a curiously flat voice. She leaned back in her chair, looking at the wall before her.

"Let's hear it, Mrs. Kingscrown."

"Ben told Gussie who gave him the whisky," said Lily. "And Gussie told me."

"Who was it?"

There was a silence.

"I gave it to him," said Virginia.

"Virginia!" cried Lurie in despair.

"It couldn't have hurt him," she said. "There must be at least ten drinks in a pint and I only put in two capsules for each drink. Even three drinks wouldn't have really hurt him. He was hounding and tormenting me for money from morning till night and I had to get away. I had to have a little peace—and I knew he'd never let me get away. You couldn't possibly expect anyone to drink a *whole pint!*"

She spoke with indignation, as if Ben had betrayed her. Her inner defenses were complete, unbroken; she did not know what she had said, what she had done for herself.

"Maybe this was just a mistake," said Lily. "But Gussie said Ben told her the whisky was a present for me."

"I had to tell Ben that," said Virginia. "It would have looked too queer—suspicious—for me suddenly to give Ben a bottle of whisky. I knew he'd never dream of giving it to you."

There was another silence.

"Miss Chatsworth," said Rutgers with no expression at all, "we'll have to detain you for further questioning."

"Yes," she said. "I expected that. I knew there'd be trouble when I told the truth. But after all, just keeping out of trouble or danger isn't the chief thing in life."

Aunt Evie... thought Malcolm.

The young policeman unlocked the handcuffs, and Malcolm was free. Virginia stood with Rutgers on one side of her and the policeman on the other. Her dark face was a little pale, but there was no shadow of uneasiness on it. She still didn't see, didn't know; she felt no compunction, and no fear.

"Captain Rutgers," said Lurie, "as—as an old friend of the family's— may I accompany Miss Chatsworth?"

"Sorry," said Rutgers. "No."

Nobody could accompany her where she was going. She looked back at Malcolm. "Try not to worry, Malcolm!" she said.

Lurie stood by the window with his back to the room.

"They can't possibly—" he said. "I don't think there'll be any—very serious penalty. She—acted for the best."

Arthur gave a loud snort. Maybe it was a laugh, only that this wasn't funny.

"I don't know what'll happen to her," he said. "I don't think she'll be convicted of murder. Not deliberate, premeditated murder. She just went ahead, acting for the best, as you said. And if people got killed, it was their own fault."

"In my considered opinion," said Lurie unsteadily, "the person responsible for all this tragedy and suffering is Malcolm Drake."

"Shut up!" said Arthur.

"He was the one who first suggested that Mrs. Chatsworth should take
a drink. He's led Virginia on—"

My fault? Malcolm thought. Lurie went out, slamming the door
behind him. My fault? Did I lead her on...?

Arthur was moving about the room in the dusk, fingering things, pick-
ing up things.

"Nice news for Helene," he said. "Poor kid! Poor kid."

He was standing at the mantelpiece; he touched something on it, and
gay, delicate little music came. *For He's a Jolly Good Fellow.*

"Oh God!" said Arthur. "I like that."

Lily got up and turned on a lamp and then another one. Malcolm sat
leaning forward, his hands clasped between his knees, looking up at her.
Her face looked tired, and sad, and wise, he thought. She knows about
things, she understands about things. All right, what do *you* think, Lily?
My fault, all this?

Their eyes met, in a long, long look. He waited, with a mounting anxiety, for her to speak. What she said would be wise, and just, and right.

She sighed a little.

"Well, boys," she said. "What about a drink?"

Not my fault, Malcolm thought. Not guilty!

THE END

If you enjoyed this book, you might enjoy the following from

Stark House Press

0-9667848-1-2
CALENTURE by Storm Constantine $17.95
Fantasy novel set in a world of floating cities.

0-9667848-0-4
THE ORACLE LIPS
by Storm Constantine $45.00
Signed/Numbered/Limited Edition
hardback collection of the author's stories.

0-9667848-4-7
**THE THORN BOY & OTHER
DREAMS OF DARK DESIRE**
by Storm Constantine $19.95
Nine voluptuous, erotic fantasies.

0-9667848-3-9
SIGN FOR THE SACRED
by Storm Constantine $19.95
Novel about the search for an elusive messiah.

Mystery Classics

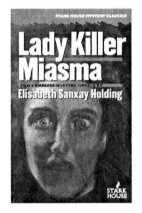

0-9667848-7-1
LADY KILLER / MIASMA
by Elisabeth Sanxay
Holding $19.95
Two classic novels of
suspense from the
author of *The Blank Wall.*

Noir Classics

0-9667848-8-X
THE BOX / JOURNEY INTO TERROR
by Peter Rabe $19.95
Two hardboiled thrillers from a master of crime fiction.

0-9667848-2-0
INCREDIBLE ADVENTURES
by Algernon Blackwood $16.95
Fantasy stories that defy categorization.

0-9667848-5-5
PAN'S GARDEN
by Algernon Blackwood $17.95
Fifteen stories of fantasy and horror.

0-9667848-6-3
**THE LOST VALLEY
& OTHER STORIES**
by Algernon Blackwood
$16.95
Ten stories for a long,
dark night—includes
"The Wendigo."

If you are interested in purchasing any of the above books, please send the cover price plus $3.00 U.S. for the 1st book and $1.00 U.S. for each additional book to:

STARK HOUSE PRESS
STARK 1945 P Street, Eureka, CA 95501
HOUSE (707) 444-8768 griffins@northcoast.com

Name _____

Shipping Address _____

City _____

State / Zip / Country _____

☐ Check/Money Order ☐ VISA ☐ MC#_____ Exp. _____

Signature_____

Billing Address _____

(if different)_____

ORDER 3 OR MORE BOOKS AND TAKE A 10% DISCOUNT!